Sara of Ilinka

Sara of Ilinka

Barbara Topham

The Pentland Press Limited
Edinburgh • Cambridge • Durham • USA

First published in 1999 by
The Pentland Press Ltd.
1 Hutton Close
South Church
Bishop Auckland
Durham

British Library Cataloguing in Publication Data.
A Catalogue record for this book is available
from the British Library.

ISBN 1 85821 681 8

Typeset by CBS, Martlesham Heath, Ipswich, Suffolk
Printed and bound in Great Britain by Bookcraft (Bath) Ltd.

PREFACE

My story of Ilinka is about two men from different cultures. Ilinka is a mystical place where an Indian brave was led to dwell. You will find no dates in my story. I leave such things to the historians. And also to the reader's imagination.

This story is about people and how their destinies are linked. Some readers may ask themselves how the two men were able to speak with each other. Yet if they could not have done so, my story would never have been told.

Barbara Topham

ACKNOWLEDGEMENTS

This book is dedicated to my husband Peter who did not live to see it published. Thank you, Peter, for everything. Especially for our children: Michael, Debbie, Ashley, Mandy and Andrew.

To Everett in Canada for taking an interest in my writing and for all he has done for me.

To my lifelong friends Margerey and Harold for being there when I needed them.

To my cousin Judith, Nicola, Michelle and Lesley for typing up the manuscript.

And of course to Meleeka who somehow came into my imagination to enable me to write this story.

INTRODUCTION

As darkness fell over the city a lone figure stood staring, watching the city lights flickering. From where he stood, high on the mountain, the lights could have been a million stars in the sky above, but he knew that down there was civilization, the place where men dreamed their dreams. It had been like that since the world began. His father and his father before him had always made this remark, although Simon had never fully understood what they meant, it was now becoming clear to him, it was the meaning of the difference between good and evil.

Simon was of Indian blood, his ancestors had once roamed these lands. The city with the twinkling lights had once belonged to the Indians. It had been taken away from them by the white man, many moons ago, and what had been a peaceful Indian village with green pastures had become a sprawling modern city. Simon sat cross-legged on the mountainside and was deep in thought. He could hear the stream gushing down to the river below and he wondered how far it had to flow before reaching the sea. Other sounds of the night came to him, but he wasn't listening, all he could hear were the voices of his ancestors.

Meleeka was a powerful man, everyone listened to him, his tribe was peaceful, kind and gentle. They killed for food and skins, they did not believe in hunting for any other reason. The men hunted, the women cooked and made clothing for their families to wear, they were happy doing their daily tasks and they watched over the young ones as they worked.

The children, like all children played their own games, and as they grew older the boys would learn to hunt and fish while the girls would help with the womanly work that had to be done, and Meleeka would, as their chief, watch over them all. Meleeka was happy he had such a loving tribe, and that all the land he surveyed belonged to them. He had found this place as a young brave and had loved it from the moment he set eyes on it.

He wondered for days, surviving mostly on fish and rabbit. At night he would find a place to camp, at first being afraid of the sounds of the night, they were so loud and his imagination would run wild; once he thought he heard a bear in the brush and fully expected it to run out and attack him in his sleep, but he soon became more confident and as time passed he began to enjoy himself and used the nights of solitude to plan the next day, map his route of this day on his skin map and dream of his own future.

The test of young braves was to go out into the wilds alone and survive on their own from the beginning of one full moon to the end of the next while all the time mapping their route on skin maps to show they had travelled far when they returned. Many a young man was never to be seen again, even though, before they set out they were taught the skills of hunting, fishing, cooking, camping and how to avoid the worst they may find, such as the elements and other hostile people or animals. It was more of a game during the years of training when they went out in groups with the braves of the village, but when they finally set out alone to prove they were worthy of being braves it was another story.

PART I

CHAPTER I

When Meleeka had said goodbye to his mother and father, he felt a great sadness as it would be the first time he had ever been alone, and leaving them for such a long time seemed like it may be forever. His mother had kissed and hugged him. 'You take care my son,' she said. Meleeka looked into her eyes; he saw the tears but he knew they would not fall, neither would they fall from his; they both knew they had to be brave. His father had held him at arm's length. 'Go my son,' he said, 'and come back a brave.'

Meleeka set off without a backward glance, he walked straight and proud, as he knew a young brave would, for he knew that all the tribe were watching him. All he took with him was a pouch of water, three sharp knives and a skin map.

With every day that passed his confidence grew. Sometimes he would meet a tribe of roaming friendly Indians and would stop and share a meal with them, but mostly he was alone. At night he would make camp and after eating he would mark out his day's journey on his skin map, and today he had come across the most beautiful place he had ever seen or dreamed of. Miles of the greenest grass, a forest to the left and one to the right, and there in the middle was a large snow-capped mountain. His eyes must be deceiving him, as he was sure it was blue, surely the colour would change.

The next morning just before noon he was at the base of the mountain and it was still blue in colour and by this time he knew he wasn't dreaming. As he walked up the Blue Mountain he found bushes with blue flowers on them and many blue berries, to his right was a stream which ran swiftly down the side of the mountain to the lush meadows below and disappeared into the forest on his left. The stream was full of fish and there was plenty of game in the forest. That night he made sure that the mountain site was properly scratched onto his skin map as he wanted to make sure he could find his way back in the future. He decided he would stay there for a few more days to explore the place better and then get a day's rest before his journey home. He felt relaxed and content; the fish he had caught in the stream were the best he had ever eaten. He had picked some of the blue berries but was unsure whether or not to eat them as they may be poisonous. The temptation was too much for him, the berries looked so good and earlier in the day he had seen a bear eating them, so he took the chance and found them to be sweet and delicious and they made him a good snack before falling off to sleep.

He stayed by the mountain for five more glorious days, though he knew he would be late in returning to his village and that his parents would start to worry about him.

The night before he left for home Meleeka had a troubled dream. His dream was of many tribes of Indians gathered together, all the chiefs were having a powwow and all the braves were wearing war paint. There was so much blood and the pounding of horses hooves was deafening. He saw the women and children crying and trying to run away. He woke up with a start, his heart pounding and his body covered in a cold sweat. He lay quietly for a while until his heart returned to a normal pulse. The dream was so vivid in his mind he could not believe it was just a dream. He washed himself in the stream then had a bite to eat and sat cross-legged, staring at the mountain thinking about the meaning of the dream. He knew he had to go back to his village and get there as quickly as possible, but he could not resist staring at the Blue Mountain, a place he also wanted to keep forever in his mind until one day he could perhaps return to it.

The peace he had felt these last few days was like nothing he had ever felt before and he wanted to take that peace back to his people. At last he stirred, it was now time to go. '*You can not take the peace to your people, you must bring your people here to the peace.*' Meleeka jumped! He looked around, wondering who was watching him and could have known what he was thinking. He thought for a moment, turned and knew the mountain had spoken to him.

Each day as he made his way home he would think of the mountain. He would fall asleep, totally exhausted, for during the day he never rested, he felt an urgency to get home as quickly as possible. The second moon had already gone and everyone would be worried for his safety. He did not know what lay before him, but still remembered the troubled dream.

CHAPTER II

As he approached the camp, all was quiet, but he sensed that something was wrong. As he neared his father's wigwam he saw that all the women and children were sitting outside; they looked at him with pity as he approached. 'Hurry, Meleeka,' one of them shouted, 'or you will be too late.' As he entered he saw his father, ashen-faced, as he lie on his buffalow skin. His mother looked up as she heard someone enter, 'Meleeka, you have come just in time. Your father is dying, I think he has only held on hoping you would return soon, so that he could talk to you.' Meleeka hugged his mother and they both knelt down beside his father. As he took his father by the hand, he looked at his mother. 'Tell me what happened,' he said. His mother told him quickly of the big battle with the white settlers.

'All the tribal chiefs brought their braves to help in the fight with the settlers and nearly all the tribes were wiped out as the settlers had the soldiers backing them up. Your father and some of the braves managed to get back to the village but most have died of their wounds as your father most likely will. I was so glad you were not here to go with them, but as the days went past the second full moon, I thought I may never see you again either. Your father knew you would return and said he would not die until he saw you again.' As she spoke his father opened his eyes and said just two words, 'Tell me.' Meleeka told him of his travels and took out the skin map. He showed him the Blue Mountain, and how he had stayed there longer than he should have. He told him about his dream, which he now knew had been a reality – the dream had come on the night, of the day, of the big battle and fate for some reason had decided he was not to be there. He told his father about the voice coming from the mountain; his father listened to all Meleeka had said. He knew that his time was near and was thankful that he had seen his beloved son again before he went to the spirit in the sky. 'Listen to me, Meleeka, he said, 'before the sun rises again, I will be dead.' Tears welled up in Meleeka's eyes, but he knew that what his father said was probably true. 'When I am gone,' his father continued, 'take the rest of the tribe to your Blue Mountain, that is where your destiny lies, you must be the tribe that lives from now on in peace, the only killing must be for food and clothing. There has been too much death and destruction. Your dreams must be good dreams of peace and harmony; let others have bad dreams of hate and lies. Tell those that go with you, what I have said, if they wish to continue fighting they must be left behind. Promise me, Meleeka, you will do as I ask, for there is something special for you at your Blue Mountain, and find yourself as good a woman as your mother has been to me over these past many years.'

'I promise,' said Meleeka, 'I promise I will do as you ask.'

They sat with him all through the night and just before sunrise, as he said it would, his time on earth ended. Meleeka did as his father had wished, and talked to those that were left of the tribe. He told them about the Blue Mountain, and if they wished to come with him, they would have to be a peaceful tribe for all the rest of time. It appeared they all wanted to follow Meleeka. He thought some of the young braves (who had been too young to go to the big battle against the white settlers, but old enough to want revenge) may have wanted to go and join the other tribes who had vowed vengeance, but no, all said they would go with Meleeka, and would keep the code of peace.

CHAPTER III

A month later, after waiting to see if any more braves found their way back and to help the not too badly wounded heal a bit more, they packed up camp and set off for the Blue Mountain. Meleeka was glad he had taken his time and properly mapped the route, otherwise they surely would have got lost, and he would have lost face with his tribe. Even so, it took several weeks to get there, as there weren't enough horses for everyone, and to ride double would only have tired the horses more; anyway there was no real hurry. They would make camp early each evening to allow the horses a good rest for the next day's trek, and the children would get a bit of extra time to play which helped heal their minds of the sights they saw after the great battle. When they met other Indians on the way they never said where they were heading – they would exchange news and sometimes have a meal with them, then carry on with their travels.

When they finally arrived at the Blue Mountain, no one was disappointed, it was just as Meleeka had described it. 'Your father was right my son,' his mother said, 'your destiny is here, I can feel it.' When they had made camp and eaten the best food they had had in weeks, they sat around talking and watched the young ones playing in the stream. Meleeka sat with his mother, content and at peace.

Before he retired for the night Meleeka bathed in the stream. Everyone else was asleep; he hoped they were all as happy as he was. He stood staring up at the mountain, it looked a deeper blue with the moonlight shining down on it. The moon looked the biggest and brightest he had ever seen, and the mountain was majestic in all it's glory. Then he heard the voice again. '*You have returned Meleeka, you will not be sorry and your tribe will be protected.*' Meleeka shook himself in disbelief! The mountain had spoken to him again, but he would not tell anyone, not even his mother. The first time could have been his imagination, his mother had told him after returning to find his father dying, but his father, though dying, knew that the mountain had spoken to him and would speak to him many more times if he was to return and take the tribe and live in peace.

The next morning the young braves came to Meleeka. 'We want you to be our chief,' they said. 'We do not mean a chief who will lead us into battle. We want a chief who will teach us new things, and show us the right path to follow.'

'We will not need a chief here; we will all live as one family,' replied Meleeka.

'We are a new tribe now and have different things to learn and a new way of living, so we have chosen you to be our leader,' said Two Feathers who had been pushed forward by the others as their elected spokesman. Meleeka said he would think about it and asked that the whole tribe join together in a powwow to discuss it. Two Feathers smiled and said, 'They are already calling you Chief Blue Mountain.' Meleeka tried to hide his delight, but he couldn't.

'Thank you,' he said, 'what better name could a leader have?'

The women and all the braves sat in a circle with the children all sitting in a bunch together at one side waiting for Meleeka to arrive. They had chosen him as their leader and soon he would come, they hoped, and would accept that leadership.

The women had all worked for days making special clothes for Meleeka. The skins were dyed with the juice of the berries from the mountain, the feathers for the headdress were also dipped in the juice and hung to dry. If Meleeka would become their leader, he would step into the circle wearing the new outfit with the feathers of his headdress flowing down to his ankles. Then he would really be Chief Blue Mountain, their chief, their leader.

'Put them on, my son,' Meleeka's mother said as she held the new clothes out to him. 'They have chosen you as their chief, it would be an insult to refuse. You brought them to your mountain, to a new way of life. It is now up to you to show them the new ways.' Meleeka took the clothes and his mother stepped outside to wait for him to change.

They walked toward the circle together, and before he stepped into the circle his mother gave him a big hug. 'I'm proud of you my son and this night would have made your father even prouder of you than he was.'

As he sat down, cross-legged in the middle of the circle, they all cheered, then danced, bowing and stretching as they danced towards him. They danced around him three times before making a circle again, and then they sat down around him. Meleeka stood up, magnificent in his new blue outfit. He turned to face the mountain and then he told them to come and sit in front of him. When they were all seated, he sat down to face his people and the mountain.

'It is an honour,' he said, 'to be chosen as your chief, and I thank you. I also thank the women for making me this wonderful outfit, which is worthy of the highest chief in the land, but we came here to start a new way of life. We will not need a chief to powwow with other chiefs – we have left all that behind. I will be as a father to you and guide you through our new ways; we will work together as one family; we will all have our own homes. There are twenty families, each one with a young brave; we will build twenty cabins, one for each family. No more living in wigwams for us, we will live as the white man lives, in a warm cabin with a solid roof over our heads.' The young braves began to chuckle amongst themselves, then Two Feathers stood up.

'You may speak,' said Meleeka.

'We are not sure that we want to live in cabins. We are Indians, we may not like living as the white man lives.' Two Feathers bowed to Meleeka, then sat down.

'I understand what Two Feathers is saying,' Meleeka replied, 'but we have come here to start a new way of living, a new beginning. What the future holds for us I cannot say, but I feel it is something special. We have to change our way of living and some of our customs, and give the new way a chance. I told you before we came here our weapons were only for hunting. There will be no more killing of men, either white or Indian. It will be as it was before the white man came.

We will live in peace. Anyone who does not wish to live this way, can go now.' No one moved or said a word. Meleeka stared at the mountain as if to say, thank you.

He didn't want to lose any of his people – there were too few already. 'It is good that we are all in agreement,' said Meleeka. He rose from his sitting position in one swift movement and stood, feet astride and arms folded on his chest. His mother, watching him, thought how proud his father would have been with him this night. Her son looked every inch a chief, his stance, tall and proud.

Tonight he had gone from boyhood into manhood. She knew that when young braves passed their hunting test they were supposed to be men, but this was different. As Meleeka had risen from the ground, he seemed to grow taller and more powerful as she watched him, and this was her child and she loved him. *Please dear spirits of our forefathers, look after him for me. Let whatever he does be right for us. Do not be angered with him for changing the ways of our people, and let our people follow him, in the new way. Help them to keep their trust in him, this I ask you, spirits of our forefathers.* Meleeka's mother then raised her head from the prayer and sat gazing at her son.

She jumped as she heard Meleeka speaking, even his voice sounded different, much deeper and much more powerful. 'Tonight,' he was saying, 'we will feast and dance the tribal dance of our forefathers for the last time, for tomorrow our new life will begin. It is time for a new start. Come, everyone, enjoy yourselves.'

Meleeka stood with his arm around his mother's shoulders as they watched the braves doing the dance for the last time. They had done many tribal dances that night, showing the young children the different dances for other tribes of Indians, but this was their own war dance, and as he watched the young braves with their gleaming bodies and the proud way they were dancing, Meleeka wondered if he was doing the right thing, taking it all away from them.

The fathers who had died in the battle, would they come back to haunt him, for leaving the old way of life, or would they too have said, '*There has been too much killing and too many slaughtered.*'

His mother looking up at him, knew what he was thinking. 'Do not worry my son, you have chosen the right path.'

That night when all was quiet Meleeka sat at the bottom of the mountain although the night had only the stars shining, and all the fires had gone out. When he looked at the mountain, it was as if the sun was shining down on it, the snow on the top was pure white, and further down where the snow had begun to melt was the deepest blue anyone would ever see. He wondered why he should be sitting gazing at the mountain when he should be asleep like all the others. After all he would see the mountain every day for many years to come, he hoped.

He turned away and looked at the vast land before him, as if in a vision he saw the cabins already built, his people all serene and happy, all working together, the children all running about and laughing as they played.

Once again he turned to the mountain. 'If what I have just seen is true,' he spoke to the mountain as if speaking to another person, 'I thank you for bringing me here and know that all will be well,' then he bowed to the mountain and retired for the night.

The next morning he called his braves together, 'I want six of you to go hunting and exploring,' he said, 'the rest of us will chop trees and start to make the cabins, the women and children will help carry the logs, while the old women do the cooking. Every other day the hunting braves will change places with the logging braves, then there will be no disagreements. We must build the cabins and stock up with food before the snows come.'

For weeks they worked like beavers, and like beavers they found a way to build. Though none of them had ever built a cabin before, they found a way to slot the logs together, they plastered the slots with mud from the stream, then tied the logs together with strips of skin. They worked from sunup to sundown. Then everyone had a meal together which the older women had cooked for them.

When the first cabin was finished it was about fourteen feet long and twelve feet wide, with a doorway on the left side and two windows at the front. The women had cut skins to fit the doorway, one for the inside and one for the outside; they could be rolled up like a blind to let in the warmth of the sun or dropped down to keep out the cool night air. They covered the windows the same way.

Meleeka wanted to build all the cabins before anyone went to live in them. The tribe had other ideas – they said Meleeka and his mother should have the first one as that would be the proper thing to do.

As yet they had not thought about white man's furniture or how to cook inside the cabin. They would only be sleeping in it, and if it was alright the others would also have cabins. 'It would not be good to build and not like what we are building,' said Two Feathers. Meleeka saw the logic in this and said they would give it a try.

The women brought rugs for them to sleep on, and skins with pictures on them that the children had painted with berry juice.

The next day Meleeka worked on the edge of the forest with some of the young braves. They heard shouting coming from down the valley. It was Two Feathers and one of the other scouting braves. When they reached Meleeka, they told him that they had been hunting further down the valley and had found a wagon with a white man and woman in it. 'They are sick, very sick,' said Two Feathers.

'We will go and bring them back here, we cannot leave them to die,' said Meleeka.

He told the braves to get horses and fresh water from the stream; Two Feathers took Meleeka and the braves to the wagon. Meleeka told two of the braves to take the water and see if the white people could drink, if not, to wipe their faces with the cool water. He and Two Feathers would put the horses to the wagon shafts and get the white people to the Blue Mountain. At the camp, the women waited for the braves to come back, although some of the older ones were against bringing the white ones there. 'They may have the fever and spread it to all of us,' they muttered to one another. 'We should leave them to die. The white man killed our menfolk, why should we try to save them?' asked Red Feather's widow. No one answered. They heard the braves approaching and Meleeka telling them to take the man and woman into the cabin while he went to find his mother.

She told him what the older woman had been saying about the fever, and what Red Feather's widow had said.

'We can't leave them to die,' said Meleeka. 'We have left the past behind us, so we must look after them. If they have got the fever and pass it on to us, so be it, at least we will have tried to help them. You take two of the young women to the cabin. They will assist you. I will speak to Red Feather's widow – she still has bitterness in her heart.'

He watched his mother and two girls go into the cabin, then he went to find Red Feather's widow; she looked at him in defiance as she watched him approach. He took her hand gently and led her to a quiet place. As they sat down, he took both her hands into his; she sat with head bowed. 'Look at me,' he said; she raised her head slowly. The defiance had gone from her eyes. He could only see sadness. 'I am sorry you had the feeling of hatred in your heart,' he said. 'I can understand why, you lost your husband and father of your children, a brave man, a man we all respected. I myself looked on him as an older brother, and felt great sadness when he did not return. We all lost loved ones in the battle with the white man; we will not forget them. They will be remembered always. It is the hatred and bitterness we have to forget. Not all white men are bad – they too have left loved ones to grieve over them. Wives without husbands, children without fathers. That is why we have come here to seek a new life, and hopefully a better life.'

When he had finished speaking, she smiled up at him. 'I am sorry,' she said, 'for having bad thoughts; it is not good to think this way. I have been happy living here, as happy as I could be without my husband, I should not spoil it. Come, I will go and help your mother.' She rose to her feet as Meleeka rose to his. They walked towards the cabin together.

Inside the cabin his mother was sponging the girl's face. As Meleeka looked down at the girl, his heart leapt, for she was not only beautiful, she was of Indian blood. But what was she doing travelling with the white man?

'They are both very sick,' his mother said without turning around. 'They both burn with the fever and we do not have any medicine.'

'I will see if the older women have any herbs,' said Meleeka. He did not want them to die, especially the young girl. As he left the cabin he looked up at the mountain. Why do I always look at the mountain when I am troubled? he thought; he had not long to wait for an answer.

The mountain was speaking to him again. '*Send braves for some snow, tell them to wrap the snow in skins and bring it back to the cabin.*'

'Then what?' asked Meleeka.

'*Pack the skins of snow round the sick ones, it will cool them, and take the fever away.*'

Meleeka did not hesitate, and sent the braves for the snow.

They thought he was mad but did not argue. His mother also thought he had lost his senses when he burst into the cabin with the skins packed with snow, and told her to wrap them around the man and the girl.

Like the braves she did not argue, but did as she was asked. She had no idea where to put the snow packs, so she put some down the sides of the bodies and some to the chests, then she covered them with bearskins. She looked at Meleeka to see if she had done it right. He shrugged his shoulders.

'We will have to wait,' he said. How could he tell her the mountain had told him what to do? She would think he had gone mad. Before the snow had melted, the fever broke, first in the man. As the man started to shiver Meleeka took away the snow packs and put blankets around him.

'We will keep him warm, he will be alright now,' said Red Feather's wife. 'We will watch the girl and do the same when her fever breaks.' As she spoke the girl started to shiver. His mother went to attend to her.

Meleeka left the cabin, looked up at the mountain. 'Thank you,' he said.

When the white man opened his eyes his vision was blurred, and he wondered where he was. He knew he wasn't in his wagon, and also knew he wasn't in a bed, although he felt warm and comfortable. He lay there waiting for his vision to clear, he could hear voices but he couldn't tell what was being said. He realized he was in some kind of cabin, with skins on the walls. Dear Lord, he thought, the Indians must have captured us. His heart started pounding as Meleeka came into the cabin.

'You feel better now, maybe you feel like having some food?' Meleeka asked as he looked down at the white man. He smiled as he spoke. 'You have been very sick, you and the girl. We have looked after you both, the girl still sleeps, but will soon be awake.'

'My daughter is alive?' he missed seeing the frown on Meleeka's face as he said, My Daughter. 'But we had the fever, we were dying,' he looked at Meleeka for an explanation.

'You eat first, then we talk,' said Meleeka.

His mother had prepared some soup and some herb tea. 'It will give the white one his strength back,' she said.

'My name is Joseph,' said the man, when he had finished eating, 'and that is my daughter,' he pointed to the corner where the girl still slept. This time he saw the frown on Meleeka's face. 'My wife died with the fever three weeks ago. We were on a wagon train; ten others died with the fever; they went down like flies one after the other. When we had buried them, the wagon train split up. My daughter and I headed north, the others who were left went to the west. After a week of travelling, my daughter Sara became sick with the fever, then I too went down with it. I thought we were going to die. We must have been in the wagon for days before you found us, and apparently saved our lives. For this I must thank you. We will always be in your debt.'

So saying, he shook Meleeka's hand. 'It was the young braves that found you,' replied Meleeka. 'For some reason you must have had to come to the Blue Mountain, but do not worry, we will look after you. We are a peaceful tribe, no harm will come to you, now you must rest; we will speak some more later. My mother will look after your daughter.'

Meleeka left the cabin and went in search of his mother. When he found her he told her all that Joseph had said.

'But the girl cannot be his daughter as she is pure Indian; she is no half-breed, so his wife wasn't Indian. If she had been, it would have shown – you can always tell when there is mixed blood.'

'Perhaps we will find the answer when Joseph is stronger,' said Meleeka thoughtfully. His mother looked at him, and smiled to herself. Her son had fallen in love with the girl. He may not know it himself. But she knew.

When Sara opened her eyes, the first thing she saw was an Indian woman bending over someone in the corner. As Sara tried to sit up, the women turned towards her. In a flash she was across the room looking down at Sara. 'Good,' she said, 'at last you have come out of your deep sleep. We were beginning to get worried about you.'

'Who are you?' asked Sara, 'and where is my father? Did he die?'

'To answer your first question,' said the Indian woman, 'I am Buta, mother of Meleeka, and no! your father did not die – he is over there. He is sleeping now, you have both been very sick, but soon we will have you both healthy again. I will go for some water to sponge you down, then you must try and eat something. When your father wakens it will please him to know you have eaten as he has been worried about you.'

Within a week Joseph and Sara had become much stronger; though they had not been strong enough to leave their beds, they could sit up and talk to one another.

'The Indians have been kind to us and looked after us well,' Joseph said to Sara. 'If they had not found us, we surely would have died.'

'I wish that mother had been with us and that she also could have been saved,' replied Sara.

'It wasn't meant to be,' said Joseph. His eyes filled with tears as he thought about his dead wife; she had been a good wife, and a good mother to Sara.

'She should not have died,' Sara said. 'She was so kind, it is not fair.'

'And would it be fair to fill heaven with only old people? No it would not,' Joseph answered himself. 'We all have to die when our time on earth is done. Age has nothing to do with it.'

'I know,' said Sara. 'It is just that I loved Mother so much, I hope that I take after her, and will always be kind and gentle.'

'You will be what you are meant to be,' said Joseph. Dear God! he thought, I will have to tell her the truth about her birth. He knew that Meleeka and his mother had guessed that Sara was Indian. As soon as they were both stronger he would tell her.

Sara looked across at her father. He is in a pensive mood this morning, I wonder what troubles him, she thought. Perhaps he is getting bored, now that he is feeling better. She would ask Meleeka to bring a piece of wood, so her father could do some whittling; it was not like her father to do nothing, but he had never had the fever before and it did leave you feeling weak and helpless, in fact, she could never remember her father having any kind of sickness.

When Meleeka and his mother brought them some food, Sara asked about some wood for her father. 'Good idea,' said Meleeka, 'it is good to be occupied.'

'I have been thinking,' said Joseph, 'there is a table in the wagon, and chairs tied on the sides. Could we have them brought here?' Meleeka shouted to the braves to bring them. Within minutes they were put in the middle of the cabin. 'Good,' said Joseph, 'we will eat at the table; will you and your mother sit with us?' he asked Meleeka. When Joseph stood up he felt a bit dizzy, but it soon passed. Sara felt weak when she stood up and Meleeka helped her to the table.

Joseph and Sara enjoyed the meal of fish; it was beautifully cooked and the best fish they had ever tasted. Buta saw how much they enjoyed it. When they had finished she brought them each a dish of berries. It was the first solid food they had eaten in weeks. 'You will soon be strong and fit again, now that you can eat proper food,' said Meleeka.

Sara asked if she could sit outside, as the fresh air would do her good. Meleeka carried a chair out for her, then helped her outside. The first thing she saw was the Blue Mountain. She could not take her eyes off it as Meleeka helped her to the chair; he watched her as she sat down, her eyes never leaving the mountain. It was as if he wasn't there – nothing existed for her at that moment, only the mountain. He watched her for a long time, as her body relaxed and a beautiful expression came to her face; she leaned back and closed her eyes – it was as if all the power of the mountain was flowing through her body. She lifted her hands, palms open towards the mountain, as one lifts one's hands to get warmth from a fire. She has the same feeling for the mountain as I have, Meleeka thought.

Sara opened her eyes and looked up at him. 'Oh Meleeka, it is so beautiful here. This is where I will sit every day, and soon all traces of the fever will have left me.' His heart missed a beat – when Sara and Joseph were well again, they would want to leave and go wherever they were going to. Looking down at Sara, he knew he wanted her to stay.

'I will go and see if your father wishes to come outside,' he said to Sara.

As he entered the cabin his mother was on her way out. 'I was just coming with a rug to put around Sara's shoulders; we must not let her catch a cold.'

'A good idea,' said Meleeka, 'I am going to see if Joseph wants to sit outside.'

Joseph said he would rather stay in the cabin. 'At least for now; maybe I will venture out later.'

Meleeka sat down at the table with Joseph. 'When you and Sara are better I suppose you will carry on with your travels?' he asked.

'I haven't thought about it,' said Joseph. 'When my wife died, and the others, Sara and I just headed north, we had no plans to go anywhere special. We thought if we found a settlement we would stay for a while and see what happened, then we came down with the fever. You know the rest. We are thankful that you found us and saved our lives. How you managed to save us I do not know; we must be the only ones to have had the fever and live to tell the tale. We could find no way of bringing down the temperature of those who had it; even the doctor who was travelling with us died.'

'We packed snow into skins and placed it around you; your temperatures broke before the snow melted.'

'That was clever; how did you know it would work?' asked Joseph.

'I didn't,' said Meleeka. He did not tell him what the mountain had said.

'It must be fate that sent us here,' Joseph said thoughtfully. 'Do you believe in fate?' he asked Meleeka.

'Oh yes, I certainly believe in fate,' he answered.

Joseph looked around the cabin. Though it was well built, he could see that it hadn't been built by white men. And looking through the open doorway he could see only Indian tents. 'Tell me about this place,' he said. 'I feel that you haven't been here long, yet for some reason you know your destiny lies here.'

Mekeeka smiled at Joseph. 'You are very perceptive for one who has been very sick.' Meleeka told him how he had set off as a young brave and what had happened to him, all that is, except about the mountain speaking to him.

'I don't doubt whether you believe in fate,' said Joseph. 'It is a strange story you tell me. What a pity all men cannot live the way you intend to do here. We left the last settlement because Indians and white men were always fighting and killing one another. Little did we know the fever would get us, and some would not make it. It is strange that we left the other survivors and ended up at your Blue Mountain. Would you call that fate, Meleeka?' Without waiting for an answer Joseph continued, 'Some men say we have a choice in what we do with our lives but we didn't choose to come here so it must be fate.'

'I think,' said Meleeka, 'you were sent here so I could marry your daughter.'

'Marry my daughter!' Joseph shouted. 'But you hardly know her.'

'Exactly,' said Meleeka, 'but we are talking about fate.'

'Maybe you are right.'

'I know I am,' said Meleeka.

Joseph stared at him for a long time. As if deciding whether he could trust him. He liked Meleeka, who seemed a good and honest Indian. And what he had told him about finding the Blue Mountain, then finding himself and Sara and saving their lives, it seemed to Joseph that for some reason they had all been brought together.

At last he spoke, 'You have guessed, haven't you, that Sara isn't my daughter.'

'Maybe not by bloodline,' answered Meleeka, 'but she is a true daughter to you. Sometimes the bond can be stronger than to a natural parent. But my mother and I have guessed the truth.'

'I thought you had,' said Joseph. 'The thing is, Sara doesn't know, my wife and I never had the courage to tell her. We loved her so much and we always thought of her as our own, always knowing in our hearts that one day we would have to tell her. Yet always making some excuse not to.'

'I think,' said Meleeka, 'the time has come for you to tell Sara the truth. My mother and I saw at once that Sara was pure Indian; others will also see it, especially the older women. Even Sara herself may feel she is different from other white girls and is afraid to question you.'

'You are very wise for your age,' said Joseph. 'No wonder the braves want you for their chief.'

Meleeka smiled, and shrugged his shoulders. 'It is funny,' said Joseph, 'that none of the white people we have known ever mentioned that Sara could have Indian blood in her.'

'How could they?' asked Meleeka. 'She was yours and Rosa's daughter. If they suspected anything, they would not tell you, though between themselves they may have said many things. Would you like to tell me how Sara became your daughter? Perhaps then, it will be easier for you to tell Sara.'

'Maybe so,' said Joseph, 'maybe so. I will start from the beginning then you will know all about me. I was brought up on a farm in the north of England. I was never interested in farming, and anyway my brother would inherit the farm, being the eldest. In my younger days I was a bit wild and drove my father to distraction with my drinking and gambling. When I met Rosa I fell madly in love with her; she was the sweetest, kindest girl you could ever have met. But she wasn't good enough for my family. Father was a social climber, mother a snob, and my brother, he was chasing after an upper-crust wench. When I told my father I wanted to marry Rosa, he couldn't believe it.

'"Marry a serving wench from the local tavern – now I know you're mad," he shouted at me. "Think of the disgrace you will bring to the family. Is the girl pregnant? Give her some money and send her away. You will not bring shame to this house, Joseph. Is it not enough that you disgrace us with your drinking and gambling? Now you want to marry a serving wench." By this time my father was so red in the face with his temper, I thought he would have a heart attack.

'"Father," I said, "you can rant and rave all day, it will do you no good. For whatever you say, I am going to marry Rosa, and no, she is not pregnant, for I have not touched her." I gave him no opportunity to say another word, for I walked out of the room. It did not matter to me what any of them said. I was going to marry Rosa.

'A week later, after many family squabbles, it was decided I would be given a generous amount of money, on condition I started a new life, with or without Rosa. That was up to me, and never had I to set foot on the farm again! Of course, I agreed.

'Rosa and I were married and we came to America. With the money my father gave me, we set up a small trading post. One day an Indian girl arrived; she was big with child. The poor girl was exhausted, she had been walking for days. Rosa, being Rosa, felt sorry for the girl. She left me in the store and took the girl into the house part. Rosa filled the bath for the girl and told her to get in it. She gave the girl soap and towels and said she would find her some clean clothes. "I will make you something to eat while you are having a bath," Rosa told the girl. Rosa came back into the store and said we would be having our meal in half an hour.

'"How's the girl," I asked.

'"She is worn out," said Rosa. "I have made up the spare bed and found her some night clothes. When she has had a bath, we will eat, then she can go to bed."

'"We don't know anything about her," I said.

'"There will be time for questions tomorrow," said Rosa. "At the moment, all I know is her husband was killed, and she has been wondering about for days," Rosa told me.

'The girl was quiet as we all sat around the table eating our meal. Rosa told me not to badger the girl with questions, if she wanted to speak, she would speak. I did not want to stare at the girl. Yet I did not want to ignore her. And I must say, she looked a damn sight better, sitting there in Rosa's nightdress, than when she walked into the store.

'When our eyes happened to meet, she would smile shyly. I could not tell how old she was; if I had to guess I would say about nineteen. She was tall, like Sara, and I suppose if she had not been pregnant she would have been slim. Yet Sara does not look like her. The girl's face was round.' Joseph could not bring himself to say Sara's mother because he never thought of the girl as Sara's mother. 'She did not have fine chiselled cheek bones like Sara,' he told Meleeka.

'Anyway, when we finished eating, Rosa took the girl and put her to bed. Later that night, we were woken by the girl's screams. Rosa took one look at her and sent me to get some hot water. The girl must have had some kind of premonition, for she asked Rosa to look after the child if anything happened to her.

'"Nothing is going to happen," Rosa told her, "and when the child is born, you can stay here for as long as you want to. We will look after you and the baby." "Won't we?" Rosa said to me as I came into the room with the hot water, soap and towels. "Yes," I said, not really knowing what I was saying yes to. The girl died in childbirth. We thought the baby was also dead; it did not cry. Then Rosa shook it, more in desperation than anything. The poor mite looked like a skinned rabbit. "It won't live, you are wasting your time, leave it be," I told Rosa. Then we heard a small whimper. "Put some warm water into the bowl," Rosa shouted. "Then warm some of that pure oil the Mexican left for us." As Rosa washed the baby, I warmed the oil, though I thought Rosa had gone mad. When she dried the baby, I poured the warm oil into her cuffed hands. Rosa massaged the baby all over with the warmed oil. The baby was still breathing, though it was still very shallow. Every half hour Rosa would massage the baby with warm oil, then wrap a warm blanket around it. By morning Rosa was exhausted. But even to my inexperienced eye, the baby looked stronger.

'Rosa managed to get some milk down the child, only a few drops at a time, but at least it was something. After a week of constant attention, the baby began to look human. "She will survive now," Rosa said to me. "I hope she is worth all this trouble," I replied. "Just look at yourself, woman. You are worn out, you haven't slept for a week. Your beautiful hair, all lank and greasy." "Do not worry about me, I will soon be my old self again, and now we have a daughter to look after. All the trouble, as you call it, will have been worth it." As she spoke Rosa placed the baby in my arms. I cannot explain the feelings I had at that moment – apprehension, I suppose. I had not thought of the child as a daughter; someone might come looking for the girl and take the baby away. I looked down at the baby. A feeling of great joy came over me! I held the baby in one arm and pulled Rosa to me with the other. The love in

Rosa's eyes as she looked up at me, and the tenderness on her face when she looked at the baby, brought a lump to my throat. I kissed the top of Rosa's head and hugged her closely. "And what are we going to call our daughter?" I asked, praying silently that no one would come and claim the baby. "We will call her Sara, after my mother," Rosa answered. "Welcome to our world, Sara," I said, kissing the child on the forehead. I swear the baby smiled at me, and stole my heart.

'As the years past we thought of Sara only as our daughter. Sometimes Rosa and I would think about telling her the truth, then we would decide not to. I nearly told her when Rosa died, but Sara was so upset, I thought it best to wait.'

A shadow fell across the doorway as Sara entered. She went to her father and put her arms around him. 'I know it is wrong to eavesdrop, but I could not help it. I was coming back inside when I heard you talking to Meleeka. I heard what you said about my birth and how you and Mother looked after me. Yes she will always be Mother to me. As you will always be my father. It does not matter that we are not blood relatives – you both loved me as if I was your own child. I could not have wished for better parents. And I am glad you did not tell me when I was younger.'

'I would not have kept you in ignorance much longer; I had decided to tell you when we reached the new settlement,' her father said.

Sara kissed her father on the cheek, 'I love you, Father,' she told him. 'There is no need for any more explanations.' Joseph's eyes filled with tears as he hugged his daughter.

'I will leave you two alone,' said Meleeka. 'You may still have much to talk about.'

'Wait, don't go yet,' said Sara. 'With my eavesdropping I nearly forgot what I was coming to tell you. I don't know if I had fallen asleep and was dreaming, or whether it really happened. But I am sure the mountain spoke to me.'

Meleeka reacted involuntarily. 'It did. I mean, did it?'

'Don't be silly,' said Joseph. 'You must be dreaming. How can a mountain speak?'

'What did it say?' asked Meleeka.

'You can't believe the mountain spoke to her,' Joseph asked Meleeka.

'Let us hear what Sara thinks the mountain said.' Meleeka could hardly contain his excitement.

'Well,' said Sara, 'this is what I heard. "*You and your father have been brought here for a reason. Your lives were saved, so that you could stay here. This will be your new home, there is no need to travel any further. You will both be safe here.*"'

Joseph was thinking how their lives were saved with snow from the mountain. How the others had died with the fever. He remembered the doctor saying there was no cure. Yet Sara and himself had been cured. He looked at Meleeka. 'What do you make of all this?' he asked.

'Earlier,' Meleeka answered, 'we were talking about fate. Was it fate that my braves found you? Was it fate that your lives were saved when by all accounts you should have died of the fever? And, was it fate that at the very moment you were telling me about the birth of Sara, she was coming to tell us what the mountain had said?' Whether it be in a dream or not Meleeka knew it was the mountain that spoke to Sara. But for the moment he would not tell them.

'I cannot take all this in,' said Joseph. 'A mountain telling Sara we must make our home here.'

'Surely it is I that is having a dream, and will wake up at any moment,' said Sara.

'It is no dream,' said Meleeka. 'The three of us are all wide awake. Maybe it is your destiny to settle here. Who can tell? We will wait until you are both in better health, then see what you wish to do. If you decide to stay with us, my people will make you welcome. Now I think you should both get some rest. There has been too much excitement for one day.'

CHAPTER IV

Two weeks later Joseph and Sara were strong enough to go for a walk. Their convalescence had been long but Buta was a strict nurse. Each day she would sit them outside the cabin. 'You need much sun to get your strength back,' she would tell them. 'Later you will take short walks to keep your legs moving. That way, you will get better much quicker.' She had been right. Joseph and Sara felt as though they had never been ill as they set out to explore their surroundings.

They followed the stream through the forest; the water was so clear, they could see the fish dashing about. When Joseph said he felt tired, they rested awhile by the stream. Joseph, watching the antics of the fish in the stream, said to Sara, 'Being here reminds me of when I was a boy in England.'

Sara looked at him in surprise, for her father seldom spoke about his earlier life, neither had her mother for that matter. 'Why?' she asked him.

'If I was bored, I would go fishing,' he told her. 'Sometimes alone, sometimes with friends. We caught the fish with our hands. Tickling trout we called it. You could catch as many as a dozen, if you were lucky. If the children from the village were with me, I gave the fish to them, for some of them were very poor. If I was on my own, I would give them to the cook when I got home. She would give me a couple of buns in return. I wonder if I can still catch fish by tickling them,' Joseph said, more to himself than Sara. 'We will have to be quiet though.' He lay down and slid his hands under a flat stone in the water. Within minutes he threw a fish out of the water, the fish just missing Sara, who stood behind him. Without more ado, Joseph plunged his hands back into the stream, feeling like a young boy again. He wasn't satisfied until he had caught four.

To Sara's disgust, Joseph took out his penknife and gutted the fish before stringing them together and slinging them over his shoulder, before setting off back to the cabin.

'Have you ever seen anything so breathtaking?' asked Sara, as they came out of the forest.

Joseph turned quickly – he knew without asking where she was looking. Once again Sara was mesmerized by the mountain. Many times as they sat outside the cabin, Joseph had caught her staring up at the mountain. It seemed to have some strange effect on her that Joseph did not understand.

After a few moments gazing up at the mountain, Sara would close her eyes, her face transformed with love and tenderness, like a mother's when she sees her newborn child. A smile would appear upon Sara's face, as though Sara and the mountain shared a secret. Joseph knew he was not the only one to notice Sara's behaviour. Meleeka had also noticed. 'Yes it is breathtaking,' replied Jospeh, more sharply than he intended. 'We had better hurry, we have been away long enough; Meleeka will be worried about us.' With a sigh, Sara followed her father, her thoughts still with the mountain. Did it really speak to me? Or was I dreaming? she thought to herself. I was so weak it could have been an hallucination. Yet I feel as though it is giving me some sort of power and is also trying to tell me something. I wish I could speak to my father, or even Meleeka about how I feel. But if I try to, an inner voice seems to say, not yet, the time is not right, we will tell you when.

As they reached the cabin, Meleeka came towards them. 'Have you liked what you have seen?' he asked Joseph.

'Yes, it is beautiful. You could not have chosen a better place to start a new way of life,' Joseph told him.

'I have spoken to my people. If you wish to stay with us, also making a new life for yourselves, you will be welcome; it was agreed by everyone,' Meleeka told them.

'I will have to think about it, but we are grateful for your offer,' Joseph answered thoughtfully. He did not take kindly to the effect the mountain was having on Sara.

'Would you not like to settle here?' Sara asked her father as they entered the cabin.

'I will have think about it, Sara. It may not be wise for us to settle with a tribe of Indians. Good Indians, I admit, but Indians none the less.'

'Well,' Sara said, 'I think it is kind of Meleeka and his people inviting us to say. Anyway, we could always move on later if we found being here unsuitable.' Sara looked pleadingly at her father, and before he could say anything she continued, 'Meleeka's aim is to live as the white men live; you could teach them many things. Look at this cabin, for instance. The next one, with your help, would be much improved. If we only stayed for a year, we could be of help to them. It is the least we can do. After all they did save our lives.'

'I know,' said Joseph, 'and I am truly grateful – what you say makes sense for we have nowhere else to go. So there is no reason why we should be in a hurry to move on. I just wonder if this is the right place for us! Whether you realize it or not, Sara, that mountain has a strange effect on you. I have seen you looking at it many times and whether you are standing or sitting, something strange comes over you. As if you are drawing some kind of power from it. I just don't know what to make of it all.'

Sara took hold of her father's hands. 'I admit,' she said, 'I do get a strange feeling when I look at the mountain. But it is not a bad feeling, it is as though I am being revitalized. A warm glow comes upon me; I feel that all the world is full of love, as it was meant to be when the world was created. It cannot be wrong to feel like this, surely, Father. But if you want to move on and not accept Meleeka's offer, we will do so,' Sara told him.

'I do not know what to do,' replied Joseph, 'but from what you have just told me, it would do us no harm. And as you say, we could be of some help to Meleeka. Yes, I think we will give it a try,' Joseph told her.

Sara took hold of her father's hands, kissing the palms. 'You won't regret it, Father,' I promise.

'Don't make promises you cannot keep,' he said. 'We do not know what lays before us.' He hugged her to him, then pulled away, looking into her eyes. He was smiling as he said, 'Come what may, lass, the dye is cast.'

'We will go and tell Meleeka right away before you change your mind,' Sara said, taking hold of her father's hand, as she took him to find Meleeka.

'I am glad you have decided to stay,' Meleeka told them. 'My people will be pleased also; we all feel you have been sent here to help us. The way your lives were saved from the killer sickness must be for a purpose. For what, as yet, we do not know. But my people think it is a good omen.' Meleeka took hold of Joseph's hand, shaking it vigorously. 'You must keep the cabin for your home; it will be our gift to you,' he told them.

'Thank you,' said Joseph.

'But you do not like it,' interrupted Meleeka. 'Come, speak the truth, we are friends and will remain friends for a long time, I hope. So do not be afraid to tell me what you feel.'

'The cabin itself is alright – it just isn't big enough,' Joseph told him.

'Not big enough?' said Meleeka. 'Why, it is much bigger than any of our tents.'

'You asked me to speak the truth, so let me explain,' replied Joseph. 'If we stay here, we will need beds and furniture; there will have to be a stove for cooking. Also, Sara will need a bedroom for herself, and so will I.'

Meleeka listened to what Joseph was saying. 'But when we found you, the wagon was your home, and that is not big. I thought you would be pleased when I gave you the cabin. It is like the one of the white man.'

Joseph knew he had hurt Meleeka's feelings and would have to be careful. 'Did you ever enter the white man's cabin?' he asked.

'No, I only saw one from the outside,' replied Meleeka.

'If you had seen the inside, it would have been something like the one I have described,' Joseph told him. 'The wagon was our home, because we were travelling. We would build another home when we arrived at our new settlement. I am honoured that you have given us the cabin. You must not think otherwise. If I have hurt your feelings, I am sorry. But if we are to stay, it will have to be altered and you may as well know now. For it is better to make things right in the beginning than to gamble about them afterwards.'

'I understand,' said Meleeka. 'Now that you have explained, we will build a new home for you and Sara. With you to help us, we can build a real white man's cabin.' Meleeka held his hand towards Joseph. 'Agreed?' he asked.

'Agreed,' replied Joseph, shaking Meleeka's hand.

That night Joseph drew a plan for the new building of a cabin, so it would give Meleeka an idea of what it should look like. The next morning as Joseph lay the plans on the table, he explained to Meleeka the layout. 'This large room is where the cooking will be done; we will also eat and relax here. The other two rooms are bedrooms for myself and Sara. You see, it is just like this cabin, only split up into three rooms.' Joseph unrolled another drawing. 'And this is how it will be when it is furnished.' He pointed to the fireplace he had drawn. 'We will need stones from the river and the mountainside to build that,' he said. 'I can make some furniture. There are tools in the wagon. Rosa always said I should have been a carpenter. We have mattresses, pots and pans and things. There should also be supplies in the wagon. Rosa was always one for stocking up in case of emergencies.' Joseph looked up to see Meleeka grinning at him.

'What are you trying to do, my friend – convince me or yourself?' Meleeka asked him.

'I am sorry. I must have been thinking out loud,' Joseph replied.

'I am impressed with the plans you have shown me. If you tell me what you need regarding the stones and logs, I will see to it that my braves acquire them for you.'

CHAPTER V

In the weeks that followed, everyone worked hard. The braves felled the trees and stripped them of their branches; even the children helped by collecting stones in a sled-like basket that Joseph made for them. The children could not have been given a better task, for they did not throw any old stone into the basket. Being children, they searched for stones of different colours and shapes.

Joseph supervised the building of the cabin and with the help of two braves, made a bed for himself and one for Sara. Later he would make some drawers, but for the moment there were more important things to do.

The highlight of the building was when Joseph built the fireplace and the chimney that went outside the house. When the cabin was finished, the children gathered small logs so Joseph could light a fire and they could watch the smoke come out of the chimney, as he told them it would. Joseph smiled when he heard their squeals of delight as the first puff of smoke emerged.

He stood back to admire his own handiwork, for he was delighted with the way the different coloured stones reflected their true colours with the flames from the fire, and he silently blessed the children for being so selective in their choice of stones. He had built the fireplace from floor to ceiling with a mantle shelf across the middle, while a hole was inserted on the left side of the fire, making an oven for Sara.

The raised hearth was built with smooth, flat stones. On each side of the fireplace, the shelves that Joseph and Meleeka had made were filled with Rosa's best blue dinner set; pans hanging on the wall beneath them also caught the glow of the firelight.

Joseph placed a framed picture of Rosa on the mantle shelf, where he had also placed a few of her treasured knick-knacks. 'It is looking more like home by the minute,' he said to Sara. Sara agreed with him – the room was cozy and warm, the flames from the log fire giving a welcoming effect.

'When we get some more furniture it will be really comfortable,' she said.

'What about your bedroom?' Joseph asked her.

'I love it, like here, the furniture is a bit sparse but what does it matter?' Sara wasn't bothered about the furnishing of her bedroom; she could see the Blue Mountain from her window and for some reason that was all she cared about.

Joseph and Sara were surprised when Meleeka and Buta arrived, bringing gifts for their new home, Meleeka carrying what looked like a carpet. He placed it in the middle of the floor and unrolled it. It was a hugh rug woven in many colours with two smaller rugs hidden inside. 'The women of my tribe send you these to welcome you. They wish you, as my mother and I also do, much happiness, good health and long life in your new home.'

'And these,' said Buta, placing an assortment of wall hangings and carved animals on the table, 'are from the young braves and the children. They have also sent a message. They hope you will stay with us for many many moons.' Both Joseph and Sara were touched with the kindness showed to them by their new-found friends.

'How are we ever going to thank you all?' asked Joseph. 'First you save our lives, then you invite us to make our home with you and now all this.'

'The rugs are beautiful,' said Sara. 'I will have to thank the women for them, and also thank the braves and children for their gifts.'

'They will be pleased that you like them,' said Buta. Meleeka told Joseph how much he admired the cabin and how different it was from the one they had built.

'We can build others like it,' Joseph told him. 'If you wish your tribe to live as the white man lives, well,' Joseph said, waving his hand around, 'this is how we live. This is the white man's home, though as yet, we are a bit short of furniture. It will take time,' he told Meleeka, 'to build more cabins like this one, but between us we can do it.'

While they were talking, Sara showed Buta the workings of the oven at the side of the fire. Though Buta herself admired the fireplace, and the oven, she wondered if the women, including herself, would ever come to terms with living (as Meleeka wished them to do) like the white man. She voiced her thoughts to Sara. 'Maybe us womenfolk will not want to cook inside a cabin, it will be strange for us to do so,' Sara smiled at Buta.

'You and the other women must come here and I will show you how to use the oven.'

'That is a good idea,' Buta told her.

'Who knows,' Sara said, 'by the time winter comes, you may all be thankful for the protection the cabins will give you.'

As they rejoined the two men, Joseph was telling Meleeka they would have to stake the land. 'We will do it tomorrow. We will include the forests and the river, then go into a half circle staking whatever land we need. That way no one can take it away from us, as long as we do it legally.' Meleeka was thoughtful.

'What's troubling you?' Joseph asked Meleeka.

'It is the talk of owning all this land; it was foolish of me, an Indian, to think I could keep it. That it was there for the taking. For is that not why the white men are fighting us, so they can take our land? It is you, Joseph, who must stake the land and do whatever the white men do, when they have stolen land from the Indians.' Joseph gasped. So did Buta and Sara. 'It is alright,' said Meleeka quickly, 'I do not mean to insult you with what I say. But don't you see, if you own the land, Joseph, it will be safe. If I own it, one day I could also lose it.'

Joseph saw the logic in what Meleeka was saying. 'And you would trust me with all this land? But Meleeka, you hardly know me.' Joseph could only just keep his voice steady.

'It is better for you to have the land now, Joseph. For if other white men come and find it belongs to Indians, they could kill all my tribe and seize the land for themselves. Do I not speak the truth?' Meleeka asked Joseph.

'Yes, I suppose you do,' Joseph answered. 'But you have plans for you and your people, you told me so yourself.'

'You asked me a moment ago if I trusted you,' said Meleeka. 'The answer is, yes, I do trust you. All I ask, when the land is yours, my plans will be fulfilled and my people can stay here.' Joseph stared at Meleeka and marvelled at the wisdom in one so young, for he knew what Meleeka said was true. If he did not take the land, one day, others might come and kill for it.

'I will do as you ask,' he told Meleeka, 'but in my heart the land below the Blue Mountain will always be yours, any other land I claim will be my own. But I promise whatever happens in the years to come, whatever I do with the land, I will include you in the planning of it. As I hope you will also include me in your plans. Do you agree?' Meleeka nodded in agreement.

As they shook hands, Joseph smiled at Meleeka and said, 'You have the word of an English rogue. I cannot say English gentleman, for I never was one.' They both laughed. Sara made them some coffee and brought it to them.

'I am going with Buta to thank everyone for the gifts,' she told them, as she placed the coffee pot and mugs on the table. As Sara and Buta left the room, Joseph poured the coffee. 'You will not regret your decisions,' Meleeka said to Joseph, 'for I knew when my braves found you and your lives were saved that our destinies would be entwined. How or why, I did not know. But I think today, we have found the answer. You are here to protect this land for us.'

'Thank you for trusting me,' Joseph replied. 'Though by rights, all this land belongs to the Indians. You were there long before the white man. By the way, if we are going to build some more cabins, I will have to get more supplies and we will need furniture; we cannot make it all.'

'My braves tell me white men sell things near the great lake, where the boats come in to land. It will take many days for you to get there with the wagon.'

'All the same, I will have to make the journey,' Joseph told him.

'Then my braves will escort you to the great lakes when you decide to go,' Meleeka said.

That night when Sara retired to her room, she lifted the blind and gazed up at the Blue Mountain. All was quiet, as if the whole world was asleep. For a long time, she gazed at the mountain, letting her thoughts drift. Then she heard the voice. It was deep and clear.

'*It is good that you and your father make your home here with us. We guided you here and told Meleeka how to save you both. For here is where your true destiny lies. When your father Joseph claims the land, you will suggest the name Ilinka to him.*'

'Why?' asked Sara involuntarily.

'*Your true parents were from the Ilinka tribe,*' the voice answered, '*but you must always look upon Joseph as your father, for you have known no other. And he loves you as a true daughter.*'

'I know,' said Sara, feeling a bit foolish talking to a mountain. Then a thought struck her. If I am foolish enough to speak to a mountain, I may as well ask a question.

'If,' she said, with hesitation, 'the destiny of my father and myself lies here, why was my mother Rosa not allowed to dwell here with us? For did she not give me all the love of a true mother? Why was she not cured of her fever?'

Sara waited for an answer; there was nothing, but the silence of the night. She shrugged her shoulders and sighed. I might as well get into bed, she thought. As she turned away from the window, the voice spoke once again.

'*Only the great white spirit in the sky can answer your questions, as to why someone lives or dies. This I am telling you for it will always be so. Time on earth ends for all when their allotted time is spent.*'

'Yes, my father says much the same thing,' answered Sara.

'*He is a wise man,*' answered the voice. '*But do not speak to him of this conversation. In fact, tell no one. I am going now. I will speak with you again soon.*'

Well, Sara thought, as she got into bed, there is no doubt about it this time, the mountain did speak to me. But I wonder why it said, '*We guided you here.'* Oh well, I don't suppose it matters. She snuggled under the blankets and fell into a dreamless sleep.

CHAPTER VI

Joseph showed Meleeka a map of all the land he had staked. Meleeka gasped when he saw the size of it.

'I know there is a lot of land there,' said Joseph, pointing to the map, 'but we have to think into the future.' Joseph unrolled another map on which he had drawn twenty cabins; at the side of each cabin stood a wigwam.

'This is the immediate area,' he told Meleeka. 'The mountain, the forests, and where we will build the cabins.'

'As you see, I have spaced the cabins to give everyone plenty of room. The wigwams we will also keep for at first some of your people may not take kindly to living in the cabins. It will be better for them to have a choice.'

Meleeka grinned at Joseph. 'You are good for us,' he said. 'You think of everything. Some men would kill for this land and rape our women, if it suited them,' Meleeka told Joseph.

'I know,' Joseph replied, 'my people, the English, have captured many lands and killed many natives of those lands. One day, maybe a hundred years from now, the future generations of those lands may not wish to be ruled by the English. And I shudder to think what will happen then. If everyone could work together like you and I do, Meleeka, the world would be a better place.'

'I agree,' said Meleeka 'but as my father would tell me often, some men have good dreams, some men have bad dreams. But dreams, all the same.'

'Yes, that is true,' said Joseph, nodding his head in agreement. 'Well, at least our dreams are good dreams, Meleeka. We will just have to make sure they stay that way.'

Sara watched her father as he pinned the plans he had shown Meleeka onto the wall. They had just finished supper and, as usual, would sit and discuss the day's events before going to bed. 'So Meleeka was pleased with your plans?' Sara asked.

'Yes, he was,' answered Joseph. 'And do you know, I am getting excited with the prospect of it all. I wish your mother was alive. It would have amused her, living with a tribe of Indians. But she would have loved it.'

'Yes, she would,' answered Sara. 'Have you and Meleeka decided on a name for when the buildings are finished?' she asked, as Joseph sat down on his chair in front of the fire.

'Not as yet,' Joseph answered. 'Why? Do you have a name in mind?'

'I think Ilinka would be a good name,' Sara replied, as though the name had just popped into her head.

'We will have to speak to Meleeka, he may already have chosen a name. What made you think of Ilinka? It is a strange name, though I must confess, I like the sound of it.' Sara refrained from answering her father.

The next day Joseph told Meleeka about Sara's suggestion of the name Ilinka. 'Don't ask me how she came to conjure up a name like that. But the more I think about it, the more I like it,' Joseph told Meleeka.

'I also like the name,' Meleeka answered, 'but I will go and ask Cheeka, as she is the eldest of my tribe. If Cheeka agrees with the name Ilinka, the whole tribe will agree.'

Meleeka stepped into Cheeka's tent and sat down cross-legged before her. She was glad too see him, for she liked the young ones to come and talk with her. Most of her days were spent in her tent as she was too old to do much else. Soon her time on earth would be over, and she waited patiently for it to come.

Meanwhile, she would tell the young ones tales of the old days. It pleased her to talk about the past and it amused the young ones. 'You have a problem?' she asked. From being a young boy, Meleeka had always gone to Cheeka if he was troubled. Cheeka smiled at him, her blue eyes bright and alert. They could have been the eyes of a much younger woman, except that her face was all wrinkled with age, her hair white as snow and when she smiled, only two teeth could be seen in the front of her mouth.

Meleeka wondered what it was like to be old and waiting to die. He would miss her when the time came.

'Well,' she said, as if she had waited long enough for him to speak. 'You have come for something. What is it?'

'I have been speaking with Joseph, the white man. He said his daughter Sara suggested a name for the new settlement. I told him if you thought the name was suitable, we would agree to it.'

'So, you still value old Cheeka's wisdom,' she said laughing.

'Yes, I do,' Meleeka replied.

'What is the name the girl has chosen?' asked Cheeka.

'Ilinka,' he replied. He saw the surprise in her eyes.

'That is a strange name to come from a white man's daughter,' she told him. Meleeka did not miss the emphasis on white man's daughter. Did Cheeka know about Sara.

He had told no one except his mother about the conversation with Joseph. He would not have told his mother if Joseph had not given permission to do so, for it is not good to repeat the secrets of others.

Cheeka chuckled to herself as she watched Meleeka wrestling with his own thoughts. She took hold of Meleeka's hands, holding them tightly, then said to Meleeka, 'Through the flap of my tent I have watched the white man's daughter. She is very beautiful; it was her beauty and grace that caught my eye. Yet, something about her always puzzled me, though she dressed and acted like a white woman. Never could I think of her as one. When you mentioned the name Ilinka, I knew I was right. I am right, aren't I? The girl is of Indian blood.'

'Yes,' replied Meleeka, knowing he could not fool Cheeka for she had lived through many moons. 'But if you want to know more about Sara, you will have to ask Joseph, her father.'

'I will,' replied Cheeka.

'Why were you surprised when I mentioned the name Ilinka?' Meleeka asked her.

'The Ilinka tribe,' Cheeka told him, 'came from Asia thousands of years ago. They had the power to heal by touch. The healing power was given to them from the Lord of the sky. It was meant to be a gift for all humans. But the Lord of the sky became angry with the men of the earth, for they brought greed and hate to the world. Only the Ilinkas kept the pureness of heart and goodness of the soul. So the Lord of the sky let the Ilinkas keep the healing power on condition the tribe divided into four and went to the four corners of the earth. The ones that came to this land settled down to a peaceful life. They would only kill for food.

'Other tribes of Indians would fight among themselves but all would go to the Ilinka to be made well again, if they were wounded or became ill. Sometimes a brave or squaw would leave the Ilinka tribe to marry, though this was frowned upon. From generation to generation, the power was passed down. Then the white man came and wanted the land of the Indians. It did not matter to the white man whether an Indian was good or bad, as long as he got the land. That was all that mattered. In one fell swoop, so legend has it, the Ilinka tribe was massacred. For they would not, could not fight. What happened to those that left the tribe, I do not know. That is why I was surprised when you said the name Ilinka.'

'Do you not think it strange that the girl should choose the name?' Cheeka asked Meleeka.

'I think it very strange, very strange indeed,' he replied, 'and thank you for telling me; it is a part of history I did not know about. I do not wonder that you keep the young ones amused with all the stories you tell them.'

'I have told no one about the Ilinkas,' she answered.

'Well, thank you for telling me; it has been very interesting.' He was deep in thought as he went to find Joseph.

When he entered the cabin, Joseph was sitting in the chair by the fire. 'Where is Sara?' Meleeka asked, sitting down opposite Joseph.

'She has gone with your mother. Why, is anything wrong?' Joseph asked.

'I have been speaking with Cheeka and she told me such an

extraordinary tale,' Meleeka replied. 'I know she is old, but her mind is sharp, so I am sure it was not the ramblings of an old women. Do you not know anything about the parentage of Sara?' he asked Joseph.

'No, only what I have already told you. Is it important?' Joseph asked.

Meleeka repeated all that Cheeka had told him. 'I see what you are getting at,' Joseph said. 'Why did Sara think of the name Ilinka? Do you think there is a connection between Sara and the Ilinka tribe?' Joseph asked Meleeka.

'I do not know what to think,' Meleeka replied, 'but Cheeka thinks it a good name for our new settlement. So Ilinka it will be. Meanwhile, you can try to find why Sara chose the name.'

As the weeks went by, more and more cabins were built. Under Joseph's supervision, the braves learned quickly, not only with the building of cabins, but with the making of furniture such as chairs and tables.

When Joseph went to the great lakes for more provisions, he knew the tasks he set before the braves would be done willingly. At the trading post he would exchange beaver pelts and rugs the women had made, for whatever he needed. Or sometimes he would sell them if it was a better deal. No one bothered him. To the traders he was the man who lived in the mountains and at the moment Joseph liked it that way. The less people knew, the better.

One day as he was about to set off on the long trek home, he met a farmer who wanted to sell two cows and a bull. On impulse, Joseph decided to have them. After much haggling with the farmer, a deal was finally struck. Joseph tethered the animals to the wagon and set off to make camp for the night. That night as he sat by his campfire, with only two cows and a bull for company, he laughed out loud as he wondered what his father and brother would say if they could see him now. As he settled down for the night, his thoughts once again returned to his father, which surprised him, for over the years his father had faded from his memory. It must be the cattle that is making me recall memories of him tonight, he thought. What a pity he will never know that today the farmer in me emerged.

With this thought, Joseph fell into a deep sleep. He did not know that when he awoke his father would be dead and he would be a rich man.

CHAPTER VII

At the very moment Joseph was thinking about his father, so too were his father's last thoughts upon Joseph. For years he had regretted being so harsh with his youngest son. He should have realized that the lad was only doing what most lads do at that age. And by all accounts, Rosa was a good lass, even though she worked at the tavern. It was his eldest son Nathan who turned out to be no good. Nathan's hopes of marrying into gentry were cut short by the girl's father. He was not having his daughter marrying a farmer's son. Even though they were gentlemen farmers and supposedly rich. Nathan, in his disappointment, took to drinking and wenching. He also showed his true colours, becoming mean and cruel with his parents.

The animals even suffered at the hands of Nathan, until one day, three years after Joseph had left, Nathan got his just rewards. He was gored by a bull and died instantly. As the years passed, Joseph's father hoped that one day Joseph and Rosa would return, bringing with them a brood of grandchildren, though his wife told him many times that he was living in a fool's paradise. 'Joseph will never return. For one thing, he will obey your orders when you told him "never to come here again while I am alive". That is what you said to him. And for another, you hurt him deeply.' Aye, thought the old man, Joseph was not the only one I hurt that day. For did I not watch you over the years die a slow death. Not from any disease, but from a broken heart. Knowing you would never see your favourite son again. And I hope when I meet you in heaven, Alice, you will have forgiven me for what I did. For in the end, I have done my best for your beloved son.

When his beloved wife Alice died, Joseph's father went straight to see his lawyer, John Rhoder, an old friend of the family. John was surprised when his friend, Nat Tyler, was shown into his office. Not so much because Nat's wife Alice had just died, for if Nat wanted any business attending to, John was summoned to the house. He did not have to wait long to find out what was bothering his old friend. 'I have come to do something that should have been done a long time ago. At least then, it would have given Alice some hope and she may still have been alive today.'

John spoke only one word, 'Joseph!'

'Aye, Joseph,' Nat replied.

'I want him found. I know I have been a stubborn man, waiting for Joseph to come home, yet doing nothing about it. Good God, John, what kind of husband and father have I been? For years I watched my wife shrink into a shadow of her former self, knowing all the time, it was Joseph she was worried about. The hardest part for her was not knowing whether he was alive or dead. And all I could do was hope the lad would fall on hard times and come crawling back. Not only that, I was prepared to wait even if it took forever. But now I want him found. If I cannot make amends to Alice, at least I can make them for myself.'

'I am relieved you feel that way,' said John, putting on his lawyer's voice. 'After the funeral, I would have had to try and find Joseph anyway, for Alice left all her assets to him in her will. And over the years, the money she received from her father's will has grown considerably. So you see Nat, you coming here today has taken a load off my mind. At least you are in agreement about finding Joseph.'

'Aye,' said Nat, 'the lad must be found.'

'But what if we cannot find any trace of him? It must be nigh on fifteen years since you turfed Joseph out and sent him to that Godforsaken land. I don't like to say this, Nat, but he may already be dead, killed by them savage Indians.'

'Don't you think I know that,' Nat replied. 'Though Alice didn't think so. For just before she died I said the very same thing to her about the Indians. "Joseph is not dead," she told me. "For if he was I would know."'

'Well,' said John, 'All we can do is find the best men suitable for the job and send them to track him down.'

'Let us hope they find him,' Nat replied, 'and after Alice's funeral, I will set my own affairs in order.' That had been five years ago, and still Joseph had not been found.

When the doctor told Nat he had only three months at the most to live, he sent for his friend John to make sure his will was watertight. He had left everything to Joseph or his issue. If he died before Joseph was found, John and his son Adam, who were the executors, would see to the running of the farm, the house and all his other assets. When John arrived, he was saddened to hear the news from his friend Nat. He reassured Nat that everything was in order and they would do their best for him as they had always done. 'I am just saddened by the circumstances, and wish we could do the impossible – find Joseph and get him home, before it is too late.'

'Just keep on trying, that is all I ask,' Nat replied, 'then he will know I forgave his foolishness. I have suffered deeply for not understanding the ways of youth.'

Through the last days of his illness, he lay in bed, hoping against hope that by some mircale, Joseph would walk through the door. When the housekeeper came to make him comfortable for the night, he thought it was his wife Alice. 'Our Joseph hasn't come home,' he said. 'I did so wish to see him before I died but I cannot wait any longer.' When the housekeeper reached his bedside her master was dead.

When Joseph awoke that morning, he had no idea he was a rich man.

CHAPTER VIII

When Buta took Sara to visit Cheeka, the old woman was happy to see them. She was always glad of some company, for when one gets old the only thing left is to sit and talk. If you wish to do something, the body is too tired, even though the mind is active. The days can be long and dreary if no one comes to visit.

'Come, sit down,' Cheeka said, as Sara and Buta entered the cabin. 'I am pleased that you find time to come and speak with old Cheeka.'

'We came,' Buta told her, 'to see if you would like to see one of the cabins.'

'What would I wish to see a cabin for?' asked Cheeka. 'I am happy living in my tent, as I have always done. I am too old to change my ways, besides, from my tent I can watch all the activity going on. So, I would rather you both sit and talk with me. This is the first time I have met the white man's daughter. Though I have seen her many times from a distance.'

Buta shrugged her shoulders at Sara and they both sat down. Cheeka's keen eyes swept over Sara. I knew she was no white man's daughter, Cheeka thought. And I am thankful that Meleeka did not lie to me, though I can understand him not wanting to break a confidence. The way the girl dresses and acts is the way of the white women and could fool many people, but it does not fool Cheeka. The girl is pure Indian. Cheeka closed her eyes as many thoughts raced through her head.

Buta thought Cheeka had fallen asleep as old people sometimes do in the middle of a conversation. After a few minutes when Cheeka had still not spoken Buta mimed to Sara that they would leave quietly. As they made a movement to leave, Cheeka spoke to Sara. 'Your father

Joseph told Meleeka you had suggested the name Ilinka for this new dwelling place of ours. It is an interesting name. What made you think of it?' The question was so unexpected. Sara nearly blurted out that the mountain had told her. Just in time she answered, 'I don't know, it was just a thought.' Cheeka did not miss the intake of breath and the hesitation before Sara answered her. The girl isn't being truthful with me – no matter, it will wait until I speak with the girl's father. 'It is a good name,' she told Sara. 'A true Indian name. I think Meleeka will also agree.' Had she told Meleeka what the name meant? Cheeka could not remember. As Buta and Sara said they would have to go, Cheeka asked them to send Meleeka to her.

'My mother says you wish to speak with me,' Meleeka said, as he sat down crossed-legged, facing Cheeka.

'I have seen the white man's daughter and I wish to know more about her,' Cheeka told him.

'You will have to wait for Joseph's return. I told you before, it is from him that you must learn about Sara.'

'I know you told me before. I am not senile, though I may be old,' Cheeka said irritably. 'How long before he returns?' she asked.

'Why is it of such importance to you?' Meleeka wanted to know.

'Because,' Cheeka answered, 'now that I have spoken with the girl and observed her more closely, I am convinced she is from the Ilinka tribe.'

'But,' said Meleeka, 'you told me the tribe was wiped out.'

'So the legend says,' replied Cheeka. 'But do not forget, I also told you some left the tribe before the massacre. Maybe I am just an old woman with too much time to think. Yet I have this deep conviction about the girl.'

'Well, I can tell you truthfully that Joseph does not know what tribe Sara comes from. When he returns I will ask him to come and speak with you. Will that suit you?' Meleeka asked.

'It will have to do, though I would have liked to have spoken with him before now,' Cheeka answered.

'He has been very busy,' Meleeka replied. When Meleeka left the tent of Cheeka, his thoughts fell upon Sara. If she was of the Ilinka tribe, would she hold the healing power that Cheeka had spoken of?

Since Cheeka had first told him the tale, he had watched Sara, looking for any strange trait she might have. As yet he had seen nothing and Joseph had never said anything about Sara acting strangely. Meleeka shook his head. He did not know what to make of the things Cheeka told him, now that it involved Sara. He hoped the legend of the Ilinka tribe was untrue; that it was only the figment of Cheeka's imagination. They say old people have strange thoughts. Yet deep in his heart, he knew all that Cheeka said was true. Even about Sara being of the Ilinka tribe. Before he went to bed that night Meleeka sat at the foot of the Blue Mountain hoping the voice would speak to him. For secretly, he thought it was his magic mountain and because he was troubled about Sara and the Ilinka, the mountain would speak and help him with his troubled thoughts. He waited a long time. But nothing happened.

He went to bed that night with disappointment in his heart, for his magic mountain had let him down.

Sara had also been looking at the mountain. She lay on the bed and felt as though she was going into a deep sleep. Her arms began to raise slowly. She opened her eyes. From where she lay she could see the top of the snowcapped mountain. Her arms came to a halt, the tips of her fingers beginning to tingle. She tried to lower her arms, but could not. Her fingers opened. If my fingertips had eyes, thought Sara, I would swear they were looking at the mountain.

Strangely enough she did not feel frightened. Her fingertips began to burn, as if she had put them on hot coals. The whole of her hands went icy cold. She could not believe what she saw. Gold threads seemed to be coming from the mountain into her fingertips. At last her arms began to move. They came slowly down and lay palm upwards on the bed. Sara lay there feeling relaxed, yet full of wonder. What is happening? she thought. Surely I did not imagine the gold threads. Then she heard the voice. '*Do not worry about what has just happened. Soon you will be coming into womanhood. You will be given the gift of your ancestors. The gold threads will give you the power to heal, not immediately but in the future. The power will be built up slowly but it will come. There are other things to be taken care of. You and your father will travel over much water. Tell no one about what has happened.'*

Sara wondered what the voice meant when it spoke of travelling over much water. Her father had never mentioned about going anywhere. This was their home now. She smiled to herself. The secret smile that Joseph did not like. The mountain will tell me when the time is right. Sara, like Meleeka, thought it was a magic mountain. She closed her eyes, happy with her thoughts and fell asleep.

CHAPTER XI

The aroma of fresh-baked pies and scones wafted towards Joseph as he walked into the cabin. 'The food smells good,' he said, smiling at Sara as she came running towards him and threw her arms around him.

'The young braves saw you in the distance and came to tell me you were on your way home, so I thought I would do some baking,' Sara told him.

'What better way should a man be greeted when he returns home after a long journey,' Joseph said as he hugged her.

'Two young braves came to meet me,' he said. 'I was glad of their company on the last part of my homeward journey. You'll never guess what I've brought home with me, so I will tell you. Two cows and a bull,' he told her.

'Your right,' Sara told him, laughing at the look on his face, 'I would never have guessed.'

'The smell of that food is making me realize how hungry I am,' Joseph said. 'I will wash and shave then come and devour it. Afterwards we will go and look at the cattle.'

As she waited for her father, Sara wondered if she should tell him about the mountain. She did not like keeping secrets from him, for he was a good and kind father to her.

As she pondered about it, an inner voice said, '*The time is not right to tell your father, trust us. We will let you reveal all to him when the time comes*.' She went to the window and looked up at the mountain. 'Forgive me,' she said, 'for thinking of telling my father when you have told me not to speak of you to anyone.'

'Who are you talking to?' asked Joseph, as he came back into the room. Sara spun around, a sheepish look on her face.

'No one, I must have been thinking out loud,' she answered.

'And what must you have been thinking about?' he asked her. Joseph could see the mountain as he looked at her. Surely, he thought, she hasn't started talking to the mountain. I'd best keep an eye on her.

'I can't remember what I was thinking about, you broke my train of thought,' Sara told him as she turned to get the food. Joseph let the matter drop.

He was glad to be home and all he wanted was a good meal, then to relax by the fireside. As they dined, Joseph told Sara about his trip to the great lake and how he had haggled with the farmer over the cattle. 'One day we will have a large herd roaming around here but for now, the ones we have got will do to start with.'

Sara, catching the excitement in her father's voice, asked him if he was thinking of starting a farm.

'Maybe I will,' he answered, there is plenty of lush pastureland; it might be a good idea. I wonder what my father would say if he could hear us talking about starting a farm.'

'Do you ever think of going back to England?' Sara asked him (thinking about the mountain saying they would travel over much water).

'What gave you that idea? Of course I never think of going back. This land is our home, though I must confess that is the second time in the last few days I have thought about my father. Do you know,' Joseph said, 'my father told me more than once that I would never make a farmer, and here I am planning on having a herd of cattle roaming around, as well as the hens and pigs.'

'Have you spoken to Meleeka about your plans?' Sara asked, then continued before Joseph could reply, 'The Indians like to hunt for their food. It is their custom to live as nature intended. They say the Great White Spirit in the sky provides everything they need. It has been so for thousands of years.'

'So,' Joseph said, 'you have been having history lessons on Indian culture while I have been away.'

'No,' replied Sara, 'I have just been talking to the women and they tell me things.'

'Well,' said Joseph, 'it wasn't my idea to build the first cabin here if you remember. It was a cabin we awoke in after being sick with the fever. It is Meleeka who decided his tribe would live as the white man, and yes, I have told him about the plans for the cattle and he agrees with me.'

'I am not bothered one way or the other,' Sara said. 'It is just that some of the older women seem to prefer the old customs. They tell me they will use their own methods of cooking.'

'What about the younger women?' Joseph asked.

'Most of them think it is a game we are playing,' she replied. 'They laugh and giggle, but on the whole, I think in time they will prefer our way.'

'There you are then,' Joseph said, 'it is the young ones that will like this place; times change, Sara. Not always for the better, I admit, but change they do.

'One day this beautiful sprawling land will have millions of people living here. They will come from all walks of life and from all nations. They will build their houses and churches, then before you know it, there will be towns and cities. Just like other civilized places in the world; it is not always for the better, but it will be done. They call it progress. I think what Meleeka is doing is right. For when the white man really takes over, this land will not belong to the Indians any more. What will become of them remains to be seen, but it will all happen, mark my words.'

Joseph pushed his plate away and drank the remainder of his coffee. 'That was the best meal I have eaten in ages. Even our solemn conversation couldn't spoil it. Now, I am going to do what every man should do after a good meal – relax in his favourite chair.'

Within two minutes he was asleep. As Sara washed the pots, she mulled over what her father had said. He had spoken many times about people from other lands coming to settle here, yet she could not imagine the vastness of the change her father spoke of. She remembered one day asking her father about England and receiving a short history lesson.

'England,' he had told her, 'was once an uncivilized, barbarous country to be invaded and fought over. It is also shrouded in mysteries and legends. People came from many lands and settled there bringing their customs and religions with them.' He told her of the palaces in which kings and queens resided.

'England is abundant in history,' he said, 'I cannot tell you how many lords and ladies there are in the land, with their heraldic coats of arms. They all have servants to do their fetching and carrying. Even the lower gentry who live in more stylish houses have a cook and a maid.' When her father said that he burst out laughing. 'I am forgetting,' he told her, 'that my family also had servants. Well, we had a cook that lived in and two girls from the village that helped around the house. We also had a farm manager and lads from the village to help on the farm. I am trying to describe to you, Sara, the different classes of society that exist in England. They go from the top of the ladder to bottom and at the bottom of the ladder you find the very poor. They live in hovels not fit for animals to live in. The children go barefooted and hungry even though their mothers starve themselves to give their children a little extra food. I have seen a father who had toiled and sweated all day go home and say he was not hungry, so his wife and children would eat the meager meal that had been prepared for him. And all because the people he worked for pay him a pittance.

'It is the same all over the world, the men with money get the best of everything, the poor survive the best way they can.' Sara sighed and hoped what her father said about this land would never come to pass, for she did not want it to become like England with all the different classes of society. Sara had never known the affluence of wealth, nor the poverty of the poor. It must be awful to be very poor, she thought, as she stacked the plates on the shelves.

She was just about to sit down when Meleeka arrived. He saw Joseph asleep in the chair and motioned for Sara to go outside. 'Do not wake your father, he must be tired after his journey. I only came to tell him that Cheeka would like to see him. Have you seen the two cows and the bull?' he asked Sara.

'No, we were going to see them after we had eaten but Father fell asleep,' she told Meleeka.

'Would you like me to show them to you? The fresh air will do you good,' he asked her.

'Yes, a breath of air would be nice. I will get my shawl,' said Sara.

As they walked to where Joseph had let the cattle roam, Sara asked Meleeka what he thought about her father's plans to raise more cattle and cultivate the land. 'I know you plan to live like the white man,' she continued, 'but you have always hunted the animals and looked to nature for food. Surely your way is the best. Since I found out about my true parentage, I have become very interested in your culture. I love my father dearly and would want no other, but the fact remains, though I was brought up as a white girl, I now know I am of Indian blood. It is like having a foot in each of your shoes and taking both sides into consideration. She told Meleeka of the conversation with her father and said how awful it would be if millions of white people took over this vast land.

Meleeka stared at her. It was the longest speech he had ever heard Sara make. Usually, though always pleasant, she was shy in his company. 'Your father has seen other lands,' he told her, 'maybe what he says will come to pass, maybe not. You and I know only of this land, we cannot image any other. As to his plans, well, I think your father is a good and honest man. I would trust him with my life. What he is planning will be for the good of us all. Do not ask me how I know, I can only say I feel it in my heart. As for my braves, they will always fish and hunt for food, I do not think they will change overnight.'

Meleeka took hold of Sara's hand as they made their way back to the cabin. 'Whatever happens,' he told her, 'we will watch this place grow together.'

Joseph was awake but still relaxing in his chair. Sara gave him the message that Cheeka would like to see him. As Joseph entered Cheeka's tent she motioned for him to sit facing her. She liked to see the face of the person to whom she was speaking. 'Do not think me a nosy old woman,' she said to Joseph, 'but what I am going to ask you is very important. So I will come straight to the point. I can see that Sara is no white man's daughter, she is pure Indian. Do you know anything about her parents?' she asked bluntly, then continued, 'I have asked Meleeka if he knew anything; in fact I have asked him twice, but he told me very little. He said it was you I must ask. Meleeka is very loyal to you,' Cheeka told him.

'As I am to him,' Joseph replied.

'Yes, yes,' said Cheeka impatiently.

'But what about Sara? Why is it so important to you?' Joseph asked her.

'Is she gifted?' asked Cheeka.

'She is a good cook and can sew. In fact, she can make anything she turns her hand to. Some day Sara will make someone a good wife,' Joseph said proudly.

'No, no,' Cheeka said, irritably, 'can she make sick people better?'

'Make sick people better? Of course not,' Joseph answered in a raised voice. 'She is not a doctor.' Was the woman becoming a bit senile, he wondered.

'Well,' persisted Cheeka, 'does she have any strange ways?'

Joseph could feel his temper rising. 'This is my daughter you are speaking of,' he shouted. 'She may not be of my flesh but my late wife and I looked after Sara from the day she was born, probably saved her life. And you sit there and ask me if Sara is alright in the head.' He rose to his feet.

'I am sorry,' said Cheeka quickly. 'I did not mean to insult Sara or you. Please sit down and let me explain.'

Cheeka told Joseph about the Ilinka tribe and how she thought Sara was in some way connected with the Ilinka. Joseph listened intently to Cheeka, for she repeated word for word exactly what Meleeka had told him weeks ago.

'I am sorry, but I do not know which tribe Sara's parents came from. I can only tell you the circumstances of her birth.' Cheeka listened to all that Joseph had to say.

'Now you know as much about Sara as I do,' said Joseph. 'Anyway,' he asked, 'what does it matter which tribe her parents came from?'

'It will matter a great deal to Sara if she is of the Ilinka tribe,' Cheeks told him, 'for she will be truly gifted.'

'In what way?' Joseph asked.

'She will have the power to heal with the hands,' Cheeka said.

'Well, as far as I know,' Joseph told her, 'Sara is the same as she has always been. I have seen nothing different.' But he hesitated as he said it.

'Did something just bother you?' Cheeka asked. 'Why did you hesitate?'

'It is the mountain. I think it has some strange effect on Sara,' he told her.

'In what way?' she asked.

'Sara said the mountain had spoken to her, but it was when she was recovering from the fever. She has not mentioned it since,' Joseph told her. 'Yet today, just after I arrived home, I could have sworn she was talking to the mountain. Well, I heard her talking, yet there was no one about. When I asked her who she was speaking to, she looked at me sheepishly and said she must have been thinking out loud. Then through the window I saw the mountain behind her and I knew that Sara was not being truthful with me. Yet it is unusual for Sara to lie. So I let the matter drop.'

'You will have to look for any changes in her ways,' Cheeka told Joseph, more convinced than ever after what Joseph had told her that Sara would have the gift of the Ilinka. Sara is not really being untruthful to her father or to me, Cheeka thought, she has been warned not to speak of these things.

'Do you not think,' asked Joseph, 'that we should tell Sara about the Ilinka tribe and that she may be one of them?'

'No. It will be better to wait and see what happens,' Cheeka replied. 'You and she are very close, like a true father and daughter should be. If strange things begin to happen to her – which they already have, Cheeka thought – she will tell you.'

'I hope you are right,' Joseph replied, 'for it seems to me we could be wrong not to warn her; she could become frightened.'

Cheeka took hold of Joseph's hands. 'Trust me,' she said, 'nothing will frighten her and when the time is right she will speak to you of it. Now, I think we have talked enough, it is past my bedtime. Thank you for coming and satisfying an old woman's curiosity.'

When Joseph got back to the cabin Sara was fast asleep.

CHAPTER X

Meleeka and Joseph shook hands as the last cabin was finished. Twenty-five had been built, with plenty of space between each one.

'We should be pleased with ourselves,' said Joseph, 'the best craftsmen in the land couldn't have done any better.'

He turned to the young braves. 'I take my hat off to you all,' he said to them. He doffed his hat and bowed. 'You have done a wonderful job. Meleeka tells me some of you wish to stay in your tents. I understand, some things are hard to change. And the way one lives is the hardest of all. There are more than enough cabins for each family. It was better to build too many than too few. It is up to you; I will make use of them.'

He stepped back and Meleeka came forward. 'I am proud of you all,' he told them. 'You have worked hard and made this a wonderful place. When we came here I said it would be to live as the white man lives. I am disappointed that some of you do not wish to live that way. Yet I will not force you to do so. Joseph tells me you cannot change people overnight. I think I understand what he means. Our people have lived in tents for thousands of years. So what does it matter if it takes a few years to learn how to live like the white man. But whether we live in tents or cabins, we must have a name for our new abode and I call upon Sara to name it.'

Meleeka held out his hand for Sara to take it and brought her forward. 'I think you have a special name, would you like to tell us?' he asked.

Sara hesitated. Joseph standing behind her could see them all waiting for Sara to speak. He saw Cheeka watching Sara intensely. He wondered what was going on in the old woman's mind. Then Sara turned suddenly to face the mountain.

'I wish to name this settlement Ilinka,' she gave a slight nod before turning back to the crowd. Only Joseph saw the look on Sara's face as she said the name Ilinka. Quickly he glanced over to where Cheeka was standing. The old woman was nodding her head, a smile of satisfaction on her face. The braves and womenfolk cheered and chanted 'Ilinka, Ilinka' several times.

Meleeka turned and smiled at Joseph, 'it seems they all like the name Sara has chosen,' he said. Joseph forced a smile to his face. He wasn't thinking about the name, he was wondering why Sara turned to nod at the mountain, as if it was something sacred.

I will ask her about it, he thought as he went to join the others.

The women had prepared a feast to celebrate the opening of the settlement. Meleeka sat cross-legged on the ground, happily watching the young ones playing, their laughter ringing out all over the camp. The women also seemed to be enjoying themselves. Some were busy with the food, others talking and laughing together.

This is going to be a happy place, he thought, it has been good how we have all worked together and now everyone can enjoy the fruits of all the hard work.

Tomorrow they would start preparing for the long winter that was expected. The braves would hunt for meat and gather wood to stockpile. Joseph would go for new provisions before the snows of winter arrived. But today was a day for celebration for everyone to enjoy.

He turned towards Joseph to tell him what he was thinking. Joseph lay propped up on his elbow staring at the mountain.

'You are not happy this day when everyone else is enjoying themselves?' Meleeka asked.

'I am happy enough,' replied Joseph, without taking his eyes off the mountain. 'It is Sara that is bothering me.'

'Why?' Meleeka asked. 'Is she ill or something?'

'Not physically sick,' Joseph replied, 'but sometimes I wonder if she is getting sick in the head.'

'Sara, sick in the head? What makes you think that?' Meleeka asked in disbelief. 'Come, Joseph, tell me what is bothering you. I cannot believe you have such thoughts about your daughter.'

As he replied Joseph turned to face Meleeka. 'Of late Sara has been acting strangely. She does silly things that I do not understand.'

'What sort of silly things?' Meleeka asked him.

'Well,' said Joseph, 'take today for instance. I may have been the only one who noticed, but as Sara said the name Ilinka, she gave a slight nod in the direction of the mountain, as though she was acknowledging it in some way, and more than once have I not caught her speaking to the mountain? She denies it of course.'

As he listened to Joseph, Meleeka thought about what Cheeka had told him of the Ilinka tribe. Joseph too, was thinking about what the old woman had said.

'What do you think I should do, Meleeka?' Joseph asked. 'Should I make Sara tell me what fascinates her so about the mountain? Or should I wait and see if anything else happens? For it is unlike Sara to be secretive with me.'

Meleeka wondered what to say to Joseph. If the mountain was speaking to Sara, as it was to him, he could understand her not wanting to say anything. For he himself could tell no one.

'I think if I was you,' Meleeka told him, 'I would not say anything. It would be best for you to wait until the time comes and Sara can speak to you about it.'

'Why? Do you know something I don't. You have been very friendly with Sara of late,' Joseph said sharply.

'I can say, in all truth,' Meleeka answered, 'that Sara has never mentioned anything to me. It is just a feeling I have that it would be better to wait and see what happens. Sara loves you. If she was troubled, who better could she turn to than her father?'

'I will take your advise and hope you are right,' Joseph told Meleeka.

'Don't worry,' Meleeka answered. 'One thing I am sure of, is that your Sara is not sick in the head.' Both men laughed. 'Come,' said Meleeka, 'let us enjoy ourselves with the others. They will wonder what is wrong with us, having such a deep discussion when we are supposed to be celebrating.'

CHAPTER XI

When the first snow came, it fell gently at first. The young ones ran about catching the snowflakes. Within hours a blizzard raged. Joseph was glad they had built sheds for the cattle. He had purchased four more cows on his last visit to the great lake. If the bull gave a good performance, they would have some calves next year.

For three days the snow and wind never let up. Apart from going outside to feed and water the cattle or get wood for the fire, Joseph and Sara never left the cabin. He assumed the others also stayed in their tents or cabins and knew which would be the most comfortable in this weather. Sara seemed content. He had not seen her gazing at the mountain for some time.

Through this bad weather, he helped with the housework, then got his knife to do some whittling, for he was making toy soldiers, while Sara was making rag dolls to give to the young Indian boys and girls.

As he listened to the wind howling Joseph was glad, in a way, that they would not have to milk the cows, for they had dried up just before the snow came. He hoped the cattle felt as snug and warm as he did.

Anyone venturing out in this weather without good cause was asking for trouble. When this weather is over, Joseph thought, it will show that the cabins have been well built and all the hard work was worth doing.

Sara was thinking the same as Joseph, about being warm and snug. The heat from the fire was as warm as the sun on a hot summer's day. She put the sewing down on the table beside her and lay back in the armchair and closed her eyes. She wanted to be alone with her thoughts and her father would not disturb her if he thought she was asleep. Sara wanted to remember the night before. She had gone to bed and huddled under the blankets to get warm. When she felt warm and cosy, she lifted her head from under the blankets and lay on her back. She tucked the blankets under her chin so only her face was showing. How long she lay there or whether she had been asleep and something had awoken her, Sara could not remember.

At first she thought that somehow the snow was blowing into the room, for what looked like snowflakes seemed to fill the room and were falling down on her. Her first impulse was to jump out of bed, as it would get wet with the snowflakes. She could not move. Then she realized it was not snow, it was like hundreds of tiny silver stars twinkling above her. Then more tiny stars appeared, mixing in with the silver ones.

They were of the most beautiful greens, blues and gold. Surrounding them all was a purple mist. Sara felt movement coming back into her body. She felt a relaxed, warm feeling come over her. She lifted her hands from under the blanket and tried to catch the tiny coloured stars. She could not catch them, but her fingers started to move as though strumming a harp. Then both her hands came to rest on her forehead. With the first finger of each hand, she drew three half circles above her eyebrows, then drew a line through them. At that moment all the tiny coloured stars disappeared. Sara lay there for a few moments, thinking. What is happening to me? And why am I not frightened? If the blizzard was not raging outside, I would go to the window and see if the mountain would speak to me. But I have no way of seeing it through all this snow, I will have to wait until the weather clears.

With these thoughts still in her head, she put her hand back under the blankets and lay there with her eyes open. Then she heard the voice. She felt relieved as she listened to what the voice said.

'You, Sara, are of the Ilinka tribe. Tonight the power of Ilinka was being given to you. It is the power of good so do not be afraid. The power will come to you slowly. It will be built up, little by little. Do not worry, no harm will come to you and soon you will be able to tell your father, Joseph, all that is happening to you.'

The voice faded away and Sara drifted off to sleep. Sara was so deep in thought as she sat in the chair in front of the fire that when she opened her eyes, she was surprised her father was staring at her.

'Are you alright?' he asked her.

'Yes, why?'

'You were making some very funny noises and moving your hands about. Have you had a bad dream?' he asked, knowing by some instinct she had been pretending to be asleep.

'No, I have not been asleep,' she answered. She wasn't going to lie to him, but neither could she tell him the truth.

'Something is happening to me, Father,' she told him. 'At the moment I cannot tell you about it, but I promise, when the time is right I will tell you everything.'

So, Joseph thought, the old woman was right. Sara is connected with the Ilinka tribe.

'It is alright, Sara,' he said, 'I think I understand.'

'Thank you, Father,' was all Sara said.

When Joseph awoke the next morning the first thing he noticed was the silence. It took him a few moments to realize the wind had stopped howling. At last, he thought, the blizzard has blown itself out. He went to the door and looked out. There were deep drifts of snow all around, some as high as the cabins. He looked over towards the forest – what a beautiful sight! The white snow was glistening on the branches, the trunks half white, half brown, depending on the way the snow had fallen. The rays of the rising sun were flashing through the forest like someone signalling with a mirror. Only Mother Nature could paint a picture so beautiful.

His eyes moved across to the mountain. 'Even you aren't blue any more. Mother Nature can even cover a mountain as big as you with her white snow,' he shouted out. 'And while I am talking to you, though I must be going soft in the head talking to a mountain, I hope what you are doing to my Sara will bring her no harm.' Joseph turned back into the room, disgusted with himself. Fancy speaking my thoughts out loud to a mountain. If nothing else, after breakfast, he told Sara, he was going to see to the cattle.

'Be careful,' she told him, 'the snow looks very deep in places.'

'I will be alright,' Joseph replied as he went outside.

When Sara finished her chores she went to her room. She lifted the flap from the window and took deep breaths of the cold air. She had missed going outside these last few days, and the snow was still too deep for her to venture out. She felt pure joy as the coldness hit her face. The air she breathed seemed to cut her throat before making an impact on her lungs. She took several deep breaths before standing back from the window. I needed that, she thought, though I was happy enough to be in the cabin during the blizzard, but I felt stifled.

She went back to the window to see if there was any movement outside. All she could see were the tracks her father had made to get to the animals. She glanced over at the mountain. How different it looked all covered in snow. It was just like any other mountain, there was no magic in it today. She was just about to turn away when she heard the voice.

'*We are still here, Sara. The snow cannot hide us from you. Your father spoke to us this morning. We listened to him, though we could not answer. He is worried that harm may befall you. He has watched you closely and thinks you are acting strangely. The time has come for him to know the truth.*'

'What is the truth?' Sara asked, 'and why are you always saying we, when I can only hear one voice?'

'*Because I speak for your ancestors, of the Ilinka tribe. When we came from our homelands thousands of years ago, we settled here. At the very spot where you have built the new settlement. In a blizzard, such as the one you have experienced; many of our people died. They were laid to rest at the bottom of this mountain. When the snow melted, the tribe moved on. For thousands of years they lived a simple life as the Great Lord of the sky wished all mankind to live. To be content and happy in their daily lives. Legend will tell you that all the Ilinka tribe were massacred by the white man, but two escaped.*

'*Until your birth, your mother, Azenia, was the last descendant of the two that escaped. Your father, Eleacon, was of another tribe. The history of the Ilinkas would take too long to tell and is of the past. It is the future that concerns you, Sara. Being a descendant of the Ilinka, it was not by chance you were brought to this place, nor was it by chance that Meleeka found you. This is where the Ilinkas should have stayed all those years ago. Now it is your destiny to keep this place for future generations.'*

'How can I do all this?' Sara asked, 'I am only a young girl, I do not understand. First you tell me you are giving me the power of Ilinka. Now you say the settlement is in my keeping for my ancestors are buried here.' Tears whirled up in Sara's eyes. 'Sometimes I think I am going out of my mind, listening to a mountain. At first it felt like magic, it was exciting. But now you frighten me, for I do not think I can do all that you ask. I do not wish to listen to you any more. Besides, I am cold.'

'Go and sit by the fire,' the voice told her. *'I will explain everything to you.'*

'There is something else you told me – I would be going over much water. Is it true?' Sara wanted to know.

'Come,' said the voice, *'go to the fire where it will be warm.'*

Sara, as if in a trance, walked from the bedroom to the chair beside the fire.

'Well,' she said, as she sat down on the chair, 'I am waiting.'

'My name is Silver Jayot,' the voice told Sara. *'I am your guide. I have been with you since the day of your birth and will be until your mission on earth is complete. It was I who inspired Rosa to massage you with the warm oil; you were so tiny, you would have died had I not been sent to watch over you. It was I who brought Meleeka to the Blue Mountain, for your destiny is linked with his. But for the moment, I cannot reveal how it is linked, for that is of the future. There are things to be done before then.'*

'What things?' Sara asked, looking at her father's chair as she spoke, for she felt as though someone was sitting there having this conversation with her.

'When the snows of winter have ceased,' the voice continued, *'you and your father will go to the land of his birth. That is when you will travel over much water. Your father must go to his homeland for his inheritance. This is why I said it is time for your father to be told the*

truth. Messengers have been sent to look for him. They have no idea where to look, for your father has not been in contact with his homeland since he left.'

'How can I tell him?' interrupted Sara. 'He will never believe that I have had a conversation with someone I cannot even see.'

'You will repeat to your father what I have told you about the Ilinka tribe and how you are a descendant of the tribe. He will not be surprised, as both Cheeka and Meleeka have spoken with him about the Ilinkas. You must also tell him about me, your guide, Silver Jayot. For now I have given you my name, no more will I be the voice from the mountain. Now, Sara, do you understand all that I have been telling you.'

'I think so,' answered Sara hesitantly, 'but I do not think my father will want to go to his homeland,' she told Silver Jayot. 'For this is his home now and he loves it here and rarely speaks about his life before he came to this land.'

'He will go,' Silver Jayot told her, *'for his going will determine the events of the future of Ilinka.'* Then Silver Jayot continued, *'when he returns from seeing to the cattle you will give him this message. Tell him that his family are all dead, his father's last thoughts were of him and that his father regretted sending him away. The farm and everything now belongs to your father and he must go home to claim his inheritance. You will go with your father for it will please him. Also there will be someone you have to help, and remember, wherever you go, I will always be near to guide and watch over you.'*

It was a few minutes before Sara realized the conversation had ended. She sat quietly in the chair pondering on what had been said. Now she could understand about having a guide and Silver Jayot seemed quite nice to talk to. It had been much nicer sitting in front of the fire having a conversation with Silver Jayot than looking through the window at the mountain. And it must be alright to have a guide, for she heard one of the women say Cheeka had one.

With this thought, she rose from the chair and smiled to herself. Sara wondered how long her father would be and threw some more logs on the fire. He would be cold and hungry when he returned. I will make some broth, she thought.

Joseph came in and went to stand by the fire. 'Don't stand there,' Sara told him, 'go and change your clothes or you'll catch your death. Your so wet, the steam from your clothes will put out the fire. So come on, move yourself. There will be some hot broth and dumplings ready when you get changed.'

Joseph laughed and said, 'Your worse than your mother used to be, bossing me about. And not a word about how the animals were or was there anyone else out in this weather.'

'We can talk about that when you get out of those wet clothes,' Sara answered. And we will have plenty of other things to talk about, she thought to herself.

As Sara ladled out the broth, Joseph told her that Meleeka had also ventured out to see if the animals were alright. 'It was a good thing we built those sheds or we would have lost the cattle. We have left them plenty of food and water in case we have another snowstorm.'

'Meleeka told me he made everyone go into the cabins for shelter. Old Cheeka wasn't very pleased to be moved but Meleeka told her there would be more protection in the cabin than her wigwam and she would have himself and his mother for company.'

(*'Many of your ancestors died in a blizzard such as this,'* Sara heard a voice whisper).

'So everyone is alright?' she asked.

'By some miracle, yes,' Joseph answered. 'For I have never seen a blizzard like it before. I cannot remember one as bad even in the bleak, exposed moors of northern England, and believe me, Sara, we got some harsh winters there.'

He was silent for a moment as though listening for something.

'What is it?' Sara asked.

'Nothing really,' he replied. 'It is just that for years I have never thought about the past. Yet these last few weeks, I have done nothing else, since I bought the animals. In fact, perhaps I am getting old. They say when age creeps up on you, you look back instead of forward.'

'Don't be silly, you are not old, you have plenty to look forward to,' Sara told him.

'I,' said Joseph, 'I suppose I have.'

Now, thought Sara, I must tell him now.

'Come and sit by the fire, I have something to tell you.' Joseph lit his pipe and sat down.

'Well, lass, let's have it. What is on your mind?'

Without hesitation Sara gave him the message from Silver Jayot, about his inheritance and his family. 'You have to go and collect your inheritance, Father, for Silver Jayot says it determines the future of Ilinka.'

'I will think about it,' her father said. 'Is there anything else you wish to tell me?'

'Yes,' Sara replied, relieved that now she could be open with her father. She told him everything. How she had thought the mountain was a magic mountain because it spoke to her. But now she knew that it was Silver Jayot, her guide.

She also told him of the night in her bedroom when she was being given the power of Ilinka. 'I was told that same night that my destiny was here and was linked with Meleeka. But first you and I would travel over much water, then we would return. I wanted so much to tell you all this before, But I was told not to speak of it. You understand, don't you, Father?'

'Yes, I understand,' he told her.

Joseph had listened intently to all that Sara told him. He did not dispute any of it, for had not Cheeka tried to warn him that Sara could be of the Ilinka tribe? He did not even question the telling of Silver Jayot and how Sara felt he was sitting in Joseph's chair, and though she could not see him, was having a conversation with Silver Jayot, as she would with a human being.

'What do you make of it all?' Sara asked, interrupting his thoughts. 'You seem to be taking it all very calmly, and here I was wondering how best to tell you. In fact, I was a bit frightened of telling you, especially about Silver Jayot.'

'Sara,' he told her, 'you must never be afraid to tell me anything. In fact, I feel much better now that I know what is happening. For have I not found you doing some strange things of late, and I must confess, that more than once I thought you were going soft in the head. It is a relief to know you were only speaking with your guide.

'For, you see, I know of people having guides. We had an old biddy used to frequent the tavern where I went drinking in my younger days. And incidently, where I met Rosa. Everyone called the old biddy a witch. She would sit in the corner and often you would see her muttering to herself. The landlord did not mind her being there. After all, she was doing no harm. But then the landlord would say, "If I throw her out and she is a witch she might put a curse upon me." So he played it safe and let the old biddy sit there. Anyway, what I am getting at is that one day I was bored, so I bought the old biddy a drink. She seemed so lonely when I took the drink over to her that I sat down next to her. As she turned to thank me for the drink, she pulled the shawl away from her head, revealing the most beautiful auburn hair I had ever seen. Her skin was like ivory, with just a hint of colour on her high cheek bones. When she looked at me her eyes were like two sparkling emeralds. I looked at her awestruck. Why, I thought, she is not an old biddy, she is beautiful. I wondered why she hid herself in those filthy clothes and sat in the corner alone. I could not wait to tell the landlord about her. I made a movement to leave her. I was so dumbstruck, I had not even spoken one word.

'"Don't go," she said, "I have willed you to come to me."

'"Willed me. You can't do that. It was my choice that I came."

'"You came because I wanted you to," she told me. I was thinking what folk said, about her being a witch. Yet I was gazing into those beautiful green eyes that sparkled like emeralds. I shook myself to see if I was dreaming. No, the beautiful woman was still there. Then she spoke to me again.

'"I have a message for you," she said. "That is why I willed you to come to me. Soon, you will leave your family and take a wife. You will go to a new land and make your home. One day you will return but not for long. You will do what has to be done then return to your new homeland."

'I do not remember taking my eyes off her face. But when the message ended I was looking at an old biddy with grey matted hair. Her face wrinkled like a prune. How long I had sat with her I do not know.

'The old biddy picked up her ale with filthy dirty hands, then told me my guide had spoken to me. I had no idea what she was talking about and could not get away quickly enough. Not, as I had thought earlier, to tell the landlord that the old biddy was not an old biddy at all but a beautiful woman. I just up and fled and never saw the old biddy again.

'A few months later, what she had predicted about leaving my family, having a wife and going to a new land all came about. And from what you have told me, it seems the other part of her prediction is going to come true. I must confess I had forgotten all about the old woman until you mentioned Silver Jayot. But why I was able to see that beautiful face when I was looking at an old biddy, I have no idea. In fact, it scared the pants off me. I ran all the way home.'

'So,' said Sara, 'when the snow melts and spring time comes, we will travel over much water?' she giggled as she said it.

'Well,' Joseph answered, 'if the future of Ilinka will benefit by us going, and if I have to prove the old biddy was right, yes, we will go and collect our inheritance,' he grinned at Sara as he said it.

'Your inheritance, don't you mean?' Sara asked.

'No, it is our inheritance,' he told her. 'For whatever I have will one day be yours. I wonder what happened for my father to leave everything to me. You must thank your guide, Silver Jayot. But for him, we would never have known about the inheritance. For not a soul in England has any idea where I am or what I have been doing these past twenty years, and it is certain that I would never have been found. If I was a drinking man,' Joseph told her. 'I would drink a toast to the spirits of your ancestors.'

They both whooped with laughter.

CHAPTER XII

Later in the day Meleeka fought his way through the snow to go and visit Joseph and Sara. When he left Joseph that morning he had looked up at the mountain.

Why, he asked himself, does the mountain not speak to me any more? I did as the mountain asked and brought my people here. I only hope we can survive the winter, for never have I seen a blizzard like this one. And this is only the beginning of the winter. Now my mountain is not blue any more, it looks just like any other mountain. Perhaps the magic has worn away. He felt disappointment in his heart, as if in some way the mountain had let him down. When the mountain was blue, I felt so proud every time I gazed up at it, as though it belonged to me, now I will have to wait until spring before I feel that way again. Meleeka was so deep in thought that at first he did not hear the rumbling sound. When he did, it sounded as though the bowels of the earth were opening.

He ran back to the cowshed. He did not know what was happening and for a moment, wondered why he had not run home, for that was nearer. He took refuge with the cattle. They were restless, stamping their feet and swaying from side to side as if in unison with the rumbling earth. After a few minutes, everything went quiet, even the cattle stood still, as though they were listening for something.

Meleeka peeked out and looked towards the cabins. Everything was quiet. In fact, it was so quiet he felt an eerie calmness. He shivered involuntarily. Not through coldness or through fear, for he felt neither. He pulled open the bottom half of the door and stepped out. As he turned to close the door he looked up. There, in all its glory was his

Blue Mountain. Meleeka stood there mystified. How can this be? he thought. Before I heard the rumbling the mountain was covered in snow. Now it is like a man who has shaken the snow from his clothes before entering his house. This surely is a mysterious place, if ever there was one.

Then the voice he had so longed to hear, spoke again. *'You wanted to see your Blue Mountain again, now you see it.'* For a moment Meleeka was startled upon hearing the voice.

'From this day,' the voice continued, *'the mountain will never be covered in snow again. Only the peak will catch the snow. The rest will always stay blue. No matter how fierce the blizzards of the future might be, however large, Ilinka grows. Your Blue Mountain will dominate the background.*

'My Blue Mountain?' asked Meleeka, in awe.

'Yes yours,' replied the voice, *'you had faith enough to bring your tribe here. You have done all that was asked, without questions. One day you and Sara will be proud of your Ilinka. But there is yet much more for you both to do. When next you see her, she will tell you many things.'*

As Joseph opened the door to get more wood, he saw Meleeka approaching.

'Get the kettle on, Sara,' he shouted, 'we have a visitor.'

As Meleeka entered, Joseph followed carrying an armful of logs. 'Get up to the fire and get warm,' he told Meleeka. 'You look frozen to death. Whatever brings you out visiting in this weather? Though don't think you are not welcome. You are. I am just surprised to see you, that's all.' Joseph threw the logs down onto the hearth.

'Come, sit here,' he said. Pulling the chair nearer the fire. 'Sara will have some coffee ready in a minute.' Meleeka stretched his hand towards the warmth of the fire. He had not realized how cold he was but the heat from the fire soon warmed him. When Sara gave him the coffee, he sat back and relaxed.

'Now Meleeka,' Joseph wanted to know, 'whatever is so urgent for you to come visiting on a day such as this?'

'It isn't that bad,' answered Meleeka, 'at least the wind has died down and the snow has stopped. I only had to fight my way through the drifts.' Meleeka waited until Joseph and Sara sat down, then he proceeded to tell them all about the mountain. He was disappointed when they just accepted all that he had told them. He thought at least they would have shown either disbelief or excitement, but no, they both looked at one another and smiled.

Meleeka leapt from his chair. 'Come,' he said to them, 'see the mountain for yourselves. Then maybe you will show more interest in what I have told you. I suppose you do not believe me?'

'Oh we believe you alright,' Joseph told him. 'And you are wrong about us not being interested. We were very interested. Are we not, Sara?'

'Yes,' Sara answered, looking up at Meleeka and smiling.

Meleeka's disappointment softened with the smile he got from Sara. 'I am sorry for my outburst,' he told them, 'but I thought what happened today was so unbelievable. I cannot understand why you two seem to take it so calmly.'

'Meleeka,' Joseph said, 'if you had said the mountain had moved away completely, today of all days, I would not have been surprised.'

'Why today of all days?' Meleeka asked him.

'If you sit down and listen to what Sara has to tell you, I think you will understand.'

When Meleeka was seated, Sara told him all that had been happening to her. How Silver Jayot had told her about the Ilinkas and the message he gave for her father.

'What do you mean,' Meleeka interrupted her, 'when you say you are going over much water?'

'Wait until Sara has finished,' Joseph told him. There is much more she has to tell you.'

Meleeka tried to hear everything but he felt agitated. If Joseph took Sara to England, they may not wish to come back. Over the last few months he had looked upon Joseph as a father figure and Sara, he hoped, one day would be his wife. He was so deep in thought, he had not realized Sara had finished speaking.

Sara and Joseph waited for Meleeka to say something. Sara knew what she had told him seemed unbelievable, even more unbelievable than what Meleeka had told them. But she thought Meleeka of all people would understand. She had not expected this long silence.

'Well,' said Joseph impatiently, 'what do you think?'

'About what?' asked Meleeka, coming out of his reverie.

'About everything Sara has just told you.' Joseph was puzzled by Meleeka's attitude.

At last Meleeka answered them. 'I can understand about Sara's guide, and her being given the power of Ilinka. What I cannot understand is why you wish to go and collect your inheritance. I thought you were settled here. That this was your home. Why do you need this inheritance? It will be of no consequence to us and why, if you must go, has Sara to go with you? We would take care of Sara while you were away. Or do you think that once you see your home again you will not wish to return?'

Joseph studied Meleeka during this long speech. I will have to be careful how I answer him, he thought, for Meleeka thinks if I take Sara away he will not see her again. Joseph cleared his throat before he spoke.

'Do you remember,' he asked Meleeka, 'we once had a long discussion about fate and destiny? Well, I think that fate, for some reason, has decided that I go back to England and Sara must come with me. She has told you what her guide Silver Jayot said. Are we to question what he told her, and don't forget, Silver Jayot did say, our going over much water would determine the future of Ilinka.'

Joseph went over to Meleeka and looked him straight in the eye and told him, 'Do not worry, my friend, I will bring Sara back, safe and sound.' Joseph lowered his voice, as he said, 'To you, Meleeka, to you.'

They shook hands and smiled at each other.

CHAPTER XIII

During the winter, the young braves hunted and trapped beaver. The women busied themselves making blankets, pouches, purses and even Indian dolls. They were all for Joseph to sell. By the time the snows of winter melted, everything was ready.

Joseph and Meleeka had sorted the beaver pelts. 'The best ones I will take to England, they will make a better price,' Joseph had told Meleeka. 'The others I will sell at the great lakes.'

The women bundled all they had made into moose and bear skins, making sure they were secure enough to stand the long journey.

The night before Sara and Joseph were to leave, Meleeka and his tribe gave them a farewell party. The young braves persuaded Meleeka to wear his chieftain outfit and to let them dance in the old tradition.

'We know you said we had danced them for the last time,' said Two Feathers, 'but surely this is a special occasion – one we could never have known would happen. Think how much Sara and Joseph will enjoy it. Think what happy memories will go with them on their travels.' Two Feathers looked pleadingly at Meleeka.

Meleeka grinned broadly at Two Feathers. 'Alright, if you think it will please them, that is what we will do. We will also have a huge bonfire, for the evenings are still cold. Get the braves and the young ones to help you stack it,' Meleeka told Two Feathers.

Before the party began, everyone came to wish them a safe journey and hoped they would not be long away. The children shouted with joy when the bonfire was lit. Later they entertained the grown-ups with a song or dance. Everyone did a party piece, either solo or in a group.

Joseph felt saddened at the thought of leaving these wonderful people, although he knew it would not be for long. As the fire was dying down, Joseph noticed Meleeka and the young braves were missing.

'I think it is time we were away to our beds, we have to make an early start tomorrow,' he said to Sara.

Buta, overhearing, ordered more logs to be thrown on the fire. Then said to him, 'You cannot go yet, we have a surprise for you.' Buta turned, signalling to the others. The women began to chant, slowly at first as the beat quickened, the young ones joining in.

Buta told Joseph and Sara to look towards the fire. The new logs thrown on minutes before had taken hold. With sparks flying and the flames rising, Meleeka's head appeared, his feathered headdress quivering slightly. Slowly inch by inch Meleeka grew to his full height. Sara could not take her eyes off him. Her young heart beating faster with every movement he made.

The contrast of his chieftain robes and the flames of the fire was a sight to behold. As Meleeka came to his full height, he spread his arms out wide, looking like a great bird rising up out of the fire. The chanting grew louder, louder. Meleeka folded his arms and slowly disappeared behind the flames. Without taking her eyes away from the scene, Sara grabbed hold of her father's hand. He held it tight to reassure her.

The women, still chanting, moved behind Joseph and Sara. Meleeka and the braves came out from both sides of the fire, dancing as they did so; as they reached Joseph and Sara, the women stopped their chanting. Meleeka gave a deep bow towards Joseph.

'Tomorrow,' he said, 'you will leave us to go on your long journey. All my tribe wish you a safe return. In a moment my braves and I will dance the tribal dance of our forefathers. But before we commence, I would like to say what is in my heart. I hope that while you are away you will often think about Ilinka and its people. For my tribe is sad that you must leave us. It has been good that the white man and his daughter live among us. It was my dream when I brought my tribe here to live as the white man lives and leave the Indian way of life behind. But you have taught me that it would be wrong to wipe out the skills and arts of our ancestors, and from my heart I thank you for it.'

Meleeka bowed and saluted to Joseph. As he did so, the women began to hum softly. The braves stamped their feet and folded their arms. Then Meleeka and the braves began to chant. As they chanted they swung their arms from side to side then they looped them twice around their bodies. Sara could not take her eyes off Meleeka. His movements were so graceful, the whole camp seemed to be chanting.

'Sha, sha, sha, sha, sha, sha.'

As the chants became louder and louder, Meleeka bent his left leg and leaned his body into it. His right leg stretched outwards. In unison with the chants. He stretched his arms forward, fingers pointing to the ground.

Joseph, as he watched, was fascinated by the gracefulness of Meleeka's moving arms. Up, down, across, from left to right, and back again in a half circle. One by one the braves followed. Sara and Joseph found themselves chanting as loud as anyone.

Meleeka swung from his left to his right, still doing the same actions with his arms. Once again, one by one the braves followed. When all were in position, the chanting began to slow down. Then, as if ın slow motion, Meleeka and the braves began to raise their bodies, swaying from left to right. The chanting became softer and softer as they raised their heads up to the sky, lifting their hands above their heads and clasping their fingers together.

For a moment all was quiet as Meleeka and the braves were still as statues carved of stone. Then everyone cheered as Meleeka brought his hands to his side. After the momentous cheering, Meleeka and the braves bowed to their audience.

'Meleeka, that was wonderful,' Sara told him as she walked towards him, the sweat glistening on his forehead. 'I shall never forget this night as long as I live, it has been so exciting. And when you rose above the flames, I thought my heart would burst, thinking you might fall. I even grabbed hold of my father's hand for reassurance.'

'There was nothing to be afraid of,' Meleeka told her. 'My braves are strong, they would not let me fall.'

'But,' said Sara, 'you were so near the flames, you could have fallen into them.'

'I do not think so,' Meleeka replied as he sat down crossed-legged next to Joseph, the long feathers of his headdress trailing on the ground behind him.

'I too have enjoyed this night,' he told them. 'I have not worn my chieftain clothes for many moons. When first we came here, the womenfolk, unbeknown to me, made them for me. My tribe christened me Chief Blue Mountain and presented me with these clothes. I told them I did not wish to be their chieftain, but would be as a father to them all. Tonight as I danced with the young braves, I felt so proud of them all. The way they have worked so hard, not only in the building of Ilinka, but with the care and thoughtfulness given to the women and children. Always seeing there was plenty of wood for the fires and food to eat. And most of all, tonight I felt great joy when once again they called me Chief Blue Mountain.'

'Can you not be called that all the time?' Sara asked him.

'No,' he answered. 'for tomorrow I will be Meleeka again. It is better that way.'

'Speaking of tomorrow,' said Joseph, 'it is time Sara and I turned in. Thank you for tonight Meleeka. It was a pleasure to be here.' They bid everyone goodnight. And Meleeka walked with them to the cabin.

The next morning when all the goodbyes had been said, and the wagon packed to the hilt, Meleeka and some of the braves escorted them on the long trek to the great lakes, where they would start the first steps of their journey to England.

CHAPTER XIV

Sara was fascinated with the docklands of Liverpool. When they left the boat she dare not let go of her father's arm. The bustle of the docks with people rushing hither and thither had been too much for her and the stench made her sick.

They had found lodging nearby and for the first two days Sara never left the house, preferring to sit at the window and watch the antics of the people as they passed by.

On the third day, her father said she was to go out with him. 'You cannot stay cooped up here all the time,' he had told her. That was a week ago and now she did not mind the hurly-burley of the docks, neither did she mind the stench. And today they were going to town – her father had sold the pelts and everything they had brought from Ilinka. There was a fortune to be made there, if you had the right things to sell.

'When we get into town,' Joseph said to Sara, 'we will get ourselves some new clothes, the best money can buy, for when we get to the farm, we are not going to look like something the cat dragged in.'

Like two children, they gazed into shop windows, going up one street and down another. Sara would see something she liked then changed her mind before entering the shop.

'We could be doing this all day,' said Joseph laughing. 'Let us go and have something to eat and get our breath back.'

They found a tea house and Joseph ordered hot toasted muffins and tea for two. The tables were laid out nicely with lace table clothes and a bouquet of flowers on each. The waitress was friendly and struck up a conversation when she brought their order.

Joseph told her they had been window-gazing for hours. 'My daughter needs a new wardrobe. Can you recommend anyone?' he asked. The waitress eyed them both and hesitated before answering.

'There is Miss Traverns just around the corner. But she is very expensive.' They did not look as though they had much money but then you could never tell, the waitress thought.

'That does not matter,' Joseph said, interrupting her thoughts.

'Well, that being the case,' she told them, 'if you take your daughter to Miss Traverns you will not be disappointed, sir. Take my word for it. Why, only this morning was I not admiring a green velvet skirt and a cream silk blouse displayed in her window.'

'Right then, it is to Miss Traverns we will go and thank you for your help, miss,' he looked at the girl questionably.

'Jenny Crook, sir, but everyone calls me Jen.'

'Well, thank you, Jen,' said Joseph.

When they entered the shop, Miss Traverns herself came forward to serve them. 'May I be of assistance?' she asked snootily. They were not her usual clientele, in fact, they were positively shabby. If they did order anything, she would insist on them paying in cash. Too many of her customers made her wait for their money. The girl would be interesting to dress as she had an unusual kind of beauty.

All these thoughts went through Miss Traverns' head as she approached them.

Joseph, detecting the snootishness in her voice, felt like walking out of the shop. Only the look on Sara's face as she gazed at a blue velvet coat stopped him.

'Well, I was,' Joseph emphasized the was, 'thinking of asking you to rig out my daughter. But if it is too much trouble for you, we will go elsewhere.' Joseph could not keep the sarcasm out of his voice.

'No, it will be no trouble at all,' Miss Taverns answered. She liked the man's honesty. 'I apologise if I sounded a bit off hand, but to be honest, you do not look like my usual clientele.'

'Oh, and who are your usual clientele?' asked Joseph. 'The posh gentry folk who do not pay the bill? Have no worry on that score, madam, you will be paid for whatever we purchase.'

Sara turned to her father – she had never heard him speak to anyone like that before. Whatever is the matter with him? she wondered.

'And furthermore, madam,' Joseph continued, 'you should not judge people by the way they dress. We have travelled a long way, my daughter and I, and from where we come from, how one dresses is of no consequence, for we have not the time for wearing finery, but now we are in England, I wish my daughter to be dressed like a young lady.' Joseph saw the expression on Miss Traverns' face and burst out laughing. 'If you could only see yourself,' he told her. 'I know what you are thinking: shall I throw the man out for he is mad? Yet if I do I may lose a valuable customer.'

Miss Traverns gasped. That was exactly what she was thinking. Joseph, feeling sorry for his outburst, apologized to her.

'I have been away from England so long I am forgetting my manners,' he told her, 'but I cannot do with snobbery, never could. It gets my hackles up. Shall I go outside and come in again? Then we can start afresh.'

'No, no,' said Miss Traverns, 'I was also at fault. You have taught me a lesson today. Never judge a man by the cut of his clothes. That is what you meant, is it not?'

'Something like that,' Joseph replied. As they smiled at one another, Miss Traverns said to Joseph, 'It will be a pleasure, as you put it, to rig out your daughter.' Joseph sat down as she led Sara away to the fitting room.

He was truly sorry for being so hard on the woman, for she was probably quite nice when you got to know her. And what must they have looked like to her? All the clothes they possessed had been made by Rosa and Sara and not of the best quality material. He grinned to himself – it had been a long time since he had seen such fine clothes as these. And he had made up his mind that when they went to see the family solicitor, they would not be dressed in shabby clothes.

For all he had said to Miss Traverns about judging people by the way they dress, he would buy Sara all that she needed. Then get a new rig-out for himself. They would make a grand entrance when they got to the farm.

He could not understand why he was thinking this way, for there would be no one to impress, according to what Sara's guide had told her. So why was he bothering to make a grand entrance with the old family lawyers and at the farm? Pride he supposed, to satisfy himself. His father had told him he was a rascal. So he would return to all intents and purposes a gentlemen and a man of means.

Thinking of his father, he marvelled how he had accepted without question the message that Silver Jayot had given Sara for him, and had come thousands of miles to collect his inheritance.

'What do you think?' Miss Traverns voice broke into his reverie. Joseph, who had seen Sara only in clothes that Rosa or Sara made, could not believe the transformation. Sara even looked taller. Whether it was the clothes she wore or because Miss Traverns had plaited Sara's hair into a chignon, he could not tell.

She wore a pale blue blouse with a small stand-up collar. The yoke was embroidered with midnight blue rose buds, the sleeves, from shoulder to cuff, were jointed together with the most intricate of lace work. The midnight blue velvet skirt hugged Sara's tiny waist, then flowed to her ankles. Showing a hint of silk stocking and midnight blue shoes.

'Aye, lass, you look really beautiful,' Joseph told her. 'Now, how about trying on that blue velvet cloak you have had your eyes on?'

The cloak fitted perfectly. He smiled at Miss Traverns and told her. 'You have transformed my daughter. If I had met her walking down the street, I would not have recognized her.' Miss Traverns smiled, pleased with the compliment.

'By the way,' Joseph asked, 'I hope she is wearing all new undergarments beneath all this finery.'

'Of course,' said Miss Traverns blushing.

'Good,' Joseph replied, 'we will have another two complete outfits for her.'

'They will have to be especially made,' Miss Traverns answered. 'Sara is such a tall girl. It was only by chance that I had these clothes in stock.'

'How long will that take?' Joseph wanted to know.

'At least a fortnight and I would have to take on extra staff to get them ready so quickly,' answered Miss Traverns.

Joseph did not want to stay in Liverpool so long, but looking at Sara in her new outfit, he knew it would be worth it.

'Alright,' he said, 'two weeks it is then.'

'I will need Sara to come for fittings, we will arrange the times as we go along,' she told him. 'I have a new batch of materials coming in tomorrow,' Miss Traverns said as she parcelled up Sara's new clothes. 'So if you call in the day after, we will make a start. And thank you for your custom,' she said, handing Joseph his change.

'You're welcome,' he answered, as he doffed his hat and gave her a wink.

CHAPTER XV

Every morning Joseph took Sara down to the docks. He was interested in the buying and selling. A plan was beginning to form in his mind. With the right contacts, he could send beaver pelts from Ilinka. There could also be a market for the Indian blankets and rugs, even the dolls. With the prices he got for the things he had brought from Ilinka, it was worth thinking about. He would plan everything out before they went back, then speak with Meleeka.

Sara loved going to the warehouses – the smell of spices from the East made her forget the stench she encountered on their arrival. Also from the East came bales of silk, the colours a sight to behold. Sara would watch fascinated as they unravelled the bales to sell to the highest bidder. Sometimes while she waited for her father she would listen to the men unload the boats, some speaking foreign languages she could not understand. Others she knew were of the English-speaking race, but with all the different accents, Sara could not understand what was being said.

One such day, among all the hustle and bustle of the docks, Sara's thoughts returned to Ilinka. How quiet and peaceful it all was compared to this. For a moment she felt homesick and wondered what Meleeka was doing. How sad he had looked when they said goodbye to him and the braves. She thought for a moment he was about to kiss her, but no, he gave a slight nod of the head, telling her to take care of herself, shook her father's hand and before turning quickly towards the empty wagon, then drove away, the braves following behind. As Joseph walked towards her, he could see her mind was miles away.

'Penny for your thoughts,' he said, grabbing her by the shoulders.

'I was just thinking about Ilinka and how different it is from Liverpool.'

'And I suppose at the same time, you were also thinking about Meleeka,' laughed Joseph, as he took hold of her arm and led her away. 'We will go and see how Miss Traverns is getting along. The sooner your clothes are ready and our business is settled, the sooner we will be back in Ilinka.'

Before they reached Miss Traverns, Sara told her father she felt hungry. 'Can we not have something to eat before we go to see Miss Traverns?' she asked.

'Aye, perhaps it will be best,' Joseph answered, as he was feeling peckish himself.

The tea shop was quite full when they arrived but Jenny saw them and waved them over to a corner table. They had become quite friendly with her over the last two weeks. Every time Sara went for a fitting, they would call in to the tea shop for refreshments. If there were no other customers, Jenny would sit with them. She would talk ten to the dozen and have Sara and Joseph doubled up with laughter, when she told them of the silly things that had happened to her.

Today Jenny was very busy. There was no time for idle chatter. They ate a good dinner of beefsteak pie, followed by trifle, then a mug of coffee.

'I enjoyed that and could not eat another morsel,' Sara told Jenny as she came to clean the table.

'You had better watch it,' Jenny said, 'or when you get to Miss Traverns, nothing will fit you, as you will be a size bigger.'

'Speaking of Miss Traverns, we had better make a move or she will think we are not coming,' Joseph told them.

They said goodbye to Jenny then made their way to the shop. As Joseph passed the window, he noticed the cream blouse and green velvet skirt was still on display. Miss Traverns greeted them with a broad smile upon her face. Different than when we first came into the shop, right hoity-toity, she was then, Joseph smiled to himself as he remembered.

'You will be pleased to know that everything is ready,' Miss Traverns told Joseph. 'If Sara will go to the fitting room and you are both satisfied, I will parcel them for you.'

The clothes fitted Sara perfectly, and no one could complain about the workmanship that had been done.

'We are pleased with everything,' Joseph told Miss Traverns. 'And thank you for all the trouble you have gone to have them ready so quickly.'

As he was about to pay her, he remembered the blouse and skirt in the window. At the prices Miss Traverns charged, it would be quite a while before Jenny could afford them.

'I would also like to purchase the green velvet skirt and cream blouse displayed in the window,' he told Miss Traverns.

'But,' she answered in surprise, 'they will not fit Sara, they are far too small.'

'They are not for Sara. Do you frequent the tea shop around the corner?' Joseph asked her.

'Yes I do, quite often as a matter of fact,' she replied.

'Then you will know the waitress Jenny; do you think the skirt and blouse will fit her?' Joseph asked.

'Yes, I suppose so,' answered Miss Traverns, wondering of what interest Jenny would be to Joseph.

'Good, then would you be so kind as to have them delivered to her,' Joseph asked.

Miss Traverns pondered a little before asking Joseph her next question, for she was intrigued by his generosity. 'Would you not rather take them yourself? I think Jenny would be pleased with her gift and it is only around the corner.'

'No,' answered Joseph. 'It will be best if they are delivered. I would not wish to embarrass the girl. You can include a note with them, and as we are leaving tomorrow, she cannot refuse to accept them.'

Miss Traverns was getting more interested by the minute.

'And what,' she asked, raising an eyebrow, 'would you like the wording on the note to say?'

Joseph could not help the mirth that bubbled up inside him when he saw the expression on Miss Traverns' face. She thinks I have been having an affair with Jenny and the clothes are Jenny's reward.

'If you will give me a card, I will write the message myself,' Joseph told her. He could not hold back his mirth any longer when Miss Traverns had the decency to blush as she read what was on the card: 'Please accept the enclosed in appreciation for the kindness you have shown to two strangers. From Sara and Joseph.'

'Do you always know what I am thinking?' asked Miss Traverns, embarrassed by the way Joseph was laughing at her.

'Only when it concerns me,' Joseph replied. 'Now I will go and find a carriage to take us to our lodgings.'

No sooner had the shop door closed than it opened again. 'We're in luck,' he told them. There was a carriage outside. Sara said goodbye to Miss Traverns and thanked her for everything. Joseph also thanked her and reminded her not to deliver the things to Jenny until the next morning. He could not help but add as he stepped into the carriage, 'Just think what a good customer you would have lost had Jenny not sent us to you.' He dropped his cap at her as they drove away. Miss Traverns stood on the pavement waving until the carriage was out of sight, a thing she would never think of doing with her other customers. Well, she thought, meeting those two was quite an experience. She smiled to herself. Come morning she would give Jenny the gift.

The next morning as Joseph paid for their lodgings, the landlady hardly recognized them in their new finery.

CHAPTER XVI

Joseph was relieved to find he and Sara were the only passengers travelling in the coach. Well, at least for the first stage of the journey. As they left Liverpool behind, they both became pensive, each wondering what lay before them.

Sara gazed out of the window and wondered how her father would handle the situation. Joseph was also thinking what to do for the best. He could neither go to the lawyers nor the farm and tell them the truth. He supposed John Rhoder was still the family lawyer and would be taking care of everything. Or perhaps, he too had died and his son Adam had taken over. Joseph gave a deep sigh as he thought about Adam as from boyhood until his leaving they had been great friends. His one regret when he left England was being unable to say goodbye to Adam for he was away in France. Joseph now wondered why he had not taken Rosa's advise and written to Adam.

'Are we going straight to the farm?' Sara asked, bringing Joseph's thoughts back to the present.

'No,' Joseph replied, making up his mind. 'The coach will drop us off in town, we will stay the night at a hotel and be refreshed for whatever lies in front of us.'

Joseph decided they would stay at the Ford Hotel. He would be less likely to meet anyone there from the past – though he did not think anyone would recognize him after all these years – than at the White Horse.

'Are you tired?' he asked Sara when the porter left the room.

'Yes, a little,' she replied. 'Why?'

'I was wondering if you wanted a nap before dinner. Or whether you would rather go for a walk and stretch your legs after sitting for hours in the coach.'

'If you don't mind, I think I will rest,' she told him. 'What are you going to do?'

'I think I will do the same,' he replied.

As Sara went to her room Joseph gazed around him. He was lucky to get this suite; it was the only one in the hotel with two bedrooms. He walked over to the window and looked out. The town square was exactly as he remembered it. Across the road from the hotel was a row of shops selling every commodity. To the right was the White Horse, right next to the bank.

Around the corner on the left, which he could not see from the window but he knew would still be there, were the doctors, herbalists and solicitors. Beyond the square was the river and the market place. The river, Joseph thought, that seemed to split the town in two halves. The gentry on one side and the poverty-stricken on the other.

Yet surrounding both sides was the beauty of the countryside, the farmlands and the rolling hills. Yet even with the farmers, one would be scratching around to keep his family fed, while another, like his father, would be rich and affluent.

Joseph sighed as he turned away from the window, his thoughts turning to Ilinka and wondering what changes would take place in the next fifty years. As he lay down on the bed to rest before dinner, he did not know the future of Ilinka was in his hands.

The dining room was quiet as the waiter led Joseph and Sara to their table. Joseph said good evening to the few customers in the room, except for the two men in the corner. They were so deep in discussion that neither of them looked up as Joseph and Sara entered.

Joseph and Sara were halfway through their meal when one of the gentlemen left. The other ordered a brandy then sat back and relaxed, a look of satisfaction on his face.

Sara, in conversation with her father, saw the waiter place the brandy on the gentleman's table. As the customer picked up his glass, he casually glanced around the room, and before the glass touched his lips, his eyes let upon the table where Joseph and Sara were dining.

Without having a sip of his brandy, he put the glass down and sat staring at them. Sara tried to give all her attention to what her father was saying but out of the corner of her eye she could still see the man, his drink untouched, staring in their direction. Joseph, not knowing, saw a deep flush come upon Sara's face.

'Are you too warm?' he asked.

'No, I am alright,' Sara replied, her face getting redder as she glanced over to see the man still staring.

'Something is ailing you, what is it?'

'I don't want to cause any trouble,' Sara told him, 'but that man over there keeps staring at us.'

'He won't be staring at us, more like he will be besotted by you,' Joseph told her smiling.

'I don't think that has anything to do with it; he looks as though he has seen a ghost,' Sara replied.

Before turning around to see who was taking such an interest in them, Joseph said to her, 'It is a hundred to one chance that I would be recognized but it is a possibility.'

Sara, watching her father, saw a broad smile come upon his face and his eyes light up in delight. She saw the same expression on the stranger's face as he picked up his brandy and came over to their table.

Her father pulled out a chair for the man to join them but before he sat down, they shook hands vigorously and to the amusement of the other diners, hugged one another unashamedly, tears welling up in their eyes.

Joseph turned to Sara, his face still beaming with pleasure. 'Sara, this is Adam, the best and truest friend a man could ever have known.'

'So good a friend,' Adam told her as they shook hands, 'that not a word have I heard from him in twenty years.'

'I know, and I apologize,' Joseph told him.

'I'll forgive you,' replied Adam.

'Where's Rosa? Is she resting?' Adam wanted to know, but saw the sadness come upon Joseph's face as he mentioned Rosa.

'Rosa died of the fever, Sara and I were saved by a tribe of Indians but Rosa died before they found us,' Joseph told him.

'I am sorry to hear that. Rosa was a grand lass.'

'Aye, she was,' said Joseph sadly. 'But life has to go on and Rosa would be the last person to want us to go around moping.' He smiled at Adam as he spoke, for he could see his friend was embarrassed.

Then Adam told him, 'I moped for weeks when I came back from France and found you had had a rift with your father and had gone to America, taking Rosa with you. I thought at least you would have left me a note. Speaking of your father,' Adam continued, 'why are you staying here? Why did you not go to the farm?'

'The farm?' Joseph asked, feigning surprise.

'Yes, the farm, it is yours, your father willed it to you.'

'Did he now?' Joseph asked sarcastically.

Adam looked at his old friend quizzically before asking, 'If you did not know about the farm, what brought you here?'

'When we were young,' Joseph said to him, 'we made a pact never to lie to each other so for the moment I will not say anything.'

'Fair enough,' Adam told him. But he did not miss the relieved look Sara gave her father. 'I have an idea,' he said, smiling at Sara. 'It is early and a beautiful evening, why don't we order a carriage to take us to the farm, it is only a couple of miles away. What do you say Joseph?'

'If Sara feels up to travelling we will go,' Joseph told him. They both looked at Sara for her answer.

'I think it a good idea, it will pass away the evening,' she told them.

As they travelled through the town and into the countryside, Sara only half listened to her father and Adam as they recalled the days of their friendship long ago, for the changing scenery was more interesting.

She was beginning to understand what her father meant when he spoke of the rich and the poor. Upon leaving the square and crossing the river, Adam pointed out to her the grand, imposing houses of the wool and cotton merchants, before the carriage skirted the market place.

Travelling through the town, Sara saw the ragged, bare-footed children and the hovels they lived in. Her father told her there could be nine in a family living in a two-roomed house. He pointed out the factories where the children worked for a pittance, and the mansions of the mill owners.

Now, as the horses slowed their pace climbing the long steep hill to the open countryside, Sara lay back enjoying the majestic views. Joseph and Adam also relaxed and became quiet as if they to were taking in the scenery. But in truth, each was deep in his own thoughts. Joseph was thinking how fortunate it was that Adam, of all people, had decided that evening to dine at the Ford Hotel, for Adam had told him it was a place he seldom visited.

Joseph smiled to himself when a picture of Meleeka came into his mind and he heard him say, 'It was fate, Joseph, it was fate.' Whatever it was, Joseph was thankful, for he had not relished going to the farm or the lawyers with some cock and bull story. And now everything would take its course. For Adam would see to everything and there would be no questions asked. Until Joseph was ready to tell Adam what circumstances had brought him home, he smiled again wondering what Adam would make of it when he told him the truth.

Adam was also deep in thought. He was overjoyed to have his friend back home. Ever since old Tyler died, leaving everything to Joseph, he hoped and prayed that Joseph would be found, alive and well. And that he would not be too stubborn to come home.

Yet Adam was puzzled by the mystery of Joseph's appearance. Adam glanced across at Joseph, his mind racing. He knew about the farm even before I mentioned it to him, but how? None of the messengers had found him and apart from myself, he has not spoken to anyone else since he arrived. No matter, Adam thought, I will do as Joseph asked and not question him, for he will tell me soon enough when he thinks the time is right.

All three came out of their deep ponderings when they heard the driver shouting at the horses. 'Woa! Woa! Woa!'

As he alighted from the carriage, Joseph was surprised at the delight he felt upon seeing the farm again and knowing that all he surveyed belonged to him.

He voiced his thoughts to Adam who smiled more to himself than at Joseph as he knew just how rich a man his friend really was. For old Tyler had bequeathed not only his farm to Joseph but also his stocks and shares. And there were also monies from his mother.

CHAPTER XVII

Sara gaped in amazement as she looked up at the large stone farmhouse with its mullioned windows and small courtyard surrounding the front of the house, with steps leading down to the large garden. She was so taken aback, she did not realize she was standing there gaping until she heard Adam calling to her.

'Come along, Sara,' he shouted, 'we are going around the back way. Bessie will be in the kitchen.'

As Adam knocked on the kitchen door and entered, he beckoned Joseph and Sara to follow him.

'Why, Mr Rhoder, what a surprise,' Bessie said, as Adam entered the kitchen. She was sat at the kitchen table having supper with John, the farm manager, and Jamie, his son.

'I have a much bigger surprise for you all,' said Adam, smiling at them as he introduced Joseph and Sara.

'Well I never. Oh I am so glad they found you, sir,' Bessie said, slightly flustered as she shook Joseph's hand.

'And the same goes for me,' said John.

Sara was watching Jamie as the introductions were being made, and saw him cringe as her father went towards him. As her father put out his hand, Jamie backed away and bolted out of the kitchen. Jamie's father excused himself and ran after him.

'You will have to be patient with the lad. He is afraid of strangers,' Bessie told them. 'Sit yourselves down and I'll make you all a mug of tea. Kettle's just boiled. Are you planning on staying the night?' Bessie asked them as she placed their mugs of tea onto the table. She had noticed they'd brought no luggage with them. It was Adam that answered her.

'I was thinking of asking John to drive us back into town later, then Joseph and Sara could bring their luggage tomorrow after spending the night at the hotel.'

'It is up to you,' Bessie said. 'But if you wish to stay, it will be no trouble, for all the rooms are aired and everything is in order.'

'I think it is a good idea,' Joseph told her. 'Yes, we will stay. Then in the morning I will go and collect our things and go with Adam to his office. Besides,' Joseph continued, 'John seems to have his hands full with the lad.'

'He has,' said Bessie, 'poor Jamie is a bit short in the head.'

'Is that alright with you Adam?' Joseph asked.

'Yes, of course,' Adam replied, draining the last drops of his tea, 'and if it is alright with you, I will show Sara around the farm while you have a chat with Bessie.'

When Adam and Sara left them, Bessie made Joseph and herself another mug of tea. She told him how glad she was that he had been found and was able to come home. Joseph, meanwhile, did not enlighten her on the being found bit – he let her assume that is what happened.

As Bessie handed him his tea, Joseph rose from the table. 'Let us sit over here by the fireplace,' he said. 'I loved sitting here with cook when I was a lad. I thought the kitchen was the best and friendliest room in the house. And you know what, Bessie,' he said smiling at her, 'I bet it still is.'

'Why, thank you, sir. I take it that was meant to be in way of a compliment,' Bessie asked.

'It was so,' he replied.

'It be a right pity, sir,' said Bessie, 'that you could not get home and see your father before he died. He told me many times how he rued the day you went away. And even on his death bed his last thoughts were upon you. I was with him most of that day. I think he thought I was your mother for he would ask, "Has our Joseph not arrived yet, Alice?" Or perhaps your mother was by his side, for I have heard it said when someone is dying, a loved one comes and takes their hand. Anyway, as I went to make him comfortable, I heard him whisper, "Alice, I cannot wait any longer for our Joseph to come home," and then he was gone, sir.'

Bessie dabbed her eyes on her apron as she finished telling Joseph about his father. For a moment Joseph felt a sadness as he thought about his father, alone except for the servants in this rambling house, waiting and wondering if the son he'd sent away in anger would ever return. Perhaps he loved me after all, then he hardened his heart.

No, he thought, my father never loved me. If Nathan had married and been blessed with sons, my father would not have given me another thought. Then silently he said to himself, I forgive you, Father, for what you did and said to Rosa and me, but I will never forget. Yet in a way I thank you for my going away with Rosa, she was the best thing that ever happened to me, even though Rosa had to die of the fever.

Joseph heard Bessie's voice as if coming from afar.

'I'm sorry,' he said, 'I was miles away. What were you saying?'

'I was just saying,' Bessie replied, 'that when I came to work for your father after your mother died, I was instructed to keep the house ready at all times, in case Joseph came home unexpectedly and brought a brood of grandchildren with him. Even after your father's death, I kept on with those instructions, for Mr Rhoder told me to carry on as usual, so I hope you will find everything in order, sir.'

'I'm sure I will,' Joseph told her. Before he could say anything else, Bessie continued.

'John was instructed to look after the farm. He also worked for your father before he died. John employs men and lads from the village to help him. I have two girls to help me with the housework. It is a big place for one body to look after on her own. Since John's wife died three months ago, I give him and Jamie their meals; 'tis company for me and for them. And I hope I may continue to do so if it be alright with you.'

Joseph smiled at her, then said, 'Bessie, you carry on as if I were not here. Adam gave me a good report on you and John as we travelled here. In fact, he spoke most highly of you both and said it would be a hard task to find anyone better.'

'Why thank you, sir,' Bessie said beaming with pleasure. Joseph did not like being called Sir – he was not used to it – for years he had been called nothing else, only Joseph.

'I'd best go and stoke the fire in the drawing room, the evening air is getting chilly,' Bessie said, rising from her chair. 'Would you prefer to go in there?' she asked.

'If you don't mind,' Joseph answered, 'I will stay here and wait for Adam and Sara to return. Besides, as I said before, this is my favourite room.'

They both smiled as Bessie left the room. Joseph relaxed in his chair and gazed around the room, everything was spic and span. For a moment he could not believe the farm really belonged to him. Here I am, he thought, the master of it all and not even interested in looking around as Adam and Sara have done. Did I hate my father and the farm so much that I would rather sit in the kitchen with my housekeeper discussing things that, by rights, should be discussed elsewhere in the house? He wondered how long Sara and Adam would be, and if he should go and look for them. Then he smiled to himself, it was Adam who had brought them in by way of the kitchen, anyone else would have hammered on the front door. But Adam knew he would be more at home going in the back way for when they were both young, they would always creep in the back door. Joseph knew it was Adam's way of saying 'Welcome Home'.

No man could have a better friend than Adam, even after all these years of absence; it was as if they had not been apart. Adam had brought him up-to-date with the happenings of the last twenty years. He told him about Nathan being jilted and turning into a cruel drunkard, and how he was gored by the bull. And how his mother had pined away knowing she would never see her youngest son again. And when she died, his father wanted everything possible done to find Joseph. All this, Adam told him as they travelled to the farm.

Yet never once, though Joseph knew it must be the uppermost question in Adam's mind, did he ask, 'How did you know to come home?'

I will tell him tomorrow, Joseph thought. We will invite him to supper.

CHAPTER XVIII

The next morning it was decided that Joseph would stay at the farm and Adam would collect their things from the hotel. 'It would be foolish, both of us going into town,' Adam told Joseph, as they ate their breakfast, 'especially as I will be dining here tonight.'

'But I was going to come to your office,' Joseph said.

Adam thought a moment before replying, 'Well, being as my father is away on business, I will bring the will and everything to the house when I return and then we can discuss everything; it does not have to be at the office. Besides you have a lot of catching up to do around the farm, why waste the day travelling to town?'

Joseph, seeing the logic of Adam's words, finally agreed with him. As John drove him into town, Adam chuckled to himself at the thought of seeing Joseph's face when he found out just how rich a man he was.

Upstairs in her bedroom, Sara awoke to the sound of voices that all at once faded away. For a moment she wondered where she was, then she remembered Bessie bringing her to this room the night before. Bessie had found her a nightie and stayed until she got into bed.

'Now you have a lay-in in the morning, you must be worn out with all that travelling,' Bessie said to her.

'I will send one of the girls with your breakfast so you can stay in bed as long as you like.' She had thanked Bessie then said goodnight and within minutes was fast asleep.

Now wide awake, and not being used to laying about in the morning, she slid out of bed, her feet sinking into the deep pile of the carpet, went to the window and drew back the curtains.

The view was breathtaking – far away in the distance, no matter which way she looked, were great sprawling hills, each one mingling into the next. The tallest hill of all seemed to dominate the rest, its peak reaching into the clouds, the shape of it reminding her of the Blue Mountain and Meleeka. Just then there was a knock on the door and a young girl entered.

'Ho, you're up then, miss. Bessie sent me to see if you were awake. I have brought your breakfast.'

'Thank you,' said Sara, as the girl laid the tray on the bedside table. 'I have just been admiring the view. You can see for miles through that window, and all those hills, they look majestic in the morning sunlight.'

'Aye,' the girl answered, 'and on a clear day you can see the hills of Derbyshire and them be many miles away. Will there be anything else, miss?' the girl asked as Sara sat down on the bed.

'Will you not stay and talk with me?' Sara asked. 'I would be so grateful for your company. Stay at least until I have eaten my breakfast.'

'Alright, just for a few minutes, mind, or Bessie will be after me. She told me about you and the Master arriving unexpectedly last night, a right shock you have her in, I can tell you.'

'The Master,' said Sara. 'Why do you call my father the Master?' she asked.

'Well, miss,' replied the girl, 'he be owner of this place so 'tis obvious he be the new Master.'

'Forgive me if I seem stupid,' Sara said, 'but I am unfamiliar with the ways of the English and how they live. You see, where I come from, my father has always been known as Joseph and I as Sara. By the way, what is your name?' Sara asked.

'My name is Jessica, miss.'

'There you are then,' Sara said, smiling at her, 'you're Jessica and I am Sara, so in future you must call me Sara and not Miss Sara.'

'I cannot do that, Miss Sara,' Jessica said in disbelieve. 'It wouldn't be proper. I would get into trouble. I am only a servant, well skivvy more like. Oh, no miss, it would not do at all.'

'Well, I certainly do not wish to make trouble for you but I do hope you will be my friend.' Then seeing that Jessica did not know how to answer, Sara changed the subject and said to her, 'Tell me about the young boy Jamie, who we saw last night.'

'He's a bit short in the head,' Jessica told her, 'probably with his mother always hitting him on the head when he was younger. He be that timid, he will run a mile if he sees a stranger.' Jessica paused, before continuing. 'Jamie must have had the fright of his life when you and the Master walked in last night. For to be honest, Miss Sara, we all thought your father was dead, not a word had anyone heard about him all these years. 'Tis strange how the Master came home now as if he knew everything would be his.'

'What makes you say that?' Sara asked her, surprised at how Jessica would think of such a thing.

'I don't know,' Jessica replied. 'Take no notice of me, sometimes I get these silly notions in my head and they just pop out before I can stop them. Bessie says they are predictions, whatever they may be. Speaking of Bessie, I best be off.'

She whipped up Sara's tray and without another word, left the room.

A moment later Joseph popped his head around the door and said to her, 'How do you fancy going for a ride? 'Tis a beautiful morning.'

'Yes, I'd like that,' Sara told him.

'Here then, put these on,' he threw a pair of riding breeches and a shirt onto the bed. 'I'll go and see to the horses.'

The ride over the moors was invigorating and they both enjoyed the freedom of the wild countryside. They jumped wall after wall that separated the farms until both horses and riders were out of breath. They dismounted and walked the horses for a while. They came to a stream and let the horses drink, then tethered them to a tree, letting them rest before setting off home.

As they themselves rested upon the grass, Joseph told her that Adam would be coming to supper.

'I would like to tell him about Silver Jayot, but it is for you to decide whether we tell him or not,' he said to her. 'Make no decision now, think about it and let me know later.'

'Can we trust Adam?' she asked.

'I once said,' replied Joseph, 'that I would trust Adam with my life. Seeing him again, I have no reason for changing my mind. You saw him last night when I said not to ask any questions – he was bursting to ask a thousand but he did as I asked him, and I know he senses there is something uncanny about me returning home. Adam and I were great friends when we were young. In fact, there was a closeness between us that went beyond friendship. Sometimes we could tell what the other was thinking. What I do know, Sara,' Joseph continued, 'is that if we do tell Adam about Ilinka and the strange effect it has upon you and that I came home because your guide, Silver Jayot, gave you the message for me and that it seemed the most natural thing in the world for me to take heed of it, I know that Adam will believe us. Let others think it was a coincidence that we arrived here when we did, for they might think upon it as some form of witchcraft if they knew the truth. The English are renowned for not understanding the unknown. And I would not like people to think you were some kind of witch.'

Joseph untethered the horses. 'Come,' he said, 'it is time we made our way home.'

CHAPTER XIX

Adam could not take his eyes off Sara. She wore a dark green plain velvet dress, yet it looked superb on her. He could not imagine any other woman he knew wearing such a dress. He wondered where Sara had purchased it from, for he hadn't seen another like it. If he had asked, Sara would have told him she had designed it herself.

'I do not want another frilly, fancy dress,' she told Miss Traverns. 'I want one like this.' She showed Miss Traverns a sketch she had drawn of a long straight dress tied at the waist with a tassel; the neckline rounded at the base of the throat was joined in open stitch work to the yolk, the long sleeves with half-inch tassels, draping from elbow to cuff. When Miss Traverns inspected the drawing, she was shocked at the plainness of it.

She sniffed and turned up her nose to show her disapproval, but said she would make it, for she could not refuse. She did not know it was a longer version of the Indian dresses the women wore at Ilinka. The dress finished, Miss Traverns herself was surprised how lovely it looked upon Sara. It was the plainest dress she had ever made. Yet never had she seen a dress have such a stunning effect on any of her clients. But then none of her clientele had the figure or the grace of movement that Sara had.

Adam was thinking on the same lines as Miss Traverns, as to Sara's movements. He liked Sara, there was no pretence or coyness about her and he felt at ease with her and there were not many women he could say that about.

I wish I was twenty years younger, he thought. I would go with her to the ends of the earth.

During supper Adam was intrigued as Joseph and Sara told him about their lives at Ilinka, especially as they were the only white settlers. He realized when Sara spoke about Meleeka that she was in love with him – he wondered if Joseph realized that his daughter was in love with this Indian fellow. Adam pondered for a moment on what Joseph would do if Sara insisted on marrying Meleeka.

For Adam could not imagine Joseph having a Red Indian for a son-in-law. Between them, Joseph and Sara told him all there was to know about Ilinka. Except, of course, the magic of the Blue Mountain and Silver Jayot.

Then Joseph told him of his life before they went to Ilinka. How he and Rosa fared when they reached America and of course, how Sara became their daughter. Adam felt a sense of relief when Joseph told him about Sara, for if she did wish to marry Meleeka, there could be no objection from Joseph.

'So, there you are,' Joseph told him. 'You know all that has happened to me from when I left England.'

Adam gave a ruthful smile as he thought, Not everything, for I know there is something you are keeping from me. For the life of him, he could not think what it was, or why his instinct made him feel so positive about it.

Later in the drawing room, Joseph was thunderstruck when Adam told him how much he was worth.

'Dear god in heaven,' Joseph shouted. 'Whatever is a man to do with such an amount of money. Are you sure about all this?' he asked. He could not believe what Adam had just told him; that besides the farm, he was to inherit seventy-five thousand pounds. He knew his father had always been classed as a rich farmer, but always assumed it was because the farm was well run and been in the Tyler family for generations.

'I am very sure,' Adam replied 'and everything is straightforward enough, there are no complications between them, your parents have left you well provided for. Your father was a very shrewd investor, he knew when to buy and when to sell, not one penny did he lose. And now it is all yours, Joseph, you are a very rich man indeed, and if I was in your shoes, I would think long and hard before deciding whether to return to Ilinka.'

'Maybe, maybe,' replied Joseph, still in a state of shock. Fancy his father playing the stock market and making a fortune – he couldn't believe it. He thought about the simple, happy life he had lived all these years, with his beloved wife Rose and Sara.

They had never been really poor and destitute, but neither had they been rich. Yet there was always warmth and comfort and a companionship between them that no amount of money could have bought. If only he could have said to Adam, 'You keep the money and bring Rosa back to me.' Joseph would have been a happy man.

Sara, watching the different emotions on her father's face, guessed what he was thinking. She also knew without a shadow of a doubt they would return to Ilinka. And if Adam hoped to talk her father into staying here, he was in for a disappointment. Adam was already disappointed – he had expected Joseph to jump for joy upon being told what a rich man he was; he also expected some response from Sara. But no, they both sat there deep in their own thoughts.

In all his years as a lawyer, Adam had never seen such an unresponsive attitude as Joseph was showing. Oh, Joseph had been shocked by the amount of his legacy, but Adam knew it was not that as to why Joseph was so deep in thought.

Through narrowed eyes, he observed both Sara and Joseph and remembered what they told him about Ilinka. The place has a hold on them, he thought, I don't know what it is, but there is something.

He had been fascinated and amused during supper when they had told him about being saved by the Indians and how they built the cabins.

'And you live with a tribe of Indians? You, the only white man. I can't believe it' he had said to Joseph.

When Joseph told him they would be going back to Ilinka, he had said to him, 'I must say you have portrayed a pretty picture of Ilinka, but to go back there. You must be out of your mind. Perhaps you will think differently when you see your father's will and other legacies you have to come.'

'Then,' Joseph had replied, 'nothing my father says in his will can make me change my mind.'

Adam could stand the silence no longer. 'Well, say something, Joseph. I have waited a long time for you to find out what a rich man you are and all I get is silence.'

Joseph looked up and smiled at him. 'I am sorry,' he said, 'if I did not whoop for joy. Is that what you expected me to do? And I admit it is a pleasing amount of money for any man to inherit.'

'Than what is the problem?' Adam asked.

'There is no problem,' replied Joseph. 'I was just thinking of Rosa and wishing she could be here with us.' As he said it, he could have sworn he felt Rosa's presence and heard her whisper to him, 'I am here Joseph, I am always with you.' He glanced swiftly at Sara. Was his imagination running away with him? Or was it really possible for someone you loved and lost in death to stay by your side. Sara smiled at him. The same smile he had seen so many times at Ilinka, then nodded her head in answer to his unspoken question. Joseph felt a warm glow inside him, for sometimes, when he was alone, he had spoken to Rosa as if she was with him – now he knew that she was.

Adam saw the look that passed between Joseph and Sara. It made him feel uneasy, there seemed to be an uncanny closeness between them as if they could have a conversation together, yet not have spoken a word. He felt himself shiver involuntarily. He coughed nervously, wanting to cut the atmosphere in the room.

'I'm sorry, Adam,' Joseph said, seeing his friend's discomfort, 'but there are so many thoughts going through my head.'

'And what are your plans now you are a rich man?' Adam asked. Not wanting this conversation or Joseph to go into a decline again. 'Don't tell me you are still thinking seriously of returning to Ilinka.'

'Yes, we have to go back,' Joseph told him.

'You have to!' Adam said in surprise. 'What do you mean you have to? From now on you don't have to do anything, not unless you really want to.'

'I have to go back,' said Joseph raising his voice. 'My destiny, fate or whatever you wish to call it belongs to Ilinka.'

'I should think,' said Adam in his lawyer's voice, 'that your fate lies here, if only out of duty to your father.'

Joseph gave him a withering look, then said, 'I owe nothing to my father, least of all duty. Do you think if my brother was alive or had he been married and left sons to carry on the farm, that I would be sitting here now? No, my father would not have given me a second thought.'

Adam realizing how Joseph's mind was working, thought it best to agree with him.

'But what about the farm?' he asked. 'It has been in the Tyler family for generations, surely that means something to you.'

'I haven't given it a thought,' replied Joseph, 'but seeing I am the last of the Tyler men and as I cannot see myself getting married again and producing a son, I cannot see what good it will do keeping the farm, for it will soon pass out of the Tyler family anyway.' Then Joseph continued, 'If we were able to stay here and Sara could marry a farmer, then things might be different. But Sara's fate also belongs in Ilinka. Still, I will give some thought as to what I will do about the farm. It is early yet, and you will be the first to know when I have made up my mind.'

'Fair enough,' Adam said, not wanting to pursue the subject further – he assumed that Joseph was raking up old wounds, for never had he seen anyone so disgruntled after being left such a huge legacy.

'To change the subject,' Adam asked Joseph, 'why are you so sure that your destiny is waiting in Ilinka?' Once again he saw that strange look pass between father and daughter. He also saw Sara give a slight nod. For a moment Adam thought Joseph was not going to answer.

Then Joseph turned to him and said, 'Tonight we have told you many things about Ilinka, but there is something we have not spoken about.'

'I thought there was something, I could sense it,' Adam told him. 'What is it Joseph? Don't you trust me? Does our friendship of the past mean nothing to you?'

'Of course I trust you. I told Sara today I would trust you with my life,' Joseph replied, 'but it was up to Sara whether or not we should speak of it.'

Adam was intrigued. Whatever could be of such importance that Joseph had to have permission from his daughter? He presumed that the nod Sara gave her father was a signal.

He heard Joseph say, 'It was no coincidence that I came home when I did. And you could have sent a hundred men to look for me, but I do not think there would have been any chance of them finding me.'

Then Joseph told him about the Blue Mountain and the effect it had upon Sara, the first time she saw it. How both Meleeka and Sara thought it was a magic mountain because it spoke to them. And lastly, he told Adam about Sara's guide, Silver Jayot, and the message he had given her. 'Sara was told to tell me my father had died and men had been sent to look for me and I was to come home and collect my inheritance. Sara was also to come with me. Why? As yet we do not know. Then we were to return to Ilinka. So,' Joseph continued, 'you could say we have been sent here for a purpose. For some reason I have to collect my inheritance then go back to Ilinka. What good all this money will do there, I have no idea, for we live a simple life where money is of no consequence. Though I must confess, when I sold the things we brought from Ilinka and got such a good price for them, a plan was beginning to form in my mind. But I will have to speak to Meleeka about it.'

Adam listened to Joseph with great interest, in fact, he was fascinated with the whole story. Earlier when they had spoken about Ilinka, it was just a place where they lived. But now, as Joseph talked, Adam saw everything in his mind's eye. As though someone was painting pictures and showing them to him. Everything was so clear, he was so engrossed he did not realize Joseph had stopped speaking.

He was brought out of his reverie when Joseph, seeing the faraway look on Adam's face, and what he took to be a smile of disbelief around his mouth, said, 'You don't believe a word I've said, do you, Adam?'

'On the contrary, I believe it all,' Adam replied. 'I was just carried away with the pictures forming in my mind, of the mountain and Ilinka. In fact, it was as if I was there, seeing everything as though it was happening now. No wonder you have to return. For I have only heard the telling of it, yet the effect it had on me was very strange. Promise me one thing Joseph, that when you do go back you will not let another twenty years go by before you get in touch with me again.'

'I promise,' said Joseph. 'And you promise that what you have heard tonight goes no further.'

They smiled at each other and shook hands. 'It's a deal,' said Adam.

CHAPTER XX

Jessica brought Sara her breakfast tray and laid it upon the table, then sat down on the edge of the bed.

'I am going to miss our little morning chats,' she said to Sara. 'And we will all miss you and the Master; you have been ever so kind to us. Bessie was just saying how you've treated us more like friends than servants, and how its been like one big happy family. And Bessie says she can't get over young Jamie and how he followed you everywhere. He will be like a normal lad now, not timid and frightened of his own shadow. Jamie's father said it would be like some miracle happened to the lad.'

Sara smiled to herself as she listened to Jessica prattling on – it had been the same every morning. Jessica would bring her tray, sit on the edge of the bed and chatter ten to the dozen while Sara ate her breakfast.

When Jessica took the tray away, Sara lay back on the pillows and thought to herself, I wonder what Jessica would say if she knew the truth about Jamie.

She lay there recalling it all. When she'd retired on the night that Adam came to supper, she heard the voice of Silver Jayot. *'Your father was right to tell his friend the secrets of the Blue Mountain. It will help him to understand as to why you must go back. He will be of great help to your father in the future, for all your destinies are linked. You will see as time goes by what I mean. So do not worry about Adam, you can trust him.'*

'Yes I know,' Sara replied. 'I felt that he would be a true friend to my father and myself. I felt so at ease with him over supper. It could have been Meleeka that I was talking to.'

Then Silver Jayot told her the real reason he had come to her this night, *'You must help the boy Jamie.'*

'Help Jamie, how? He would run a mile rather than speak to me. So how do you expect me to help him?'

'Have you forgotten,' Silver Jayot asked, *'what was told to you at Ilinka? You have a special gift, Sara, to heal the sick.*

'What will I have to do?' Sara wanted to know.

'Firstly,' Silver Jayot told her, *'you will make friends with him, it will be easier than you think. Jamie has a malfunction in his brain, that is why he acts peculiar and cannot do the simplest of tasks.*

'When you are alone with him, you must place your hands above his head and circle them around the crown. You do not have to touch him, so he will feel nothing. Slowly, day by day, Jamie will begin to make progress.'

'Can I really make him better?' Sara asked, excitement in her voice. 'But what will his father and Bessie think when Jamie suddenly becomes normal?' Sara wanted to know.

'He will spend much time with you,' Silver Jayot replied, *'and they will not see you touch him. To all intents and purposes, you will be teaching him things and giving him the confidence he lacks. This is what everyone will believe.'*

And that was just how it happened. The very next day when Sara went to the stables, Jamie was sitting on the wall throwing stones at nothing in particular; he was not even looking where the stones were landing.

Sara wondered what to do. If she shouted to him he would just take off. He is so engrossed he doesn't even know I am here, Sara thought.

She bent down and picked up a handful of small stones then crept over to where Jamie was sitting. She leaned on the wall and held out her right hand that was full of the small stones, her left hand ready to grab the back of Jamie's jacket if he attempted to run off.

'I bet I can throw my stones farther than yours,' she said to him. She felt Jamie stiffen and grabbed the tail of his jacket. 'Don't run away, Jamie,' she said – he reminded her of a scared rabbit, not knowing what to do or which way to turn.

'I only want to be your friend,' she told him gently. He looked up at her and saw the sweetest smile he had ever seen.

'Would you not like to be my friend?' Sara asked him. He did not answer, but neither did he try to get away.

'I get lonely too,' she told him. 'But that is because I am in a strange land and do not know anyone. So if you would be my friend, I would not be lonely any more.'

Without taking his eyes off her, he took a stone from her hand and threw it, not even looking where or how far it went. Sara knew she too would have to throw a stone, and to do that she would also have to let go of his coat. Then what? Would he make a bolt for it? They say that those who are sick in the mind can be very shrewd when it suits them to be. It was a chance she had to take.

She let go of Jamie's coat and threw a stone as far as she could. To her relief, Jamie took another stone and this time watched to see where it went. They continued throwing until all the stones were gone.

'Well, that proves one thing, you can throw better than I can,' Sara told him. Jamie did not answer her – he sat on the wall staring in front of him.

'Would you like to help me with the horses?' she asked him. 'I don't think Tom, the stable boy, will mind if we go and give him a lift, do you?' She saw Jamie flinch when she mentioned Tom's name. 'Or would you rather go for a walk?' she said quickly.

Jamie nodded and swung his legs over the wall and jumped onto the path.

'You show me the way and I will follow,' she told him. He took her across the fields until they came to a small ravine with a stream running through it. Without speaking, he motioned for Sara to sit down on a tree stump. She sat down and for a moment thought Jamie was going to make a dash for it as he ran to the edge of the stream. Then he lay down and put his hands into the water, just like her father had done at Ilinka.

Sara relaxed, for she knew that Jamie was doing what her father called tickling trout. Within minutes Jamie had caught a large fish. He lay it down beside him and plunged his hand back into the water. Sara, watching him, dared not speak – she was satisfied that Jamie allowed her to sit and watch him. Jamie caught four fish and tied them together with a piece of string he took out of his pocket. Without so much as a word or a smile, he gave the fish to Sara and sat down beside her.

'Thank you, Jamie,' Sara said, 'these are the finest trout I have ever seen. If we give them to Bessie she will cook us a fine supper. Would you like that?' For an answer he just stared at her and nodded his head.

Sara put the fish on her knees – what did it matter if they made her clothes smell? Making friends with Jamie was more important. They both sat there deep in their own thoughts. Sara was wondering how she could get her hands above Jamie's head without him thinking she was going to touch him.

Just then Jamie got to his feet and started to walk back the way they had come. There was no one more surprised than Bessie when Jamie walked into the kitchen and Sara followed him carrying the trout.

'Well bless my soul, what have we got here?' Bessie asked.

'Jamie caught these,' Sara said, plonking the fish onto the kitchen table. 'And if you wouldn't mind cooking them, Bessie, we will have them for supper.'

'That is what we agreed upon, isn't it, Jamie?' Sara asked him.

With both Bessie and Sara looking at him, Jamie nodded his head then ran out of the kitchen.

'That be a turn up for the book,' Bessie said, as she poured Sara a mug of tea. Sara plopped down on the nearest chair.

'Thanks, Bessie,' she said, picking up the mug. 'I'm ready for this. Then I must get changed – I stink of fish.'

Bessie's jolly laughter could be heard in the yard. 'If you don't mind my saying so, miss, I agree with you. You do stink of fish. But however did you get Jamie to catch them for you?' Bessie asked, dabbing the tears of laughter from her eyes.

Sara told her about the stone-throwing game and then of Jamie taking her to the ravine. 'I think that Jamie is lonely,' Sara told Bessie. 'And if he will let me spend some time with him, I will be quite willing to do so. Though I must confess, he never spoke one word to me all the time I was with him.'

'Be thankful for small mercies,' Bessie said. 'You be lucky he would have anything at all to do with you.'

'By the way,' Sara said, 'when I asked Jamie if he wanted to come with me to the stables and give Tom a hand, Jamie actually flinched. Is he frightened of Tom? I mean, really frightened.'

'Well,' Bessie replied, 'I think Tom is always making fun of Jamie and if he sees him anywhere near the stables Tom will run Jamie off.'

'Does he now,' said Sara, rising from the chair. 'Jamie and I will have our supper in the kitchen if that is alright with you, Bessie. That is, if Jamie turns up.' Sara added as an afterthought.

'I will cook the trout to perfection,' Bessie told her.

CHAPTER XXI

Sara entered the kitchen wearing an old blouse and skirt. Bessie had set the table for two.

'I will make myself scarce, if and when Jamie arrives,' she told Sara. 'I have cooked you a trout apiece – they are so large I thought one each would be enough. There is some crusty bread and butter to go with it and I will leave you some jam. Jamie always likes a jam butty to finish off with.' As she spoke the kitchen door opened and Jamie stood there.

'Come on in and shut the door,' Bessie told him. He came timidly into the room. Sara thought he looked different, then realized what it was. She had never seen him without his cap on. His blond curly hair had been brushed until it shone, his face scrubbed clean, showing a pale complexion with rosy cheeks – not wearing his cap seemed somehow to make him look taller.

Somewhere at the back of her mind she recalled Jessica saying Jamie was about eleven years old. She wondered if the girl was right for tonight he looked older.

'Who's a bonny lad then?' Sara heard Bessie say to Jamie. Sara, watching him, saw his face turn red with embarrassment and thought he was going to turn round and flee.

'Come, let us sit at the table,' she said quickly. 'Bessie has cooked the trout for us and we will enjoy them all the more because you caught them.' Bessie served them their supper and poured them a mug of tea, then said she had something to take care of in the pantry.

When she had gone, Jamie sat staring at his plate. 'Shall we eat it like the Indians do at Ilinka?' Sara asked him. Jamie looked up – he had never heard of Indians. Sara smiled at him, broke off a piece of fish and put it in her mouth. Jamie hesitated for a moment then did the same.

'It is much more fun eating fish with your fingers. Don't you think so, Jamie?' She was rewarded with a smile.

All through the meal she talked to him about Ilinka and the Indians. It did not bother her that he never answered, at least he was listening.

When Jamie finished eating his jam butty, as Bessie called it, Sara poured them both another mug of tea then went to sit on the fireside chair.

'Come and sit on the rug,' she said to Jamie, placing his mug of tea on the floor next to hers. Jamie sat down where Sara hoped he would, at her feet with his back to her. He picked up his mug of tea and began to sip it. Sara continued to tell him about Ilinka. As she did so, she moved both her hands above his head. As if moving of their own accord, her hands began a circling movement, just above Jamie's crown. The palms of her hands became so hot Sara wonderced why Jamie could not feel the heat.

But no, he sat there content to listen to her story. After a while, her hands stopped moving and she rested them upon her lap. She finished telling Jamie about the young braves then bent down to reach her mug of tea. As she made a movement, Jamie picked up her mug and passed it to her. She smiled at him and thanked him.

The tea was cold but she drank it slowly for she felt sure that Jamie was going to speak to her, and in drinking the tea she would not break the silence and put him off. She looked at him as she drank, her eyes smiling above the rim of the mug. At last she was rewarded.

'I'd like to thank tha for being kind ta me this day, an' for having tha supper we me. I bin happy today and I lik tha story about the Indian braves. But a must go now. Me dad ill be wondering bout me. Good night,' he said and dashed out of the kitchen.

For a moment Sara sat there nursing her empty mug. Well, at least I have got him talking to me, she thought.

Every day she spent some time with Jamie and somehow always managed to get her hands above his head. When she did so, her palms would go hot and begin to circle just as they had done the first time. As the days passed, she could see Jamie becoming more confident and he asked all manner of questions. One day she took him to the stables and to her delight he stood up to Tom.

As usual, Tom tried to belittle Jamie, but this time Jamie wasn't having any of it. When the fight started, Sara leaned over the stablc door to watch them, though Tom was bigger than Jamie and certainly older. Sara had no qualms about letting them fight. It was time Tom got his come-uppance, and it was time for Jamie to stand up for himself.

When Jamie's nose started to bleed, Sara felt she should stop the fight, but something held her back. As the blood poured from Jamie's nose, Tom, thinking the fight was over dropped his guard. Jamie wiped the blood away on his shirt sleeve and lunged at Tom. Tom fell to the ground and Jamie dived on him. He sat astride on Tom's chest and pinned his arms down with his knees.

With fists clenched, he pummelled Tom in the face. When the blood spurted from Tom's nose, Jamie raised his fist to give one last blow. Then he heard Tom whisper. 'Enough Jamie, enough.'

Sara, sensing the fight was over, grabbed a pail of water she had got ready to give the horse before the fight began.

'Alright you two,' she said, putting the pail down beside her. 'Shake hands then get the blood washed from your faces. And let's have no more of this tomfollery.' They shook hands, then bumped their heads together as they both bent down at the same time to wash their faces.

All three of them burst into peels of laughter.

CHAPTER XXII

'You've done wonders for that lad,' Bessie said, as Sara finished telling her about the fight. 'His father doesn't know how to thank thee. There has been such a change in him, if I hadn't seen it with my own eyes, I would never have believed it. It is the best thing that has happened to Jamie, you taking such an interest in him.'

'I am glad I have been able to help him and bring him out of his shell,' Sara replied, knowing all the time it was the healing that helped Jamie, but not being able to tell Bessie that. For Silver Jayot had told her she could mention the healing of Jamie only to her father, for others would not understand.

'But what will they think?' Sara asked him, 'when Jamie becomes normal to them?'

Silver Jayot told her, *'It will look as though with Jamie spending so much time with you and the patience and kindness you showed upon him, brought out the confidence that he lacked.'* And Silver Jayot had been right.

There had been no miracle cure with Jamie changing overnight. No, the healing worked gradually. First the frightened look disappeared from his eyes and his thinking became clearer. Some days Sara would take him to the village.

At first he was shy and timid, especially when other children tried to become friends with him. But slowly, with Sara's healing power, his confidence grew.

Joseph was also watching the change in Jamie, but of course he knew the secret. And he marvelled at how the timid, frightened lad, who had dashed out of the kitchen on the night of their arrival, could be turning into such a bright young lad. He was so impressed with Jamie that he told Sara he would hire a tutor for him if Jamie's father would agree.

A week later it was settled, Jamie was to have a tutor. Joseph told Bessie he wanted to see her and John in the drawing room at seven o'clock that evening.

'Don't worry,' he told her, 'you have done nothing wrong.'

'I wonder what the Master wants with us?' Bessie said to John as they walked towards the drawing room.

'We will soon find out,' replied John, as he knocked on the door.

'Come in,' shouted Joseph.

As they entered, Jospeh told them to sit down and make themselves comfortable. Joseph poured out five glasses of sherry and put them on a tray.

'Ha, just in time,' he said, as Sara and Adam entered the room.

When they were all seated with a glass of sherry, Joseph looked at John and Bessie. 'I suppose you are wondering what all this is about? Well, I will put you out of your suspense. As you know Sara and I have to go back to Ilinka. When we came here, it was never our intention to stay. So I have asked you to join us, to let you know my plans.

'I hope you, John, will carry on running the farm. You will have carte blanche, of course. But if you have any problems, or are worried in any way, you go and see Adam. Also with your permission, I would like to hire a tutor for Jamie. I would also like you to teach Jamie all you know about farming – only if Jamie is interested, that is. There has been a great change in the lad's behaviour these last few weeks. I think we have all noticed that. So if he gets some schooling and hopefully takes an interest in farming, who knows what Jamie could be capable of. So John, what do you think?'

John thought he was the kindest master in the whole of England. Who else but Joseph would have their servants sitting in the drawing room, drinking sherry and discussing not only his future, but his son's as well?

'I think I've a great deal to thank thee for,' John answered. 'Not only for trusting me with looking after the farm, but for taking an intrerest in Jamie as well. And of course, I don't mind you hiring a tutor for him, if you think it's not too late for Jamie to have some schooling.'

'It is never too late for learning,' Joseph said. 'And for some, like Jamie, it is better to be schooled when they are older than not to have any schooling at all. And don't worry, Adam will keep an eye on Jamie's tutor and make sure he is teaching him properly.'

'Well,' said John, 'I don't know how to thank thee. I am so grateful for all that you are doing.'

'There is no need to thank me,' Joseph told him, 'if you take good care of the farm, that will be good enough for me.'

Joseph turned his attention to Bessie. 'And what about you, Bessie, will you be agreeable to carry on as housekeeper?'

'Of course I will, sir, you know that.'

'I would also like you to do me a favour,' Joseph said, 'though you are under no obligation to do so, it is entirely up to you.'

'What is it, sir?' Bessie asked.

'I would like you to train Jessica to become a housekeeper. The girl seems like a willing worker and she has been a good friend to Sara. You can get another girl from the village to take Jessica's place. But as I say, it is entirely up to you.'

'It will be a pleasure to take Jessica under my wing,' Bessie told him. 'She is a good lass and a good worker. Jessica will be so pleased when she finds out.'

'Then you can have the pleasure of telling her,' Joseph said.

'I think you are doing the right thing, not selling the farm,' Adam said to Joseph when John and Bessie left the room.

'Aye, maybe you are right,' Joseph replied. 'At least I know I am leaving it in good hands.'

'You are also leaving your money in good hands,' Adam was smiling as he said it.

'I know I am, you scoundrel,' laughed Joseph. 'Talking me into not selling the farm and keeping most of my money invested. I can't think why I've let you get away with it. Or even how you talked me into leaving most of my inheritance in your hands.'

'Well,' said Adam, 'at least it will not be twenty years before I see you again. You have something to come back to now, even if only to see how much money I will be making for you. And don't grumble, you are taking quite a substantial amount of money with you, though for the life of me, I can't think what you will be spending it on.' Adam paused. 'I'll not say "in that godforsaken place", but you know what I mean.'

'Yes, I do know what you're getting at,' Joseph replied. 'You'll be thinking, what does Joseph want to be taking all that money for, when he lives with a few Indians on a small settlement. Am I right? Is that what you're thinking?'

'Yes, I suppose so,' Adam replied.

'Ilinka may be small now,' Joseph said, 'but I have the feeling all that will change and Meleeka and myself will be responsible for the changing of it. I cannot say why I have this feeling. I just know that in a few years Ilinka will be a very different place.'

'In that case,' said Adam, 'who knows, I might even come to visit you.' They both laughed.

'I hope so,' said Joseph, 'I certainly hope so.'

Sara jumped when Jessica came back into the room. How long have I been mulling over the events of the last few weeks? she wondered. But I must keep things fresh in my mind for I have so much to tell Meleeka.

Jessica came over to the bed, 'I thought you had fallen back to sleep. Your father sent me to see if you need any help.'

'No, I'm alright, Jessica, thank you. I wasn't asleep, I was deep in thought, that's all. Tell Father I will be down presently.'

When Jessica had gone, Sara jumped out of bed and ran to the window. She wanted to take in the view for the last time. Meleeka would never believe her when she told him how far she could see from her bedroom window.

Adam was alone in the drawing room when Sara went downstairs.

'Your father's gone to tell John we will be leaving shortly,' he told Sara. John was taking them to town, then a private coach Adam had hired would take them to Liverpool. Adam was accompanying them and spending a few days with Joseph and Sara before they left for Ilinka.

Sara felt saddened when she said her goodbyes to Bessie and Jessica. But it was nothing to what she felt when it came to saying goodbye to Jamie.

He was standing in the yard with his father when he saw Sara – he ran across the yard and threw his arms around her. She hugged him, then kissed the top of his head before holding him at arms length. She saw the tears well up in his eyes and hugged him close.

'Don't cry Jamie,' she said gently, 'you will be alright. And mind you do some learning while I'm away. One day I may come back and will be hoping you have grown into a clever young man.'

He looked up at her and smiled. 'I will do my best,' he told her, 'and thank you for being my friend.' He took hold of her hand and walked with her to where Joseph and Adam were waiting. He dare not ask her when she would be coming back for she had only said she may do. But one day, when Sara was telling him about Ilinka and the young braves, she had told him when he was older he would be able to go to Ilinka for himself. And if Sara did not come back, he would go to Ilinka to see her.

When Sara bent down to kiss Jamie goodbye, she was puzzled as to why there was a secret smile upon his face. She hoped that one day they would meet again when Jamie was fully grown, so that she would see him as a man – hopefully with his tutoring, a clever man – and know she herself was responsible for the healing of him.

Sometimes, even now, with Jamie as proof, Sara could not believe that she was responsible for the healing of him and of this wondrous gift she held in her hands.

CHAPTER XXIII

Adam was surprised when they reached Liverpool that Joseph insisted they book in at a small hotel.

'I know I am a rich man,' Joseph said to Adam, 'but I cannot stand hoity-toity folk, never could, and you above anybody should know that. And I ask you, what would the best hotel in town be like? I'll tell you,' Joseph continued, before Adam could reply, 'it will be full of silly people, each one thinking they are better than anyone else. Some of the women will have spent money their husbands can ill afford just to be better dressed then the woman on the next table.'

'Alright, alright, a small hotel it is,' said Adam laughing at Joseph. 'I can see being a rich man is not going to change your way of thinking.'

That evening Adam took them to see a musical comedy. Sara was enthralled with the costumes and the music. She had never been to a theatre before and really enjoyed herself. Later when they were having supper, Sara became pensive. Adam, noticing how quiet she had become, asked if she had not enjoyed herself at the theatre.

'Very much so,' Sara answered, 'but I was just thinking of Ilinka and how Meleeka and the young braves danced for us the night before we left.'

'Now that was something to see,' said Joseph. And proceeded to tell Adam all about it.

'The more you tell me about Ilinka, the more I want to see it for myself,' Adam tolf them.

'Well,' said Joseph, grinning, 'when I went to the docks they told me the ship would be sailing on time, so you have two days to make up your mind and sail with us.'

'I wish it were possible for me to come with you,' Adam said. 'But one day I promise you, I will see your Ilinka.'

The next morning at breakfast, Joseph decided they would all go on a shopping spree. First he bought two huge leather trunks and told the man at the shop to deliver them to the hotel at five o'clock that evening.

'We should have brought enough to fill them by that time,' Joseph said as they came out of the shop.

'I only hope they will have room on the ship for them,' laughed Adam.

In each shop they visited, the shopkeeper thought Christmas had come early. Joseph wanted everything parcelled and delivered to the hotel, so everything would go straight into the trunks.

When Adam said he was in need of some refreshments before he dropped dead with hunger, Joseph told him he knew where they served the best steak pie he would ever taste.

'Just lead me to it,' Adam said, 'and I will devour it.'

When they entered the tea house, Jenny was busy taking an order so did not see them arrive. Joseph ushered Adam to a table in a corner alcove. Adam was surprised, for he was about to make his way to a table near the window.

'I don't want the waitress to see us yet,' Joseph said, 'I want to surprise her.'

'Why are you being so secretive,' Adam asked. 'Did you have an affair with her when you were last here?'

'No, it was nothing like that,' Joseph replied.

'Whatever it was, I think I am about to find out,' said Adam, 'for the waitress is heading this way.' When Jenny arrived at the table, she asked Adam if he would like to order, wondering why this man whom she had never seen before was taking such an interest in her.

'My friend here tells me you serve the best steak pie in town.' Adam was looking up at her with a broad grin upon his face and pointing a finger in the direction of Joseph and Sara.

For the first time, Jenny looked at the two other customers. 'Oh, sir. Oh, miss,' she said, delighted to see them both again. 'I am so glad to see you and I must thank you for the beautiful present. I nearly died when a parcel was delivered to me from Miss Traverns of all places. And the other girls were green with envy when I opened it. I got some snide remarks, I can tell you, them wanting to know what I'd done to warrant such a gift. I knew that I had done no wrong, so I never let them bother me. But I must confess, I did wonder myself why I was sent it.'

'Because,' Joseph told her, 'you were kind to two strangers and that meant a lot to me. Besides, I was feeling generous that day and, seeing the blouse and skirt in the window, reminded me of you. And the look on Miss Traverns' face, when I told her to deliver them here was worth every penny. Now, let us hear no more about it, for my friend here will die of starvation.'

Adam agreed with Joseph about the pie – it was the best he had ever tasted. They said goodbye to Jenny and when they had gone, she found they had left her a huge tip. As they came out of the tea house, Sara decided to visit Miss Traverns. She would get a shawl for Buta and Cheeka and for the other women she would get some ornatmental decorations for their hair.

Miss Traverns, remembering the amount of money Joseph spent with her last time, greeted them like long-lost cousins. Joseph was quick to notice and smiled to himself. Sara chose what she wanted and also purchased three blouses for herself.

Miss Traverns, pleased once again with their custom, walked with them to the door and wished them bon voyage.

The next day Adam stood on the quayside until the ship sailed out of sight.

I am going to miss Joseph, he thought. For when we met again it felt as though Joseph had never been away. Still, some say that is a sign of true friendship. And Sara, yes, I will miss Sara. She may not have been Rosa's child by birth, but she was certainly Rosa's daughter in her ways. The same kind and gentle nature, always thinking of others, putting them before herself. If I had married, I would have loved a daughter like Sara.

As he walked back to the hotel, he wondered if he would have had the courage to do what Joseph did, all those years ago – pack his bags and with the women he loved, go to a strange land and make a fresh start. Yes, he thought, I would have done the same given the same circumstances. Especially, though I never told anyone, I too was in love with Rosa. But Rosa had eyes only for Joseph.

CHAPTER XXIV

Meleeka was worried. Before long, the snows of winter would be here and if Joseph and Sara did not return soon, they would have to wait until the spring. He was also troubled about the white men – the braves had seen two of them trapping beaver at the lower end of the river. Luckily the braves kept out of sight and observed what the white men were doing.

Maybe the white men will not return, Meleeka thought, and if they do, will only want the beavers and not bother us. His thoughts returned to Joseph and Sara.

What a surprise was in store for them when they arrived home! Though the summer had been hot and the tents were still erected, his tribe was happy to use the cabins. Sometimes when he looked down upon the camp from the mountain, he was awed at the sight it made. It was like an Indian reservation and a white man's settlement all rolled into one, each complementing the other. He hoped it was an omen that one day the Indians and the white man would live together in peace.

Even Cheeka spent most of her time in Meleeka and Buta's cabin, which had pleased them. But sometimes Cheeka decided she wanted to be alone and would return to her tent for a few days. No one bothered, they let her do as she liked.

'We are lucky,' Buta told Meleeka, 'old people do not like change, they want to do as they have always done.'

Meleeka gazed up at the Blue Mountain. Though he knew after what Sara told him it was his guide that spoke to him and not the mountain, he still felt as he had done many times before. That the mountain held some kind of magic, and when he was worried about anything, it was the mountain he would go to.

The voice had spoken twice while Sara and Joseph were away. The first time he was told they had reached their destination and on the second occasion, the message was longer. *'When Joseph returns, there will be many changes that come to Ilinka. The changes will come gradually and will be of great value to Ilinka and its people.'*

Meleeka asked what kind of change.

'I cannot tell you,' the voice replied. *'You must wait for Joseph to return then you will have much to discuss.'*

All this had been said weeks ago and the voice had not spoken since. Now he turned away from the mountain disappointed, for he thought the voice might have reassured him that Joseph and Sara would soon be home.

He headed towards the pasture to attend to the young calves and their mothers. The young braves had fenced off a large piece of land circling the cowshed, so neither the cows nor the calves would roam away.

He smiled to himself as he remembered the day the first cow calved. It caused a great deal of excitement. Meleeka and two young braves were returning home after a day's hunting. One of the braves stopped suddenly and told the others to listen. As they listened, Meleeka realized it was a cow bawling. He made his way to where the noise was coming from, the two braves following him. They found the cow laying on her side, the calf struggling to get out. Meleeka bent down and stroked the cow lovingly.

'Don't give up now,' he said gently. 'Stand up. We are here to help you.' The cow looked at him with hopeful eyes and the next moment its calf was born where the cow was lying. Meleeka picked up the calf and lay it near its mother to be licked clean. Before the calf was fully cleaned, the cow started bawling again.

'There's no need for that,' Meleeka said, as if talking to a human being, you have your calf here with you.' The cow, taking no notice of him, bawled again, louder than ever.

'I think,' said the young brave who was standing at the rear end of the cow, 'she is going to produce two babies.' And he was right, for soon afterwards another calf was born.

When both calves were cleaned, the two braves carried them to the cowshed. The mother cow made so much noise as she followed that the whole tribe came to see what all the fuss was about. The children squealed with delight when they saw the twin calves. Within three weeks, the other cows also calved.

Meleeka, walking home after tending the cattle, caught sight of Joseph's wagon, and stopped in his tracks. How silly of me, he thought, when Joseph and Sara arrive at the great lakes, they will need transport home. Tomorrow I will send four of the braves with the wagon to meet them. They can wait for Joseph until the full moon. If he has not arrived by then, they will have to come home, for if the winter snow falls, they will not get back.

The next morning he asked Two Feathers if he would take the wagon down to the lakes. 'I would go myself, only I think it best I stay here in case the beaver trappers come back.'

Two Feathers said he would go, willingly. 'I too have been wondering about Joseph and Sara,' he told Meleeka.

'Take three of the young braves with you and be careful,' Meleeka said. 'Make camp at the edge of the forest, from there you will see when a boat crosses the lake. It may not be wise to stay too long in the town, for there are many white men who do not trust Indians. If Joseph and Sara have not arrived by the night of the full moon, you must return.'

Two Feathers said he would do all that was asked, and went to find the other braves.

CHAPTER XXV

On the night of the full moon, Meleeka could not settle. His mother, seeing his agitation, told him to sit down.

'It will do no good,' she told him, 'to keep wandering about hither and dither. We can only wait for Two Feathers before we know if Joseph and Sara will be home.'

'I know,' Meleeka replied. 'It is foolish of me but tomorrow if Joseph and Sara have not arrived, Two Feathers will follow my instructions and return.'

'And if he did not follow your instructions, you would be displeased with him,' his mother told him.

Meleeka smiled. 'Yes, you are right, it would not please me if my orders were disobeyed.' Later he was outside and with his head bent against the wind, felt a wetness fall upon his face.

The first snows of winter, he thought, and the braves have not yet returned, if we have a blizzard, they might be trapped in the snow. I must get help and search for them before the snow falls heavily.

He began to run. There was no time to lose even if Joseph had not arrived – his braves could be in danger. As he dashed into the cabin, his mother looked up wondering whatever was so urgent, for Meleeka was usually calm and not one for dashing around.

'What is it my son?' she asked.

'I am worried about Two Feathers and the wagon. If this snow turns into a blizzard, they may get trapped. And I cannot find any young braves to come and help me search.' He got no further, for his mother began to laugh.

'It is no laughing matter to get trapped in the snow,' he told her sharply.

'Oh, Meleeka, I'm sorry,' she told him, 'when you came rushing in I thought something was wrong. Now I realize you haven't heard.'

'Heard what?' he asked.

'The braves have gone to help with the wagon, the axle broke and Two Feathers sent for help. I thought you had gone with them.'

'Are Joseph and Sara with Two Feathers?' Meleeka asked.

'Yes, of course,' answered his mother.

'We had better light a fire in the cabin – they will be frozen when they get here.'

'It has all been taken care of,' his mother interrupted him. 'The cabin will be warm and a meal waiting for them, so there is nothing to worry about.'

'In that case, I must go and help them with the wagon,' Meleeka said, excited at the thought of seeing Sara.

'Have something to eat first, you also must be cold and hungry,' said his mother.

'No, it is better that I go now,' he told her.

'Go then,' she said, 'for I know you cannot wait any longer to see Sara. You will find them beyond the beaver dam.'

He untethered the first pony he came across and rode at great speed towards the dam. By this time the snow was falling so thick it blurred his vision. Yet he still urged the pony on. 'Faster, faster,' he kept repeating.

As he approached the dam, he brought the pony to a halt. I must be mad, he said to himself, riding like that in this weather, if the pony lost its footing anything could happen.

He dismounted and gently stroked it, whispering in the pony's ear as he did so. It was then that he heard the voices. Thinking they may be trappers, he steered the pony behind a tree.

As he watched and listened, he saw two horse riders heading his way. With the heavy snow, he could not tell if they were the beaver trappers – he hoped not, for they might shoot him. Before his thoughts could go any further, a great excitement ran through him. It was one of the braves and Sara. I just know it is, he said to himself. Throwing caution to the wind, he ran towards the riders, shouting her name as he ran.

Sara, hearing her name being called, reined her horse to a halt. She saw Meleeka running towards her. With a cry of delight, she dismounted and ran to meet him. They crashed into each other's arms, both laughing with joy at seeing one another again. Meleeka with his arms around her, swung her into the air. Then held her at arm's length with snow falling upon their faces and they gazed at each other, the love shining in both their eyes. Meleeka pulled Sara to him, kissing her gently on her cheek.

'Welcome home, Sara,' he said.

Sara, at that moment realizing how much she had missed Meleeka, threw her arms around him, her lips finding his, and kissed him passionately.

Meleeka felt the unison of their hearts beating, as he put his arms around her and drew her closer to him. He could also feel the manhood in his loins. Not wanting to embarrass Sara, he drew quickly away. He saw the hurt in her eyes as he released her.

'You have to get home,' he told her.

Sara, feeling confused, turned and made her way towards Two Feathers. Meleeka grabbed hold of her wrist, wondering what he could say.

Sara was upset and he was the cause of it. Yet he could not tell her it was because of his manhood and embarrassment that he had drawn so quickly away.

He had dreamed often of Sara kissing him so passionately. But in his dreams it was their wedding night and they would be shy and gentle as all young lovers should be, then as the night wore on, their passion would rise and merge into one, uniting them forever.

It was a dream he wanted to become a reality. If he had not drawn away from Sara, the dream would have ended.

The falling snow and Two Feathers would not have existed for the passion rising within himself, and Sara could never have been stopped.

Sara, in her innocence, thinking that Meleeka was rejecting her, tried to pull herself way from his hold. He pulled her towards him, taking hold of her chin, and forced her to look at him.

'Sara, I love you,' he told her. 'I love you more than life itself. I was not rejecting you. That is what you are thinking, isn't it?' he asked.

Sara could only nod, for he still held her chin.

'Am I also right in thinking you feel the same love for me?'

Again Sara nodded.

'Good, now we understand one another,' he said, taking his hand away from her.

He led her towards Two Feathers. 'Take her home,' he told Two Feathers. 'I will go and help the others.'

CHAPTER XXVI

Sara felt the warmth of the cabin as soon as she entered and closed the door quickly, not wanting the heat to escape. Buta, throwing a log on the fire, looked up and saw the snow-clad figure of Sara. She was so glad to see Sara home safely, she threw her arms around her, even though the snow from Sara's coat fell upon her.

As Sara took off her coat, she told Buta that Two Feathers had brought her home, how they met Meleeka and that he had gone to help the others.

Buta did not miss the blush upon Sara's face as she spoke of Meleeka.

'Come,' said Buta, 'get out of those wet clothes. There is plenty of hot water if you want a bath before the menfolk arrive. No one else will disturb us. There are clean clothes warming by the fire if you only wish to get changed.'

'A hot bath in front of that roaring fire will be lovely,' Sara told her.

'Then I will prepare it for you,' said Buta. As Sara bathed she told Buta of her visit to England, omitting for the moment the healing of Jamie. Buta laughed as Sara mimicked the different accents she had heard.

She told of how her father was now a very rich man and of the shopping spree in Liverpool. 'I think that may have something to do with the axle breaking, for the wagon is full to the very top.'

When Adam's name was mentioned more often than Buta cared for, and Sara said he wanted to visit Ilinka as they had told him so much about it and he wanted to see Ilinka for himself, Buta wondered if Sara had fallen in love with him, or was it he who had fallen in love with Sara and would follow her to Ilinka.

She had no idea that Adam was Joseph's friend or that he was as old as Joseph. All she knew was that Sara spoke so enthusiastically about the man and it seemed as though he had spent a lot of time with Sara.

Buta, not wanting to hear any more about Adam, reached for a towel, holding it ready for Sara to wrap around her as she stepped out of the bath. As Sara dried herself, Buta emptied the bath.

I do not know who this Adam is, she thought, but one thing I do know, my son is in love with Sara. He will take no other woman for his wife. If Sara does not become his bride, my son, though he may be living, the heart inside of him will have died. And a man with a dead heart is of no use to anyone. I will have to make sure that Sara takes only Meleeka, my son, for her husband. With this thought still ringing in her head, Buta glanced over at Sara. Sara, with the towel wrapped around her, was sitting by the fire combing her wet, tangled hair.

She was also thinking of Meleeka. What had possessed her to kiss him so passionately. The thought of it brought a flush to her cheeks. She could still feel herself close to him and his manhood stirring. With this thought the flush deepened. She wondered about their wedding night and what mystery it would reveal.

At that moment a rapturous look came upon her face. Buta, seeing it, misread the look. She had no inkling that Sara's thoughts were upon Meleeka. For only minutes before, had not the conversation been dominated by the name of Adam. Buta's mind was in turmoil.

Was it possible that Sara and the white man Adam . . . No, I must not think such a thing. But the look upon Sara's face, it is the look of a woman who loves and knows the love she gives is returned. If Sara has lost her virginity to the white man, it will be disastrous for us all.

Buta called upon the Great White Spirit in the sky to take the bad thoughts from her head and to guide her in her actions, for if she told Meleeka of her suspicions, and he and Sara were to marry, the tribal law of virginity would have to be performed upon Sara. Yet if she did not speak and Meleeka found on his wedding night that Sara was not a virgin, it would break his heart and his pride. Buta called once again to the spirit in the sky. Let it be that my thoughts are of an over-protective mother, who wishes only happiness for her son and that I have wronged

Sara, thinking such bad thoughts.

'Buta do you feel unwell?'

Buta, not realizing she was standing with her eyes closed and lips moving in silent prayer, heard Sara's voice, as if it was coming through a long tunnel.

She opened her eyes and pulled herself together.

'I am alright,' she told Sara. Sara took hold of Buta's hand and led her towards a chair. As she sat down, Buta looked up at Sara.

'Are you sure there is nothing wrong?' asked Sara.

Concern in her voice, Buta replied softly. 'No, I am alright. Do not worry: get dressed and we will have something to eat.'

CHAPTER XXVII

By the time Meleeka reached the others, Joseph and the braves were fixing a makeshift axle to the wagon. All the luggage was strewn about in the snow.

Meleeka, coming upon the scene, realized how vulnerable were his braves. For if he had been a white man and seen the braves near the wagon with luggage thrown about, he would have thought it was an Indian raid, and a white man would shoot first and ask questions later.

He edged his pony towards them – no one heard him for they were all watching Joseph as he spun the wheel around to make sure it was safe. They all cheered when Joseph shouted, 'Load the wagon.'

Joseph raised his eyes and saw Meleeka grinning down at him. Meleeka leapt from his pony and landed in Joseph's outstretched arms.

'Welcome home, my friend, I was beginning to think you had stayed in England.'

'I told you,' said Joseph, 'I would be back before the first snows of winter. It isn't my fault if the snow had other ideas,' he grinned at Meleeka.

'Perhaps if the wagon had not let you down, you would have arrived before the first snowflake,' Meleeka said, enjoying the banter with Joseph.

'Does that mean you forgive me for being late? And that I kept my promise?' Joseph replied.

They both burst out laughing. Joseph decided to put only the heaviest of luggage into the wagon. Between them the braves would take the rest. They also used Meleeka's pony as a packhorse for Meleeka would be travelling with Joseph.

The snow was falling heavily as they made ready to go. Joseph, with Meleeka beside him, watched the braves as they set off ahead. He still marvelled at the way their lives had been brought together and at the joy he felt being among them again.

A broad grin came upon his face. Meleeka, seeing the grin upon Joseph's face, asked him what there was to smile about, when they were both chilled to the bone and did not even know if the wagon would make it home.

'Well,' said Joseph, 'if you promise not to be offended, I will tell you my thoughts.' Meleeka promised. 'To put it crudely,' said Joseph, 'in the first place, I was wondering what the hell am I doing here driving a wagon in all this snow, with a bunch of Indians for company, when I could be living like a gentleman if I was in England.'

He glanced at Meleeka and saw that his words had hurt him. Before Meleeka could say anything, Joseph continued. 'I was smiling because of the joy I feel, being amongst you all again. Broken wagon, snow and all. But 'tis only natural for me to compare the two, and I did ask you not to take offence.'

'I did not like you calling us a bunch of Indians,' Meleeka said. 'Those words were hurtful to me but I now realize you did not mean them to sound insulting. It was only a figure of speech. I was also thinking,' Meleeka continued, 'that my friend Joseph was a changed man. But I was wrong to think such thoughts. For you still speak the truth that comes from the heart.'

By the time they reached the settlement the snow had ceased. Meleeka glanced towards the mountain and was delighted when he saw it was blue, though everywhere else was covered in snow.

Though he would never disbelieve whatever the mountain said to him, it was still an awesome sight, seeing the blueness of it standing out against the pure white snow.

Joseph was intent on guiding the horses but nearly dropped the reins as Meleeka shook his arm, then pointed towards the mountain. Joseph could hardly believe his own eyes when he realized what Meleeka was pointing at.

Then in his down-to-earth manner, he said, 'Well, you were told, were you not, that the mountain would never again be covered in snow. Did you not believe what you heard?'

'Of course I did,' replied Meleeka. 'I will always believe what my mountain tells me.'

When they finally reached the cabin, Meleeka was surprised that his mother was not with Sara. He told Joseph he would go home and come back later to help him unload the wagon.

'I think we have done enough for one day,' said Joseph. 'It is a hot bath for me, something to eat and then bed. We can see to the wagon tomorrow.'

Joseph saw the disappointment on Meleeka's face. He guessed it was not the unloading of the wagon Meleeka was interested in, but Sara. Joseph relented after all – had it not been for Meleeka and the braves, they would not be here now.

'Alright, you win,' he told Meleeka, 'come back later but not to do any work. We will sit by the fire, for there is something I would like to speak to you about.'

Joseph was rewarded with the broad grin which came upon Meleeka's face before he turned to leave them.

When Meleeka returned Joseph felt refreshed and alert. His soak in the hot bath relaxed his tired bones, then when they had eaten he dozed in his armchair.

When he awoke, all the tiredness he'd felt was gone. He was glad now that Meleeka would be returning for there were things to be talked about. The three of them were still sitting around the fire into the early hours of the next morning.

At first Joseph told Meleeka light-hearted stories of their adventures in England, and Meleeka listened with great interest. He also noticed that Adam's name was often spoken. Not by Sara, but Joseph. Meleeka had no qualms about Adam for he realized Adam was Joseph's friend from boyhood. No, it was the name of Jamie that troubled Meleeka. For Sara as well as Joseph spoke with great affection about Jamie, and Meleeka could not understand the look that passed between them whenever Jamie's name was mentioned. He was puzzled just as Adam had been when they were together in the drawing room.

Joseph, noticing that for some reason Meleeka was becoming disturbed, asked Sara if she would make some coffee. As Sara made the coffee, Joseph filled his pipe with tobacco for he needed time to think. He wanted to tell Meleeka of his plans but felt the time was not yet right.

He new something had upset Meleeka but for the life of him could not think what. As he toyed with his pipe, he saw Meleeka watching Sara's every movement and all the love that Meleeka felt for Sara was written upon his face.

At that moment Sara, bringing the coffee pot to the table, smiled at Meleeka, her face also lighting up with love.

Joseph, watching them both, missed nothing. He felt his own heart stop beating for the two of them reminded him so much of how himself and Rosa used to gaze upon one another. And once again, he felt Rosa's presence.

'They love as we once loved,' he heard Rosa whisper in his ear.

They drank their coffee in silence, each of them needing time to gather their thoughts. Joseph was the first to move. He threw some logs onto the fire, then stood with his back to it, looking down at them.

He coughed to bring them out of their reverie. As they gazed up at him, he thought how young and innocent they looked. And wondered if he was doing the right thing in what he was about to say to them. He thought of Rosa and remembered how they were once young and innocent.

Then he said, 'I think it is time for us to make plans for your wedding. And in my opinion, the sooner the better.'

He was rewarded with Sara leaping from her chair and throwing her arms around him. He looked over her shoulder at Meleeka, and saw a broad grin upon his face.

When Sara released him, he poured himself another mug of coffee. More for something to do than anything else. For when Sara sat down, Meleeka took her hand in his and they sat gazing at one another.

Then he heard Meleeka say, 'Thank you, Joseph, you have made me very happy this night. For I love Sara deeply and I thought she also loved me. But earlier when you both spoke with such affection for

Jamie, and when you mentioned his name, I felt there was something I did not know or understand. I also felt that something happened between Jamie and Sara that you were keeping from me.

'In my heart I felt suspicion and hatred, then I felt ashamed of myself for having such thoughts. For to love someone as I love Sara, you must always have trust in them.'

So, thought Joseph, that is why Meleeka seemed disturbed, he thought there was something between Sara and Jamie. The poor lad must have been thinking that Sara and Jamie were lovers. Just the thought of it made Joseph want to roar with laughter but he dare not, for Meleeka would not understand.

So instead, he controlled the laughter that bubbled inside him and said to Meleeka, 'I think there is something you should know about Jamie and Sara. There is no need to look so startled, it is not what you think.' Seeing Meleeka's discomfort he went on, 'I think it best that Sara explains it to you, for it was her doing and you will have to know about it sooner or later.'

Joseph puffed contentedly on his pipe while Sara told Meleeka about Jamie and the healing.

'Oh, Meleeka,' she said at last, 'if only you could have seen the transformation, it was so incredible you would not have believed it, remembering Jamie as I first set eyes upon him, timid as a scared rabbit he was. Yet when we left him, he was confident and keen on his schooling. I could not believe that I was responsible for such a change in him. Isn't it wonderful?'

'So,' said Meleeka, 'old Cheeka was right about you. You are from the old Ilinka tribe and have the gift from the Great White Spirit in the sky. It is a wonderful gift Sara. Do you not agree Joseph?'

'I certainly do agree,' Joseph replied, 'and don't forget I saw Jamie before Sara started healing him. What a pathetic sight he was.'

Meleeka, happy now that all had been explained to him, said it was time he went home. The snow lay thick upon the ground as he made his way to his cabin. He was glad that Sara was home for he'd missed her so much.

Soon when spring arrived, they would become as one; he could not wait to tell his mother the good news. Though it was late, Buta was waiting for him.

He noticed when he told his mother that he and Sara would soon be joined together she did not seem happy.

'Is anything wrong?' he asked.

'Today,' she answered, 'Sara spoke much about a white man called Adam. I did not like it. It is not good when a woman likes one man and marries another. It brings trouble between them.'

Meleeka put his arms around his mother and smiled down at her. 'You do not have to worry,' he told her, 'Sara loves only me. Adam is a friend to Joseph and has been since they were young. It is only right that all three would be together many times and that Sara would speak much about Adam.'

Buta silently thanked the Great White Spirit in the sky – she was wrong in her thinking of Adam and Sara.

Joseph was also thinking about Adam. Sara was in bed and he was smoking his pipe of tobacco before retiring. He was glad now that before leaving England he'd told Adam to send craftsmen and materials to Ilinka, for he knew that he wanted to give Sara and Meleeka a real white man's house for a wedding present.

PART II

CHAPTER I

Meleeka paced the dining-room floor, his heart saddened knowing that Cheeka would soon be with the spirits in the sky. He would miss her, though he knew that Cheeka was happy that her time on earth was ending.

He remembered how delighted she had been when he went with Sara to tell her of their forthcoming marriage. Her eyes lit up with pleasure as she told them.

'Your news does not surprise me, for nothing on this earth could have prevented the merging of your two bloods. And with this merging, a new generation with a special lineage will be born to you. Their nature will be one of gentleness and goodness in both heart and mind. Through Sara, they will be given the power to heal which will be carried on for generations to come. It will be a great gift that comes from the Great White Spirit, for he knows that many, many moons from now, bad medicine will be made. At first they will think it a cure for all, but it will be discovered it can sometimes kill.

'It is then the people of all nations will turn once again to the true way of medicine. They will turn to the plants of the earth, that grew even before the coming of man, the Great White Spirit putting them there, knowing that the humans he would create would need them.'

She had taken hold of Sara's hands, telling her, 'And those like you, Sara, who have been given the healing touch, will be sought after from all walks of life, from the lowest of birth, to the highest. Perhaps, then peace will come upon the earth, as it was meant to be when time began.'

She had let go of Sara's hands, taking hold of his own, saying, 'You have done well, Meleeka, in bringing what was left of the tribe to this place. Your father would be proud of your achievements. It was a sad day when he was called to the spirit in the sky. But who knows, if it had not been, we might all have been killed. Your father died, not wishing to fight with the white men, neither did the other tribes, but it was only natural, wanting to keep the lands they dwelled upon. Yet, for all the fighting which still goes on, this land of ours will be taken from us, no matter how long the battles rage. Though you must not worry about Ilinka, Sarah's prefathers watch over her, they will protect Ilinka. Yes,' she said, looking at Sara, 'the true blood of the Ilinkas runs through your veins.

'Many secrets went to the grave with your forefathers, but one day the secrets will be found and in fact, you will see and hear many things. Listen to all you are told, write it down for your future lineage. I can reveal to you, Sara, that from your lineage will be born a boy blessed with special gifts. He will be the one chosen to find the sacred writings of the Ilinkas. All this will come about in the distant future when great silver birds fly high into the sky and people from all nations travel upon them.'

As he paced to and fro, Meleeka could not imagine what Cheeka had spoken about; he only knew if Cheeka said these things, they would come to pass, and it would be so.

There were so many memories he held stored away of Cheeka and now she was dying it seemed they were all to come flooding back. He remembered the interest she took watching the building of the stone house that Joseph was having built. It was a wedding present for himself and Sara. At first Cheeka was distrustful of the white men who had come from England to build the house, but when she saw how hard they worked and settled in with the tribe, she loved to watch them. She'd taken a great liking to John and James Grant, the carpenters, and also to Ray Peters, the stonemason.

Meleeka stopped his pacing, knowing it was time to go to the tent of Cheeka. Sara and his mother would be expecting him. The spirit in the sky was already near to take Cheeka. As he walked across the settlement towards Cheeka's tent, he saw the others of his tribe gathering outside. Inside the tent, Cheeka took hold of Sara's hand saying, 'Remember all I have told you.'

Then she was gone.

At that moment, Meleeka came into the tent. Going swiftly to Cheeka, he kissed her forehead, her palms and then her feet. He then ordered his mother and Sara to prepare her for burial, before going outside to tell the gathering crowd of Cheeka's passing. With all eyes upon him, he told them that this was a sad day with the loss of Cheeka. She was a wonderful old woman, who he hoped would live in their hearts forever. 'I know,' he said 'that even the youngest among you will have a special memory of Cheeka. I only ask that you will not let that memory fade, for Cheeka loved us all.'

He could say no more, his voice beginning to choke him. He stepped back inside the tent, closing the flap. Not wanting to disturb the two women, he stood with his back to them. His eyes filled with tears that would not fall. Then he remembered something Cheeka said to him when he was a young boy. He had fallen from his pony, hurting himself badly. Many were watching him, so he held back the tears. Cheeka swooped him into her arms, carrying him into her tent. Then she told him, 'Cry, Meleeka, cry. It is not good to hold back the tears, they wash away the pain.' With these thoughts, the tears came and he let them stream down his face. When Sara called to him, he walked towards her, tall and proud, letting the tears flow.

Cheeka was buried in the place she had chosen herself. She had taken Meleeka to the very spot telling him, 'Before the next moon I will be gone to the spirit in the sky. This is where you will lay me to rest. You will give me a white man's burial. If you want to live as the white man, then I will be buried as the white man buries his own. I ask only that you will let me die in my tent. I have been happy here, Meleeka, and I am sure that when my time on earth is over, I will be content for my body to lie in this place, where the river will flow past my grave. The birds will rest upon it before they continue their journey home, and the beast of the forest will look down upon me as they pass by. Promise me Meleeka, you will do as I ask?'

'You have my word upon it,' he told her, though his heart was sad, knowing that Cheeka would soon be gone from his life. 'I will miss you like a child misses his mother,' he told her.

'I know,' was all she answered him by.

CHAPTER II

Nine months after Cheeka's death, Sara's first child was born. Meleeka, like all fathers, could not believe he'd been responsible for producing such a tiny being. His heart swelled with pride as he gazed down upon his son. He kissed Sara, thanking her for giving him such a beautiful son.

'But he looks so tiny, I think I am a little afraid of him.'

'There is no need to be afraid of him,' said Sara. 'Take him into your arms to show him he is loved.'

Meleeka gently took hold of the baby, whose eyes were already open. A surge of pride ran through him, making him forget the anguish he and Joseph, his father-in-law, went through while waiting for the birth.

He looked up to find Joseph grinning at him, then carried the baby towards Joseph saying, 'Come meet your grandfather.'

As Joseph took the newborn infant into his arms, he too felt a surge of pride run through him. He, like Meleeka, was relieved that it was all over and both Sara and the baby were alright. His eyes shone with pride as he looked down at his grandson. For a moment he felt a twinge of regret, knowing no blood of his ran through this child. He hugged the child close, saying to himself, But I will love you always, as I loved your mother when she too was placed into my arms.

He asked, 'Have you decided on a name?' as he handed the baby back to Sara, regretting for the first time having no sons of his own.

The answer, when it came both pleased and surprised him. Once again it had seemed as though Meleeka had read his thoughts when he heard him saying, 'Sara and I will be naming our son after his grandfather, Joseph Simon Tyler.'

Meleeka saw Joseph's eyes fill with tears of happiness and knew that his father-in-law was pleased.

When Joseph felt the lump in his throat disappear and was able to speak he said, 'I feel proud that you wish to give the baby my name, but surely Meleeka, your first-born should carry your name.'

Meleeka smiled, telling him, 'Sara and I gave this much thought, then we decided that if it had not been for yourself and Rosa saving the life of Sara, she would not have been here this day to give me a son.'

Joseph took a gold coin from his purse, placing it into the baby's hand, saying as he did so, 'Joseph Simon Tyler it is then,' he squeezed the tiny hand around the coin saying, 'may your life be long and happy.'

When the two men had left the room, Buta made Sara comfortable, then told her to rest. As she lay on the soft pillows, Sara felt a glow inside her for this wondrous gift she'd brought into the world. Her labour was not long, even though Meleeka had thought differently, yet it had not been easy. She'd known from the beginning, a son would be born to her, for on the night of Cheeka's death, Silver Jayot spoke to her, telling her, *'Tonight Meleeka will put a seed of life into you. The outcome will be a son. You will name him after your father Joseph.'*

'Will this be agreeable to Meleeka?' she asked. 'Surely Meleeka will want his first-born to have at least a tribal name, if not his own.'

Silver Jayot replied, *'Meleeka will understand why his first born should carry the name of your father. However, if Meleeka should insist on a tribal name, you must suggest the name of Washrek, a true Ilinka name.'*

'I will do as you say,' Sara told Silver Jayot. Her heart was still filled with sadness at the loss of Cheeka, but she remembered Cheeka's warning to take heed of everything she was told.

Meleeka agreed that their son would take the name of her father. 'There must be a reason for Silver Jayot telling you this,' he said. 'Besides, I am sure it will please him and I do not mind. I love your father as if he was my own. I have much to thank him for, especially as he gave his beloved daughter to me.'

Sara's eyes lit up with all the love she felt for Meleeka, as she asked him, 'But what about the tribal name Washrek? If it is a true Ilinka name should we not include it?'

'I do not think that will be necessary,' Meleeka replied. 'But if there ever comes a time when our son will need a tribal name, then that will be the one that we will use.'

As she closed her eyes, Sara was sure they had done the right thing. The pride she had just seen on her father's face as he held the child which bore his name, was a joy to see. With these thoughts, she drifted off to sleep.

While Sara slept, both father and grandfather were being congratulated by the rest of the tribe, on the birth of a boy child.

When Meleeka left Joseph, he went to stand below his beloved mountain. He raised his eyes, silently giving thanks for the safe arrival of his son and for the peace that reined over Ilinka. As always, when he'd spoken to the mountain, he bowed before turning away. He was about to make his way home, when he heard the voice of the mountain. He spun round, wondering what he would hear. Usually, the mountain only spoke when he was worried about something, or to warn him. He felt his guts churn as he'd never felt them do before. Whatever I am about to hear, he thought, is not good, for never before have I been afraid to listen to what my mountain has to say. The happiness he felt a moment ago was gone in a flash, when he heard the voice telling him,

'I regret the bad news I bring you, on a day that should be filled only with joy, but you have to be warned. You must stay in the vicinity of Ilinka. Let Joseph see to your needs. Fighting looms in every direction between the white men and the natives. Tribes are being slaughtered, even the meekest of them. The bloodshed you saw with your father and his braves is nothing compared with what is happening now, and it will become worse. The earth will shake with the thunder of hooves. The screams of the natives of this land, will be heard for generations to come.'

When the message ended, Meleeka felt sick as he imagined the slaughter of both the natives and the white men. Yet, he wondered why the Great White Spirit in the sky let the blood of the natives flow into the ground like water from a stream. Surely it would be better if they were struck down with the killer fever, and let the white men take the land if it meant so much to them. For a moment he felt like gathering all the braves together, then join another tribe and help them fight. Instead he went to his friend, Joseph, to tell him of the message.

Joseph was sitting outside his cabin, whittling away. He looked up as a shadow fell across his path.

'Is Sara alright?' he asked seeing the serious look upon Meleeka's face.

'Sara is fine,' Meleeka replied.

'Then what is it?' asked Joseph. 'I know there is something troubling you.'

'Come, let us go inside,' Meleeka said. 'Then I will tell you.'

'So what am I to do?' Meleeka asked, after telling Joseph about the message.

'You will do as you've been told to do,' Joseph replied.

'But I feel like a coward,' said Meleeka. 'Doing nothing while others are being slaughtered. And what about my young braves? They too may wish to fight when I tell them.' Meleeka looked at Joseph with pleading eyes.

As always when Joseph needed time to think, he lit his pipe. Then when he was ready, he told Meleeka, 'As I see it, you were brought here for a reason. When you came, you vowed to be a peaceful tribe.'

'Yes, I know,' Meleeka interrupted him, 'but this is different. What is happening now will effect the natives of this land for generations to come.'

'I know,' said Joseph. 'Yet if you go to their aid, yourself and a handful of braves, what good will it do? It is more than likely you will leave a wife without a husband, as well as a son without a father. Also there will be mothers weeping for their lost sons. Think about it, Meleeka, remember what it was like when you went home to find your father dying, and the women of your tribe weeping for their loved ones. Do you wish that to happen here?'

Joseph got out of his chair and walked towards the window. Though he did not know why he did so, he gazed up at the mystical mountain which affected his daughter and son-in-law so much. He waited for

Meleeka to answer his last question, but before Meleeka could do so, Joseph spun round saying, 'Perhaps, your mystical mountain is testing you to see if you keep your vow.'

He knew it was a terrible thing to say, but if it was the only way to make Meleeka see sense, then so be it. He saw the look of disbelief on Meleeka's face, then softened the blow by adding, 'Or perhaps there is another way you are to be of help to the tribes of this land.'

'How can there be?' asked Meleeka. 'If as you say, I am to obey the mountain and stay in the vicinity of Ilinka.'

'I cannot answer your question,' Joseph told him truthfully, 'though I am sure there must be a reason why you have to stay. I too am shocked by what you have told me and can understand your reaction. In your shoes, I would feel the same. Yet at this moment I feel we must have time to think. So tell no one about the message, not even Sara, for I am sure, Meleeka, when the time comes when you can be of help, you will be shown the way.'

Meleeka looked into Joseph's eyes – he had trusted this man in so many things, surely he could trust him now. He sighed, saying, 'I hope you are right, my friend, for in my heart, I know I should keep my vow. Neither do I wish for Sara or the womenfolk to mourn for any of my tribe. Yet I do not want them, if they found out, to think me a coward.'

'Then you will bide your time and keep your silence?' Joseph asked.

'Yes I will do that for the time being,' Meleeka replied.

When Joseph went to say goodnight to Sara and his grandson, he prayed that no harm would come to them or any of the tribe. They had worked so hard with the building of Ilinka. He was troubled by the message Meleeka received from the mountain. Over the years he'd been there, he'd come to believe the old mountain had some mystical power that he could not understand.

His face must have shown his troubled thoughts as he went into Sara's room.

'Is anything wrong, Father?' she asked him.

'No,' he replied not wanting to alarm her. 'I am just a bit tired, that is all. I have just come to say goodnight, then I will leave you.' He kissed her and then went over to his grandson and watched him sleeping in his crib.

I hope, he said to himself as the baby stirred, that Cheeka was right in saying your ancestors will protect Ilinka. He had once seen how some of his own countrymen treated the natives of this land and he did not like it. He was so choked by the thought of it, that when he turned again to Sara, he could only nod his head to bid her goodnight before he turned to leave the room.

'Father,' Sara called as he was about to leave the room, 'I know there is something troubling you and whatever it is, I know Meleeka is also worried about the same thing. Can you not speak to me about it? Perhaps, I can help.'

'It would not be fitting,' Joseph replied, 'to upset you in your condition.'

'What condition?' she asked. 'I am not sick, I have only given birth. Come and sit down and wait for Meleeka, he should not be long. Then we can discuss whatever is bothering the pair of you.'

Joseph did as Sara wanted, sitting down in the chair beside the bed, wondering how much he and Meleeka should tell Sara. Sara took hold of his hand, then lay back on her pillows saying, 'Relax, Father, we shall not speak another word until Meleeka arrives.'

Sara closed her eyes wondering what was troubling her father and Meleeka, when earlier, they were both so happy with the birth of the baby.

Joseph, thinking Sara was dozing, let his mind wander to when they first came among Meleeka and the tribe. How they had built the cabins with love in their hearts. Why, even the men who had come all the way from his own village to build this house did so with loving care. When it was finished, though, they were glad to be going home to their families. They were also saddened to be leaving Ilinka. For as Ray Peters had remarked as he was leaving, 'If God needed a paradise on earth, this is the place.'

Both himself and Meleeka had been pleased with this comment, for it proved the white men and the natives could work and live in peace. Meleeka was especially pleased. Apart from himself, Meleeka had never encountered an Englishman, let alone be their host. Yet, when he suggested that Meleeka should go with him when he escorted the men down to the lake, Meleeka refused saying he had no wish to leave Ilinka.

The wagon had been so packed with beaver pelts, blankets and furs, ready to be shipped to Liverpool, that John and James Grant rode the ponies Meleeka lent them. Meleeka waved goodbye to them from the veranda of his new home. He'd been so pleased with his white man's house, as he called it, that he even carried Sara over the threshold. Then he asked, 'How can I ever thank you, Joseph?'

'Perhaps,' he replied, 'one day you will be agreeable to me building more houses like this on the bottom land, well away from Ilinka.'

Meleeka smiled saying, 'One day, Joseph, yes, one day, but not yet.'

Joseph came out of his reverie on hearing Sara scream. Jumping out of the chair, he asked, 'What is it Sara? Are you in pain?'

At that moment, the door flew open and Meleeka rushed in. With one leap, he was across the room, taking Sara in his arms, asking her the same questions as Joseph. She pushed him away. He took hold of her hand, gently stroking it. Her father, on the opposite side of her, took hold of her other hand and did the same, looking at Meleeka as he did so. He saw the unspoken question in Meleeka's eyes and nodded to assure Meleeka he'd said nothing to Sara about the message.

They both looked at Sara as she gripped their hands tightly. Her eyes were glazed and staring, not seeing any of them. Then she began to speak of villages being burned. 'Women and young girls are being raped, the innermost parts of their body being ripped from them. Those who do not die from shock are scarred for life. Not only mentally, but physically, in that the so-called gentlemen, when they are done, slash them with their knives. The fires are raging all over this land, the brutality is like none we have ever seen. There will be shame and hatred with the natives of this land for generations to come. But it is not the end, we will never forget.'

Joseph and Meleeka, still holding Sara's hands, were mesmerized with what she said. For though Sara was with them, she seemed not to be, with her glazed and staring eyes. Neither of them dare hardly breath in case they disturbed the trance-like state. They saw her blink and then the tears came, flowing freely down her cheeks, as if to wash the vision she'd just seen from her mind.

They waited patiently for the tears to stop and when they did, Sara's eyes became normal and she asked, 'I spoke to you of what I've been seeing, didn't I?'

'Yes!' they both said in unison.

'But you already knew, I could tell there was something bothering you both.'

It was Meleeka who answered her saying, 'We did not know it was as bad as you described.' Then he told her of the message from the mountain. 'I told your father about the message, but no one else. Perhaps we should call a meeting tomorrow with the rest of the tribe.'

'You must do nothing of the sort,' Sara told him. 'Not yet at least. We must wait. For in waiting, a solution may come to us as to how we can be of help.'

'Perhaps you are right,' Meleeka said, 'Though, I must confess, when I first heard what the mountain was telling me, I wanted to gather my young braves together and join another tribe to help them fight against the white men. Your father persuaded me not to do so.'

'My father is a wise man,' Sara told him. 'For what good will that do? With your handful of young braves and a father figure who vowed only to kill for food. No Meleeka, we must wait. I do not want my vision to become a reality. Here on Ilinka soil. I know these bad things are happening elsewhere, but as yet we are safe. I know Cheeka said my forefathers would always protect Ilinka, but did that prediction also include its people?'

Neither Meleeka nor her father dare interrupt her. They were so used to Sara speaking in gentle tones.

'I think,' said Joseph, when Sara had finished speaking and he saw she was calmed down, 'that we should sleep upon the matter. We also need supplies, so if I go to the trading post, perhaps I will find out something.'

He rose from his chair saying it was time he went home.

CHAPTER III

When Joseph reined the horses to a halt outside the trading post, he heard roars of laughter. As he tethered them, he hoped that Meleeka would keep his word and do nothing until he got back to Ilinka with the supplies. He'd left Meleeka in low spirits, wanting to tell his braves about the fighting, for he did not like keeping things hidden from his braves, but at least Meleeka had smiled when he'd said to him, just before leaving, 'I am sure, Meleeka, when the time is right, you will be shown a way of how you can help without breaking your vow.'

There was another roar of laughter as he opened the door of the trading post. Then the laughter ceased as he entered. He saw the proprietor sitting at a corner table with four men. He nodded in their direction, then went to the counter where a young boy was serving. The men in the corner, seeing he was taking no interest in them, continued their conversation. At first their voices were low, their laughter loud. Then as their excitement mounted, the voices became louder. Joseph, hearing the word 'Indian' mentioned, pricked up his ears, though he appeared not to be listening.

He heard them saying how they raided an Indian village and after the killing and raping, how they burned the place down. The laughter came again when one of them said, 'Them young squaws fought like hell to keep their virginity. Look I have the scars to prove it.'

'Did you kill them all?' The storekeeper asked.

'No, three of the bastards got away,' one of the men said in disgust.

'You'd better not tell our leader,' said another.

'They won't last long anyway,' said the first man. 'Not with their wounds. Besides, there's no place for them to go.'

As he listened, Joseph thought of Sara. What the man was saying was just like Sara described in her trance-like state. He tried to fathom where this raid had taken place. He dare not ask any questions for the men might wonder why he was taking an interest. It would be best to keep a low profile. When he had visited the store before, he had kept himself to himself, speaking only when spoken to.

As the boy helped him to carry what he had purchased outside, the storekeeper looked up, asking, 'Is everything alright?' 'Yes, thank you,' he replied and bid him goodday.

Driving away from the store, the men's lurid conversation rang in his ears. He decided to drive a few miles to the east, as he knew there was an Indian village thereabout, and though it was out of his way, and he would be late back to Ilinka, he felt he must go there.

Once again he thought about Sara and the night she'd had the vision. As he travelled, he wondered of the destruction men brought upon themselves. Why did they have to destroy before they could build? Go and kill because a man's skin was different to their own. It was all so senseless when those that invaded this land could learn so much from the natives they called savages.

Meleeka had once told him of the many tribes with their own secret writings that were given to them when the sun and the moon had first appeared. No white man, Meleeka had told him, would ever find out about these writings. He also told him of tribes that could heal, not as Sara heals, but in other ways. They touch and press different parts of the body. Even, some tribes say, the rubbing together of fingernails can cure some ailments. And of course, there are many medicines that came from the earth.

'Believe me, Joseph, the natives know many things the white man does not understand,' Meleeka had said.

All these Joseph thought about as he travelled to find the Indian village. When he came upon it, he could not believe the sight which met his eyes. Among the ashes lay partly charred bodes. He leapt from the wagon. Everywhere he looked there were mutilated bodies. The most sickening sight of all was of four young boys speared to the totem. He retched and retched until he thought he could have no stomach left.

'Dear God in heaven,' he shouted. 'Why have you let such atrocious deeds happen to these people? What are you letting the world come to when men do such things to their fellow men?'

He pulled the spears out of the young boys, letting them slide into a sitting position around the pole. Then in a frenzied rage, he threw himself into the river as if it would wash the bloodiness from his mind. When his rage was spent, he sat in the cold waters, his eyes glazed like a madman. He dragged himself from the river and looked around him, asking himself what he was to do with all the dead bodies. He could not leave them. Yet it would be impossible to bury them all. Not really knowing what he was about to do, he walked towards the wagon. His clothes, dripping wet, left a trail of water behind him. His boots squelched with every step he took. Without thinking, he took hold of the shovel and began to dig. How long he dug for, he would never know. When the shadows fell across him, the hole was deep and he was soaking wet, not from the water from the river but with sweat. He looked up from the deep hole to see Indians astride their horses looking down at him. Thinking it was an illusion, he returned to his digging.

'That is enough, white man,' he heard a powerful voice say. Once again he raised his eyes with blurred vision. He saw someone dismount and jump down, landing next to him. He felt two strong arms engulf him, lifting him to the outstretched arms above. They carried him towards the wagon, sitting him down, resting against the wagon wheel. Someone gave him water to drink.

When the mist from his eyes cleared, he saw the Indians bending over him, concern showing on their faces. The one he took to be their leader asked if he was feeling alright.

'Give me a moment,' he answered, 'then I'll be fine.' His whole body was shaking, not from fear but exhaustion. When he felt able he spoke to them saying, 'Never in my wildest dreams could I imagine coming upon a sight such as this. How men can do such a thing to their brother men, I do not know. May their God give them their just rewards for doing such atrocious murderings of these people. For I am sure their God will not forgive them.'

'Neither will we,' said the leader, raising himself to a proud stance.

'My people will never forgive this,' he gestured towards the dead. 'Or other atrocious deeds my men and I have come across these past few weeks. No tribe in all the land will forgive or forget what is being done to its people. Neither will they let their children or their children's children forget. The hatred we feel will live in our hearts for generations to come. They will not forget you either,' he said to Joseph, 'for you took the task upon yourself to try and bury the dead before the beasts or the birds of prey would come to devour them. But the wise spirit in the sky saw this task was too much for you alone and guided my men and I to help you. You must rest now, we will see to all that needs to be done.'

From nowhere, it seemed to Joseph, a blanket appeared ready folded to rest his head upon, another to cover him. Within minutes he was asleep, his mind could not forget the horror he had seen. When he awoke the first thing he saw was a mound of earth where he'd been digging. He assumed the dead lay beneath it. He shivered involuntarily and turned away, not wanting to remember. As he raised himself, he saw the Indians squatting by a campfire, then the leader walking towards him.

'Drink this,' he said to Joseph, holding out a cup. 'It is medicine that will reduce the shock and heal the mind. Then you must eat.'

The hot liquid tasted like sweetened mud, yet it was not vile.

While he drank, the leader went over to the fire, returning with a plate of fish. Giving it to Joseph, he sat down beside him, asking 'What is your name, white man?'

'Joseph, Joseph Tyler.'

Then he heard the leader telling him, 'My name is David. Like you, I too have a white man's name. How this came about does not matter. I wish now to thank you, Joseph Tyler, for what you attempted to do this day and hope that I can call you friend.'

Joseph put down his plate and shook hands with David. As he did so, he looked around him for the first time. There was no sign of any massacre, even the totem was missing. If it had not been for the mound of earth, he would have thought it all a dream. He told David what he had been thinking then said how surprised he was everything was cleared away so quickly.

David gave him a rueful smile, telling him, 'It is not the first massacred tribe my men and I have come across. There are so many tribes being slaughtered in such a way as these were. We know they are not killed by the soldiers or in disputes with the settlers. My men and I are guided where to find the villages of these tribes, killed unlawfully by the men with cruelty in their hearts, and we bury them as we have done today. It is a gruesome task, yet we take pride in doing that task well.'

'What about those that are only wounded and are left behind?' Joseph asked him.

'These white men,' David replied, 'leave no wounded. They want no witnesses to their barbarian ways, and they call us savages,' he said in disgust.

'There were some escaped from here,' Joseph told him, 'but what I overheard at the trading post, they were not expected to survive. That is how I came to be here, to see if I could find any survivors.'

'Instead,' said David interrupting him, 'you came upon a scene so dreadful, it deranged your mind.' He touched Joseph on the shoulder saying, 'The medicine I gave you should take away the shock, and I hope in time the scene you came upon will fade from your mind. How do you feel now? Are you fit enough to travel or perhaps you might like to do what you came for and help my men and I to search for those men you say escaped.'

'I am alright now,' Joseph told him. 'The medicine has calmed me. But I think it will be a long time before I forget what I have seen.'

They searched long and hard but could find nothing.

'I think,' said David to Joseph 'the white man was mistaken in saying some escaped. My men are keen eyed. If there was anyone to be found, they would have done so by now.'

Joseph replied by telling him he didn't think the men at the store were mistaken. At that moment they heard a loud cawing sound. Joseph saw David stiffen and was about to ask him what it was when David motioned for him to be quiet. A second cawing sound came, then a third. David relaxed saying his men had found something.

Joseph followed David who seemed to know where the sound had come from. When they reached the others, Joseph saw they were standing near a mound of yellow flowers.

'What is it?' he asked.

'They are the flowers of life and death,' David told him.

'I do not understand,' Joseph said.

David smiled at him saying, 'Only a few hours have I known you, yet I do not think of you as a white man who knows not the highly kept secrets of some of our people.' Then he explained. 'It is said by some tribes, the yellow flower holds great healing curatives. Most tribes have their own magic medicines but those who dwell where the yellow flowers grow always use it.'

'I still do not understand about that,' Joseph said pointing to the mound.

'Then I will tell you,' David said. 'For I know you will keep what I tell you safe in your heart. If a wound is straight, a leaf from the flower is wrapped around it and the wound will heal. If the injuries, whether they come from man or beast, are so bad the blood will not stop its flow, then the flower is gathered in abundance. The injured ones lay themselves down then cover their body with the healing flowers. If the flowers stop the bleeding, they will live and the wound will eventually heal. If not their time has come and they go to the spirit in the sky.'

Joseph glanced over to the mound of flowers. He presumed there was more than one body lying beneath them.

'What do we do now?' he asked.

'So,' said David, 'you do not disbelieve what I have just told you?'

'Why should I disbelieve you?' asked Joseph. 'If they have so much faith to do that,' he waved his hand towards the healing plants.

'We must wait,' said David. 'We will make camp here for the night.'

'Should we not see if they are still alive?' Joseph asked him.

'No,' replied David. 'We must not disturb them. They will sleep until the yellow flower does its work. If they are to live, the leaves will crumble, if not they will be dead. Usually, there is someone to watch over them, another member of the tribe who sees to their needs when the leaves wither.'

David already knew that two who lay there were dead and one would live. He did not tell Joseph for he did not want Joseph to see what they would find when they removed the flowers, which would be at the hour of morning sunrise.

They made camp, the two of them talking together long into the night, David sensing Joseph was afraid of sleep, for what he might recall. When he knew the time was right, David put some powder into a cup, mixing it with water.

'Drink this, my friend,' he said, 'for you are now ready to sleep. I cannot promise a dreamless sleep, but it will soothe you.'

Within minutes Joseph was fast asleep. He awoke with the hot sun blazing down upon him, feeling refreshed as though he'd not a care in the world. As he lay there, he remembered the dream he'd had sometime in the night, of lying naked on golden sand. The greenest of waters ebbed to and fro at his feet, then up over his body. As the water reached his chin, he thought he should move in case he drowned, but the waves were so soothing he just lay there, letting the waves lap over him. Not even closing his eyes, he'd watched the green waters flowing past him. Then the water began to sparkle with brilliant colours as if the rays from the sun were shining through. As the waters ebbed away, he heard a voice saying, 'Like the water slowly ebbing away from you, so too will the harrowing sights you have seen ebb away from your mind. So be not afraid that what you have witnessed will send you mad.'

Aye, he said to himself, last night I was afraid to close my eyes, in case I awoke deranged.

He raised himself slowly and was surprised to find there was no sign of David and his men, or the mound of yellow flowers. He wondered what had been happening while he slept and where the men had gone to. They must be up to something, he thought, for I am sure they would not leave me sleeping. He decided to wash and shave. Perhaps they will be back shortly, he thought, as he made his way back to the wagon.

As he dried his face and though he heard no one approach, he heard David asking, 'How are you this morning, my friend?'

He spun around, grinning as he told David, 'I feel like a new man, light of spirit and clear headed.'

'Good,' said David smiling. He'd expected no other answer.

'Did any of them survive?' Joseph asked.

'Yes, a young girl,' David told him. 'But her wounds are so deep and wide open, I do not know how she has done so. Her mind is also deranged, shocked to the core. I think it would have been better for her to have died like the two which lay beside her. They were two young braves. Their groins were severed, their chest and back slashed to the bone. It was not a sight I would have wanted you to see, Joseph.'

'What have you done with the braves? And where is the girl?' Joseph asked.

David told him, 'We have bound the girl with more of the yellow flowers, then carried all three to the burial ground. The two braves now lie with the others. I held the girl while my men saw to the two braves and explained to her what was happening. Whether she understood, I do not know. Her eyes are glazed as if she cannot see. My men will soon be here with the girl. I came on ahead to see if you were alright. The problem now is what to do with the girl.'

'There is no problem,' said Joseph. 'The girl will come with me to Ilinka. You and your men must also come. I think it will be of advantage to us both. I am sure my son-in-law will want to meet you. My daughter will take care of the girl. She will be in good hands with Sara.'

CHAPTER IV

Sara and Meleeka, with baby Joseph in his arms, were sitting outside their home waiting for Joseph to return. A bed was already prepared for the injured girl. Earlier while out hunting, Two Feathers came across Joseph, who sent him to warn Sara that he would be returning with a very sick girl, as well as David and his men.

'It is unusual,' said Sara to Meleeka, 'for my father to bring strangers among us.'

'I was thinking the same,' Meleeka told her. 'Though I know there must be a good reason for him doing so. Anyway, if your father gets his way, there will be many strangers that will come here, once he starts to build. Yet he's not spoken to me of those plans since the day we moved into this house. Has he mentioned anything to you, Sara?'

'No, none at all,' Sara told him.

'Your father is a wise man,' he said. 'He will only set his plans into motion when the time is right.' Then he continued, 'I wonder what he found out at the trading post? He has been away much longer than we expected. Perhaps the strangers he brings with him have something to do with that.'

'We will soon know,' said Sara, glancing towards the edge of the forest. 'The girl must be very sick. See how they are walking in front of the wagon, removing anything that will make it jolt.'

As soon as Joseph reined the wagon to a halt, David's men lifted the girl from the wagon. Sara, seeing her father was impatient to get the girl into the house, led the way. Once that had been seen to, Joseph introduced David and his men to Meleeka.

'You have a wonderful settlement here,' David said as he glanced around. 'You also have a beautiful wife.'

'All due to my father-in-law,' said Meleeka smiling. 'It was the happiest day of my life, when he said I could marry his daughter.'

Joseph looked up when Sara came outside. 'How is the girl?' he asked.

'She is in a deep sleep, it will do no good to disturb her.' She could not tell him how horrified she'd been by the girl's wounds.

'You are right. Let her sleep,' said David. 'She has seen much horror and unmerciful cruelty.' He shuddered involuntarily.

Meleeka saw Joseph react in the same way. He could not wait to find out what had happened to the girl, so he said to David, 'My mother and womenfolk are preparing food for you and your men, but if you would like to dine with us, David, you are welcome.'

'That would please me.' David replied.

'Good,' said Meleeka, 'then go inside with Joseph and Sara. I will see to your men and Two Feathers will see to the wagon.'

When he returned, Meleeka found Joseph and David sitting at the kitchen table drinking coffee, Sara was nowhere to be seen, for which he was thankful. Sitting down between them, he asked, 'What have you both seen? I know it is something awful by the way you reacted when David mentioned the girl.'

When he'd been told of all that had happened, he felt physically sick. So sick, he thought he might have to leave the room. Then rage took over, more so when he thought of the girl, here in this house, suffering in mind and body. He was so enraged, he jumped up from his chair, flinging it to the floor as he did so. Then shouted at Joseph, 'Do you still think I should stay in the vicinity of Ilinka when such atrociously wicked things are being done to the people of this land? No, Joseph, I will break my vow. I and my braves will fight. No longer will we be a peaceful tribe.' He turned away from them, walking towards the door.

'Where do you think you are going?' Joseph shouted.

'To tell my braves, of course.'

'You will sit back down. I have something to say to you.'

Meleeka was so surprised at the way Joseph had spoken, he did as he was told, though he retaliated by saying, 'Nothing you have to say, Joseph, will make me stay here in safety and pretend this wickedness is not happening.' His eyes were blazing as they looked into Joseph's.

'You seem to have forgotten,' Joseph said in his normal voice, 'that I know what is happening. I have seen it with my own eyes, and believe me, Meleeka, I do not wish to see anything like it again. I would not wish my worst enemy to attend to what I and David here attended to. Yet I know as I speak, my best friend, you Meleeka, and David, with your young braves, will come upon this scene many times.'

'What are you talking about?' Meleeka asked.

'I was going to have a quiet discussion with you and David after we had eaten,' Joseph told him, 'that is why I brought David home with me.'

'So,' said David, getting the drift of what Joseph was saying after listening to them both, 'that is what you meant when you said my coming to Ilinka would be of advantage to both Meleeka and myself.'

'I wish someone would tell me,' Meleeka said, raising his voice in annoyance.

At that moment, Sara entered the room asking what all the shouting was about.

'Nothing,' Meleeka told her, not wanting to alarm her with what he'd been told.

'Come,' he said to Joseph and David, 'we will go outside while Sara prepares us something to eat.' He could not wait to continue the conversation.

'Try to be quiet then,' Sara told them as they were leaving, 'We have a baby sleeping, as well as a sick girl.'

When they were outside, Meleeka looked at Joseph saying, 'Tell me Joseph, what it is you are planning in that head of yours. It had better be good.'

'May I speak first?' asked David, looking at Joseph, 'I think I know what is going through your mind. Especially with what Meleeka said about breaking his vow. If I am wrong, you must correct me.' When Joseph nodded for him to do so, he turned to Meleeka saying, 'I can understand your outrage at what we have told you, but you must understand, Meleeka, me and my men are not at war with anyone. We are guided to where these outrages are taking place, then we clean up the mess. I think Joseph, your father-in-law, is of a mind that if you join forces with me and my men, you will be of help, without breaking your vow. But I must warn you, the task is gruesome, neither do we know which village we will be called upon next. Not all the tribes are at war with the white men. Neither are me and my men, although the evil we have seen disgusts us. So I suggest that you and your braves join forces and follow our lead. That way you will not be breaking your vow. I am sure that is what Joseph also has in mind.'

He glanced at Joseph for confirmation, so too did Meleeka.

'I could not have put it better myself,' said Joseph to them both, though he knew that Meleeka would not give an answer until he had spoken with the mountain. So he was not surprised to hear Meleeka saying, 'Yes it is an excellent idea, but I will let you know my answer later. Yet, I cannot understand, from what you have told me, why these small tribes are slaughtered in this way. For what reason would anyone do such a thing?'

'I have thought about this also,' David told him, 'and have suspected that there is a man who hates the natives of this land so much, he has banded together a gang of cut-throats who will help him with his dirty deeds. What Joseph overheard at the trading post more or less confirms my suspicions. I only hope we can find this man, then justice will be given to him. Is it any wonder, with the likes of him, the soldiers and the settlers who fight us, that our people are outraged with what is happening, making their hearts fill with hatred.

'Yet not all white men are bad, Meleeka, some of the new settlers are kind to our people. Others are frightened for they have heard we are all savages and they believe what they hear. They do not accept their own kind are the ones who started the war with the natives and that the chiefs who fight as your father did, do so to protect what is rightly theirs, for they have dwelled in this land for many, many moons.'

At that moment, as David was speaking, a great roar of laughter filled the air. All three looked up to see David's men playing with the children. David smiled as he watched them saying, 'It is good to see my men with laughter in their hearts. I cannot remember when last I saw them as happy.'

'You must stay here with us until you get your next calling,' Meleeka told him. 'Perhaps, by then your minds and bodies will be refreshed.'

All three men, with smiles on their faces, watched the antics of the children and David's men, until Sara called them to come inside.

Later, when Meleeka had spoken with the mountain, he told Sara of their plans, of how he would be joining David and his braves. She looked at the three men who were all sitting around the kitchen table. They'd been in deep discussion for most of the evening, while she had seen to the baby and the girl. She smiled in their direction, glad now that Meleeka had come to a decision of what he was going to do. She knew her father would not be joining David and Meleeka, which she was thankful for. She could tell by looking into her father's eyes that he had witnessed something which deeply disturbed him. 'You must bring any wounded you come across to Ilinka,' she told them, not noticing the look that passed between the three men, each knowing what the other was thinking. 'I think I will go outside,' Joseph told them. 'I need some air.' Though in truth, he wanted to be alone to calm his mind from recalling the horror he had seen.

Half an hour later, when Sara went to find him, he was sitting on the veranda smoking his pipe, deep in thought. She was saddened to see the expression upon her father's face. It was as if he had witnessed the bowels of hell. He was so deep within himself, he'd no idea she was there until she wrapped her arms around him, kissing him on his cheek. She was rewarded as he gazed up at her, his eyes lighting up with fatherly love. That was how she liked to see him, for from her earliest recollections her father was always smiling.

She had come outside to question him, now she hesitated, not wanting to bring the pain back into his face. Yet she had to know, so she took hold of his hand saying, 'Father, if I ask you something, will you answer me truthfully?'

'Of course I will, you know I would never lie to you, Sara. What is it you wish to know?'

'I have just been to see the girl,' she told him. 'The yellow flowers of life and death seem to have done their work well. The wounds are healing, though they are deep. I bathed her body and my hands of their own accord glided over her wounds. For a moment, the girl opened her eyes; they were unseeing eyes. I spoke to her, but she gave no response. I think I know the reason why.'

'What reason may that be?' he asked, but he knew what Sara was about to say, even before she began to tell him.

'That both you and the girl have seen the vision I told you about, become a reality. Am I right, Father? Tell me the truth.'

'Yes Sara,' he told her, 'you are right in your thinking, I cannot deny it. But in all truth, it was much worse and it is a sight I do not wish to witness again. I also think it would have been a blessing if the girl had died with the others, for I am sure, what she must have seen will for ever plague her mind. Yet, from what David told me about the yellow flowers, it must be her destiny to live.'

'As it was ours,' Sara said, hugging him close.

'Aye, as it was ours,' he repeated, 'when we were saved from the fever.' He gave a sigh as he raised himself from the chair, saying, 'I'll tell you now, Sara, I will not envy Meleeka and David when they set out on their mission, for God only knows what will lay before them.'

CHAPTER V

Meleeka had seen so many horrendous sights, he wondered if he could cope with seeing any more. It was over twelve moons since he'd left Ilinka, now all he wanted was to go home. When he had ridden out of Ilinka, he'd no idea of the horror that lay before him, even though Joseph had tried to warn him of the gruesome task he and his braves were about to undertake.

They'd ridden to the east where David said he was being guided. They travelled for days, sometimes meeting a wandering tribe, warning them to be careful. It was one night when they'd made their own campsite, that he was awakened by David. When he'd opened his eyes, seeing David bending over him, he became alert, asking 'What is it?'

'Get your braves, we must go,' was all David said before going to waken his own men.

Meleeka went quickly to rouse his men. As they made ready, he knew his braves, like himself, were apprehensive of the unknown. There was no time for talking as they rode swiftly through the night. He was glad the moon was full, making the night as light as day, as they crossed stone-filled rivers and rode through thickets of trees.

When, at last, David signalled them to come to a halt on the edge of a forest, they looked down onto a peaceful settlement. He gave a sigh of relief on seeing no burnt-out tents or mutilated bodies, then looked questioningly at David, who answered by telling Meleeka, 'I cannot understand why all is calm and peaceful, for this is the place to where I've been guided. The sun will soon be rising; we will rest until there is movement in the camp.'

So they waited, keeping watch over the settlement. But when the sun broke through there was no movement, only an eerie silence. Not even a birdsong could be heard to welcome the coming of a new day.

Meleeka and David, with their men following, ventured down to the encampment. As David opened the flap of a tent, Meleeka felt his guts begin to churn, the hairs on the back of his neck tingling. They stepped inside, suddenly coming to a halt, unable to believe what their own eyes were seeing. Even David was sickened by what he saw. Meleeka, used to a gentle way of life, spewed and retched until he thought his whole innards had spilled forth.

David's eyes took in the scene before him of three young boys, their bodies, it seemed to David, mutilated and scalped as they'd slept. A squaw with a suckling child at her breast, also mutilated. He felt Meleeka tap him on the shoulder and asked him without turning round, 'Are you alright Meleeka?'

'Yes,' Meleeka answered, 'and I apologize for being squeamish.'

David dragged his eyes from the scene saying, 'There is no need to apologize, it is understandable, for until you have seen with your own eyes how gruesome it is, you can not imagine the things you are told, and even I feel like vomiting on seeing this.' He gestured his hand towards the dead bodies. There was something puzzling David about the whole scene, yet he could not fathom what it was.

Then as Meleeka forced himself to look upon the gruesome sight, he asked David, 'Had they been drugged before they were killed?'

David looked at Meleeka, knowing now why he'd been puzzled. All the same he asked, 'What makes you think that?'

'Their eyes are closed,' Meleeka replied. 'they could not all have slept while such atrocious acts were being performed.'

'You could be right,' said David thoughtfully, 'in fact, I think you are, so prepare yourself, Meleeka, for what we will find in the other tents.'

They came outside to the waiting men, David telling them of the gruesomeness, then saying, 'Prepare for mass burial.'

As the men went into action, he and Meleeka went from tent to tent finding the same gruesomeness in each one.

All day they toiled. The hot sun blazed down on them, blood and sweat covering their bodies. By nightfall, everything was cleaned away, there was nothing to show that it had been a dwelling place. David was pleased with Meleeka and his braves. They'd shirked at nothing, working as hard as his own men. He told Meleeka that they should go to the river to wash their bloodstained flesh.

'You must be proud of your men, they have done well,' he said. 'It could not have been easy for them to come upon such horrific sights, then have to dig the graves.'

'I am proud of them,' Meleeka said. 'For today they showed great courage in what they have done.' Then he asked, 'But who could have drugged them before they were slaughtered and how was it possible? It seems to me as though they had all retired for the night.'

'That I cannot answer,' David told him. 'Neither do I expect we shall ever find out, for as usual there was no one left alive to tell the tale. Though I must confess, I have never come across a tribe that has been drugged before.'

'Perhaps,' Meleeka said, 'when we return to Ilinka, the girl will be able to tell us something.'

'It is unlikely,' said David. 'Her wounds may heal, but her mind will not want to remember.'

As he scrubbed himself in the waters of the river until his body was gleaming, Meleeka could not believe what David said about the girl's mind. He watched the men as one by one they left the cold waters, with the filth they left behind flowing downstream. As he made to follow them, he said to himself, 'We might be cleansed on the outside but I know our minds are still sickened by the events of the day.'

He walked over to his men, thanking them for doing their work so diligently. 'I am proud of you all,' he told them, 'and no more shall I call you my young braves, for today you have become men.' He smiled for the first time that day. Then his heart soared with pride when his men smiled back at him.

Later as they ate around the campfire, he thought of Sara and the girl, hoping that Sara would heal the girl's mind and that David was wrong in saying that the girl would not want to remember.

CHAPTER VI

Sara and the womenfolk were busy sewing. They had congregated at Sara's house. She and Buta were sat by the window so they could keep an eye on the children who were playing outside. Young Joseph was toddling now and the older children loved to play with him. Everyone smiled as they heard peels of laughter coming through the open window – everyone that is except the young girl sitting outside on the veranda. Her wounds were healed, even the scars had nearly disappeared, but not a word had she spoken since she had come out of her deep sleep.

While the children were still laughing and playing their game, Sara went outside to see if there was any reaction from the girl as the children played. Once again, Sara was disappointed. The girl was sitting on the chair as lifeless as ever. Sara went over to her, looking into the girl's eyes which did not move. Sara shuddered, wondering at the horror that must lay behind them. She called them unseeing eyes, not because the girl was blind, for she knew she was not, but the expression in them never changed, which in Sara's opinion was a pity for they were the most beautiful eyes she had ever seen – the colour of midnight blue and the lashes thick and long. If only the girl's eyes would light up with laughter, she thought, taking hold of the girl's hand.

Once again she marvelled at how quickly the wounds had healed, leaving only the finest scars. Whether that had been the yellow flowers, her healing or a combination of both, she did not know. She only wished the girl's mind would release the terrifying sights she must have seen.

Sara glanced up as she heard her father coming toward her. She smiled but said nothing, returning her gaze towards the girl. As he sat down, her father whispered to her, 'At least she does not tremble any more when I come near her.'

Sara smiled saying, 'I think she knows she can trust you. I only wish her mind would heal as quickly as her wounds have done.'

'Sara,' he said, 'be patient. I only saw the aftermath of what she must have seen and believe me, I still have nightmares about it. And to think my own countrymen were responsible for those horrendous deeds.'

'We cannot prove that, Father,' Sara said to him.

'Maybe not,' he replied, 'but we both saw the reaction when she first opened her eyes when I came to help you change her sheets. There is no denying, Sara, she was scared of me and why else would she be scared of me except that I am a white man?'

Sara could not deny her father's way of thinking as she recalled that day. He'd lifted the girl from the bed as he had done so many times before. She'd opened her eyes and he had been shocked by the fear he had seen in them.

'It's alright, you are with friends,' he had told her in a soft and gentle voice. Her body stiffened then began to shake. 'I think she is having a fit,' he said. 'Hurry up and get the sheet onto the bed.'

When he laid her back on the bed, she shook more violently than ever, her eyes never leaving his face.

'You'd better leave us,' she told him. 'I think she is afraid of you.'

'Will you be alright with her in this state?'

'Yes of course. If I need you I will call out.'

When he had gone, she caressed the girl's brow, all the time whispering to her that she was safe and no more harm would come of her.

'There is no need to fear the man who held you. He is my father, he brought you here to be cared for and all that we want is for you to become well again.'

All this she had said many times over until the trembling ceased. She made the girl comfortable, then called her father to come to the door but not to enter the room. She dare not risk the girl becoming frightened again. She asked him to bring soap and towels, then when she had sponged the girl down he could bring a bowl of soup.

While she waited for her father to return, she held the girl's hands and, speaking softly, told the girl about Ilinka, all the time looking into the girl's frightened, staring eyes for any manifestation into the state of her mind. But it was to no avail, she just lay there as if she was both deaf and blind.

When her father returned and asked about the girl, she told him, 'She is calmer now but she must have gone through hell for she is lying there like a zombie.'

'I am not surprised,' he'd said, then told her, 'We had best prepare ourselves to give that lass a lot of tender loving care for it's going to be a long time before she will be able to speak of what befell her tribe and until she does, she will not come out of the shock of it.'

His words are proving to be right, she thought, coming out of her reverie as she felt young Joseph tugging at her skirt. She smiled at him, then swept him up into her arms, hugging him close. He was her pride and joy. She wished Meleeka was here to see how his son was growing, then said to him, 'Are you hungry, my pet? Then Mummy will make us all something to eat. You stay with Grandpa and I'll call you when it's ready.'

As she went inside, she found the women getting ready to leave and Buta already in the kitchen preparing the evening meal.

Later that night when Buta and her father left her, she sat alone by the fireside drinking a mug of coffee before retiring. As she did so, she felt the presence of her guide, Silver Jayot. *'Yes, I am with you,'* she heard his familiar voice saying.

Her eyes left the flickering flames of the fire which she had been staring into and went towards the chair where Meleeka would have been sitting if he'd been at home. She could not see Silver Jayot, but she knew that was where he would be. Then she heard him telling her. *'I have come to warn you of danger, but if you listen carefully it will be avoided.'*

'I am listening,' she said to him, speaking to him as if he was a human being.

Then he began to tell her, '*A preacher man is heading this way. He is evil, it is he who puts hatred for the natives in the white men's hearts.*

He pretends to be the messenger of the white man's God, though he is no messenger. He gets his men to kill our people but does no killing himself.'

'But what am I to do?' Sara asked in alarm. 'There are no men here except my father. We would be powerless against such a man.' She felt her heart quicken in fear as she spoke, remember the girl's wounds when she took away the yellow flowers.

Silver Jayot again began to speak, telling her, '*At first the evil one travels into the camp sites alone, then pretends friendship. Later he sends his men to do the killing. They show no mercy, not even to the smallest child.*' Sara shuddered involuntarily as she thought of young Joseph, then heard him continue, '*Before entering the encampment, the evil one spies out the land. If he is made think that Ilinka is a white man's settlement, you will be safe. So you must make sure the women and children are dressed as the white people dress. Then Ilinka will be of no interest to him.*'

'I will do as you say,' Sara told him 'But what if he decides to come here for food and shelter?' She could see the logic in what Silver Jayot said about disguising themselves, though in doing so, there was a chance the evil one might come upon them anyway.

She gave a sigh of relief when she heard him saying, '*It is very unlikely the evil one will do so. He spies from afar through his long glass. He has no wish to visit a white man's settlement lest they see through his deceitfulness.*' When Sara thanked him for the warning, he told her, '*I will always be near to protect you.*'

'What about Meleeka and the others? Can you give me news of them?' she asked.

'*They are all safe,*' he answered, '*But their hearts weep for they have seen much that has horrified them. Right now David and Meleeka are speaking with other chiefs, for they too are enraged with what has been happening. What the chiefs have been told by Meleeka and David is beyond their understanding. But do not worry, Meleeka will return to you with his men.*'

Once again, she thanked him for the information, then said to him, 'I am worried about the girl. Why can I not heal her mind as I did for

Jamie? And can you not tell me her name?'

'*Her name is Aljana,*' he replied. '*As to the answer to your first question. If you remember, Jamie had a malfunction of the brain. He had not seen his family and friends slaughtered. So do not doubt your powers to heal, nor compare Aljana with Jamie. Each day, with your help, she becomes stronger but to unleash her mind from the horror she saw will take time. And when that time comes, I will be with you to guide you in all you must do. Until then, I must leave you.*'

She felt his presence leave the room. She laid her head on the back of the chair and thought about all he had told her, and was thankful that she had a guide such as Silver Jayot. In the morning she would tell her father of all he'd said, then they would prepare for whatever lay before them.

CHAPTER VII

Meleeka and David sat together in silence. They had spoken with the chiefs, telling them of the horrific sights they had seen and the burials they had performed. Now the chiefs were speaking among themselves. Meleeka hoped he would be returning to Ilinka soon, his men and David's needed to rest. He also felt he was needed at home. He sensed that Ilinka was in danger, perhaps even from the very ones who'd travelled before them to the settlements they'd come upon, finding so much death and destruction. He shuddered at the very thought of it. As he saw Chief Whiteband coming towards him, he nudged David and they waited for the chief to speak.

'You say there are no survivors from these raids?' he asked them.

It was David who answered, 'Only one girl. She is in the care of Meleeka's wife, but I think it is unlikely she will tell us anything. We found her beneath the flowers of life and death. She lay between two boys who were dead. We carried all three to the burial ground of their tribe. I held the girl in my arms while my men buried the boys, hoping the girl would comprehend what was happening. Whether she did, I cannot say, her eyes were open at the time, then she went into a deep sleep, which she was still in when we left Ilinka. I must confess, I wish she too had died, for her wounds when we saw them were horrifying and I could tell her mind was shocked to the core.'

'We have no control over life and death,' Chief Whiteband told him. 'And if the flowers saved her life, there must be a reason for the spirit in the sky to want her to live. But what are we to do about these raids? If there are no witnesses, we have no idea who is committing these atrocious deeds. It has been suggested by some of the chiefs that we raid the white man's settlements and chop the hair from their heads as they have done on so many of these raids.'

'We cannot do that,' shouted Meleeka. 'It is cruel and barbaric. It is not fitting if we lower ourselves to their standards.'

'Then what do you suggest?' asked Chief Whiteband. 'That we let the barbarians get away with it?'

'No,' Meleeka answered. 'But neither do I wish to see innocent people slaughtered. I have seen enough of that already. Besides, David and I think these raids are organized by one man who has hatred in his heart for the natives of this land. It is he and his band of savages that we must find and bring justice to them. Otherwise there will be many uprisings among the white men and the natives. This must be avoided.'

'I am in agreement with you,' said Chief Whiteband, 'but we will have to convince the others. Some are saying that when a white preacher man reads from his book, he reads about an eye for an eye, so they think this is what they should do.'

Meleeka began to laugh, a thought coming into his head, relieving the tension he'd been feeling. Then he said, 'That is the answer to what has been puzzling us, David.'

'What is?' David asked, dumbfounded.

Meleeka smiled at him saying, 'How many campsites did we come upon and think the people were drugged before they were slaughtered? We could not understand how this could be done, but now I think I have the answer. The preacher man reads his book to the tribe, somehow he manages to drug them, then sends in his murder squad.'

'I think Meleeka is right,' said Chief Whiteband. 'We must warn our people against him. If all the tribes are warned, perhaps soon this evil one will be captured, then he will be brought to me. My men and I will be prepared for when that day comes. We will speak now with the others, I think they will agree with our plan. If they do, your mission will then be ended, for over twelve moons you have seen much that sickened you. I am sure you must wish to return to your homes.' Then he smiled saying, 'There must be many spirits in the sky grateful for what you have done and I thank you on their behalf.'

Meleeka's heart was fearful, so too were the hearts of his men, as they gazed down upon Ilinka. There was not a soul to be seen. He looked fearfully across to David remembering other sites they had come upon looking much like Ilinka did now, and what they had found when they went into them. There was no need to tell David what he was thinking, David already knew. So did the others. Then one of the men shouted, 'Look over there!'

They gave a sigh of relief as they gazed over to where he was pointing and saw Joseph coming out of his cabin with the children following him.

Meleeka was so relieved that for a moment he could not move, until he heard David saying, 'What are we waiting for? Everything is alright.'

As he raced home, Meleeka saw Sara come outside holding young Joseph in her arms, his mother and the other women following her. They waited with broad smiles upon their faces to welcome them home. When he reached them, he leapt from his horse, sweeping Sara and his son into his arms, hugging them close. Thankful to be home, finding them all safe. He released Sara, keeping one arm around her, then with the other arm, drew his mother to them, drawing her into the fold. He looked around him, seeing David and his men smiling as they watched mothers and sons in their joyous reunion.

They smile, he thought, yet they must be saddened not to be with their own tribe. They'd all decided to come home with Meleeka when David said he would like to see how the girl was. As if reading his thoughts, the women after greeting their own sons, went to David and his men, hugging them.

Meleeka scanned the crowd for Joseph. It was unusual for him not to be there. Then he felt a strong grip on his shoulder and his father-in-law was saying, 'Welcome home, lad.'

Meleeka swung round to see Joseph grinning at him, Meleeka's chieftain outfit draped over his arms. He'd been to Buta's house to collect it.

'What is this in aid of?' Meleeka asked touching the outfit.

Joseph, still, smiling, told him, 'Tonight we celebrate your homecoming and you will wear your chieftain robes. It is a long time since you last wore them. There are to be no arguments, we have all waited a long time for your return, hoping all would be well when you did so and that David and his men would return with you. If this happened, we said there would be a celebration. Now I see no excuse for not doing so. You have all returned safely. Besides, young Joseph has never seen his father in his chieftain robes.'

Meleeka smiled, saying, 'Don't ever change, Joseph. For always you know what is best for us, and there is no need to cock your eyebrow, I know what you are thinking.'

'And what might that be?' Joseph asked.

'For a start,' Meleeka replied, 'I do not think it is for my son's benefit you wish me to wear those robes. You want this night to be special, to celebrate with our loved ones and be thankful we are home safe on Ilinka soil. Knowing that the celebrations will help us relieve our minds from the sights we have seen.'

Joseph's eyes twinkled, knowing what Meleeka said was true and asked, 'So what is wrong with that?'

'Nothing at all,' replied Meleeka, trying to keep his face serious as he added, 'Except we can only stay for a short while then we will be travelling again.' He loved to banter with Joseph and felt the mirth bubble up inside him as he saw the twinkle in Joseph's eyes fade away, the expression upon his face became concerned. He could contain himself no longer, letting out the laughter. He said to Joseph, 'It is truly good to be home. I will tell David what you have planned.'

He returned a few moments later telling Joseph, 'David thought it was a good idea.'

'You go into the house with Sara,' Joseph told him, 'I will help organize the men.'

Young Joseph, seeing his grandfather walking away, let go of his mother's hand and followed him. Sara and Meleeka went into the kitchen where Aljana was sitting by the fireside. She did not move as they entered.

'How is she?' he asked.

'Much better,' Sara told him. 'But not one word has she spoken.'

He walked over to Aljana. He smiled at her as he introduced himself.

There was no response, only a blank expression. Her midnight-blue eyes staring as if he was not there. Sara poured out three mugs of coffee and gave him one for Aljana. She took it from him and began to sip it. He went across to the table, sitting down next to Sara. Leaving his own mug untouched, he watched Aljana. Knowing now the horror which must be locked in her mind, he wondered if she was badly scarred as only her face and hands were uncovered. He wondered why she was dressed this way and thought it was to hide the scars. Sara had dressed her in some of her old clothes. Then he remembered the other women were dressed in the same fashion. So were the young girls and the boys wore breeches and shirts. He'd meant to ask why this was so when they were outside but with all the excitement, he had forgotten. He was distracted again from asking when he heard Sara saying, 'Aljana's scars are healed now, even I cannot believe there is no trace of the wounds she received.'

'Does she sit like that all day?'

'Mostly,' she told him. 'But sometimes I take her outside to watch the children play, yet never once has her expression changed. Though I know she is better in other ways. At first I had to dress and feed her, she can now do these things herself.'

'What about the healing?' he asked. 'Does that not work?'

'At the moment, no. But one night Silver Jayot came to me. He said that when Aljana was willing to release the horror that is within her mind, only then will the healing begin.'

'That may be never,' he said. 'When you think of what she must have seen. But if the wounds are healed as you say they are, why is she dressed in clothes that cover her all over and why are the others dressed in this way?'

She was about to tell him of the warning from Silver Jayot when Joseph and David came in.

'Is there any coffee brewing, Sara?' her father asked as he and David sat at the table. Then he told them that young Joseph was with his grandmother. 'There is too much going on outside for him to want to come home with me.'

David glanced across the room to where Aljana was sitting. If Joseph had not told him about the girl he would have thought she was completely whole again. As he sat down he heard Joseph asking Sara, 'Have you told Meleeka about the preacher man?'

David's eyes fell on Meleeka as they said in unison, 'What is this about a preacher man?'

Sara finished pouring out the coffee, then said, 'I was just going to tell you, Meleeka, when you asked why Aljana and the others were wearing those clothes.' Then she told them about the message from Silver Jayot and the clothes being a disguise. 'We got the children ready earlier today, just before you arrived. My father was taking care of them in his cabin while the women got themselves changed. My father saw you on the edge of the forest and spread the word.'

'So that is why the place looked deserted,' Meleeka said. 'You'll never know what a shock it gave us.' He told her then of how they had come upon other settlements where no one was about and how they had found the people dead in their beds. He also told her that Silver Jayot was right about the preacher man, for they had come to the same conclusion.

'But if he is a man of God,' said Sara, 'why does he do these awful things?'

'Any man can carry a Bible,' said Joseph, 'and pretend to spread the word. Silver Jayot warned you that this was so. And I believe that this is how it is happening.'

'What I cannot understand,' said David, 'is why whoever he is goes to all that trouble. I know that in the beginning the settlements were just raided and the people slaughtered where they stood.'

All eyes turned to Joseph, as if he knew the answer. Joseph's eyes let upon Aljana, then he told them, 'I may be wrong, but perhaps they changed their way after they raided the tribe she came from. Granted the men at the store thought the three which escaped would die from their wounds, but they did get away so they could not be sure that none survived. I know their leader was not with them because I overheard one of them saying their leader must not find out about the three that got away. You can draw your own conclusions from what I have told you.' He drained his coffee and rose from the table. 'I will go and see how the preparations for tonight are getting along, then fetch young Joseph back with me.'

He glanced over at Aljana and saw her lips beginning to move. She was straight in his line of vision and as the other three were looking up at him, he sat down again and nodded his head towards Aljana. He dare not speak of what he was seeing. All three turned towards Aljana. A mumbling sound was coming from her lips, then they heard her saying in a very low voice, 'I saw him, I saw him.' She kept repeating these words.

Joseph whispered to Sara, 'She knows what we have been talking about, perhaps now is the time to clear her mind of the evil which is trapped there. Go to her, Sara, and see what you can do.'

Sara went over to Aljana. Taking the girl's hands into her own, she said in a gentle voice, 'Tell me, Aljana, tell me who you saw. You are among friends, all we want is for you to become well again. If you do not speak, I cannot help you.' She felt Aljana's hands begin to tremble, saw her eyes glance towards the table. 'Do not be afraid,' she told her, 'those men are your friends.' Aljana brought her eyes back to Sara, then rested her head on the chair back. At that moment Sara heard the voice of Silver Jayot giving her instructions in what she must do. '*Go and stand behind Aljana*,' she heard him telling her, '*Soothe her brow with your fingertips. Then massage her scalp and temples*.'

All three watched in silence as Sara's hands worked upon Aljana, who had become silent once again. David was fascinated by the movement of Sara's hands. He raised his eyes to see Sara's face. Her eyes were closed, but at that moment, with the serenity which was upon her face, he felt the spirit of all healing was within her. He hoped he was right for Aljana's sake.

Sara heard Silver Jayot saying, "*Aljana is about to speak. When she does continue what you are doing*.'

Then she heard Aljana speak for the first time. Her voice was calm as she began by saying, 'The preacher man came to our people as a friend. He stayed with us for three days. He read to us from the book about his white man's God, telling us stories of Jesus and his disciples. After three days he told us he was going away, but would return with his own disciples. He did return, bringing with him twelve men. We ran to greet him, welcoming him and his disciples. Food was prepared for them all as well as us. Later, we sat in a circle, the preacher man in the middle reading to us. While he was reading, his disciples brought us drinks, they said it was good medicine from the land of Jesus. I did not like it. The medicine burned my throat. I pretended to drink, then poured it away. My brother Rhyta was sitting next to me. I told him not to drink the medicine. "I do not like it anyway," he told me, "neither does Nonica." Nonica was Rhyta's best friend. "Tell him to tip it away," I said. We all three sat listening to the preacher man, pretending all the time to be drinking the medicine.'

Sara felt Aljana's body stiffen, then she ceased speaking. Sara knowing it would be hard for Aljana to speak about what happened next, said to her as she stroked Aljana's temples, 'I know it will be painful, Aljana, to speak of what happened, but you must do so or I cannot help you. And the preacher man must be caught for he is evil and has killed many other tribes.'

Aljana began to tremble so violently. Sara opened her eyes, and saw the three men waiting with baited breath for Aljana to continue. Silently, she asked Silver Jayot for help. Her own body was wreathed in sweat, her clothes sticking to her. She gave a sigh of relief when she heard Silver Jayot saying, '*I am still with you Sara. You must continue, help Aljana through her ordeal. Prompt her if need be. She must rid the badness from her mind now or it will be locked there forever.*'

Not knowing why, Sara went in front of Aljana, lifting her chin so their eyes met. Then said to her, 'Tell me, Aljana, tell me everything.' She pulled a chair over, sitting down in front of Aljana, taking hold of her hands, placing them together as if in prayer. While her eyes looked into Aljana's, she kissed her fingertips.

After what seemed to Sara like an eternity, Aljana once again started to speak saying, 'As the moon rose, I was watching the preacher man. There was much merriment around me, but I could not take my eyes off him. His face in the moonlight looked evil. There was a scar from his forehead to his upper lip which I had not noticed before. At first I thought it was a reflection from the buckle on his shoe, then realized this could not be. He was all dressed in black and all I could see was his evil face with the scar.

'I became frightened and looked around me. Everyone seemed to be enjoying themselves, there was much talking and laughter. My gaze fell upon my brother. He too was staring at the preacher. "I am frightened," I whispered to him. "What is frightening you?" he asked. "I do not know, but I do not like how I feel," I said. He saw me shudder, then turned to Nonica to tell him of my fear. Nonica was the eldest of us and always protected Rhyta and me. Nonica rose to his feet and taking hold of my hand said, "Come, it is a warm night, we will get away from here and go for a swim. No one will miss us."

'He was wrong. We had not gone far when someone shouted, "Stop them. They must not get away." We looked around and the preacher was on the edge of the circle pointing in our direction. Three of his disciples ran towards us. We were so petrified we could not move. I felt strong arms circle my waist then swoop me off the ground. From the corner of my eye, I saw the other two men do the same to Rhyta and Nonica.'

Sara felt Aljana begin to tremble violently, then said to her, 'Spit out the vileness, let it all spill from you. It is the only way to rid yourself of this nightmare.'

Sara thought all was lost when Aljana began to writhe about, her eyes darting from side to side before she slumped into the chair. She heard her father saying, 'That is enough, Sara, let Aljana be, can you not see she has had enough? We can guess what happened next.'

'We saw the aftermath of it all, didn't we, David?'

He looked towards David for support but David's eyes were on Aljana, as if willing her to continue. Sara, hearing the anguish in her father's voice, wanted to obey him, although she knew that to do so would not help Aljana. She gripped Aljana's hands telling her, 'Spit it out, Aljana. Spit out the vileness buried within you.'

A moment later Sara felt relief run through her body as Aljana began to speak. 'The three men carried us towards the preacher. As we got near to him I saw that his eyes were full of hatred. His face red with rage. The men stood before him, still holding on to the three of us. I thought they were about to release us when the preacher got onto his horse. He looked down upon us and shouted, "Kill them. Kill them all!" Then he rode away. I screamed when I saw the knives appear in the men's hands. Then Rhyta and Nonica began to scream as the knives slashed into us. As I writhed about I saw one of the women pointing in our direction. Everyone looked our way, then ran to help us. There was no chance for them to do so, the other disciples were ready with their knives and began to slash out at those nearest to them. Through my tears I saw our people could not fight them, they were all reeling about in a stupor. I was dropped to the ground, so too were Rhyta and Nonica. There was much blood seeping from me. I thought that soon I would be with the spirit in the sky. Then I saw Nonica crawling towards me, he was also covered in blood. So too was Rhyta who lay not far from me. "What are we going to do?" I asked Nonica. "We must try and make it to the forest," he said.

'All three of us began to crawl the best way we could. Inch by inch with the blood oozing from us, we managed to reach the edge of the forest, all the time hearing the screams and turmoil that was going on behind us. Not until we thought it was safe to rest did we look back. I saw the rest of our tribe was being slaughtered. Some were being tied to the totem, then speared. I turned away when I heard Nonica's weak voice telling me we must find the yellow flowers of life and death, or it would be too late. I wondered why we were trying to save ourselves, when no tribe would be left for us to return to. Then I heard Rhyta screaming, "No, no, that is evil!"

'Nonica and I turned towards Rhyta to see what was upsetting him. Three men were throwing a child into the air, slashing it with a knife as they did so. I could not move. I was mesmerized, yet could not believe what my eyes were seeing. A bloodstained hand gripped me. It was Rhyta. I looked at his face. It was covered in mud and wet tears. Then Nonica was saying, "Come, we cannot help them. We must help ourselves. But if I live, the white man will pay dearly for what he has done." We found the yellow flowers, covering ourselves with them as we'd been taught. Before we lay down, we asked the spirit in the sky that the flower of life and death would heal our wounds. We knew that if the flowers did not heal us then the spirits in the sky would wish for us to join them, and that would be where we would next meet. We said our goodbyes. Then waited for our fate.'

Sara felt the teardrops falling onto her hands. She'd no idea whether they were her own or Aljana's, neither did she care, so relieved was she that Aljana had told her story.

'Let your tears flow, Aljana,' she said. 'Cry for your loved ones. Cry for your tribe. Wash away the horror from your mind. Wash away the hurt of it all. I will leave you now, Aljana. When you are ready, come into the other room. I will be waiting for you.'

Sara rose to her feet and went across to the table. Meleeka, her father and David were all staring at Aljana, their faces ashen from what they had just heard. Sara motioned for them to leave the room. David was the first to speak, asking, 'Is is safe to leave Aljana alone?'

Before she could answer, her father asked, 'Should we not be putting Aljana to bed?'

'It will be best to leave her, until Aljana has washed away her grief,' she told them. They did not question her again as they went silently out of the room.

Meleeka, standing with his hand on the mantle shelf, was deep in thought, visualizing in his own mind all that Aljana had told them. For Aljana's sake he was glad she had spilled forth the horrific sights that had been locked within her. He hoped that now Aljana would recover completely from her ordeal. His gaze fell upon Sara, who was deep in thought. He marvelled at the power she held within her. Yet wondered why it had taken so long before the horror could be erased from Aljana's mind. He shrugged his shoulders and, as always, thought that there was a reason for all things. It was Joseph who broke the silence in the room.

'Well, now we know,' he said, 'it is a "so-called" preacher man who is responsible for the vileness we three have seen. We have, thanks to Aljana, now got a clue as to what this villain looks like. But how on earth do we go about finding him?'

'He will be found,' said David, his voice full of venom at the thought of what Aljana had suffered. 'Tomorrow my men and myself will ride to Chief Whiteband. When he's been told about Aljana, Chief Whiteband will spread the word across the land about the preacher man and of what Aljana has told us. Then, no place will be safe for this vile person and his evil disciples. They will be sought after by every tribe, and when they are caught they will beg and beg for mercy, but their cries will fall upon deaf ears.'

As he listened to David, Meleeka thought about the vow he had made never to kill another human being, yet he'd been so enraged when Aljana was speaking about the preacher man, he would have killed him and his disciples there and then if it had been possible to do so. He glanced over to his father-in-law and guessed by the look on his face as he looked back at him that Joseph knew what was going on in his mind. As they gave each other a rueful smile, David asked, 'What about the celebration? Will we still be going ahead?'

'Of course we are.' Sara answered. 'We cannot disappoint the others.'

'What about Aljana?' David asked. 'Will she be well enough to join us?'

'We will have to wait and see,' Sara told him, 'though I am expecting her to be alright now.'

Joseph rose from the chair. 'I will go and see how the preparations are going,' he said. 'Then I will bring young Joseph back with me.'

'I think I will come with you,' said Meleeka. 'Are you coming David?'

'No,' David replied. 'I will stay with Sara. I want to be here when Aljana is recovered enough to come to Sara.'

When Aljana entered the room, both Sara and David noticed the change in her. She seemed taller as she walked across the room, straight and stately, towards Sara. Sara took Aljana into her arms, telling her, 'You will be alright now, Aljana. Now you have spoken about the vileness that was locked in your mind.'

Then she looked into Aljana's eyes and was relieved that all the trace of the unseeing eyes had gone. She saw Aljana smile for the first time. Her midnight-blue eyes lit up with pleasure.

She's beautiful, Sara thought, even though her face is stained with the tears she has shed. David, who had risen from his chair, was thinking the very same thing. Sara introduced them.

'Now, Aljana, this is David. It was David and my father who buried your people. They brought you here.'

Aljana gave David a broad smile, showing even white teeth. David's heart leapt as he took hold of Aljana's hand and gazed into her eyes. His mind flashed back to when he first found her and when he told Joseph how he wished that she had died with the others. He was thankful now that that wish hadn't been granted. Aljana held David's hand tight as she asked, 'Was it a dream that you took me to the burial ground, or did I really see it for myself? For I know Rhyta and Nonica were not saved by the yellow flowers. I also know they are buried with my people.'

'It was no dream,' David told her. 'My men and I carried you to the burial ground. Though I must confess, that even with what I know about the flowers of life and death, your wounds were so bad I had not expected you to last the journey. As we buried the two young braves, your eyes opened. I could not be sure whether you knew what was happening, though I hoped you would somehow know your tribe had been taken care of. I am truly sorry that the flowers did not save your brother and his friend.'

He saw her eyes well up with tears as she told him, 'It was not the will of the spirit in the sky that they should live. But I thank you, David, for what you have done for my tribe and for myself.'

Sara, seeing Aljana was becoming upset, said to her, 'Aljana, I think you should rest for a while. You have just been through a terrible ordeal.'

Aljana held back the tears as she smiled at Sara. Then she took hold of Sara's hands, saying, 'I will go to my room and lie down in a moment. But first I must thank you for taking care of me. Although I could not speak I was aware of all that went on around me. I know that you and your father, as well as your people, have taken great care of me. I only hope that now I have spoken, the vile ones will be caught.'

'They will be,' David said, his voice full of hatred. 'And when we find them they'll wish they'd never seen the light of day. Now I think you should take Sara's advice and rest yourself.'

'Yes, you must,' said Sara. 'For tonight we are to celebrate the safe return of the men, and I am hoping you will feel well enough to join us, for everyone will be pleased to see you have now recovered.'

CHAPTER VIII

Pride swelled within Meleeka as he gazed down at young Joseph, who was dressed in an exact replica of his own chieftain outfit. He would have liked nothing more than to sweep his son into his arms, hugging him close to his heart. But he restrained himself from doing so. He'd been hurt earlier by his son's actions. His son had ignored him and run with outstretched arms to his grandfather who had lifted him high into the air. They were both laughing. Then his son threw his arms around his grandfather's neck, clinging on more tightly to his grandfather as he tried to pass him over.

'Give him time to get to know you, Meleeka,' Joseph said, knowing that he'd been hurt by his son's actions. 'As yet he doesn't realize you are his father. He was but a baby when you went away. Today, with your homecoming, many new faces have appeared. He does not understand. You must not be troubled by his actions. He runs to me only because he sees me every day. Soon he will be following you around like a lap dog.'

He held out his hand and his son hesitated for only a moment before taking hold of it. 'Come, my son,' he said. 'They are waiting for us.'

As they stepped outside, everyone cheered. The drums began to beat as they walked towards the waiting crowd, then someone lit the bonfire. Meleeka sat down, crossing his legs and beckoned young Joseph to do the same, but did not insist when the boy remained standing, his eyes scanning the crowd.

Looking for his grandfather, I suppose, Meleeka thought, as he gazed around, pleased to see that everyone was wearing their native clothes. He saw his mother go beyond the flames of the fire. Sara and Joseph were nowhere to be seen.

The tempo of the drums changed to a slow beat as two figures emerged from either side of the fire. At first he could not recognize who they were until they came together, joining hands in front of the flames, and danced towards him.

They have planned this night for a long time, he thought, as Sara and her father came towards him, their steps in unison with the rhythm of the drums. Never before had he seen Sara look more like a native than she did tonight. Her plaited hair hung around her shoulders. The ornate headband across her brow emphasized her beautiful features. The dress she wore was made of the finest doe skin with the most intricate looped pattern. Her father was also dressed as a native, his fringed pants and waistcoat bearing the same punched-out pattern as Sara's dress. As he watched them Meleeka marvelled at the way the father and daughter had come amongst his tribe, and for a moment wondered what the future would hold for them all. He'd no doubt that one day Joseph would develop the land below Ilinka.

As they came to a halt in front of him, Meleeka rose to greet them. They bowed before him with great solemnity, then all three smiled at each other and Meleeka gestured for them to be seated.

Young Joseph, who was awestruck by all that was happening, decided to sit down between his parents. Meleeka and Sara smiled at each other as he did so and Meleeka saw his father-in-law wink at him, as if to say, everything will be alright between you and your son. A moment later, David and his men began to entertain them. They made a magnificent sight as they came out of the darkness into the brightness of the firelight. The sound of their rattles mingled in unison with the beating of the drums. They danced their tribal dance, then gave a daring performance of acrobatic feats. Everyone went wild with enthusiasm when the performance came to an end. Not to be outdone, the men of Ilinka also gave a superb performance, though this time Meleeka did not join them. He remained seated with his son sitting beside him. As Sara watched the men she thought of Meleeka, and of such a night when he'd risen above the flames like some giant bird. Her father was also remembering that night and decided that now Meleeka and his men were home, he would perhaps be able to make plans to visit his homeland, though this time Sara would not be accompanying him. He cheered with the others as the performance came to an end. A moment later Sara rose to her feet.

'I will go and see if Aljana is awake,' she said. 'Perhaps she will be well enough to join us.'

Aljana was already dressed in the clothes which had been laid out for her. She smiled shyly as Sara came into the bedroom.

'How are you feeling?' Sara asked. 'I have come to see if you would like to join in the celebrations.'

'I think I will be alright,' Aljana replied. 'Though I have been watching from the window and was reminded of my own people as I watched the dancing. It saddened me to think I would see them no more. But, yes, I will come and join you all.'

As they walked together towards the bonfire, Sara could hear her father singing an old English folk song. When she and Aljana were seated, she wondered what Adam and Jamie would think if they could see her father now, dressed as an Indian brave. She nearly laughed out loud at the very thought of it as her father finished his act and bowed to the audience. Then her father came towards her, and David came with him. Both of them were glad to see Aljana. David seated himself next to Aljana as they watched the children do their party piece.

It was while they were eating that David felt a change in Aljana. A moment before she'd been laughing and joking with him, then her hands began to tremble and her body stiffened.

'What is the matter?' he asked. 'Do you feel unwell?'

'I feel frightened,' she told him.

He took the trembling hands between his own. 'Aljana,' he said, 'There is nothing to be frightened about. You are amongst friends.'

'I know,' she said, 'but I feel we are being spied upon by something evil.'

He saw her lips tremble as she spoke and the tears well up in her eyes. Knowing what she'd been through a few hours before, he called to Sara, then quickly told her of Aljana's feelings. Sara rose to her feet then explained to Meleeka what was happening.

'I'd best take Aljana back to the house and Joseph might as well come with me. It is way past his bedtime.'

She sat the still trembling Aljana in the fireside chair while she put young Joseph to bed, all the time wondering if Aljana was going back into herself, for Aljana had not spoken a single word as they walked back to the house.

When Sara came back to her and took hold of her hands, she was relieved when Aljana looked up at her saying, 'There is someone there, Sara, I just know there is. You must believe me.'

'I do believe you, Aljana,' Sara told her. 'And I'm sure the men will find whoever it might be.'

Sara's voice was full of confidence, but she was also beginning to feel uneasy as she knew deep inside herself Aljana was not imagining things. She was also remembering the warning from Silver Jayot as she looked down on their native clothes.

Outside the house, Meleeka, Joseph and David were huddled together.

'Could Aljana be right about the encampment being watched?' David asked.

'Perhaps,' said Meleeka, 'the celebrations have been too much for her. Maybe she was reminded of when she was last with her own people and felt the fear once again. What do you think, Joseph?'

'You could be right, Meleeka,' Joseph replied. 'But there is also a chance that Aljana's intuition was warning her of danger. I think it best if I go over to the house and see how Aljana is doing. Do not say anything to the others. It is no use spoiling the party. I won't be away long.'

Joseph was thoughtful as he walked towards the house. He'd a feeling Aljana was not being fanciful, and that the danger she'd felt was real. As he went into the kitchen he was thinking that Sara and Aljana would be in there. When they were not, he poured himself some coffee. He wanted to gather his thoughts together before going to find them. Like Sara, he was also remembering the warning from Silver Jayot. He went over to the fireplace and was reaching for his pipe when Sara and Aljana came into the room.

'Oh, 'tis you father,' Sara said, as she and Aljana went to sit down at the table.

His eyes missed nothing as he watched them both. He pretended to be having trouble lighting his pipe so that he could weigh up the situation. Sara seemed agitated, which was unusual for her. Aljana was also nervous.

'Why are you both so jumpy?' he asked, throwing the spill into the fire. Now that his pipe was lit he went to join them at the table.

'I suppose,' Sara replied, 'that David told you about Aljana and her feeling that we were being spied upon?'

'Yes, that is why I am here.'

As he spoke he saw Aljana's hands begin to tremble as she told him, 'There is someone out there. I felt so happy being amongst you all and was enjoying the entertainment. When David came to sit beside me he spoke to me as though we were old friends, and made me laugh. Then my flesh began to crawl as if something evil had descended upon us. I became frightened, yet knew not why. I gazed around me but could see nothing amiss. Everybody seemed to be enjoying themselves. David said something to me which made me laugh and the feeling passed. I thought it could have been my subconsciousness recalling the last time I was with my people, and that that was the cause of my feelings. It was later when David brought us some food and we ate together that the same feeling came again, but this time it was more acute, and I knew that it was not my imagination. You must believe me,' she said, looking into Joseph's eyes, 'I think we are in great danger.'

'I also think we are in danger,' Sara told him. 'I am also feeling uneasy and it is not like me to feel this way.'

I will go and speak with Meleeka and David,' he told them. 'Lock the door behind me. I am beginning to think that you are both right, and we must prepare ourselves for whatever may lay before us in this night. I keep recalling the warning Silver Jayot gave you, Sara.'

'So do I,' Sara told him as she bolted the door behind him.

Outside Joseph found Meleeka and David waiting for him. He told them of Sara and Aljana's fears, and that he himself believed it was the preacher man who was lurking in the darkness.

'In fact I am sure about it. For I know my guts would not lie to me. Besides, who else would wish for the need to hide their whereabouts?'

'I am beginning to believe what you are saying, Joseph,' David said. 'We must band the braves together and seek out this evil one and his so-called disciples. We can be sure they will not be far away.'

David was about to move away when Joseph restrained him. 'I do not think that would be a wise thing for us to do, David,' Joseph said. 'If it is the preacher, he and his men would have been watching our movements. They will have the advantage over us, knowing what we are about to do.'

Meleeka, knowing Joseph so well, asked him, 'You already have a plan spinning around in that head of yours, am I right Joseph?'

'Yes, I have,' Joseph replied. 'We must play this man at his own game. Let him come to us, neither the preacher nor his men can have any idea that we know who they are. We also have the advantage of knowing that he either dopes his victims, or gets them into a stupor, as he did with Aljana's people. If the preacher man comes among us we must be on our guard.'

As he spoke, Joseph saw a lone rider coming out of the forest. Without taking his eyes off the rider, he said to Meleeka and David, 'Do not turn around, we have company. David, go quickly and warn the others of what we have been discussing. Meleeka, you stay with me, but let me do the talking.'

As David moved away, Joseph was whispering to Meleeka, 'I cannot see the man's face but I think it is the man Aljana has described.'

Meleeka felt himself seething inside when he heard Joseph saying, 'There is no doubt about it. He is the preacher.'

It took all of Meleeka's willpower not to turn around as he heard a horse coming to a halt behind him. If he had the rider would have seen the hatred he was feeling. A moment later, under any other circumstances, he would have burst out laughing when he heard Joseph addressing the rider in his broadest accent.

'Tha be a long way from home, mister. What tha be doing here about at this time a neet?'

Meleeka composed himself enough to glance around, and was

rewarded with the disbelief upon the man's face as he looked down on Joseph, who looked for all the world like an Indian brave, yet was speaking with the tongue of another place. Meleeka also noticed the scar upon the man's face and knew that there could be no doubt that it was the same man Aljana spoke about. Then he could not believe his own ears when he heard Joseph saying to the man, 'If tha be lost, tha's welcome to stay the neet. Tha can have good food and shelter.'

'That is very kind of you,' said the man, speaking for the first time, 'but I am not alone. I go around preaching and my disciples and I are camped out yonder.' He pointed in the direction he had come. 'We have travelled far and did not know that there was a settlement here until we heard the drums. That was when I decided to see if I could purchase some food. We have a long trek on tomorrow.'

Joseph smiled to himself before saying, 'Then tha best bring thy men here. Tha can have as much as tha likes. As tha can see we be having a party. Tha might as well join us.'

The preacher was taken off guard and he found himself unable to assess the situation at all, especially the two men standing before him. One obviously a proud chieftain, saying not a word, and the other looking like one of the tribe and yet speaking in such an uncouth way. He looked beyond them and could see that there was certainly some kind of celebration going on.

Joseph followed the preacher's gaze and saw David and his men prancing around in front of the young ones of the tribe, who were laughing at their antics. He smiled to himself, knowing that it was only a ploy, for David would be ready to act if there was any sign of danger. Then he smiled pleasantly as he asked the preacher, 'Well, does tha want to come and join us or not? If tha does tha'll be welcome, if not tha mun cum we me and tha can take tha self some food.'

The preacher glanced at Joseph and then at Meleeka. He'd lied when he told them that they'd just made camp. He'd spotted the settlement the day before after his men had badgered him to let them rest. He'd not wanted to be delayed, neither did he wish for his men to turn upon him, which he knew that they were quite capable of doing. He trusted none of them. They had only one thing in common – the hatred of the natives! Whilst the men made camp he'd taken himself off to survey the surrounding countryside. Taking out his spy glass he spotted the blue mountain and the settlement below. Though there was no one about, there was smoke rising from the chimneys and cattle grazing. As he put away his spy glass and went back to the men, he wondered about the settlement, for he'd no idea there would have been any kind of settlement hereabouts.

That night he could not sleep, the beauty of the mountain, and the settlement below, intrigued him. So much so that when morning came he decided to take another look. Once again, as he spied out the land there wasn't a soul about. He'd have thought the place deserted except for the smoke coming out of the chimneys and the grazing cattle. He'd been about to close the spy glass, thinking that there'd been enough delay without him taking time surveying countryside, when he saw the Indians. Looking down on the settlement he wondered what the savage bastards where up to. He'd seen one of them point to the cabins below as a man and some children came out, then a child, running towards the large stone house. A moment later womenfolk came out and, with the man and the children, began to wave to the savage bastards.

'What the hell are they doing?' he'd said to himself. 'They'll have no chance against the red savages!'

Then he could not believe his own eyes when he saw the Indians riding like the wind towards the settlement, to be greeted with open arms by the women and children. At that moment, disgusted with what he had seen, he'd decided to pay the settlement a visit.

'Well, have tha made tha mind up?'

He cringed as he was brought out of his reverie by that idiotic voice. He glared at Joseph saying, 'Yes, and thank you for inviting us. I will go and get the others. We will be back shortly.' Then thought to himself, as he rode away, Ah, yes. I'll be back. Then I can get to the bottom of what goes on here.

David, seeing him ride away, came over to Meleeka and Joseph. 'What is happening?' he asked.

It was Meleeka who answered, telling him, 'Joseph has invited him and his men to the celebrations. I do not know what is going on in

Joseph's mind, but I have never seen anyone more confused than the preacher when there was Joseph, looking like a native and speaking in what Joseph calls his "broad north of England accent".'

'He'll be more confused before this night is over,' Joseph told them.

'Why? What are you planning for them?' Meleeka asked, hoping there would be no killing on Ilinka soil. Well, not if it could be avoided. He voiced his thoughts to Joseph.

'I cannot make any rash promises about that Meleeka,' Joseph told him. 'But this is my plan. We will welcome them like long-lost brothers. I know it will be hard, but it must be done. David, you will make some of that concoction you gave me to make me sleep. Can you make it taste sweeter?'

'Yes, if that is what you want.'

'Then I think my plan will work,' Joseph told them.

'When they return we will get the women to latch onto the men. Tell the women that no two men must sit together. Then you, Meleeka, will clap your hands and tell them all to be seated as the entertainment is about to begin. Let the young ones do their party piece first, but tell them that afterwards they must go with Buta. Next will come David's men to entertain our guests and food and drink will be served. You, David, will serve the men with food and your special concoction. The widow of Red Feather will look after the women. We will give the preacher no opportunity to take out his holy book, or give us drink that could dope us all. Hopefully it will be them that sleep. Is everything clear to you both?'

'Yes,' they both answered, smiling at Joseph.

'Good,' said Joseph, 'now I will go and tell Sara what we are about, and to keep Aljana indoors. God only knows what would happen if Aljana saw the preacher and the men.'

Joseph smiled to himself as he sat beside Meleeka. His plan was working.

When the preacher and his men arrived they had gone like lambs to the slaughter, the men being relieved to have the monotony of the last few days broken. They sat beside the women, eager to enjoy the night's entertainment. Even the preacher man seemed to be relaxed, though

Joseph knew he would have to be alert, so too would Meleeka and David. He glanced towards Red Feather's wife and noticed that she was pouring the last drink. David was following her, seeing to the men.

His gaze then fell upon David's men who were waiting to perform their act. For a moment he wondered why fate had brought him among the natives and here he was planning the fate of his own kind. A moment later he felt Meleeka nudge him as Meleeka raised himself from the ground. Then Meleeka began to speak in a foreign tongue as he raised his empty cup and watched the preacher and his disciples do the same. As they drank there was no way they could have known that Joseph and Meleeka only pretended to do so, having tipped the liquid away beforehand.

When Meleeka sat down the drums began to beat as David's men came into the circle and began to dance. As they did so, Joseph said to Meleeka, 'That was a neat trick, standing up and proposing a toast.'

Meleeka smiled saying, 'You have been a good tutor, Joseph. Besides I had to make sure they drank David's concoction and it would have been rude of them not to have drunk to the wishes of a chief, even though they could not understand what I was saying.'

'And what might that have been?' Joseph asked, curious to know himself.

Meleeka grinned, telling him, 'I will translate my very words, for I am sure that you will appreciate the toast that I made. I told them, I hope you will all be happy in the bowels of the earth. For that is where you will be going to. But, before you go, you will all suffer more than those you have already slaughtered. You will cry out to your white god who will not listen to your cries as death comes to you. Your god will ignore you, as you ignored the natives of the land when you savagely slaughtered them.'

'How are you going to bring it about?' Joseph asked, 'when you asked for no blood spilt on Ilinka ground.'

'None will be,' Meleeka replied. 'See, even as we speak David is giving them more of his concoction. Soon they will all be asleep, then we will prepare to take them to Chief Whiteband. It will be his tribe who will see to the evil ones. They will die as they lived, violently. Then disappear from the face of the earth.'

Joseph felt no pity for any of the men as he watched them, one by one, begin to drop to the ground.

'I think,' he said to Meleeka, 'that David's concoction is working. Come, let us go over to the preacher.'

'Whatever for?' asked Meleeka.

'So that you can translate your toast to him,' Joseph replied.

'Do you think that would be a good idea?' Meleeka asked.

'I think it a very good idea,' said Joseph. 'Even though he seems already stupefied I am sure he will understand what you have to say to him. He will also realize we know about him and that he will harm no others.'

The preacher could see them approaching, even though his eyes felt heavy. A few moments earlier he'd felt the tiredness come over him. He'd tried to stand but the tiredness was too great. It was then that he realized that he'd been tricked. He forced open his eyes as Meleeka and Joseph came to stand before him. Now that man with the idiotic voice was looking down on him. The man's eyes were full of hatred, though his voice wasn't idiotic. He was speaking like a gentleman, and an English gentleman at that. He forced himself to keep awake as he heard the man saying, 'Before you become too stupefied to stand, the chief of the Ilinka tribe wishes to translate the toast which he gave to you and your men.'

As Meleeka spoke they both saw hatred come into the preacher's eyes and knew that he understood every word before he crashed to the ground. His legs, which were still crossed, rose into the air as his body had fallen. Joseph straightened the man's legs, then spoke to him before going to fetch some rope. Then David and his men worked swiftly, preparing to leave as quickly as possible. It was a long journey to the camp of Chief Whiteband. Meleeka's men were already packing provisions for the journey.

As they secured the evil ones to their horses, none of them could have known the terrible dreams the evil ones were having, especially the preacher. After he'd felt himself being lifted from the ground his dream was of going on a long journey trussed up in such a fashion on the back of a horse that the hot sun beat down upon his face. He tried to shout but his mouth was too dry from lack of liquid. His lips were so parched that he could not open them. Then the horse came to a halt and water was thrown into his face. He forced his tongue through his lips. The few drops of water tasted salty. He gave up in despair, then felt his lips being forced open and someone pouring warm liquid between them. He knew he'd tasted such liquid before but could not remember where. Between wakeful moments he felt the hot sun, then the coolness of night. After what seemed like an eternity he heard many voices jabbering in a language which he could not understand. Then the ropes which bound him were being cut. If he had not known that somehow his ankles were tethered to his arms, he would have thought that his legs, from knee to toe, had been severed, for there was no feeling in the bottom half of his legs. As he waited, hopefully, for the feeling to return to the bottom half of his legs, he felt many hands lift him and carry him away. He managed to look down after forcing open his eyes and was appalled at the native faces which looked upon him, as they chanted he knew not what. When they lowered him to the ground he saw a long wall made of wooden stumps. It was only when they fastened him to the wall in the same way in which Jesus was fastened to the cross that he realized what they were all about. He began to rant and rave but no one took any notice. Then he became silent as he watched his men being dragged towards him. They were dropped to the ground, six on either side of him, then were fastened to the wall. He began to tremble and sweat poured from him as he saw the savages form themselves into rows, one behind another, holding gleaming knives in their hands. He watched, transfixed, as the first row began to charge, the others waiting to follow.

The bastards are going to cut us to shreds, he thought, as the first blade struck into him.

He awoke to the sound of voices, his eyes so heavy that he could not open them. This did not bother him, he was glad that the nightmare had ended. The dream had been so vivid, he was glad to know that he was still alive. That was sure some powerful drink that the Indians gave me last night, he thought.

'Do you need any of my men to go with you, David?'

Another answered, 'No, Meleeka, we will be alright, but tell Aljana I will come back as soon as Chief Whiteband has dealt with these evil ones.'

David took hold of the reins of the horse that the preacher was tethered to. Then he saluted to Meleeka and Joseph before he moved away. His men followed him with the twelve disciples trussed to the horses like the preacher. As the horses began to move, the preacher was remembering the words of the chief of Ilinka before he had crashed to the ground. He knew now that his nightmare was only just beginning and that the dream he'd just had would become a reality.

Joseph and Meleeka watched them go until they were out of sight. Then Joseph remarked, 'I would not like to be in their shoes when they arrive at the camp of Chief Whiteband.'

'Nor I,' said Meleeka. 'For two of David's men will ride like the wind to warn Chief Whiteband of the evil ones' coming. By the time David arrives, all will be ready and I have no pity in my heart as to how they will suffer.'

'Nor mine,' said Joseph as they headed towards the house.

Six weeks later Joseph left Ilinka and sailed for England.

CHAPTER XI

Joseph did not tarry long in Liverpool. His business at the wharf was soon completed. He'd been disappointed upon visiting the tea shop to find that Jenny no longer worked there, and no one knew of her whereabouts. All he could find out about her was that one day Jenny was going off duty when a gentleman came in the door as she was leaving. They spoke together for a few moments and then he ushered her to a table and ordered a meal for them both. Later Jenny told them she was leaving with the gentleman and would not be coming back. She'd given no explanation and no one had seen hide nor hair of her since.

When Joseph left the tea shop he was surprised at how downhearted he'd felt at not seeing Jenny.

A few days later Joseph arrived in the town square. Upon leaving the coach he decided to leave his luggage at the tavern and go to his lawyer's office before going to the farm. On enquiring if he could see Mr Adam Rhoder the clerk told him that Mr Rhoder was busy and did not wish to be disturbed.

'Has he a client with him?' Joseph asked.

'No, sir,' replied the clerk, 'Mr Rhoder told me that he was going to catch up with his paperwork and did not wish to be disturbed.'

'Then he will see me,' said Joseph, walking towards the closed door, 'and you need not bother to announce that I am here. I wish to surprise Mr Rhoder. It will be alright,' he said, seeing the look on the clerk's face. A look which said that to let anyone do such a thing would be unthinkable.

Joseph smiled, saying, 'I assure you that Mr Rhoder will be pleased to see me.' He put a finger to his lips as he turned the knob, and the clerk stood there as if transfixed. Joseph entered the room. Then closed the door quietly.

Adam was standing with his back to the door, gazing out of the window. He was so engrossed he neither heard the door open nor close.

Joseph crept towards him, then said, 'So this is what you call being busy with your paperwork when there is an important client wanting to see you.'

Adam spun around, the surprise and delight showing upon his face when he saw Joseph standing before him. He caught hold of Joseph's shoulder to make sure he wasn't dreaming, and said, 'Joseph, you scoundrel, I was just thinking about you and here you are. I can't believe it.' They gave each other a bear-hug, as Adam said, 'Come let us get out of this stuffy office and go across to the tavern for a bite to eat. My clerk, Mr Johnson, will have an epileptic fit, but I don't care.'

The clerk, Mr Johnson, looked up from his ledger when he heard the office door open. He raised his eyebrows in disapproval when Mr Rhoder and the gentleman came out laughing like two schoolboys. Then his disapproval turned to delight as Mr Rhoder told him to take the rest of the day off, and the gentleman threw a guinea onto his desk. He thanked them both and thought how pleased his wife and children would be when he arrived home early with a guinea in his pocket.

They found a quiet corner in the tavern and while they were eating Joseph brought Adam up to date with the events of Ilinka, even telling him about Aljana and the preacher.

'And there was I,' said Adam, 'the very moment you came into my office, thinking what an idyllic life you must be leading, while I was cooped up inside on such a beautiful day.'

Joseph laughed, saying, 'And I was the very excuse you needed to get away from all that paperwork you were supposedly doing. I think Mr Johnson was thankful to get away as well with the beaming smile he gave us before we left.'

'That would be for the guinea you gave him,' said Adam. 'He has a lovely wife and children and nothing would please him more than to hurry home and give the guinea to her so she can treat the children.'

When they were ready to leave the landlord ordered a carriage and loaded Joseph's baggage, for which Joseph gave him a tip.

As they travelled to the farm, Adam brought Joseph up to date with his investments which were flourishing, also with the events on the farm. 'Wait until you see Jamie, you'll not recognize him; he's becoming a right young gentleman. Jessica is not there, she left a few months ago. She's married now and moved away with her husband. They seem to be faring well, according to Bessie, and Bessie is well pleased with the young woman I found to take over Jessica's place. And I think you will be too.'

When the farmhouse came into sight, Joseph wondered, not for the first time, what he was going to do about the farm. It seemed to him there was no reason to hold on to it, yet he could not bring himself to make a decision about selling the farm. Neither could he bring himself to discuss the matter with Adam.

He thought of Sara and Meleeka, but it was unlikely they would ever want to come to the farm. Perhaps one day he could bring his grandson here. He smiled to himself at the thought of bringing young Joseph, then dismissed the thought of selling the farm from his mind as Adam was saying to him as the carriage came to a halt, 'I bet Bessie will be as surprised to see you as I was.'

A moment later they crept into the kitchen to find Bessie taking her afternoon nap in the chair by the fireside. Adam gave her a prod on her shoulder – she could not believe it when she opened her eyes that Master Joseph was standing before her.

When she recovered from the shock of it, she said, 'Well I'll be blessed,' then welcomed Joseph like a long-lost son, and when Joseph apologized for disturbing her, she thought how lucky she was to have a master such as him.

When she'd composed herself, she said, 'I'll put the kettle on and make us a cup of tea.'

'You sit yourself down,' said Joseph, 'I'll brew the tea.'

Bessie was so excited at seeing the master, she did as she was told, saying, 'If you fancy a piece of chocolate cream cake, you'll find a cake in the pantry; made it myself this morning.'

The two men laughed, for Bessie knew how partial they were to her chocolate cake.

'I'll take your luggage upstairs,' said Adam. It was the excuse he needed to go and find the new housemaid, and give Joseph the surprise of his life.

When Adam left the room Joseph asked Bessie about Jessica. 'I hear she is married and left the district.'

Bessie told him the latest news about Jessica, then Joseph asked, 'And what about the new girl? Is she to your liking?'

'She is that,' Bessie replied. 'She be a fine lass, and everyone likes her!'

Joseph could not have guessed that upstairs Adam was grinning at the new housemaid as he said, 'The master's home. I have come to take you to see him.'

Her face lit up with pleasure as she said, 'Give me time for a quick swill and a change of clothes before I meet him. I feel a bit scruffy.'

'You look fine to me,' he said, 'but if it will make you feel better go ahead, I will go and find Jamie, then we will meet you at the bottom of the stairs.'

Joseph was sitting at the table with Bessie when he heard the door opening. He glanced up to see a tall, smartly dressed young man entering the room.

The young man was standing before him saying, 'Welcome home, sir, I trust you have had a pleasant journey?'

Joseph glanced at Bessie for confirmation as to what he was thinking. Bessie smiled, saying, 'Aye, 'tis Jamie alright. I knew you would be surprised when you saw him.'

Joseph took hold of Jamie's outstretched hand and as he shook it said, 'Well, Jamie, they have certainly turned you into a fine gentleman, though I hope you are not going to be so serious to keep calling me "sir". I am not used to such formalities as I have just been reminding Bessie. Now sit yourself down, Jamie. We are about to have some tea, and Bessie's chocolate cake.' He was just about to say, 'When Adam decides to join us,' when Adam entered the room.

As Jamie sat down, Adam looked at Joseph and said seriously, 'The new housemaid is outside awaiting the master's approval.'

Joseph was flummoxed by the solemnity of Adam's remark – it was so unlike Adam to speak this way to him, after all he was Adam's friend, not just one of his clients, so he said, 'Well, don't leave the lass dithering out there. Bring her in. She might as well join us.'

He was even more bewildered a moment later when Adam returned with the girl. She was wearing a cream silk blouse and a green velvet skirt. Then it dawned on him who it was. He rose from the table. 'Jenny,' he cried, 'what the devil are you doing here? Don't tell me it's you that is the new housemaid.'

'I'm afraid it is,' she laughed. 'Why, do you not approve?'

They all began to laugh as Joseph said, 'Adam, you scoundrel, why did you not tell me?'

As they settled themselves around the table Adam replied, 'I was tempted to when we were in the tavern. Then decided I would surprise you.'

It was Adam's turn to be surprised when Joseph said, 'So t'was you who took Jenny away from the tea shop, eh?' Seeing the look upon Adam and Jenny's faces, he went on, 'I called in the tea shop while I was in Liverpool. I was told that Jenny just up and left with a gentleman, and was never seen or heard of again. God only knows what they thought of her. Now tell me, how did all this come about?'

Adam smiled as he told Joseph, 'It was coincidental. I decided to visit the farm before going to see your agent in Liverpool. Bessie told me Jessica had given notice and was leaving the district. When I went for a bite to eat at the tea shop, Jenny was just leaving. I asked her to join me, and during our conversation I told her about Jessica and that I would have to find someone to take Jessica's place. Then Jenny here,' he nodded towards Jenny, 'said to me, "You need look no further, if you think me good enough, I will take the job willingly." So here she is.'

'And a better worker you'll not find anywhere,' Bessie chipped in.

'Well,' said Joseph, 'if that is all the surprises over with, I suggest we get tucking in to this chocolate cake.'

As they did so Joseph thought of how glad he was to see Jenny safe at the farm for there were so many bad things that could have happened to the lass in Liverpool.

It was later in the evening that Joseph discussed the reason for his returning to the farm with Adam.

'For a long time now,' Joseph said, I have been mulling over in my mind a plan to develop the land at the bottom end of Ilinka. The land is so vast, my plans will not interfere with, or spoil Ilinka itself, and as I travelled from Liverpool I was more and more convinced the idea is a good one.'

'And what made you so sure?' Adam asked, so Joseph told him.

'The slums with their back-to-back houses. The poverty, and the people looking old before their time from lack of fresh air after working long hours in the mines and factories.'

'I presume,' said Adam, 'you have it in mind to build a township, and if so what does Meleeka think about your plans? And how will the new settlers get on with Meleeka's tribe? I hear there is a lot of unrest between the natives and the intruders to their land.'

Joseph smiled as he replied, 'I cannot see any reason for the settlers and the natives not to live in peace, besides, Meleeka and his tribe are peaceful enough. They are also industrious, as you will know. And they care about each other's needs, which is more than I can say about some white folk. Of course it is true there are battles still being fought between some natives and the newcomers. But I am not going to let that stop me from going ahead with my plans. And as you tell me, I am a very wealthy man.

'I believe it is now time to set my plans into motion. As for Meleeka, he was not surprised after our traumatic experience with the preacher when I told him of my plans to come to England, and when I returned I would be starting the development. He's known for a long time what was in my mind. So he said to me, "Joseph, if the time has come to do what your heart is telling you, then that is what you must do. I cannot object for I have much to thank you for. You have given to me Sara, and she has given me a son. You have also taught us many things, and my people love you. I also believe that before many moons have passed the natives of this land will lose their heritage. Then the white man will come in peace. But they will sieze the land and build upon it. By then the natives of this land will have lost their homes, and also their pride. It will be a sad time and the people will distrust the white man for generations to come. But I trust you, Joseph, and I know the future of Ilinka lays in your hands, so do what you think is best."'

As Joseph spoke, Adam felt sorry for the redskin savages as he'd heard them being referred to at the gentlemen's club. He supposed Meleeka was right, and the natives would eventually play second fiddle. He voiced his thoughts to Joseph.

'I'm afraid so,' Joseph replied, 'but when peace comes to the land I can see no reason why the natives and the white man cannot live together. They could learn so much from each other. It's a pity there has been all the unrest in the first place. But now I feel it is the right time to start things moving!'

Adam looked at Joseph thoughtfully before asking, 'And does Meleeka truly not mind about your plans? After all, from what you have told me it was Meleeka and his tribe who settled there first?'

Joseph smiled before he answered, knowing how Adam's legal mind was working, then he told him, 'Legally the whole of Ilinka and beyond belongs to me. This was agreed upon between Meleeka and myself soon after Sara and I arrived. But in truth, I am only custodian, for in my heart I know Ilinka belongs to Meleeka and that is why, with your help, Adam, I want to make sure that when I die Ilinka will always belong to Meleeka and Sara and their issue. For though no blood of mine runs through either Sara or young Joseph, I feel they are truly my daughter and grandson. But we will talk about that later. Right now we have other things to discuss.'

Joseph went across to the table, then unrolled the plans he'd brought with him.

They were still engrossed when Jenny came in with a trolley ladened with food. Joseph smiled at her as he rolled up the plans, saying, 'Ta, Jenny, I did not realize it was so late. I'll get rid of these then you can set the table.'

They both thanked her as they sat down at the table, and she wheeled the empty trolley away. Then they ate with gusto for they had not realized how hungry they were until they sat down.

They did not speak again until Joseph poured the coffee, then Adam said, 'You have been thinking about all this building business for a long time, haven't you?'

'Yes, I suppose I have,' Joseph replied. 'Even more so since the men came and built the house for Meleeka and Sara. The men loved Ilinka, and you must admit, Adam, they were much fitter and healthier when they came home, than when you sent them out to me. Such a weedy crew they looked. I wondered whatever kind of men you'd sent, though they were all good workers, and as the weeks passed I could see them becoming stronger. Then they told me some of them had not worked for quite a while so I could understand them being a bit weakly when they arrived. But it is craftmanship like they gave me I will be needing. Do you think some of them might return? Then if they so desired we could bring their families out later.'

'We could have a word with the men,' Adam replied, smiling at Joseph's enthusiasm. 'And I do not doubt they will gladly come and work for you, though asking their wives and families to join them later will be another matter. They may not wish to leave their loved ones behind, and it will be one hell of a step for them to take for they will be going into the unknown.'

'You are right of course,' said Joseph. 'Though it will also be one hell of an adventure for them and hopefully a much better lifestyle to look forward to.'

They made their plans to talk to the men, then settled down in the armchairs on either side of the fireplace, stepping into an easy conversation that comes naturally between friends.

Bessie and Jenny were also deep in conversation, with Bessie saying, 'I wonder what them two are planning, they've been shut up together for an awful long time. I thought Master Joseph might have wanted to eat in the kitchen. He usually does as he's not one for putting on airs and graces. Reminds me more of one of the workers, than the owner of this place. What were they talking about anyway?'

'They weren't talking,' Jenny answered. 'They were looking at some sort of plans that were spread over the table. Shall I go and collect the dishes? They will have finished eating by now. I don't want them to think I'm being slapdash.'

'Nay, lass,' said Bessie, 'leave them be a while. The Master won't complain about a few dirty dishes. He and Mister Rhoder will be more interested in other things. It's a pity Sara could not have come, she would be so pleased with Jamie, why, if it wasn't for Sara the poor lad would still be an idiot.'

'How do you make that out?' Jenny wanted to know.

'Oh, I am forgetting,' said Bessie, 'you did not know Jamie before Sara came. The poor lad was nought but an idiot, frightened by his own shadow, run a mile if he saw a stranger. Sara took him under her wing, made a different lad of him. Sara said it was because she spent a lot of time with him. But I know's different, though I've never let on to anyone until now. Sara's got healing hands and she used them on Jamie. I've no proof, mind, but I'll not believe anything different.'

Jenny stared at Bessie in disbelief, then said, 'Well, I met Sara. I thought she was beautiful. She didn't look queer to me.'

Bessie smiled at Jenny's reaction, then told her, 'There be nought queer about having healing hands. It's the folk that think it be some kind of witchcraft that are queer. Why, it is a gift from the Almighty Himself. Yet some of the folk poo-poo the very idea of it, showing nothing but contempt. But I saw with my own eyes what was happening to Jamie, and I knew Sara was responsible, though I kept my mouth shut about it.'

'Do you think Jamie knows?' Jenny asked, interested now, yet not understanding how such things could come about.

'Of course he doesn't,' Bessie replied, 'and don't you go saying anything about it.'

'Of course I won't,' said Jenny rising from the chair, wondering if Bessie could be right in thinking such a thing about Sara, then saying, 'I'd best go and collect the dishes.'

When she entered the room the two men were still sitting beside the fireplace. Joseph looked up and, smiling, said, 'Tell Bessie that is the best meal I have eaten in ages. As you can see Adam and I have scraped the platter clean.'

As Jenny stacked the dishes Adam rose from his chair, saying, 'Why don't we ask Jenny what she thinks of your plans? At least you will get a woman's point of view about going into the unknown to make a new life for oneself.'

'That is a good idea,' said Joseph, as he rose from the chair and went to get the plans, then laid them out on the table.'

He explained them to Jenny, and told her of his intentions. Jenny gazed at the plans for a long time without saying anything. So long, in fact, Joseph was becoming impatient to know what she was thinking.

Adam was also wondering what Jenny was thinking, and if her answer would influence Joseph in any way. Yet deep in his heart, and after the conversation he'd had with Joseph, he knew whatever obstacles were set before Joseph, he would go ahead with building his township.

It was Adam who broke the silence, saying, 'This is only a rough sketch, Jenny, to show the likes of you and me as to how it will be. So what do you think?'

Both men were surprised at her insight when she turned to them saying, 'I think that one day it will be a beautiful place to live and the way the houses have been drawn, with so much space between them, why, they are like no others I've seen. But two things do bother me.'

'And what might those be?' Joseph asked, interested in whatever Jenny had to say.

Jenny hesitated before answering, not wanting to offend him. Then she told him, 'I like the style of the houses but why are some of them built so high off the ground? They seem to stand on stilts.'

Joseph was pleased with her observations as he told her, 'There are two reasons, one is because of the wild beasts that roam around. The other is because of the river – it is only a precaution, but one can never tell when water is around. Now what else is bothering you?'

She took a deep breath before answering, then said, 'I know that at the moment it is a wilderness, inhabited only by Meleeka and his small tribe. Well, I was wondering about the women and children who you hope will follow the menfolk. It will be hard for them. For the men it will be an adventure, even a challenge that they will enjoy. But for the women it will be different. There will be nothing, no butcher, baker, or candlestick-maker. Oh, I know folk can adapt to a new way of living, for have I not done that coming from the hustle and bustle of Liverpool into the quietness of the countryside? But to my way of thinking it will take a special kind of woman to do what you are expecting of them.'

She saw him watching her taking in her every word, and blushed deeply thinking she'd been too outspoken, then became more embarrassed when she heard him ask in a gentle voice, 'Are you that special kind of woman, Jenny? Could you take up such a challenge?'

She had no idea that what she had just said reminded him of his wife Rosa. For Rosa had said those very same words all those years ago when they were first married and embarked on their voyage to the New World.

He saw the perplexity on Jenny's face, then said, 'I am sorry, I did not wish to embarrass you, Jenny. It was that you reminded me of my late wife. Though I would be grateful if you would answer my question.'

She smiled shyly as she replied, 'To be honest, I do not know. It would be hard at first, but later things would become easier. I know they would, for when I was looking at your drawings, I had the strangest feeling my imagination was running away with me.'

She smiled at them both, then Joseph's eyes held hers. Instinct told her he was about to ask her something so she waited until he was ready.

Joseph, who'd lived below that mystical mountain for a long time, knew that somehow while Jenny looked at his drawings for so long, she'd seen something in them. He felt the excitement rise within him as he asked, 'What exactly do you mean when you say your imagination ran away with you? It is important that you tell me.'

She glanced at Adam, and found that he was also waiting for her to answer. 'T'was funny,' she told them, 'for I felt as though I was actually there, watching the buildings going up. Firstly there were two cabins, then the houses. I also saw a church, a school and lots of other buildings and I thought, if it doesn't stop growing there will be a township as big as Liverpool.' She saw the incredulity upon their faces, then laughed nervously saying, 'I told you my imagination ran away with me.'

'Maybe so, maybe so,' said Joseph, secretly pleased, for he knew what she'd seen would become a reality. Then he told her, 'You spoke the truth, Jenny, when you said it would be hard for the women. But we will tell them of the pitfalls, and then have to convince them that once the hardship is over with, a much better lifestyle will await them.'

'And that,' she said, whisking the dishes onto the trolley, 'will be no easy task.'

For a long time after Jenny retired to her bed, sleep alluded her. She thought of the things Joseph had told her about and remembered the pictures she'd seen in her head when she looked at his drawings.

All at once the excitement grew inside her as she cried out aloud, 'A new life. A new challenge it would be, starting afresh where no dwelling place had ever stood before, preparing the way for others who would follow.'

Her young body began to tingle with excitement when in her mind's eye she saw the people, the new settlers who would come from all walks of life. There would be men like Joseph, men of vision and courage – the great men like those since time began, who had built cities and towns all over the world.

She smiled to herself then cried out again, 'Yes, Master Joseph, I am that kind of woman, who would take up that challenge. I would like to be there from the very beginning to watch your township come into being.'

The next morning, as she served breakfast to Joseph and Adam, she said to Joseph, 'When it is convenient, sir, may I have a word with you?'

Not one for convention, Joseph cocked his eyebrow for her calling him 'sir', then told her, 'It is convenient now, Jenny, so sit yourself down. Adam will not mind, will you, Adam?'

'Of course not,' Adam replied, smiling to himself at the thought of what Joseph's father would have said about one of the servants joining them at the breakfast table.

He nearly burst out laughing then as he watched Joseph pouring Jenny a cup of coffee as she sat down beside him, making herself comfortable as if it was the most natural thing to sit with her master.

He dare not let his thoughts wander to what reaction Joseph's mother would have given if she'd come upon this scene.

He liked Jenny, she was forthright, yet there was a shyness about her. Neither was she afraid of the upper classes – he'd noticed this in Liverpool. Then, he thought as he watched her, Jenny is no country bumpkin – she is from Liverpool and has dealt with all kinds of people.

He brought his attention back to them both as he heard Jenny saying to Joseph, 'I could not sleep last night, my mind was in a turmoil with ideas. That is why I wish to speak with you and I hope you will not think me too forward in what I am about to say. But if I do not speak of it I have a feeling I will regret it for the rest of my life.'

Adam was intrigued to know what Jenny was up to as he heard Joseph say only two words, 'Go on.'

Jenny wavered only for a moment in case she lost her courage then told him, 'When you return to Ilinka, I would like to go with you. I have some monies saved, but I was wondering, and I would be grateful if you could see your way to lend me some more money.'

Joseph could not believe what he was hearing as he asked, 'Whatever do you wish to borrow money for, Jenny? You can come with me to Ilinka by all means. Apart from anything else, Sara will be pleased to see you. It will be my treat to take you there.'

'Thank you all the same,' said Jenny, 'but you do not understand. I wish to borrow some monies so I can start my own business.'

Both men looked at her aghast, then Joseph said, 'No wonder you could not sleep. What kind of business would you be thinking of?'

Jenny's heart was beating with excitement as she looked at the two men, and realized they were so interested they had not touched their breakfast.

So she told them, 'Yesterday you mentioned that when the workmen arrived they would have to rough it for a while, do their own cooking and such. So last night as I lay in bed, I got this idea that I could do it for them. If I got a cabin built with a stove and a bedroom before they arrive I am sure they would come and eat there. I know it will be rough for me and not as posh as the tea shop, but it will be mine, then, when the womenfolk arrive I could make it into a store, from which they would buy their commodities. That is why I need some money, to get me started and I hope you don't think me too forward in asking. But I know I can make my venture pay, and you can charge me interest.'

Joseph looked over at Adam as if he could not believe what Jenny was asking. But he did believe it, for even as she was speaking he knew it was a good idea and he imagined the cabin he would build for her. With her enthusiasm, she reminded him so much of Rosa. He would have helped her with her venture, wanting nothing in return. But he knew Jenny would not accept such a proposal.

Even so, seeing the smile upon Adam's face, he could not help but banter with her saying, 'Too forward, young lady. Why, I think you are as bold as brass coming to me with so idiotic an idea.' Seeing her crestfallen face he burst out laughing. Then taking hold of her hand and shaking it like a man's he said, 'Jenny, you have got yourself a deal.'

He was rewarded by seeing her face light up with pleasure, as she said, 'Oh, thank you, sir. You will not regret it, and neither will I for I just know it is going to work out.'

Adam was grinning all over his face as Joseph turned to him saying, 'Well, it seems I have got my first recruit. Let's hope others are as enthusiastic as Jenny.'

A month later, Adam travelled to Liverpool with Joseph and Jenny. He was going to miss them both after the exciting month they'd spent together interviewing the village craftsmen and their families. Jenny had been a great help in persuading the women to follow their menfolk once the development was underway.

Now as he was saying goodbye to Jenny he told her how much he admired her courage. Jenny smiled saying, 'Don't you be worrying about me. Everything will work out fine, just you wait and see.'

'I know it will,' he said, 'and you already know my good wishes go with you.' He kissed her on the cheek and hugged her close, then turned to Joseph saying, 'I will take care of everything at this end. The men will be with you by springtime and I will take care of their families while they are away.'

'Good,' said Joseph, 'and thank you, Adam, for all your help. Come spring there should be enough trees felled ready and waiting for them.'

He winked at Adam as he said, 'We might have Jenny's little goldmine ready by the time the men arrive.' Jenny retorted by saying, 'You can both mock me as much as you like, but there is nothing will dampen my spirit.' And Jenny was right, for not even the rough journey across the sea, which put Joseph into bed, bothered her.

It was only when Joseph put their belongings into storage, and bought two horses to take them to Ilinka, did she feel apprehensive. She knew it was a long trek to Ilinka, and wondered if the few riding lessons Jamie had given her would be enough for her to survive.

She watched Joseph pack the provisions they would need. Then with a twinkle in his eye, he came over to her where she was waiting beside the horse. He cupped his hands together, ready for her to step into them.

Taking a deep breath, she lifted her skirt and put her foot into his hands. A moment later she was astride the horse, and flashing through her mind was everything Jamie had told her. Her apprehension disappeared as soon as they began to ride away.

One night as they camped out under a moonlit sky, and she lay snuggled up in the blanket, she saw a falling star and wished upon it. She'd never known the moon was so big or that stars could shine so bright. The feeling deep inside her was that never once would she ever regret coming to this land.

She woke up refreshed and feeling hungry. Then smiled to herself as the aroma of bacon and coffee came wafting towards her.

As she raised herself, resting her chin on her hand, she saw Joseph smiling at her as he said, 'Come on, lazy bones, it is time we got a move on.'

They'd ridden for quite a while and she was lagging behind when Joseph came to a halt. Thinking he was waiting for her, she dug her heels into the horse and galloped towards him. As she came to a halt, Joseph leapt from his horse and held up his arms to help her dismount. As he helped her down, she looked into his eyes, then felt the excitement explode within her. She needed no telling as to where they were at. By the time her feet touched the ground she was saying, 'This is the place where it is all going to begin, isn't it?'

She did not wait for him to answer as she lifted her skirt and began to run through the lush green pastures. Joseph caught the excitement Jenny was feeling and hoped the others who were to follow would feel the same. He began to chase after her, then came to a halt as he saw her drop to the ground and kiss the earth. Then she raised herself, throwing up her arms towards the heavens above.

He became transfixed, as a ray of golden sunlight enveloped her, and she looked like an angel descended from the sky. He closed his eyes, unable to believe what he'd just seen. When he opened them, Jenny was standing with hands on her hips, smiling at him.

He was so shaken by the momentary vision that he could not move. The sound of her voice broke the spell as he heard her saying, 'This, Master Joseph, is where I will have my cookhouse built.'

He ran towards her, swooping her into the air, saying, 'How many times have I to tell you, I am not your master? You are a free agent and I will build you a cookhouse on this very spot, if that is what you wish.'

As he released her, she became serious as she thanked him for having faith in her. 'And I shall pay you back every penny that it will take you to build and stock my cookhouse.'

'I know you will,' he said, though it pained him, her being too independent to accept his help in any other way. He did not want her to pay him back. She looked into his eyes as she said, 'And most of all, I thank you for bringing me here. It is what I was born for. I can feel it in my bones. I've never felt so happy in my life.'

She turned away from him, and he watched the changing expressions upon her face as she took in the beauty of her surroundings.

He was pleased with the site she had chosen. It would be a good vantage place for what he planned. She turned towards him, taking both his hands into hers. He felt them tremble as they gripped his tightly. His eyes sought hers. Though he could not fathom the expression which lay within them, until he heard her saying, 'From this very spot, Joseph,' – she emphasized the 'Joseph' – 'we will watch your dream become a reality. My cookhouse will become the first dwelling place. Then others will spring forth. They will spread even across the river and beyond. The people will eventually come from all nations, bringing their trade and customs with them. And once again I must thank you for making it possible for me to be here, and hopefully see it all come about from the very beginning.'

He was touched by her little speech, for it seemed she had as much faith in him as he had in her. He hugged her to him saying, 'I am glad you find it so pleasurable a place.' He could not dampen her romantic spirit by telling her it was no dream he was planning, but a happening. For if he did not make it happen, someone else would. Not yet perhaps, but certainly in a few years time. Then where would Meleeka be then? Most probably moved on like so many of the natives.

He told Jenny none of this, but said to her, 'I hope you are right Jenny, though I have no qualms about when I get the project off the ground, and the first settlers arrive. I do not think the villagers will let me down, after all, unemployment was rife in the village. Did we not find that men were being thrown onto the scrap heap – good men with a trade in their fingertips. And you will remember the young ones, working for a pittance and being despised for doing so.'

He kept hold of Jenny's hand as they strolled towards the horses. If I do have a dream, he thought, it is to give folk such as those a better chance in life, taking the weariness from their faces, and giving them back their pride.

They walked the horses to the river, and as they drank he told her, 'We will not be long now before we reach Ilinka, though we will follow the river. It is the longest way, but when you see Ilinka for the first time I want it to be from the very best vantage point.'

When the horses finished drinking, he helped her to mount. Then they rode in silence, each deep in their own thoughts.

Joseph was thinking about his family and was looking forward to seeing his grandson. Then he thought of how destiny had brought them together. First Sara, and then Meleeka, and between them both, young Joseph.

Jenny was also thinking of Sara, looking forward to seeing her again.

Then she wondered what it would be like living with a tribe of Indians. She was still wondering, when she caught her first sighting of the Blue Mountain. She was so awestruck, she reined the horse so suddenly, it nearly threw her. She steadied the horse then looked down onto Ilinka. Joseph came beside her asking, 'Well, was it worth coming for?'

'It's breathtaking,' she told him. 'I have never seen the likes of it before.'

A moment later he saw her face change from pure happiness to one of sadness.

'What ails you?' he asked, puzzled by the sudden change in her.

'Oh, Joseph,' she replied, 'Ilinka looks so mystical, I feel nothing should intrude upon it. I cannot bear to think of the effect your plans and also mine will have on such a beautiful place.'

'In what way?' he asked, surprised that she should think of Ilinka as being a mystical place, so soon after her first sighting of it.

'Well,' she said, 'when the people come to settle here, and your development begins to mushroom onto the verge of Ilinka 'twould be a shame if it caused unrest between Meleeka and his tribe and it could be a possibility. Do you not think so?'

He was surprised with the profoundness of her thoughts and if he'd had any doubts about her venture not succeeding, they'd just been washed away.

'You're a funny lass,' he said. 'Fancy thinking about such a thing when you have only just arrived. But you are right, if my plans do mushroom, the township will come onto the very verge of Ilinka. But my plans will not spoil Ilinka itself. For what you see before you belongs to Meleeka and Sara and then later to their issue. As to the new settlers, I can see no reason why they should not live in peace with Meleeka and his tribe.'

He put four fingers into his mouth making a shrill whistling sound which echoed all around, then pointed for her to look towards the settlement. As she gazed down, he gave another whistle and she saw someone wave to them. Then Joseph was saying, 'Come let us ride, and you will find out what it is like to be really welcomed home.'

They rode side by side down the hillock and across the open

grassland. She saw the natives of Ilinka riding towards them. Then all at once the natives came to a halt, bringing their horses together in a row and stood waiting.

As they galloped towards the line of men and horses, she expected Joseph to begin to rein in his horse and was ready to rein in her own, but a gap was made between the waiting men and they rode past while the men cheered. Not until they reached the edge of the settlement did Joseph slow his pace and she did the same.

It was then that Jenny saw the most handsomest man she had ever seen. He was astride his horse with a child sitting up in front of him – she assumed it was Meleeka. She saw his face light up with pleasure as they approached, then in one swift movement he dismounted, bringing the child with him. Joseph also leapt from his horse and a moment later the two men were hugging each other, the child squashed between them. Meleeka was saying, 'Welcome home, my friend, we have missed you.' They came apart as Joseph said, 'It's good to be home, Meleeka. I have also missed you and my grandson.'

He held open his arms to the child, who hesitated only for a moment before going into them. Joseph hugged the child close as with Meleeka they walked towards her.

Meleeka was smiling as Joseph introduced them, then he said, 'Welcome to Ilinka, Jenny, you are the first white woman to visit my people. I hope you will be happy with us. I know that Sara will be pleased you have come and will be glad to see you.'

'As I will be to see her,' she told him.

'Then we shall waste no more time,' said Meleeka. 'We can talk later.'

While she waited for Meleeka and Joseph to remount, she thought how lucky Sara was to have such a handsome husband. Meleeka led the way as they rode into the settlement, and as they did so Jenny thought she would never, as long as she lived, forget the welcome they were given.

She felt like a queen with everyone waving and cheering. The youngsters running beside her, smiling as if she was no stranger to their camp. Inside herself she felt at home with these people as she'd never felt so at home anywhere in her life before. She glanced at Joseph and found he was smiling at her – he winked as if he too was welcoming her to this place he loved best. A moment later Sara was running towards them. For a moment there was a look of puzzlement upon her face, which soon cleared as she recognized Jenny.

Joseph leapt from his horse and ran towards Sara, who ran into his outstretched arms. A moment later they were walking towards her and Joseph was saying, 'See who I have brought all the way from England to visit you, Sara.'

Meleeka helped Jenny dismount and Sara was hugging her close saying, 'Oh, Jenny, I'm so glad to see you. Though I can't wait to find out what it is all about, after Father has just whispered to me that I'm in for a big surprise when I find out why you have come.'

She linked her arm around Jenny's waist and said, 'Come, let us go inside the house, then you can tell me all about it.'

But Meleeka would not let Jenny go until he'd introduced her to his mother and his people.

It was much later when Sara was to hear of Jenny's venture. Buta had insisted they ate with her. Then afterwards, Jenny could not get away from the young ones who were curious about her, for they had never seen a white lady before.

Now, as she spoke to Sara and Meleeka about her plans, Joseph was content to sit by the fireside with his sleeping grandchild upon his knee. He smiled to himself as he watched the changing expressions in both Meleeka's face and Sara's as Jenny prattled on about what she hoped to achieve.

He could well imagine what they were thinking. At first there would be disbelief that one as young as Jenny could have so much ambition, and bewilderment at her being so keen. Then he knew that Meleeka approved of Jenny when he heard him telling her, 'Well, Jenny, I admire you for your courage and wish you great success, and of course, I and my people will do all in our power to help you.' He gave Jenny a warm smile as he spoke to her, and as she looked into his eyes she knew that she could trust in him to keep his word. Though all the same she had to ask him, 'And you do not mind that soon there will be white settlers so near to Ilinka?'

His smile broadened as he replied, 'Jenny, I have known for a long time that Joseph would one day set his plans into motion. He tells me now that time has come. It is better that the one I trust most in this land be the one to bring the white settlers here. For if he did not, others would come and maybe they would be untrustworthy men.'

Jenny's heart went out to Meleeka and his people. Ilinka was so beautiful. It seemed to her that it should not be intruded upon and spoiled by Joseph's plans, not even the surrounding area where the building would take place. But Joseph had told her it was progress and it seemed Meleeka agreed with Joseph.

Sara took the sleeping child from her father's arms, saying as she did so, 'Come Jenny, I will put young Joseph to bed, then we will have a woman to woman talk. I am sure my father and Meleeka have much to discuss.'

No sooner had they left the room, when Meleeka, with a grin on his face, was saying, 'Well, Joseph, you've certainly got yourself one hell of a woman there.'

It took Joseph a moment to realize what Meleeka was getting at. Then he roared with laughter saying, 'Don't be daft, Meleeka. Jenny is young enough to be my daughter, why she cannot be much older than Sara. So you can get that silly notion out of your head. Now tell me what has been happening while I have been away. Tell me about Aljana and David. You have already mentioned they are now man and wife. How are they doing?'

Meleeka was smiling as he told Joseph, 'Aljana, I am glad to say is now fully recovered. It helped her enormously when David returned from Chief Whiteband and told us the preacher and his disciples got a taste of their own medicine. Apparently they were all slashed to death as they hung together side by side on a wall made of wood. It was a gruesome tale that David told us about, the way they died. And no one listened to their cries for mercy. Even David himself was surprised by the brutleness of what he saw, but he thought of Aljana and the other tribes that had suffered at the hands of those thirteen men and he felt no shame when all were dead! But soon you will be seeing Aljana for yourself, for she and David are going to make their home with us. And soon, I think, others of my tribe will follow in Aljana and David's footsteps. They are growing into adulthood and are already making sheep's eyes at one another.'

Joseph laughed at the way Meleeka said sheep's eyes. It was an expression he'd used himself about Sara and Meleeka before they became man and wife.

Then he said, 'You cannot stop the young ones falling in love, Meleeka. It happens all the time the whole world over, and will always do so until the end of time.'

Meleeka made no comment to Joseph's remark. He would have liked to banter with Joseph, asking if the same rules applied to the older generation. For he had seen it with his own eyes, how well Joseph and Jenny got on together. He smiled to himself as he thought that one day there might be more than friendship between them.

A moment later they were discussing Joseph's plans for the white man's settlement and Meleeka was quick to notice that Jenny was uppermost in Joseph's mind when he told him, 'Firstly, we must build the cookhouse for Jenny. It must be completed by the time the men arrive from England. I also want a bunkhouse built for the men who will be arriving in the spring, so that gives us plenty of time, weather permitting of course. You already know some of the men – those that built your house. Their womenfolk will come later – 'twas hard persuading the women, but Jenny was a great help and finally convinced them at least to give it a try.

'I could understand the women's plight in not wanting to leave the village, for some will be leaving behind elderly parents and their brothers and sisters. The villagers are close-knit but they have to depend on others for work. If there be none, they starve and at the moment that is what they are doing. So that too was in our favour. Of course the women more than the men asked about the unrest between the natives and the white settlers, for they had heard stories about unrest. But I assured them they would have nothing to fear from the natives of Ilinka. In fact, I told them that you were a gradely tribe. And where I come from, that means you're the best and worth your weight in gold.'

Meleeka smiled as he said, 'I hope we live up to your high esteem of us, Joseph.'

'I have no qualms about that,' Joseph replied, 'and if I thought for one moment my plans would spoil our friendship, I would not be going ahead with them.'

Meleeka looked at Joseph thoughtfully as he said, 'You know I will give all the help I can in preparing the way. My braves will fell the trees, and Jenny's cookhouse will be ready in time.' Then he thought but did not say: I only hope you are right about your villagers, for I would not like trouble to come between our two peoples.

'Thank you, Meleeka,' said Joseph. 'I knew I could count on you with what we discussed before I went to England. Tomorrow I will take the wagon, and pick up the crates of tools and our trunks from the livery stables. Then we can make a start before winter comes.'

While the two men discussed Joseph's plans, Sara was showing Jenny around the house.

'Oh, Sara,' said Jenny, 'it is so different from what I imagined; your furniture is so grand.'

Sara laughed at Jenny's enthusiasm as she told her, 'My father had the furniture shipped from England. Apparently he made all the arrangements with Adam while we were at the farm. My father knew, even before I did, that I would one day marry Meleeka. For Meleeka told my father soon after we were cured of the fever that fate had guided us to the Blue Mountain for that very reason. And my father had promised Meleeka that one day he would have built for him a white man's house. That is how the house and the furniture became our wedding gift.'

When Sara finished speaking, Jenny was smiling as she said, 'And I can just imagine your father and Adam plotting everything behind your back. They are such great friends. They are like two kids when they get together. I bet they were a handful when they were young.'

Sara agreed with Jenny as they went outside laughing.

Jenny was fascinated with the Blue Mountain and the surrounding countryside as she took in the panoramic view. Sara stood silently beside her, then was surprised to hear Jenny asking, 'Does it not remind you of another place, Sara? It reminds me of the view from the farmhouse bedroom window, with the rolling hills and open space. Only the smoke from the house chimney pots in the village is missing.'

Sara was still gazing at the view as she replied, 'Yes, it does remind me of the view from the farm window, though to me I thought about it the other way around. The first morning I opened the curtains and gazed out of the window, the scene reminded me of Ilinka. Meleeka would not believe me when I told him, even though I tried to assure him it was true.'

'Well I can confirm it now,' said Jenny as they set off back to the house.

CHAPTER X

In the months that followed the men of Ilinka worked hard. They cleared the river so the logs could be sent downstream to the building site. Even the children helped by stripping the branches when the trees were felled, then rolled the logs to the river bank.

In no time at all, Jenny could see her cookhouse taking shape. Joseph was pleased with the progress being made. He wanted as much work done as possible before the snows of winter. He also wondered silently how Jenny would cope with the winter months.

On the day David and Aljana arrived, everyone stopped work to welcome them. David was pleased to see Joseph again, and was not surprised that Joseph had already started on the new settlement. Meleeka had mentioned Joseph's plans for the land below Ilinka. What did surprise him was Jenny and what she hoped to accomplish, though he wished her well and said he would help.

Joseph was delighted to see Aljana fully recovered from her ordeal, looking as happy as a young bride should. She told him David did not mind when she suggested they make their home in Ilinka. 'He knows how safe I feel with Sara. But it was only right I should go and meet his tribe, and become as one with them. They made me feel welcome and though David has no family to call his own, it was a sad day when he left, especially for the braves who went through so much with him, in their search for the evil one. I also met Chief Whiteband who seems to think that soon the trouble with the natives and the settlers will be over.'

'Let us hope so,' said Joseph. 'If he is right then we can all live in peace.'

The next day the work continued and did so well into the winter months. They were lucky that winter – though it did snow, there were no blizzards, neither did the river freeze over.

Joseph watched the logs pile up ready for when the men from England arrived. And knew Jenny's cookhouse, though still unfurnished, would be ready and stocked before the allotted time.

Joseph watched her as she danced around the empty building. Her face was filled with joy. He hoped with all his heart that for her sake, the cookhouse would be a great success.

The men's sleeping quarters were also finished but were unfurnished and were being used as a carpenter's shop, where the furniture was being made for the two buildings. With Joseph's guidance and the tools he brought from England, the men were becoming adept at carpentry.

Joseph cocked his brow as Jenny came dancing towards him saying, 'I'm so happy, Joseph, to think that this,' she waved her hand around, 'is all my very own. I cannot wait to see it all finished and the men coming for their meals.' She linked her arm into his as they walked towards the door and stepped outside. As he closed the door he smiled at her saying, 'You will have to wait a while before that happens, lass. The men will not be arriving before spring, even though your cookhouse may be finished before then; we have been lucky until now. But there is no telling what is in store for us with the weather.'

As they walked up to Ilinka it began to snow.

Meleeka was deep in thought as he stood by the kitchen window watching the falling snow. David had just gone; they had been discussing the new settlement. David had also told him of the battles which still raged between the white man and the natives. While out hunting, David had come upon a wandering tribe who told him they were fleeing from the white man's rage. And David had said to Meleeka, 'Let us hope Joseph knows what he is about when he brings the settlers here. I hope they will not bring unrest to Ilinka.'

'Joseph will not let that happen,' Meleeka told him confidently.

'Let us hope not,' said David. 'But you must remember, Meleeka, all white men are not like Joseph. Some become greedy and take what does not belong to them. I am not only speaking about the land they take, but also our young squaws, who they rape, without giving them a second thought.'

'Joseph is a good man,' said Meleeka. 'He is also a good judge of character. So, I think people of Joseph's village will have the same goodness as Joseph.'

'I hope you are right,' were David's parting words.

But now the seed had been set in Meleeka's mind and as he stood by the window he thought over David's words. He knew that in time other settlers would come, who were not from the village of Joseph's homeland and David was more worldly than himself. David had been in the battles between the natives and the white man and also observed their wheeling and dealing where as he himself, apart from finding his father at death's door and encountering the evil doings of the preacher and his men, had never been into battle to see what they entailed. He wished that David had not spoken of these things, it was hurtful to even consider what Joseph was doing could bring the downfall of his tribe. He loved and trusted Joseph as he would his own father if he were here.

With his mind still unsettled he went outside to find Joseph. Joseph would calm the fears which David had brought to him. As he came outside, he felt the quietness which always came with the falling snow. It was as if the whole world was sleeping. He stood for a moment wondering where Joseph would be, then felt himself being drawn towards the mountain.

There was not a soul about as he gazed up to its peak, marvelling that when he was troubled the mountain drew him to it. Then he heard the voice telling him, *'Let your heart become easy. Listen not to strangers. For David's still a stranger among your tribe. Despite your banding together on his mission and becoming friends. David does not understand how your destiny was always meant to be linked with Joseph's. And that link can never be broken. So put your mind and your heart at rest. Your bloodline is safe for many generations to come.*

'Joseph does not know he is guided by us in all things. The township he will develop is also meant to be. You were warned that this would one day come about. Would you not rather it was Joseph we entrusted

it to than anyone else?' When the voice faded away, Meleeka as always bowed to the mountain before walking away.

He saw Sara and young Joseph walking towards the house and ran to greet them, his mind and heart happy once again. So much so, he did not mention to Sara his doubts about her father bringing newcomers to the settlement, nor of the mountain speaking to him.

As the winter months flew by, the men carved and sawed the way Joseph had taught them to. They made furniture for Jenny and beds for the men who would be arriving. Neither were the women idle: they made blankets and rugs for the new premises and all were completed well in advance of the workman's arrival.

Jenny was as pleased as punch as she surveyed her very own cookhouse. The long tables and chairs were a credit to the men who made them. On either side of the fireplace there was shelving stacked with pots and pans. The pans were made of copper and gleamed with the reflections of the firelight. Beneath them were spice racks. There were also tubs of commodities that she would need; and there was a room at the back for her own private use.

'Is it to your liking?' Joseph asked after watching her inspect every nook and cranny. ''Tis wonderful,' she replied, her eyes sparkling with the pleasure she was feeling, 'and don't you be worrying about me making a success of my venture. I just know it is going to be alright, and when it is no longer needed as a cookhouse I will make it into a store. I will fill it with provisions for all the family, just like a shopkeeper would do in England.'

She linked her arm into his, and as they walked towards the door she told him. 'And when I've made my fortune you can build me a white house on the top of the hill so that when I am old and grey I will be able to sit on my veranda in my rocking chair looking down on all that has been accomplished since I first arrived. Then I will think of you, Joseph, and wonder what fate would have dealt me had you not walked into the tea shop all those years before.'

He was thrilled by both her enthusiasm and her sentiment, and he wished, not for the first time, that Rosa could be with him. Rosa would have loved Jenny like a daughter, for Jenny's attitude to life was so like Rosa's had been.

Later in the evening, four contented people sat around the blazing log fire discussing the future. Then Sara and Meleeka raised themselves from their chairs and stood together, holding hands, as Sara announced that they were to become parents again.

When Joseph heard the news he congratulated them both. As he hugged Sara to him, he said, 'I hope it will be a girl, and be just like her mother.' Silently he thought it was a miracle that Sara had grown into such a beautiful woman able to bear children at all, as he remembered what a puny baby she'd been herself.

Jenny also congratulated them and said how thrilled she was that she would be here when the child was born. Meleeka smiled to himself as he thought that one day Joseph and Jenny might be announcing that they would be becoming parents. When he voiced his thoughts Joseph laughed out loud then said, 'I am too old and Jenny is too ambitious. Why, only today Jenny told me of a house I am to build for her. Not any old house, of course, but one on top of the hill so that in her old age she can look back on all that has been achieved. Is that not so Jenny?' he asked as he winked at her.

Jenny smiled as she said it was, though she could not hide the blush which came to her face upon Meleeka's remarks. 'It seems to me,' said Meleeka, 'that Jenny has a lot of faith in her own future as well as yours, Joseph.'

'If she does,' said Joseph, 'let us hope she will not be disappointed.'

'I do not think there will be any danger of that,' said Meleeka, remembering the message he'd received earlier from the mountain.

'But while we are on the subject, and before the men arrive from England, do you think you should at least have a name for the settlement?' Joseph glanced across to Sara, as he recalled her choosing the name for Ilinka.

Sara smiled at him, knowing what her father was thinking. Then she asked, 'How does the name of Petraba sound to you father?'

Joseph repeated the name several times before he answered her, then he told her, 'Yes, I like the name of Petraba, it has a good ring to it, so from now on, Petraba it will be.'

Jenny was unable to contain her excitement as she jumped out of the chair and clapped her hands saying, 'Oh fancy me, sitting here listening to a name being given to what will one day become a township. I cannot believe it. Isn't life so incredible, you never know what fate may have in store for you.'

'You never spoke a truer word,' said Joseph, as he smiled at Sara and Meleeka, knowing how the three of them had been brought together.

A few weeks later Jenny was in her cookhouse waiting for the men to arrive from England. Joseph and Meleeka had gone to meet them, but there was no telling on what day they would arrive, though it had been assumed today would be the day.

She tasted the meat, then glanced up as the door opened and Sara and Buta came into the room. After greeting each other Jenny asked, 'Do you think the men will arrive today?'

It was Buta who answered her saying, 'How do we know when we do not even know if their ship arrived on time! There could be other setbacks. You will have to be patient, Jenny. I know how eager you are to get your venture off the ground, but you cannot do so until the men arrive.'

Buta did not know what to make of Jenny. She liked her, but could not understand the ambition which raged inside of Jenny. She thought Jenny planned things as was only befitting for a man to do. Yet she was womanly in other ways. Her cooking was excellent, and there was no doubt in Buta's mind that her cookhouse would be a success, for it was spotlessly clean, and the pretty curtains showed up all of Jenny's exquisite needlework.

Buta's thoughts were interrupted when the door opened and Joseph stepped into the room. Sara was first to speak, asking him, 'Father, is everything alright, and where are the wagons? I have not heard them approaching. You also must have arrived on foot, for your horse is not tethered outside.' Her voice was so full of concern, Jenny and Buta held their breath waiting for him to answer. Then they relaxed as he laughed out loud saying, 'Why is it women always think the worst. Of course everything is alright. Why should it not be? The men will be arriving before long, Jenny, so you can get something cooking for them.'

Then to the bewilderment of them all, he swept Sara off her feet and, twirling her around, he told her, 'I have a surprise for you. That is why I came in so secretive and alone.'

'What is it?' she asked as her feet touched the ground.

'You'll never guess in a million years,' he replied as he went and opened the door. Her eyes lit up with pleasure as Adam stepped into the room, followed by another gentleman.

'Adam,' she screamed as she ran towards him. He hugged her close, kissing the top of her head. As he released her, he made no attempt to introduce the stranger who was standing next to him. For a moment Sara was puzzled as she saw her father, Adam and the stranger were grinning like Cheshire cats. Then the penny dropped as she added, 'Jamie, is it really you? I did not recognize you. It is such a gentleman you have become.'

'And that is all due to you and your father,' he said as he took hold of both her hands then kissed her on the cheek. As Sara introduced Jamie and Adam to Buta, Buta eyed up Adam discreetly. She had not forgotten how, not so long ago, she thought this was the man who she thought Sara was in love with. Now as she welcomed Adam she knew her fears were unjustified, when Jenny had welcomed Adam and Jamie saying how surprised she was to see them again so soon. She told Sara, she and Buta would manage the cooking if Sara wanted to talk with the two men.

'Are you sure you can manage?' asked Joseph. 'The others will not be long behind us and you do realize how many you'll be cooking for, don't you?'

'I can count,' replied Jenny. 'I assume all the twelve men you were expecting have arrived. There are also you three and Meleeka. I think Buta and I can manage. Anyway I can call on Sara if I need her.'

As she left them sitting at the table, she went towards the stove, put on some water to boil and coffee into the pot, saying she would bring them a brew shortly.

Joseph, watching every graceful move she made, admired her courage and determination. He knew not many women would open a cookhouse in the middle of nowhere and do what Jenny was planning to do.

He let his gaze wander around the room and marvelled at the way Jenny had made it feel so homely. He thought of the men who would be arriving shortly and there was no doubt in his mind that Jenny would look after them well, seeing to their needs in giving them good food.

He thanked Buta when she brought the coffee then turned his attention to the conversation going on between Sara, Adam and Jamie.

When he'd drunk his coffee and said he was going outside, Jamie asked if he could accompany him. Sara, watching them both leave, turned to Adam saying, 'I cannot get over how Jamie has grown up and I am so glad you both decided to come over with the men.'

'So am I,' said Adam, 'yet it seems like only yesterday that I promised you I would one day visit Ilinka. Now here you are with a four-year-old son and another baby on the way. It does not seem possible the years have gone so fast.'

'What do you think of Meleeka?' she asked. 'Do you like him?'

'Very much so,' he replied. 'And I can see Meleeka and your father get on like a house on fire. There is certainly a special friendship between them. It seems your father was right when he told me it was destiny which brought them together and who are we to argue with destiny?'

Sara smiled as she asked him, 'And is it destiny that has brought you and Jamie to Ilinka?'

'To be truthful I do not know,' he replied. 'Though I must confess it was certainly a quick decision as well as most unusual how it all came about. I went to pay a visit to the farm, though for why I cannot say. I had only been there one day before. Anyway, when I arrived Jamie and his father were having a right ding-dong of a row. Jamie's father was telling Jamie he was too big for his boots and too knowledgeable for his own good. I did not interfere, I'd known for a long time, sooner or later that things between them would have come to a head. I went to the kitchen to have a cup of tea with Bessie and before I even sat myself down Bessie was saying, 'Them two be at it again, I can hear them in here. They do nought but argue from dawn to dust. 'Tis a pity Jamie's father cannot be thankful the lad's turned out so well.' I had to agree with her, yet I was also sorry for Jamie's father, seeing his son go from one extreme to the other. I don't think he could cope with the change in his son. When Jamie's tutorship came to an end, I wanted Jamie to come and work for me as a clerk. But Jamie loves the land and wanted to stay on the farm. That is more of less how we came to be here.

'Bessie and I were discussing the excitement in the village about the men coming to Ilinka and the families would follow later. Jamie came into the kitchen while we were talking and said he wished he was going with them. Then he asked me if it would be possible for him to go and perhaps look after your father's cattle.

'I decided to let him travel with the men. I knew your father would not object, and it would give Jamie a chance to sort himself out, away from the farm. Then I remembered my promise to you and decided to travel with them, and here I am!'

'I am so glad you both came,' said Sara. 'Has Jamie spoken to my father about the farming?'

'Oh yes,' Adam replied, and your father thinks it is a splendid idea. In fact he is going to find Jamie some land and build him a house. Jamie was thrilled to bits with the idea. He said it would be a great opportunity to make a new life for himself.'

Sara agreed that it would be, as she heard the wagons outside and went to help Jenny and Buta.

Jenny flopped into her bed, fatigued but happy. She was sure, now she had met the men, her little venture would be a success. The men were a cheerful bunch – there had been a lot of laughter as they ate. Afterwards Joseph called her over to meet them.

John and James Grant, the carpenters, she was already acquainted with. She'd met them at the farm when they did some repairs. She also knew Ray Peters, the stonemason. He came to the farm to visit Bessie, who was a friend of his mother's. The others she did not know. So as she was introduced to them she jokingly said, 'You will have to wear name tags until I get used to you all.'

'That won't take long,' Ray Peters chirped in, 'seeing we'll be living on your doorstep.' They all roared with laughter at his comment.

When the laughter died down Ray thanked her for making them a lovely meal, 'And I'm sure I speak for us all when I say it was much appreciated after the long trek it took us to get here, and if that is a sample of what is to come in the way of food, then I think we will all be getting as fat as pigs.'

Then one of them shouted, without the slightest touch of malice, 'Aye, and her bank balance will be getting fat as well, then us single blokes will be chasing after her seeing as she's no wed.'

Once again the room was filled with laughter, which she herself also joined in, taking no offence at what had been said.

When the men left to go to the bunkhouse, Joseph stayed behind. He watched her as she laid everything out ready for the men's morning breakfast. It had been decided Jenny would make breakfast and an evening meal for the men, also sandwiches if need be. He was glad for Jenny's sake that the men had suggested this. He cocked his eyebrow when he saw Jenny was brewing a pot of tea.

'Are we not drinking coffee tonight then?' he asked.

'I find it keeps me awake,' she told him. 'But if you prefer coffee, I will make you some.'

'Tea will suit me fine,' he said. 'I'll not stay long, you must be worn out.'

'I'm alright,' she said. 'It was the waiting that got me down. Not knowing whether you would arrive today or next week. I can get organized now. Buta is sending a couple of the young girls to help me.'

'That's a good idea,' said Joseph. 'By the way I've put a proposition to the men. They are agreeable, but it all depends on you, and what you wish to do.'

'What is the proposition?' she asked.

'I hope you won't be offended, though I think it will be in your own interest if the men are getting all they need from you, then you can keep tabs on what they spend and I will dock it from their wages. But as I said, it is entirely up to yourself.'

'The men will agree to do this?' she asked, seeing the logic in what Joseph was saying.

'Yes, they do,' he replied. 'In fact it was John Grant who gave me the idea. We had been discussing things on the way here and I was telling him about your venture when he said to me, "Being as there will not be much to spend my wages on, only food and drink, will you keep and save most of my wages for me? It will do me no good having my pockets filled with money I cannot spend. It will be too much of a temptation if the men start gambling. I am not against gambling but neither do I like to lose my hard-earned cash, and sometimes the wagers do get a bit out of hand."

'I told him I would take care of it for him, that's when I got the idea of you keeping tabs. I spoke about it with the others, and they all agreed to do the same as John. There are some men, Jenny, who prefer to gamble than fill their bellies. I am not saying these men are like that, but you can never tell and at least doing it this way I know the men will have good food in their belly, therefore they will do a good day's work, and you will also profit from it.'

Jenny laughed out loud as she said, 'Joseph Tyler, I did not think you could be so devious.'

'I am not being devious,' he said, pretending to be hurt by her words.

'I know you are not,' she said. 'But seeing as you will be banking the men's money, you might as well do the same for me. I think you should pay us interest.'

He saw the glint of mischief in her eyes as he said, 'You never know your luck. I will have to think about it. Now I best be going and let you get to your bed, you must be worn out.'

As Joseph was walking home, he wondered how Adam would like Ilinka. He could not believe his old friend had actually come to visit. He had no idea that at that very moment the magic of Ilinka had caught both Adam and Jamie. They were enthralled by their first sighting of the Blue Mountain. Adam reined his horse as the moon rose above the mountain – he had never seen anything so beautiful. Jamie felt the same as he reined his horse beside Adam. David and two of the braves who had come to help the men settle in rode on ahead. They had seen the moon rise over the mountain many times and like so many who live among the beauty of nature, they took the scene for granted.

Meleeka was riding with them, but when he saw the moon rising he too felt the magic. Then he smiled to himself as he glanced around to see Adam and Jamie both awestruck by the beauty of it, and he knew the magic of Ilinka had touched their hearts, as he rode towards the house.

As Adam gazed upon the scene before him, he marvelled at how accurately Joseph had described Ilinka. Many times while he'd been at work in his stuffy office he'd dreamed of one day coming here. But never in his wildest dreams could he have imagined the effect Ilinka would have upon him.

Then he heard Jamie saying, 'Sara told me how beautiful it was. I actually thought she was exaggerating, now I know she was not.'

'I know how you feel,' said Adam. 'I thought Joseph was doing the same.'

In unison they tapped their horses with their heel, then galloped towards the house, where Meleeka and Sara stood waiting for them. They were both smiling as if they knew some secrets they could not tell.

Adam felt like a boy again as he went hunting and fishing with the men of Ilinka. Dressed only in doeskin pants and wearing moccasins, his white body became so tanned he was beginning to look like a native.

It had tickled Jenny when she first saw Adam and Jamie dressed this way. Especially Adam, who's attire was usually so immaculate.

When she mentioned this to Adam, he admitted he felt a bit awkward. But the awkwardness soon left him as he came to admire this incredible tribe. They were so industrious, yet went about their tasks with not a care in the world. He admired the way Joseph and Meleeka worked together in planning the new settlement. It seemed to Adam as if destiny had ordained it.

One day as Adam came out of the forest, after being out with a hunting party, he gazed down and watched the men from England and the natives working together. That is how the good Lord meant it to be, he thought. There should be no need for all the bitterness and hatred that one kept hearing about.

Adam, himself, had never in his whole life been so content as he'd felt being here in this small community. There was freedom here, both in mind and spirit. He knew that when he returned home, it was going to take him a long time to settle down into his usual way of life.

Later when he spoke to Joseph and Jenny about these things, he told them, 'At least when I return I can put the men's families' minds at rest about the natives of Ilinka. In fact I shall write a letter to the newspaper telling them about my visit and of how the white man could learn a lot from the natives of this land if they treated them with the respect they deserve.'

Jenny, who agreed with all Adam was saying about the Ilinka tribe, was not so sure about other natives as she remembered what Joseph had told her about the preacher and his men, and how they got their comeuppance from Chief Whiteband.

She shuddered at the very thought of it as she asked, 'Do you think that will be wise Adam, including all the natives? After all, you have only met Meleeka and his tribe.'

Adam smiled as he replied, 'Treat people with respect, Jenny, and they will treat you likewise. But you have a point, and I hope with all my heart that in the years to come the new settlers will not interfere with the peacefulness of Ilinka. It is an enchanting place.'

Joseph, who was only half listening to them, reflected on how earlier in the day he'd had the very same thoughts as Adam about spoiling Ilinka.

He'd been inspecting the building site and was pleased with himself on how the work was coming along. In his mind's eye, each house was surrounded with a garden. There would be no back-to-back houses in Petraba like those in the slums in England. He imagined the tradesmen who would come, bringing life to the community. There would also be a school needed for the children, and a church. Then he began to wonder how it was all going to end. He'd smiled to himself when he thought about Jenny and remembered how she kept telling him that Petraba would just grow and grow. How many times had she said to him, 'When the settlers come, they will love it here. Then they will tell their kinfolk as well as their friends. Then before you know it, there will be all manner of people coming to settle here.' She had laughed when she told him this, but he knew she believed it would come true.

Meleeka also believed as Jenny did, that it would not take long for Petraba to become a township. 'What did you expect, Joseph?' he asked when they discussed the matter. 'Surely it was never your intention to build only a small settlement. Whatever would the white man do for a living? I am sure they would not be content to hunt and fish for a living as we do. Neither could the womenfolk be like ours. Why, they would think of themselves as going back in time, instead of forward. I know the people will have to adapt to a new beginning, starting from scratch as you would say. Those who will come will push forward. For they know of the things of which we know nothing. Myself and my tribe have simple souls, we are content with our simple way of living. We do not want our way of life to change. But in our hearts we have to accept that one day soon, we will have to.

'Your friend Adam at the moment is enjoying our simple way of life. But if he lived this way for many moons he too would become unsettled. Yes, he has seen so much of the other world.

'Jamie is also enjoying himself, but even he is looking forward to when his farm is ready. That is why I say the newcomers will push forward. It would be impossible for them not to do so.'

As Meleeka finished the long speech, Joseph looked into his eyes. He could see no hatred for what would become of this land below Ilinka, or for the people who one day would reside there. No, there was no hatred, there was only wisdom.

He smiled at this good friend of his as he said, 'I know what you say is right, my friend. But now the work is in progress I keep wondering if I am doing the right thing.'

Meleeka returned the smile as he said, 'Joseph, my friend, you must not think that way. It is your destiny to build a township and we both know it is. You and I will be custodians of it all as we watch the township grow.'

He came out of his reverie when he heard Jenny saying, 'Well, Adam, I don't know about you or Joseph here but I am ready for my bed. I will have to be up at the crack of dawn if I am to cook your breakfast before you leave. Not only yours, but the men as well, and Joseph's. Why, it will be like having a breakfast leaving party.'

Joseph and Adam both laughed at her as they rose from their chairs. Only Jenny could come out with an expression like that.

Joseph was the only one to accompany Adam down to the lake where he would get a boat to take him across. They spoke about many things on the journey, of their younger days and of Rosa. They also discussed the families who Adam would be sending to Ilinka. But as they stood on the jetty saying their last goodbyes Adam was unprepared for Joseph's parting shot when he said, 'We will be needing a lawyer Adam. How do you feel about coming to settle in Petràba yourself?'

The question was so unexpected, Adam could only blurt out, 'No way, Joseph. Though I have enjoyed every moment of my visit I am too set in my ways to uproot at my age. Besides, you know in the evenings back home how I like to relax in the gentlemen's club with all my cronies.'

'And you call that living?' Joseph asked. 'Why, look at you, man, you look years younger than when you first arrived.'

'I feel it,' said Adam. 'But the answer is still no.'

'So Meleeka was right about you,' Joseph said.

'Why? What did Meleeka say?'

'That you would soon become bored with our way of life because you have seen so much of the other world.'

'I haven't become bored, far from it,' Adam said indignantly. 'You know yourself, Joseph, I have my clients to attend to. You being one of them, and with all the work you've set before me, you should be the first to understand. I cannot come to Ilinka and pretend I am a young boy again with all the fishing, which I must confess is what I have been doing.'

'But I am not asking you to do that,' said Joseph. 'You will be working, you will have your own office and clientele. I know it will take time, but that time will come. And in the meantime you would be seeing a township grow.' Joseph could not help but smile as he added, 'Who knows, I might build a gentlemen's club.'

'And pigs might fly,' were Adam's departing words as he stepped into the boat waving goodbye to Joseph.

CHAPTER XI

When Adam arrived home he put all his energy into looking after Joseph's interests. First he assured the families of the men who were already in Ilinka that all was well with them. He also sent an article to the town's tabloid about Ilinka.

Soon he was preparing for the people from Joseph's birthplace to set off to their new life. He'd been surprised after one of the meetings how many of the young men of the village had approached him, asking if they could go. They were fed up, they said. With either having no work to go to, or if they had being paid a pittance.

It was a sad time in the village as the families and the young men prepared to leave, yet the elders who were staying behind understood. They might never see their loved ones again, but hopefully they would have a better life, in a new land.

The article in the tabloid also caught the imagination of the tradesmen of all kinds. Adam received so many letters asking for information, he had to employ a clerk to answer the letters. The interest pleased him, for he'd been assigned by Joseph to find businessmen willing to make a new life for themselves and bring industry to Petraba.

While all this was going on, he took on a new partner. He was so tied up with Joseph's affairs, he'd no time to spend on his other clients' needs. He was also surprised at how much Joseph's parting words came to mind. He found he could not dismiss them. There were many times when he got a moment's peace, he would daydream about Ilinka. Then he would imagine the development of Petraba. He would imagine Jenny in her cozy cookhouse, and wonder how she was faring. He once tried to close his mind on both Ilinka and Petraba, but found he could not do so. Then one day, he had to admit to himself that he had to go back. He had the strangest feeling that the magic of Ilinka was calling him.

And so, it was on the night he arranged a meeting with several businessmen, and was walking to the meeting place, that Joseph's words kept ringing in his ears: 'We will be needing a lawyer, Adam.'

As he went into the hotel, he smiled to himself as he imagined Joseph's face when he returned unexpectedly to Petraba, telling Joseph, 'I have just seen a pig flying.'

When the vision from the past faded from his mind, Simon sat on the hillside for quite a long while before he opened his eyes. When he did so, he lifted them heavenwards then called out, 'I know you are all up there in the skies above. All of you who's destiny it was to be brought together to found the township of Petraba.

'It was your future and your story. But, now all that belongs to history. You could not have known all those years ago that other townships would spring forth filling the wilderness with tall buildings and sprawling cities. The once long trek down to the lakes takes no time at all, and from Ilinka to the village of Joseph's birthplace takes less than a day or a night. You would not have believed, as you developed Petraba, that to travel so swiftly would ever be possible. Yet I am proud of the fact that my lineage is linked with the founders of Ilinka and Petraba. The blood of Meleeka and Sara runs through me. I am the one of who Cheeka spoke about.

'I have your chronicals of history being made. I read them often. Sometimes I wish I could have been with you for I am sure it must have been wonderful. There may have been unrest and fighting in this land, between the natives and the white man, and those natives lost everything. But Ilinka was always kept from harm's way, protected by some force that brought Meleeka and Joseph together.

'Today there is still unrest between those native tribes and the white people of this land. But there is also unrest all over the world, and this world has become smaller with the development of travel. The lands of many people are different now. Joseph would call it progress; of course he would be right to do so. For there is nothing wrong with progress. It is the hearts of some people which do not change. Their hearts are greedy for land, money and possessions.

'Even here, the land where those ancient tribes dwell, is still being taken, not by invaders as it was before, but by the laws of the land. I have no malice, that it is so. I feel only great sadness that the mother earth is being spoiled all over the world by those who know not the secrets of the land, as did those ancient tribes of long ago.'

Simon rose from the ground, stretching himself as he did so. Then he walked down the mountainside to the old graveyard. From an early age he'd been fascinated with the old gravestones. Even as a young child, if he went missing his mother knew where to find him. She could never understand what made him go there. When Simon was older he was searching for something in the loft when he was drawn towards an old leather trunk. It was there where he found the chronicals of the founding of Ilinka and Petraba.

Like the generations before him, he'd been told the story of Meleeka and Sara, and also of Sara's adoptive father. At the time, he could not understand about a white man being the grandfather of Meleeka and Sara's son. But once he'd read the chronicals, everything became clear to him, and he treated them like special jewels. There were other things in the trunk which fascinated him and he would spend many hours upstairs. When he started doing this, his mother first worried about him spending so much time indoors, but she became used to it.

She could not know that, as he read the chronicles, he could see in his mind's eye everything as if it was happening. It was as if he was watching a film on TV. Yet it was more than that. He felt he was there with them, as if he was actually in the film. He lived with them, walked beside them. The people became more real to him than those who lived around him.

Now, as he reached the graveyard, he stood between the cluster of graves where they were all buried. It seemed to him that even in death they would not be parted. He sought out the grave of Cheeka. Then knelt before it making a secret sign of his ancestors as he did so.

For a moment he gazed at the simple headstone with only Cheeka's name carved upon it. Then said out loud, 'You predicted many things,

Cheeka, all of which are coming true. People are turning to those with healing hands like Sara's. No longer are they thought to be witches. The healing plants are also being used, and are now known as alternative medicine. You also told of how one day someone from the lineage of Meleeka and Sara would bring the true Ilinka tribe together. The day is now near – they will be brought together as the great white spirit in the sky wants them to be.'

He moved over to the grave of Meleeka and Sara, then said, 'Your bloodline runs through me. Like Sara, I have the power to heal. Soon I will bring your tribe together. That is my mission.'

Then he moved over to Joseph's grave. He gazed at the headstone for a long time. Of all those he'd read about in the chronicals, and saw in his visions, this was the man he loved the best.

His voice was full of emotion as he began to say, 'Your blood may not run through me, but I and the generation that came before me have much to thank you for. You gave us life when you took into your home a destitute squaw. You could not save the life of the squaw, only the life of the child. And I thank you for saving Sara. For had you not done so, no bloodline would there now be.

'You gave us wealth, though wealth was something you never cared about. Your nature was more of a philanthropist for you helped all who came to Petraba. You gave so much, yet the more you gave away, there was so much more came back to you. Not only in monetary matters, but also in friendship and love. You were blessed in all three. The townspeople loved you – whoever needed help when they arrived at Petraba were sent to you, and you saw to their needs. As the township flourished and you became a prominent man.

'The time came to leave your humble cabin, and build a house fit for your status. You chose a site on the border of Ilinka and Petraba. Your house overlooked the township you created. But a short stroll through your back garden and you were back in Ilinka. The house still stands. It is my home, and is known as the Tyler residence. Though you had no sons to call your own, your name lives on. I hope it will do so for generations to come.

'I too am your namesake. My name is Joseph Simon Tyler. Though my mother prefers me to be known as Simon. She did not want me to become little Joseph or Joey, like so many of the Tylers before me. For ever since Sara's firstborn there has always been a Joseph Tyler.

'But tomorrow, I fly to England and the Tyler roots. It is there I will become Joseph Tyler, a name to be proud of. Yes, the farm still stands. Though it is tenanted by others, it is still in the Tyler name.

'It was your destiny to come to this land, now it is mine to go to yours. I have to seek out the ones of our tribe. The time of which Cheeka predicted is now. Whether my mission will be a long one, I do not know. But the farm will be my base.'

He kissed the headstone, then glanced over to the headstone of Jenny, and then to Adam's. 'You also played your part,' he said, before turning away. He walked to the foot of the mountain then stood before it, just as Meleeka had done all those years ago.

When the voice spoke to him it was so loud he felt that those whose bodies lay in the graveyard would surely be listening, as the voice boomed out, *'The mission you are being sent upon is most urgent. There is much unrest in this world. The ancient tribes of long ago went through nothing compared with the slaughter of this age with the thunder of bombs that rage about the earth. If your mission is not completed it could be disastrous for the earth world. You will be guided in finding the separated tribe of Ilinka, but you must also use your own power in seeking them out. The Great White Spirit is becoming angry with the ways of the earth world. He wants this special tribe brought together. For it is through them mankind can be saved. Time is running out.'*

Simon stood for a long time in the silence which followed the warning. Then he bowed his head to the mountain before walking away.

PART III

CHAPTER I

When Joseph heard the captain telling everyone they were now flying over Shannon and would be arriving at Manchester on time, he felt the excitement inside him rising. Even more so than when he'd said goodbye to his parents at Toronto Airport to embark upon a journey he'd dreamed about since being a young boy. It would not be long now before he arrived at the birthplace of his pioneering ancestor.

He thought, not for the first time, how strange it was that throughout the generations before him, not one of the tribe of Tyler showed any interest in visiting the farm, even though, each and every one of them had been told the story of how the white man and his daughter Sara had come to dwell with Meleeka and his tribe and of how the Tyler name came into being.

He could understand them thinking that no blood of the white man ran through them, for their bloodline came from his adopted daughter Sara, a true Ilinka. But he was proud of their history and prouder still that he bore the white man's name, which had been passed on to the eldest son since Sara's firstborn.

During the long journey, he'd silently repeated the name Joseph Tyler to himself, for his second name was Simon, the name his mother insisted he be known by, so as not to become little Joseph or Junior like so many other Tylers before him. The name would stick, she said, even when he grew into manhood. He smiled to himself, remembering her words at the airport. 'I suppose,' she'd said, 'that when you reach England, you will be calling yourself Joseph.' Before answering her, he'd gazed at both his parents; they would never know, as he'd read the chronicles from the attic, how many times he'd wished they would call him Joseph and not Simon. He could understand his mother's reasons for not doing so, but the first Joseph Tyler had become so real to him, he thought of him, not as he had been told, as Sara's adoptive father, but as someone special, and though it was true that no blood of Joseph Tyler ran through the Ilinka tribe, if it had not been for him, they would never have existed. So when he finally answered his mother, he told her proudly, 'Yes, when I reach England, I will be known as Joseph Tyler.'

When he'd said this, it had been time to leave them. He hugged his father first, then his mother, and he was pleased when they both said in unison, 'Take care of yourself in England, Joseph.'

He felt the wheels of the aircraft touch the tarmac. As they did so he wondered if the farm would be anything like the painting of it that hung above the fireplace back home. He supposed the farm would be changed, for the painting was nearly 200 years old. It had been given as a wedding gift to Meleeka and Sara. To him, the painting always seemed to dominate the room and if he was in there, no matter whatever he was doing, his eyes would many times be drawn towards the picture. Yet others of the tribe never gave a second glance towards it. He suspected that even his father would like the picture taken down, or at least, not returned to its proper place when the room was redecorated, but he had not the courage to do so for the painting had been hung there for so long it was like a mascot.

All thoughts of the painting left him. As he stepped out of the plane, he was so excited as he went down the steps that when his feet touched the tarmac he wanted to raise his hands to the spirit in the sky and kiss the ground he walked upon. Instead he followed the other passengers and silently thanked the spirit in the sky for choosing him to come to this part of the world on his mission.

He knew that this mission was special and of great importance, for when he'd arrived home from his visit to the old graveyard, he'd showered and performed his nightly ritual. It was then that the spirit of Meleeka come to him. Meleeka told him that the time had come to find the lost ones of his own tribe. 'You will be guided,' he said, 'as to why it is your destiny to find the lost ones of my tribe and how it came to be. It is when your mission is completed that Cheeka's prediction that the Ilinkas from the four corners of the earth will be brought together will come true.'

When the vision of Meleeka faded, he'd sat for a long time wondering about what Meleeka had told him. There was nothing in the chronicles about any of the tribe leaving Ilinka and going to England. He'd read them often enough, so there was no chance that he'd missed such an important event.

He smiled to himself, as he showed his passport – he could not wait for his mission to begin.

Peter Oakley, waiting for the arrival of Joseph Tyler at Manchester Airport, wondered if the village gossip about the Tyler family was true. Once it was known a Tyler was to visit the farm, the village grapevine became rife with rumours and hearsay. Even though not one of the villagers could even remember a Tyler living on the farm it did not stop the story going around that the farm belonged to a tribe of Indians. The story, it seemed, had been told in some families for generations – even old Archie could confirm this.

Whatever the truth is, Peter thought, it is not for me to question. The Tylers can be Eskimos for all I care, so long as they don't interfere with the management of the place.

He loved the farm. So did his wife Barbara and their children, Jordana and Ashley. If they were to lose it now, it would break their hearts.

Being manager of Topmount Farm was like a dream come true. He'd been working on the land even when he was but a youngster. His mates would be off playing football or cricket but he would go and help the local farmers. When he left school he'd no option but to go and work down in the mines – his ma needed the money. And even though his heart cried out for the land and the open air, he never grumbled about the hard and dangerous work.

When he married Barbara he left the coal mines finding a job as a farm labourer. Though his wage would be a lot less than working in the mines, it did not bother them, for at least there was a rent-free cottage.

Over the years he'd worked hard until he became a farm manager. When his last employer sold the farm and all its land for development he'd been lucky to get the job of running Topmount Farm – in fact he felt that this job was heaven-sent, for never before had he worked anywhere like it.

Their home was the original farmhouse and not some pokey cottage, neither was there anyone above him telling him what to do. The farm was well stocked and he'd been given carte blanche to run the farm as he wanted. 'All we ask,' said Mr Johnson, agent for the farm, ' is that you take care of Topmount as if it were your own.'

He came out of his reverie when he heard someone call a greeting from the waiting crowd. He lifted the name sign above his head, saying to himself as he did so, Please God, let this man be here on a friendly visit and not to take the farm away from us. Not now, with Jordana starting the riding stables and Ashley home from agricultural college.

As he came out through customs, Joseph scanned the waiting crowd for some sign of the man who was to meet him. He smiled to himself when he saw the name Joseph Tyler in bold lettering. His heartbeat quickened as he walked towards the man holding up the sign, knowing he would soon be on the last stage of the journey to a place that he had dreamed about since childhood.

When Peter saw the handsome young man heading towards him, he smiled, holding out his hand. As they shook hands and introduced themselves. Peter knew he was going to like this young man whatever the purpose of his visit was about. His smile was genuine, his handshake firm like a man's should be.

He'd been worried about having a stranger come to stay with them but when Mr Johnson telephoned him saying he'd had a request from Mr Tyler Snr. asking whether it would be possible for his son to stay at Topmount Farm during his visit to England, he could do no more than say yes.

As he helped Joseph with his luggage, Peter admired the fine leather cases with the initials J.S.T. embossed on them in gold lettering. ''Tis a fine piece of craftsmanship,' he said.

'My mother made them as a going-away present,' Joseph told him.

'Leathercraft is a hobby of hers.'

Weaving in and out of the motorway traffic, Peter glanced at the young man sitting beside him. He seemed deep in thought, for which Peter was thankful – he hated having to make conversation when he was driving, especially when the roads were busy.

Joseph felt rather then saw Peter's glance but he was content to travel in silence. Through the window he could see the panoramic view of the moorlands, a magnificent sight with the different hues of green and brown.

Below him there was pastureland, where cattle grazed, oblivious to the speeding traffic above. He wondered what the first Joseph Tyler and his daughter Sara would think if they were here today, with traffic speeding all around them, yet only a glance away was the serenity of a bygone age.

A moment later, the view was gone and they came onto a slip road that led onto a dual carriageway. It was here that he saw the signpost, Maraldon Village, One Mile. He glanced at his watch, then smiled. He'd accomplished in less than twenty-four hours what must have taken Joseph and Sara weeks to achieve.

Peter turned down a side road with a few modern houses on either side, then it was like going back in time as they came upon a long, winding, cobbled road with not a house in sight. The road was very narrow with high banking covered in thistles and weeds on one side and a river on the other. Beyond the river there was a field and woodland. Joseph held his breath as he watched the wheels of the Range Rover come perilously close to the edge of the road where three feet below them the river flowed. He could also hear the overgrown bracken scraping the other side of the Range Rover as Peter manoeuvred around the narrow bends.

He gave a sigh of relief when the river went off in another direction and they came to the edge of the moorland. The hills were so high, it seemed to Joseph from where he was sitting they could be touching the sky. It was here the cobbled road came to an end, the road becoming a dirt track that led up into the hillside.

'Soon be there now,' Joseph heard Peter saying as he manoeuvred the Range Rover around a sharp bend. Joseph marvelled at Peter's skilled driving as he'd to reverse the Range Rover three times before he could straighten up to get the car around the bend, one false move and the car would have been down a six-foot drop. They then came upon a narrow lane with stone walls on either side, a lane so narrow, Joseph wondered if it was wide enough to take the Range Rover but once again Peter's handling of the machine amazed him. As the car edged its way up the lane, he could see over the walls and into the fields where cattle grazed. Peter swung around another sharp bend and the farm came into view.

It was as he'd always imagined it would be, with its grey-stoned walls and mullioned windows. He could not see the courtyard or the steps which led to the garden, but he did not doubt that they would still be there. There's so much history stems from that house, he thought, as Peter came to a halt in the farmyard at the side of the house.

Peter heard Joseph gasp. As he switched off the engine, he turned towards him, then smiled, seeing the look of awe on Joseph's face as he gazed out at the panoramic view. It came as no surprise to Peter – the view affected most people that way. Then he said, still smiling, 'It's worth the bumpy ride if only for the magnificent view, isn't it Joseph?'

Reluctantly, Joseph turned towards Peter saying, 'I've never seen anything like it. I feel as though I'm looking down from the heavens above. Why. you can see for miles and miles?'

His gaze came closer to home, to the lush mowing meadow that sloped gently downhill towards a stone wall that separated the grazing cattle from the meadowland.

Beyond the cattle there were large and small hillocks all blending together. He could not see the dangerous bend that Peter so expertly manoeuvred around but in the distance the cobbled road was visible. Above the high banking of the roadside, which could not be seen as they travelled, were row upon row of houses.

'Is that part of the village?' Joseph asked, pointing to where the houses stood.

'No,' Peter replied, 'that is a housing estate built onto the outskirts.

The village is over there to your left. We cannot get to the village from here by car, the old cart tracks have long been overgrown. In fact, it is much quicker to walk down to the village than to go all the way round by car. But come along, we cannot sit here all day admiring the view. Barbara will be waiting for us to go inside.'

As Peter unloaded Joseph's luggage, Joseph admired the front of the house, telling Peter the house was a true likeness of the painting that hung over the fireplace back home. On hearing this, Peter, leading the way towards the back of the house, towards the kitchen door, wondered why, if the Tylers thought so much about the farm as to keep a painting of it over the fireplace, none until now had ever paid a visit to the farm. He voiced his thoughts to Joseph.

'It has hung there for generations,' Joseph told him. 'It was a wedding gift, given to the ancestral grandparents, Meleeka and Sara. Who painted the picture, I have no idea. It is dated seventeen ninety-four and initialled D.C. It is a picture that I love dearly and I too have wondered why no one from our family has ever been interested in visiting the farm. When I asked my father about it, he told me that Topmount Farm belongs to the white man's country, it is better that the white man take care of it for us.'

I hope his father does not change his mind, thought Peter as he opened the kitchen door.

Later that night as he stood gazing out of the bedroom window Joseph could see the street lamps lighting up the distant towns and villages. He marvelled at the sight of them, for, with the darkness of the night, he could have been three thousand miles away on the mountainside of the Ilinka, looking down onto the city, as he'd done two nights ago; the view was much the same.

He'd known that night that when his long journey came to an end, he would feel as though he'd come home. Why he'd felt this way he could not say but he knew now that it was true. As soon as he'd entered the farmhouse, he'd felt an affinity with it that he'd never once felt in the Tyler residence back home.

Lighting a cigarette, he glanced at his watch – it was two a.m., and he'd been awake more than twenty-four hours, yet he felt no need of sleep. His thoughts turned to the Oakley family and how they'd made him feel so welcome and not as a stranger in their midst.

As Barbara gave him a tour of the house, she'd told him he must make himself at home with them, he must come and go as he pleased and was not to keep calling them Mr and Mrs Oakley, but Peter and Barbara, as everyone else did. 'Besides,' she said, 'calling me Mrs Oakley makes me feel old and I'm not decrepit yet.'

Ashley and Jordana had also been friendly towards him and the whole family had spent the evening with him in the village pub. They were all sitting out in the garden, relaxing after the evening meal, when Jordana suggested strolling down to the local. They all laughed when Ashley said, 'What a good idea, I could just murder a pint.'

Peter said it was up to Joseph, after all, Joseph must be tired with all the travelling. With all eyes turned upon him, he'd agreed with Ashley that it was a good idea and he was looking forward to his first English pint. 'That's settled then,' Jordana said, smiling at him, 'we'll walk down the back lane as it will be the quickest way.'

Coming out through the back garden gate he'd been surprised they'd to walk in single file. The lane was so narrow with its overgrown banking and stone walls on either side, separating the lane from the mowing meadows.

Making their way down the hillside, he heard Peter telling him from behind that this was once the old cart track, that led from the village to the farm. 'As you can see, it is years since it's been used for any form of transport. There are many such tracks branching out from the village square to where the people once dwelt in cottages and hamlets.'

Jordana, walking in front of him, turned her head around saying, 'I'll take you riding tomorrow. We can follow the old roads. It will be an interesting ride for you.'

'I'll look forward to that,' he told her, hoping the old roads would be wider than this one.

After walking in single file for about a quarter of a mile, they came upon a wider dirt track, with a stream running beside it, and a field and woodland beyond. Coming around the next bend in the lane, he'd been unprepared for the sensation he'd felt on seeing a grey-stoned wall cottage surrounded by a garden, so unprepared, he'd stopped dead in his track. A moment later the sensation was gone. But he knew by then the cottage would somehow be connected with his mission and he'd stood there for a few more minutes staring at it.

Peter, seeing his interest in the cottage, told him it belonged to old Archie. 'A right character he is. You might meet him tonight. He still likes his pint, even though he's ninety-eight.'

Stubbing out his cigarette, he smiled to himself. He'd met old Archie and Peter was right, he was a character, so too were some of the other locals he'd met in the pub. He'd got the feeling, though they'd made a fuss of him, that had he not been with the Oakleys and been introduced, he would not have been made so welcome. The villagers were close knit and he would have been a stranger in their midst. Close knit or not he thought, as he walked towards the bed, I know I am going to like Maraldon village and its inhabitants.

Lying in bed, he remembered the telephone conversation with his father before coming upstairs. He'd told his father all about the day's events and how he liked the Oakleys. He must have sounded enthusiastic about it all, for his father told him before putting down the receiver, 'Don't you be getting any ideas about staying there for long. I know how fascinated you have been with the history of it, but you have a mission to fulfil and when that mission is completed I want you home.'

As he put down the receiver he wondered if all fathers spoke to their grown-up offspring as if they were still a child. But, like his father, he knew the mission was important and that whatever his feelings for Maraldon and the farm, the moment it was completed, he would have to return home. He did not need his father to remind him. The warning had been given.

Switching off the bedside lamp, he wondered how his mission would begin and where it would lead him. He was not troubled about it, for he knew the spirits in the sky would guide him in whatever he had to do.

CHAPTER II

When daylight broke and though he'd slept for only three hours, he awoke alert and ready for the new day – a day he was looking forward to. He was to go riding with Jordana, then afterwards he was to visit Archie at the cottage.

Before going to the bathroom, he laid out his doeskin trousers on the bed, ready for when he returned. He showered quickly, not wanting to disturb the others, though he knew they would soon be up and about, for farmers were also early risers.

On entering the bedroom he opened the curtains and the window before taking off his dressing gown and getting into the doeskinned trousers. He walked back to the open window, breathing in the fresh morning air until he could feel it deep inside him. He held it there for a few moments, then slowly released it, making a whistling sound as he did so. This was the start of his daily ritual, a sacred rite that was performed each morning and also at night.

He took several deep breaths until every muscle in his strong, lithe body was relaxed. He swayed his body into a series of movements that to an onlooker would seem like some form of exercises done in slow motion. But to him it was a ritual, that brought the spirits of his ancestors before him. He could see them so clearly, like visitors who had entered the room. When the ritual came to a close, there was only the spirit of Meleeka standing before him, dressed in his chieftain outfit. He stood proudly before the spirit of Meleeka, waiting for Meleeka to take off the feathered headdress and hand it to him, saying these words as he took the headdress from Meleeka and placed it upon his own head,

'Let me not bring shame to these feathers.

Give me strength this day, to do what has to be done.
Let my mind be pure, my heart loving.
Protect me in all things.
Let me speak what has to be spoken,
Hear what has to be heard
And see what has to be seen.'

He stroked the feathers of the headdress that were invisible to the human eye, and bowed to Meleeka, who then disappeared. In the evening he would thank the spirits in the sky for taking care of him and return the headdress.

He changed out of the doeskin trousers into jeans and check shirt. By the time he'd finished dressing he could hear Peter and Ashley bringing in the cows for milking.

Later, out riding with Jordana, he marvelled at the vastness of the moorland. They had been riding for miles, following the old cart tracks, Jordana pointing out places of interest, like the old coal mines that once went deep into the hillsides, all capped now for safety's sake. They had also come across the ruins of an old flannel mill and the mill workers' cottages which in the days long gone would have been their own little hamlet. There was not much to show they had been there. Only if you poked about in the long grass would you find evidence that the place ever existed. It was the same when they found the ruins of what were once small farms, where the hill farmers had made their living.

'They had to leave them,' Jordana told him, 'to make way for the gathering ground, when the reservoir was built. There is so much history among these hills,' she said wistfully, 'I often wonder about the people who dwelt here.'

The farther they rode, the steeper the hills became, until at last they came to rest on the highest of them all. It was here that Jordana dismounted, telling him it was her favourite place. 'From here,' she said, 'you can view nearly the whole of Lancashire, turn around and you're looking onto the county of Yorkshire.'

He admired the magnificent views of both counties, then seeing

Jordana was settling herself on the ground, he also dismounted, saying, as he did so, 'It would make a good vantage point if ever the two counties went to war again.'

'I hope they never do that,' she said, 'for I would not know which side to take. I was born in Yorkshire, yet I love living in Maraldon. So you can guess why this place is so special to me. I can look upon both my worlds and it is only natural my Yorkshire roots still have a pull on me. Do you not think so?'

'Yes,' he replied, 'I think it would be most unnatural to forget one's roots.'

'Is that why you've come to visit the farm,' she asked, ' because of your ancestral roots?'

'Partly,' he answered, for he could not tell her the real reason for his visit, yet neither could he lie to her.

So he told her about finding the chronicles in the loft. 'Would you like to hear about them and of our history?' When she said she would, he settled down beside her leaving the horses, also in need of a rest, to graze contentedly.

As she listened to his beautiful drawling accent, she could not help but think how lucky she was, on this lovely sunny morning, to be sitting in her favourite place listening to a true saga, of history being made.

'Oh Joseph,' she said, when he finished telling her, 'what a romantic tale that was. And to think that it all began at the very farm where I now live. I have loved the farmhouse since I first set eyes upon it. I shall adore it even more now, knowing that all those years ago, a young man defied his father for the girl he loved and in doing so, changed not only his own life but a tribe of Indians as well. Although he sired no sons of his own, his name lives on through those of a different culture that he chose to live with.'

As she said all this, her face was aglow with happiness, then she became serious, saying, 'So the village gossip is true. We didn't know whether to believe it or not.'

'Why? What are they saying?' he asked.

She blushed with embarrassment before replying, 'When word got around that you were coming to visit, the gossip in the village became rife bout the Tyler clan, originating from a tribe of Indians.'

'Does that bother you,' he asked, 'knowing I am a fully-fledged redskin?'

She smiled, saying, 'Don't be daft, the colour of one's skin does not matter, it is what is inside that counts. Don't you go thinking that others will be bothered either, for now you're here, they'll be finding something else to talk about.' Again her face became serious and she turned away from him.

'What troubles you now?' he asked, not liking the look he'd seen as she turned away. As he waited for her to tell him, he wondered what he could have done or said to upset her. When at last she turned towards him, he saw the sadness in her eyes.

Then she said, 'You tell me you have come to visit the farm because you have dreamed of doing so for a long time but I also think there is another reason and you do not wish to tell me about it.'

'Whatever makes you think that?' he asked, surprised by what she said, for he knew there was no way she could know of the real reason he had come.

He was relieved when he heard her telling him, 'My father has been worried ever since he heard you were coming. He thinks you are going to take the farm away from us.'

He laughed out loud at the very thought of it, then said, 'Jordana, you would not make a farmer out of me in a hundred years, so your father is wrong in his thinking. Besides, your father is the tenant, so surely he has some rights to protect him. I could not arrive here and just take away that tenancy.'

'That is why my father is worried,' she said. 'He is only the farm manager and there is a vast difference between being a manager and holding a tenancy.'

He saw the smile come back upon her face when he told her, 'I'll speak to your father about it and see what can be done. Surely arrangements can be made to make him feel more secure? Though I cannot promise anything, for I do not know the ins and outs of the matter. But I do admit there is another reason for my visit and if it were possible for me to tell you, I would.'

She interrupted him saying, 'As long as it does not affect us staying at the farm then it is your own business, I do not wish to pry. Knowing you'll speak to my father and put his mind at rest is all that matters. Now, if you're going to visit Archie, we had better be setting off back.'

He rose to his feet, and held out his hand to help her up. He was surprised at the electrifying sensation that ran through him as their hands touched, yet Jordana gave no sign of his touch affecting her. It was the first time he'd taken hold of her hand. When Peter had introduced him to Barbara and Ashley, they went outside to find Jordana who was astride her horse, ready to go riding. She'd smiled down at him saying, 'Welcome to Topmount Farm, Joseph. I'll see you later.' Now he wondered why the sensation he got from Jordana was missing from the others.

Mounting his horse he heard her saying, 'I'll let you lead the way home, Joseph, then if you come out riding alone you'll not be getting lost.'

He grinned at her saying, 'Have you forgotten already? I'm a fully-fledged redskin and we never get lost.'

Her eyes lit up with mischief as she said, 'Prove it to me then.'

CHAPTER III

Walking down the lane on his way to visit Archie, Joseph mulled over his conversation with Peter – he could understand now Peter's anguish about his sudden visit to the farm. Especially after Peter explained to him that as he was only the farm manager, he could be given notice to quit at any time.

He hoped he'd put Peter's mind at rest, telling him that he would have a word with his father, for his father, like himself, thought that for a long time now the farm had been tenanted and would not have been seen to by a farm manager.

'It was,' Peter told him, 'but apparently the last tenant was not much of a farmer and Mr Johnson told me, rather than risk having another bad tenant, for it was a devil of a job to get rid of them, it was decided that it would be much simpler to stock the farm and then find a good manager. And I was the lucky one who got the job.'

He smiled when Peter said this, and told him, 'I'm pleased that I waited until now to visit the farm. I might not have been made welcome by the other fellow.'

'I don't think you would have been,' Peter said, 'for according to Mr Johnson, it was good riddance to bad rubbish when the other chap left.'

As Archie's cottage came into view, he dismissed all other thoughts from his mind, for he knew it was from this cottage that the first link of his mission would begin and not from the farm as he'd expected.

He could see Archie leaning over the garden gate. He wondered if Archie was looking out for him, though they'd arranged no special time for his visit. This was confirmed as he approached with Archie saying, 'I was just wondering if you would come. 'Tis surprising how many say they'd come and visit me, then never do. Why they say things they don't mean I'll never know.' He beamed at Joseph as he opened the gate for him. 'I'll make us a pot of tea,' he said, closing the gate behind Joseph.

On entering the house, Joseph thought he'd walked into a time warp. The room, much larger than one might imagine from the outside of the house, was filled with antique furniture and bric-a-brac; even the walls were filled with old pictures and samplers. Archie, seeing his surprise said, 'I told thee last night about my antiques, did thee not believe me?'

Before he could answer, Archie told him to sit down and make himself at home. 'Kettle's on boil. I'll brew the tea, you can look around later but there's naught for sale, mind.' Joseph did as he was told, though he was itching to take a look around. Even the fireplace was the cast-iron type where the kettle boiled on the hob.

He watched Archie reach for the tea caddy above the mantel shelf and put the tea into the pot. He dare not speak as he watched Archie brewing the tea. Archie had one foot resting on the rug, his other foot was over the brass fender, his trouser leg very close to the fire. In one hand he held the teapot and with a piece of rag shielding the other, he took hold of the kettle, pouring the boiling water into the pot. Not until Archie reached the table, resting the teapot on it, did Joseph let out a sigh of relief.

Archie, not knowing how worried Joseph had been watching him brew the tea, gave it a quick stir before pouring it into the two beakers as he said, 'I have an electric kettle in the kitchen but I prefers me tea brewed this way.'

Joseph could not help himself saying as Archie handed him the beaker, 'It seems to me a dangerous way to make a pot of tea.'

'It might be,' said Archie, 'but old habits die hard and I'm ninety-eight years old, so I'm not going to change me ways now, neither in the way I brew me pot of tea or giving up me baccy and me pint. Folks make me laugh, trying to tell me I shouldn't be doing this and I shouldn't be doing that. Some even think I should have been six feet under years ago, just because I like me ale and baccy. Or that it is about time I went to live in one of them old folks' homes. They think I'm too old to look after myself, having no family to take care of me, but I tell them, I was born in this house and I intend to die here.' He chuckled as he shuffled across to the chair opposite Joseph. He took a swig of his tea then smacked his lips together as if to prove his point about how the tea was brewed.

When they finished drinking their beakers of tea, Archie showed Joseph around the house. Joseph was fascinated with all the old furniture and bric-a-brac. He'd told Archie the night before about his little antique shop back home and every time he admired something, Archie would say, 'I'll not be selling any of it so don't you be asking to buy anything. Why, most of this stuff's been here long before I was born. Me great grandfather bought this house, furniture and all, so nothing will be sold until I'm dead and buried.'

'I wouldn't dream of asking you to sell me anything,' Joseph told him. 'I just love to admire anything that is old, especially if there is some history behind it and I am sure there is plenty of history which could be told about this house and its contents.'

He said this hoping that Archie would know something about it and if there was the spirits of his ancestors would let him see what had to be seen.

He was rewarded with Archie telling him, 'Oh aye, lad, there be plenty of history in this house and part of it belongs to you. Come, let us go and sit by the fire, we can have a smoke while I tell you about it. We might as well have a drop of whisky,' said Archie, going towards a cupboard and taking out two glasses and a bottle of Bells Whisky.

As he watched Archie pouring the whisky into the glasses, Joseph wondered what the old man would reveal to him. He'd known last night in the pub that he was being drawn towards Archie. He'd been standing at the bar in conversation with Barbara but his eyes kept wandering through the open door of the Tap Room onto the old man playing dominoes with Peter and two other men.

He'd ordered a round of drinks, asking the landlord to include one for the old man. Jordana, on hearing this, said, 'That's old Archie. I never saw him come in or I would have introduced you to him.' 'Perhaps your father will when I take the drinks over. Or are you coming with me?' She'd smiled, her eyes twinkling, then told him, 'Ladies are not allowed into the Tap Room, not in this pub anyway.'

As he carried the drinks into the Tap Room the game of dominoes came to an end. Peter and Archie moved over to another table letting two other men take their places. He set the drinks down, joining them at the table. By the end of the night he'd realized that in some way Archie would be of help to him in his mission.

He came out of his reverie when he heard Archie saying, 'Here's thy whisky, lad. Cheers.' They clinked glasses and Archie sat down opposite him, but it was not until Archie lit his cigarette and was sitting comfortably that he said to Joseph, 'It seems sort of queer, you sitting there and me about to tell you a tale about your ancestry. Because when I was a nipper, me and me ma spent many a cold evening sitting around the fireside whilst she told me stories. She was a good storyteller, me ma, some she'd make up but others were true. Me favourite was a true story that had been told to her by her grandfather. It was about young Master Tyler who once lived at the farm and who ran off with a wench from the tavern because his father would not let him wed her. They went to America and Master Tyler finished up living with a tribe of Indians. Nobody thought they would ever see Master Tyler again but they did and he became a legend around here, for when he did return, it was to claim his inheritance and soon after half the village followed him across the sea. But I suppose you know all about that?' Archie asked as he looked towards Joseph.

'Yes I do,' Joseph replied, 'and as you say it is true.'

'Ah, well,' said Archie, 'now we come to the interesting bit and it concerns this house. Years later Master Tyler returned to the village again. He bought this house for his housekeeper at the farm. It seems, so the story goes, that when Master Tyler returned for the third time he brought with him a young pregnant girl. You can imagine the gossip in the village after he'd bought the house and installed his housekeeper and the girl, before sailing across the sea again. Everyone thought he was the cause of the young girl's plight. But they were wrong and the gossips were in for a bigger shock when the baby was born. For it was of mixed blood: it was part redskin and a boy.'

Archie chuckled when he saw the look of dismay upon Joseph's face. 'You knew naught about that, did you?'

'No I didn't,' Joseph answered, wondering why there had been nothing in the chronicles, especially as the birth of the baby had been common knowledge in the village. But he knew now that it would be from this village the search would begin to find the lineage of the child.

Though he was disappointed when Archie told him that there were no descendants from the child ever lived in the village, the mother took the child away when he was just a bairn. It did not worry him, the spirits of his ancestors would now let him see how it came to be. They would show him the whole story, he would see it in his mind's eye as if he was watching a film on TV.

He'd known from when he first found the chronicles in the loft and as he read them, could see in his mind's eye the history of his ancestors being made, that he had been given a special gift, and now as he listened to Archie, he became impatient to get back to his room at the farm. For now, the spirits of his ancestors were ready to reveal to him the secret that had been kept from all the generations of the Tylers. For he'd no doubt in his own mind and from what the spirit of Meleeka had already told him that the boy child, born in Maraldon, was the grandson of Meleeka and Sara. Why there had been no leak ever to come from the village of the baby's birth, he could not imagine. For as Archie had said, when Master Tyler returned home after his second visit, half the village followed him. Surely he thought, there must have been some sort of correspondence between the villagers and their loved ones. He also wondered why the baby was born in Maraldon and not Ilinka, after all, the first Joseph Tyler would have been the baby's great-grandfather, so why bring the mother here and leave her?

Then he remembered something his own grandfather once told him: 'There is a reason for all things, as there is also a time.' He smiled to himself as he thought about it. For he knew the time was near for the secret to unfold, and as it did so, the reason would unfold with it.

He offered Archie a cigarette, even though he wanted to get away as quickly as possible to see what the spirits would reveal. He thought it would be impolite to just get up and leave, so as he flicked his lighter he said, 'I will have to be going as soon as I've smoked this.' As Archie bent towards the flame of the lighter to light his cigarette, Joseph saw above Archie's head the face of Meleeka. He knew then he would have no need to hurry back to the farm for it would be here in this house that the spirit of Meleeka would show to him what had to be seen. A moment later he was taking the unsmoked cigarette out of Archie's hand. Archie was sleeping like a baby, so relaxed was he in his chair. Joseph quickly stubbed out his cigarette then closed his eyes. No sooner had he done so than the things that Meleeka wanted him to know began to appear.

CHAPTER IV

Emma Kyersh left Liverpool when she was six years old. Her father was a doctor and as Emma was a sickly child, he decided that the streets of Liverpool were no place for her.

His wife worried about Emma constantly and he'd seen so much death and disease amongst young children that he could not bear to think what might happen to her.

When he'd suggested that they go and make a new life for themselves in America, his wife needed no persuading. Neither his wife nor himself had any close kinfolk and a colleague from the hospital was interested in buying the house. So within a few months from him suggesting it, they were ready to set sail.

It was whilst they were on board ship that he heard about the township of Petraba, which was still under construction. When he heard about this he decided that was where they would make their home. He knew it would be an horrendous journey but a new township and a new beginning for them. The two seemed to go together. He wondered for a moment about Emma. Would the journey be too long a trek for one so young? Then he dismissed the thought. The sea voyage was doing Emma the power of good – he'd never seen her so bright and full of life.

When they finally reached Petraba, the long journey had not taken its toll on Emma but on his wife. He was surprised to find when he reached the town that there was no hotel. He was sent to see a Mr Tyler. 'You'll be alright,' said the carpenter who sent him, 'Mr Tyler will find you somewhere to live.'

Mr Tyler found him a place to rent. The house was fully furnished and the rent he was asking was but a pittance. Besides, he had a sick wife to attend to, so he could not be too choosy. The house would be satisfactory until they found out if they liked the place, then if they did, he would have a house built to his own liking.

He did not know, as he was putting his wife into bed, that the daughter of Mr Tyler was telling her father, 'The newcomer has a very sick wife; she will die before the next sunrise.'

'Is it too late for you to help her?' her father asked.

'Yes,' she replied, 'for already the Lord of the sky calls for her.'

Emma could not understand what was happening. It seemed a long time since her father told her that they were going on a big adventure and when they arrived at their destination they would all live happily ever after.

She had to admit, though, that all the time they'd spent on the big ship, they had lots of fun She'd also enjoyed riding in a coach pulled by horses. Neither had she minded crossing the big lake in a boat that smelled of fish. Or of riding in an old cart pulled by two old nags that brought them here. She supposed all this was what her father called an adventure.

But since they arrived her father had done nothing but cry. And this morning, she had seen her mother asleep in a big box which afterwards they had put in a deep hole. As the box went into the hole, she'd felt her father grip hold of her hand and squeeze it tight. She had not glanced up at her father. He would be crying and she did not like to see him cry. He'd told her it was because her mother was dead and that they would not see her mother again. But she had seen her mother again when she'd crept into the room where she'd been forbidden to go. She thought, when she saw her mother lying there, how happy her father would be when she told him about finding her mother, who had not left and gone to Heaven, but was asleep in a big box. It would have to wait, though, until all the strangers that were filling the house had left.

But when the strangers prepared to leave, her father had lifted her up into his arms and everyone waited. A man opened the door to the forbidden room and they all went inside. She thought how glad her father would be when he saw that her mother was only sleeping, but when she looked, there was a lid covering the box. As she'd watched them lower the box into the big hole she wanted to cry out, 'Bring it back, bring it out of there, my mummy won't like being down that hole.' She saw the strangers throwing dirt down into the hole where her mother had gone. She might have cried then like her father was doing but two strong arms enfolded her and swept her off the ground. It was Mr Tyler who held her in his arms, hugging her close, then carried her all the way home with the others following.

It was not until later that the tears came, the house was full of people and she'd slipped out past them. She wanted to be alone, so she went to sit on the front steps. She kept thinking about her mother who was in that deep hole, with no one to open the lid when she woke from her sleep. She thought of her father and how he'd lied to her when he told her her mother was in Heaven, and all the time him knowing her mother wasn't in Heaven at all. When the tears began to fall, she couldn't say whether they were because her father had lied to her or because she would never see her mother again.

She'd heard the front door open but did not move, neither did she wipe away her tears. She thought it was her father coming to look for her but it was Mr Tyler's grandson Joseph. He sat down beside her. He did not speak until he saw her take a handkerchief from her pocket and begin to dab her eyes.

'Let the tears flow, Emma,' he said, 'then they will take away the pain. It is a sad day for your father and yourself, to see your loved one be buried.'

'But my father lied to me,' she told him. 'He said my mother had gone to Heaven and I saw her asleep in that wooden box. Now she won't be able to get out when she wakes up.'

'Emma,' he said, taking hold of her hand, 'look at me.' When she did so, he smiled, telling her, 'Your father did not lie to you. When your mother died, her spirit went up to the Lord of the sky, only her body remained. It was her body you saw in the coffin. She will not wake up and try to get out, though her spirit will never be far away from you.'

She felt better when he'd told her all this. He'd explained everything much better than her father had done. He must be clever, she thought, for she knew he was only ten years old, yet he could tell her what happened when someone died.

He'd asked if she was alright now and when she answered him with a smile, he said, 'Good, my mother sent me to find you. She wants to know if you would like to come home with us for a while. Your father said it would be alright for you to come, he would like to be on his own.'

She had gone with them to the Indian settlement and loved every minute of her stay there. She was sorry when it was time to leave and go back home to her father. She loved her father but the thought of seeing him still crying, which she supposed he would be, or perhaps he would be alright by now. Joseph's mother had told her that her father was very sad because his beloved wife had been called to the spirits in the sky, but hopefully the sadness would soon leave him. 'He is a doctor. He knows that when our time on earth comes there is nothing that we can do about it.'

She thought about this as she walked home with Mr Tyler and his grandson. She also remembered the day they first arrived when her mother was so ill and her father cursing himself for bringing them to this godforsaken place. 'We should have settled in one of the other towns we passed through,' he'd shouted to no one in particular.

When the house came into sight, she'd run towards it, hoping her father's sadness would be gone and he would be happy again. But her father had not been there and none of the people that were in the vicinity had seen him. Mr Tyler had told Joseph to take her to his mother whilst they searched for her father. She had been put to bed but she could not sleep. Then Mr Tyler came into the room. He'd hugged her close and his voice was gentle as he told her about finding her father's body floating down the river. Joseph's mother came into the room and gave her some hot milk.

They did not leave her until they thought she was asleep; they could not know she was still troubled by the day's events and wondering why all these bad things were happening to her.

Emma was sorry when she'd to leave the Indian settlement. She had been quite happy living with Mr Tyler's daughter since the death of her father. In fact she would have liked nothing better than to stay with them for ever.

But it was decided, when Mr & Mrs Petrie enquired if they could foster Emma, and as they had no children of their own, that it would be in Emma's own interest that she be brought up with her own kind.

The Petries were in their late forties and though they doted on her, she never really liked them. They would dress her up in fancy clothes and take her visiting when all she really wanted to do was to go and see her friends at the Indian settlement. She totally ignored the children of the Petries' friends when they came to visit.

When Mr Petrie heard about this, he forbade Emma going to the Indian settlement. He hated all Indians and thought them nothing but savages. But Emma had a will of her own and if she felt like going to the Indian camp, she went and no one was going to stop her.

She would never forget how they had brought her love and laughter back into her life after she'd cried for days because she'd no mother or father to take care of her. Sometimes she wondered how the Petries put up with her and why they didn't send her back to live with the savages, as they called them.

From the beginning she'd refused to call them mother and father, even though they'd said it was her duty to do so. Instead they had settled for her calling them Pop and Nan. She knew she should be grateful to them for taking her into their home and perhaps she would have been if only they did not treat her like some china doll that was shown off at every opportunity.

As the years passed she grew used to their ways, as they did hers. They even allowed her to visit her Indian friends, as long as she acted like a young lady when she was at home.

When she was fifteen, the Petries decided to move to a warmer climate, the winter months being too harsh for Mrs Petrie's rheumatic bones. Emma did not want to go with them but could not refuse. They had always been kind to her, in fact, they spoilt her in many ways.

She realized how much they loved her when, one evening, a week before they were to leave, they told her she would not be going with them. When she asked them why it was Pop that answered her saying, 'We have talked it over, Nan and myself, and though it will pain us to leave you here, we know it will pain you more to leave. Nan also feels, though she cannot say why, that it is your destiny to remain and if we take you with us it would not be long before you came back of your own accord.'

She could see they were both upset that she would not be going with them and for the first time she hugged and kissed them both with love in her heart. She felt the tears well up into her eyes, knowing what a sacrifice it was to them in letting her stay. She thought it strange that Nan should think it was for her destiny they had to do so. Then she heard Pop saying, 'I have already spoken to Mr Tyler about all this and to Mr Collinge, the blacksmith. As you know, Mr Collinge has been left with three children to bring up on his own, with his wife leaving him like that. So we have arranged for you to take up residence with the blacksmith and help him with the children. He will pay you, of course.'

Emma did not care who she was to take up residence with. She had been prepared to go with them. Now there was no need and nothing could have pleased her more. In fact she was quite happy with the arrangement.

CHAPTER V

Emma loved taking care of Mr Collinge's children and his home. Once the housework was done, she would give the youngsters some schooling, then afterwards take them out until it was time to prepare supper for when Mr Collinge came home.

Sometimes she would take them to visit her Indian friends, especially young Joseph, Mr Tyler's grandson. He'd been a friend for as long as she could remember and had always protected her.

It was on one of these visits that she realized that her feelings for Joseph were changing. It wasn't hero worship she felt for him any more but love. And, she suspected his feelings for her were also changing. He'd always treated her as one would treat a younger sister but now his eyes lingered on her longer than need be; he also took hold of her hand when there was no need for him to do so.

Emma, wise beyond her years, knew that a love between them could never be. It would be unacceptable with both the white settlers and the natives. She told herself she must never be alone with Joseph again, for she was growing into womanhood and him into manhood and it would not do any good to put temptation in their way. She knew it would be a hard task she had set herself, as she would still be taking the children to visit the settlement. For not to do so would need some explaining, especially as she herself had visited the settlement for years, besides, the children loved going to play with their new-found friends and Mr Collinge did not object.

For twelve months Emma was able to hide her true feelings for Joseph. It helped having the children there with her. It also helped that she did not see much of him as he spent a lot of time with his grandfather.

It was Joseph's grandfather who decided that Joseph should be taught about the outside world. A tutor-come-travelling-companion was found to take him on a grand tour, just like the son of an English aristocrat would be sent upon. His grandfather had wanted him not only educated but worldly in the truest sense of the word.

Emma was invited to the party given for him the night before he was to leave. All night she managed not to be alone with him but when he offered to walk her home and his mother insisted that he should, Emma could not refuse the offer. If she insisted on walking home alone, she would not only hurt Joseph's feelings but his mother's as well.

As they strolled down by the river, Joseph reminisced about their childhood, which surprised Emma, for she thought he would be more excited about his coming tour. Then she heard him saying, 'Let us go to our secret hideaway. We have not been there for such a long time and it was always our favourite place.'

At that moment, Emma saw them not as Joseph the young man, or herself a young woman, but as children who would go to their secret hideaway where no adults could enter. It was a place where dreams came true and you could be anyone you wished to be, even a prince or a princess.

Without thinking she lifted the hem of her dress and began to run, knowing that Joseph would give her a head start. As she reached the edge of the forest, he caught up with her and they raced together between the trees until they reached the bottom of the hillside. He took hold of her hand and did not let go until they reached the plateau above. They stood for a moment to catch their breath, then were both struck by the wonder of the night. The moon and the stars were so low in the sky they were nearly touchable. It felt magical to both of them, for never before had they been to their secret hideaway at night.

There was a childlike wonder upon their faces as they turned to face each other. A moment later, all innocence of childhood was gone. For what they had begun, as a gentle kiss, had become a raging passion that neither could control.

Later as they laid together in each other's arms and Emma gazed up at the moonlit sky, she could have sworn the moon was smiling down upon her, as if she'd committed some act that it was pleased with and that the stars twinkled more brightly as if they too were in agreement with the moon.

She thought of Nan Petrie and what she'd said about her destiny. Was this what her destiny was all about, this one night with Joseph, for she knew that there could be no other? The thing she had most tried to avoid had happened – an act of love that there was no hope for. There was so much planned for Joseph – his grandfather had high hopes for him and they did not include him marrying a white girl. That would be unacceptable, by the white settlers and the natives. Their love for each other would bring nothing but trouble in a troubled land.

She'd decided at that moment that when Joseph had gone she would make her plans to leave Petraba. She could not stay here now, the passion of this night was too strong between them. When Joseph returned it would flare up again – he'd already told her how much he loved her; how it seemed to him, he had always loved her. When he'd told her this, at the height of their lovemaking, her own heart soared with happiness. But now she realized that it was an impossible dream and she was not going to let it ruin Joseph's life, which it would if she stayed here. It would be different if they were both of the same creed and could declare their love – she would wait for him forever if need be.

She felt the tears well up into her eyes at the thought that after tonight she would never see him again. When Joseph asked why she was crying, she told him because she was so happy. It would break his heart to tell him what she'd been thinking.

It was a week later that Emma went to see Joseph's grandfather. He had always been kind to her and she could not leave without telling him she was going. She'd argued with herself all week as to whether she should just disappear. It was possible for her to do so. There was some money in the bank that the Petries had deposited for her and there was the money she'd saved from her wages. She had also thought of returning to the home of Nan and Pop Petrie. But Joseph would, when he found out, come and find her there. And he must never find her, no matter what.

Yet she could not understand why, on what had been the happiest moment of her life, some inner voice deep inside herself was warning her about the consequences of their actions, bringing to her a sadness, like as nothing she'd ever felt before, not even when her parents died. But she knew she must take heed of that warning.

A lump came into her throat as she remembered that night and of when Joseph kissed away the tears. How they'd run, hand in hand through the moonlit forest and the rest of the way home. When they reached Mr Collinge's house they sat on the front steps to catch their breath. Then Joseph reached into his pocket, taking out a tiny box. 'This is for you Emma,' he'd said. 'Don't open it now, wait until I am gone. It is our secret, inside that box, but one day you will wear it forever.' He'd kissed her then, hugging her close before silently walking away. She watched him until he was nearly out of sight and turned to wave goodbye. As he did so she got the strangest feeling that he knew he would never see her again.

She sat herself down on the steps, opening the tiny box. Inside was a ring. The tears welled up in her eyes when she saw it – whatever Joseph might have said about her wearing it one day forever, she knew she would never wear it. For Joseph would not be there to put it onto her finger.

Many times during that long lonely week she'd held the tiny box in her hand while she planned where she was to go. She never opened it, but just held it tight as if it was some kind of mascot.

She would be sorry to go, for she'd been happy here, as happy as any orphan could have been. And over the years, she'd watched the township growing and still people were coming to settle there.

By the time she went to see Joseph's grandfather, everything was planned in her mind. She did not relish the ordeal, for he was a shrewd man. Sometimes she'd even thought he could read peoples' minds and hoped he couldn't read hers. But just to be on the safe side, she'd put the tiny box into her pocket, holding onto it tightly as she explained to him her reason for leaving.

She told him that she felt more at home with the natives than with the townspeople, which was true, yet belonged to neither place and that she would like to visit her homeland, for when people talked about England, she could not imagine what it was like and she'd been born there. She could remember a little bit about Liverpool but not much and that was where she wanted to go.

She was sure her mascot had worked, when she heard Mr Tyler saying, 'I can understand your reasons for wanting to leave. Have I not watched you over the years, preferring to be on the other side of the track, so to speak? I can understand you wanting to see your birthplace. I only wish you would wait a few more years. You are young, Emma, and do not know the ways of the outside world, especially the ways of city life. But if you have made up your mind I will be the last person to try and stop you. For was I and my Rosa not much older than you when we came to this land? So I will not interfere with your plans. It is your life, always remember that and only you can know what your heart is telling you. Listen always to your heart, Emma, as I did when I knew it was my destiny to make my home with Meleeka and before that to leave my home and family for the sake of Rosa.'

As I must leave for the sake of Joseph, Emma thought as she looked into Mr Tyler's kindly eyes.

Then he'd smiled at her saying, 'I myself will be returning to England in six weeks' time. If you have really made your mind up, why not travel with me? We shall be company for each other.'

CHAPTER VI

Emma could not believe that she was pregnant but realized that she must be. The sickness she'd suffered the last three mornings was not seasickness for the ship could have been sailing on a pond. Besides, she'd seen no blood in her knickers since the night that she and Joseph had made love in their secret hideaway and that was two months ago.

She thought about Joseph and what he would do if ever he found out about the baby. She knew he would come to find her and take her back. The very thought of it made her shudder. Not because she didn't love Joseph – she did, and always would – but she'd lived too long with a foot in each camp to know that it was impossible for them to be together.

Some of the settlers distrusted Meleeka and his tribe only because of the fact that they were redskins and it would not take much for them to make things bad for Meleeka. If they found out that she was pregnant and Meleeka's son was the father, it would be like putting a powder keg in their hands to use against Meleeka and his people.

For as more and more new settlers came to Petraba, so did the stories get spread about of the white settlers being killed and their womenfolk raped for no reason at all, except for the hatred these savage natives felt about the taking of their land. Emma supposed that was reason enough but wondered why it had to be – if the stories were true, of course.

Joseph had told her long ago about the history of the Ilinka and of how the development of Petraba came to be. She hoped that peace would remain between the two settlements but she had her doubts. There was disquiet in the township and had been for some time, with men who could not hide their hatred for the natives of this land. Meleeka would need all his strength and courage to ignore the slights of these men.

And so will I, she thought, knowing the predicament that I am in. Then she remembered Joseph once telling her, if she ever needed courage she was to call upon the Great White Spirit in the sky to help her. She'd laughed at him then, telling him there was no such thing. But now she cried out to that unknown spirit to give her strength and courage for when she arrived in Liverpool, alone and pregnant. Yet she did not feel afraid of her predicament as she put both her hands onto her still flat stomach, as if protecting the seed of love that was within her. She felt her heart fill with love, for this part of Joseph that was inside her, then she said out loud, though she knew not why, 'Do not worry, my little one, we shall be alright, you and I. The ancestors of your father will protect us, I am sure of it.'

Three days later, she knew there was no doubt about it at all. For someone, somewhere was surely seeing to their needs.

It was late evening and she was on deck with Mr Tyler. He liked to stroll and then to sit in a quiet corner and smoke his pipe before he retired for the night.

It was whilst they were sitting quietly, both lost in their own thoughts, that she was shocked out of her reverie when she heard him asking, 'Emma why did you not tell me that you are pregnant? Don't deny it. Have I not heard you retching these last few mornings? And the sea so calm, it could be nothing else. Why did you not tell me before we set sail? I cannot leave you in Liverpool now, knowing that you are with child. I don't suppose that you are prepared to enlighten me as to who the father is?'

She could not help but look up at him and saw the concern for her written all over his face. Though she was shocked that he knew she was pregnant, she was not surprised at his outspokenness. He'd never been one to beat about the bush and he certainly wasn't doing so now.

She longed to tell him the truth but dare not. She stared up at him and, looking him straight in the eye, she told him. 'When we set sail I had no idea I was pregnant – it would have made no difference to my plans. I could not have married the man anyway as it would have been impossible. And I beg of you, Mr Tyler, when you return to Petraba you will tell no one of my predicament. I do not want any word about the child getting to the father.'

As he gazed into those deep blue eyes of Emma's that had not once turned away from his, he marvelled at her courage and her wisdom. She had not mentioned who the father was, but he knew, from the very first morning he'd heard her retching, the father of Emma's child could be no other than his grandson. Had he not watched them both over the last few years, fighting the love that was between them, each of them knowing it could not be. He remembered what his daughter Sara told him, when he first suggested to her about sending his grandson on a grand tour.

'It is up to you, Father,' she said, 'and I know the reason for you suggesting it. I believe you think with sending my son away, you will be sending him away from temptation. For I too have been watching him and also Emma, they are both fighting a love that cannot be. But if it is the wishes of the spirits of my ancestors, that a seed from my son enters the body of Emma, no power on earth will prevent it from doing so.' And now, he was confronted with the reality of his daughter's words.

When first he'd heard Emma retching, he'd mentally calculated the time of his grandson's leaving and guessed that the power of their love must have become too strong for them to hold back on the night of his grandson's leaving party when he had escorted Emma home. So all my plans for Joseph were to no avail, he thought. I need not have sent him on that grand tour so that he and Emma would be separated.

He felt Emma take hold of his hand and brought his mind back to the present on hearing her asking him, 'Mr Tyler, will you promise me, you'll say nothing of my predicament when you return home?'

He felt his own heart quicken its heartbeat at what she was asking: after all, by the technicality of fate, the child she was carrying was his great-grandchild, and what about Sara and Meleeka? They had a right to know, for they would be the grandparents, and so too had his grandson, the father. He thought of Meleeka and of what he would tell

Emma – if the role was reversed and it was Meleeka sitting here, would Meleeka keep such a secret? At that moment he felt his hands grip Emma's tightly and could not believe his own lips, as he heard himself telling Emma, 'Your secret is safe with me, lass.' Then added to himself, for the time being.

He saw the tears well up into her eyes as she thanked him. 'But there is one condition,' he said, putting his arm around her shoulder, drawing her close to him. 'I will not leave you in Liverpool, you must come to Maraldon with me. The streets of Liverpool are filled with all kinds of skullduggery. I realize you have been a very determined young lady with a will of your own, taking matters into your hands like this. It does not surprise me. It has always been so with you. But if you come to Maraldon with me, Bessie will take care of you and I'll know you will be safe. I know that Bessie will not pry into your affairs, in fact she will take care of you like a mother hen.

'It will also make my visit easier. Like me, Bessie is getting on in years and it is time she retired and most likely I will never return to Maraldon again, so I wish to see her settled. She's been loyal over the years and the least I can do is to see to it that she retires in comfort. Another reason I planned this visit was to put the farm up for sale. I really don't know why I have kept it all these years, certainly not for sentimental reasons. Yet even now, as I am telling you all this, I feel that for some reason the farm has not to be sold. But what good would it do to keep it? For I cannot see Sara and Meleeka or even their children ever being interested in the farm.'

'What is your heart telling you to do?' Emma asked him, remembering what he'd told her a few weeks earlier.

'Ah, you remember then do you? I'll always remember, for surely our own hearts would not lie to us. Then I shall take heed of my own advice and instruct my lawyers to find a suitable tenant. That way it will make a living for someone and still belong to the Tylers. And who knows, one day someone from the Tyler clan might take an interest in the farm and come to visit. Well, that is my mind made up, now what about yours?'

She hesitated for a moment before answering. Her heart was telling her to go with him but what he'd said about a Tyler may one day wish to visit the farm disturbed her, then she felt relief flood her body as she said to him, 'I will be coming with you, Mr Tyler, for I too am listening to my heart.'

He hugged her close once more, then taking his arm from around her shoulder he said, 'Good, that makes two of us and I do not doubt we are both doing the right thing.'

She watched him relight his pipe then go into his own thoughts while puffing away contentedly on his pipe. She did not know that when he smoked in such a fashion there was something troubling him and that he'd just given in to her and that he was far from content. The promise he'd just given to her was uppermost in his mind, yet he could not retract it. He turned his thoughts to his family and especially to his grandson.

He wished that when he returned home after completing his affairs he could take Emma back with him but he knew, deep inside himself, it could not be.

He'd lived below that mystical mountain long enough to know of what strange power it possessed and if those ancient spirits of Ilinka wanted Emma's child to be born elsewhere, it had to be so. And it seemed to him that somehow Emma herself knew this, for had she not made her plans to leave even before she knew that she was pregnant? He remembered the day when she first came to him telling him she was leaving and how he'd not pressed her to stay. In fact, he had helped her, making things much easier for her than if she would have had to travel alone. He knew now this journey was planned for them both, by some power that he could not question. Why it had to be so he could not answer. He was only thankful the child would be born in Maraldon and not Liverpool where Emma had first planned to go.

The secret he held about his great-grandchild he would keep close to his heart. Meleeka had told him many times, 'There is a reason for all things, Joseph.' Meleeka would repeat those words if he found out about the grandchild he was not meant to know about. But if there was a reason, he himself could not fathom it.

He emptied out his pipe, then pulled the blanket that was draped around his shoulders closer to him. He was ready, now that he had sorted things out in his mind, to return to his cabin. Emma, sitting beside him, had also been deep in thought. When she'd seen his pipe was lit and thought him content she too relaxed, gazing up at the moonlit sky with its twinkling stars that seemed to be smiling down on her.

Silently, she thanked the spirits in the sky for taking care of her. Now, she would not be alone and pregnant in Liverpool – she had somewhere to go and someone would be taking care of her. She thought about Joseph and wondered if one day, when their life on earth was over, they would meet again, somewhere beyond those stars. Surely there was no prejudice in Heaven. Or maybe they would be reborn again, in a world where they could flaunt their love. She hoped so, for she felt the world they lived in now was a cruel one, when it was wrong to fall in love with someone a different colour of skin than oneself. Surely, love is love, no matter what and one cannot help where one is born.

She also thought it cruel to be sitting next to Mr Tyler and him making all those plans for her, yet she had not been able to bring herself to tell him the truth about the baby. After all he would be her child's great-grandfather and he was the kindest man she had ever known. Had he not been her benefactor when her parents died? And even when the Petries left he had watched over her and was still doing so. For had he not suggested her going with him to the farm? Anything could have happened to her if she would have been alone in Liverpool. It was on the tip of her tongue to tell him the truth, then as if she had not to do so, he broke the spell by saying, 'I'm feeling the chill of the night, Emma. I think we had better return to our cabins.'

CHAPTER VII

It was in the early hours of the morning of the sixteenth of January, that Emma was awakened by the shooting pain deep inside her womb. Though the baby was not due until early February she wondered if it was the onset of her labour pains. She got out of bed and walked over to the window. She could hear the wind raging outside and wondered if the gentle fall of snow that began before she came to bed had turned into a blizzard. When she opened the curtains she could see there was no doubt about it – there were deep snowdrifts all around.

She got back into bed hoping the pain was a false alarm. She snuggled under the warm bedclothes, then waited to see if another pain would grip her – only then would she awaken Bessie.

She thought of Mr Tyler and wished he was here – if it was time for her baby to come, at least he would have seen his great-grandchild and perhaps then she might have told him the truth. He'd been so good to her, and Bessie for that matter. He had bought this house for Bessie and furnished it with bits and pieces from the farm, as well as giving them both a substantial amount of money before he'd left for home.

She remembered how he'd hugged her close on the day he was leaving, and tears welled up in both their eyes when he told her, 'Take care of yourself, Emma, and the baby. It is a precious child you are carrying.'

'I know,' was all she said as he hugged her even more tightly, then as he walked away, she'd had the strangest feeling that he knew and they both held a secret they could not share.

Mr Tyler had also been right about Bessie, taking care of her like a mother hen. Bessie treated her like the daughter she'd not had, yet never once questioned her about the father of the child. Not even with the gossip that was going around the village which Bessie had overheard. She remembered how Bessie had come in from shopping in the village all flustered, and then said to her, 'Well, Emma, I've heard everything now and I truly believe what folks don't know, they make up. They are saying in the village that Master Tyler be the father of your child, for why else would he have been so generous as to set us up in this house and provide us with money. Where they got that bit of information from, I don't know. But I was so disgusted when I overheard the woman talking, I just ignored her and came home.'

Emma smiled to herself, remembering the indignant look upon Bessie's face. Then she screamed in agony as the second labour pain shot through her.

With the blizzard raging outside, there was no chance of Bessie fetching the doctor, or the old hag from the village who sometimes helped in delivering babies, so Bessie herself prepared for the baby's arrival.

As Emma's labour pains became unbearable, she cried out for Joseph, not once but many times. Bessie, hearing her, wondered if for once the village gossip could be true, then pooh-poohed the very thought of it. Master Joseph would never abuse a young girl.

When at last the child came out of its mother's womb, Bessie wrapped it in a towel and placed it in Emma's arms. When she did so, she could not hold back the tears of relief now the ordeal was over. Emma also began to cry, but her tears were tears of happiness.

Bessie hugged her close, saying, 'There, there, lass, 'tis all over with and you've gotten yourself a baby son. So settle down while I get the water ready to wash him down. Poor little mite, he'll wonder what sort of a place he's come into with us both blathering over him.'

Emma was so overwhelmed by Bessie's kindness, she found herself saying, 'Bessie, I think it only right I should tell you who the father of my baby is. But you must promise me, you'll never tell anyone else, because it might get back to them over there and you have no idea the trouble it could cause.'

'As if I would,' said Bessie, annoyed that Emma should even think such a thing, when never once had she questioned Emma about anything.

Emma, realizing she had hurt Bessie's feelings said to her, 'Bessie, I know I can trust you, I am surprised with myself in even thinking of telling you. You do not know how many times I longed to tell Mr Tyler about the baby's father but every time the opportunity arose, something stopped me from doing so.'

'Does the father not know?' Bessie asked, interrupting Emma. 'Or did he leave you in the lurch?'

'I was not left in the lurch,' Emma answered. 'How could I have been? I did not know I was pregnant myself until I was on board ship. But even if I had known I would not have told him and he must never find out. In fact you shall be the only person I will tell the truth to.'

'That's settled then,' said Bessie, 'whatever you tell me will go no farther than these four walls. You have my word upon it.'

She smiled at Emma to reassure her, then could not hide the shock when Emma told her. 'The father is Mr Tyler's grandson and do you wonder how upset I've been, not being able to tell him, after all the kindness he has shown me.'

Bessie was so shocked by this she didn't know what to say. So she poured some water into a bowl and taking the child from Emma began to sponge it down, telling Emma she would see to her when the baby was settled.

Bessie's thoughts were in a turmoil. Though she'd promised Emma she would keep the secret of the father's identity, she felt duty bound that she should let Master Tyler know of the birth of his great-grandson. After all, he'd been good to her, letting her see to the upkeep of the farm all these years when it had been evident for a long time that he himself would never me coming back to live there. And now he had bought her this house, so she could retire in comfort. There has been no end to the man's generosity, she thought, taking the baby out of the water and wrapping it in a towel. And here we are, keeping this precious little one from him.

As she began to wipe the baby's face she realized two things. The first was, if Emma had not told her about the father, taking a good look now at the child, she would have known the father was of Indian blood. She also realized, without a shadow of doubt, that even if Emma had not told Master Tyler about the baby's father, Master Tyler himself knew whose blood ran through the child's veins. With this thought she gave a sigh of relief as she handed the child back to Emma, asking her, 'Have you thought of a name for the little mite?' Emma, taking hold of her son, would have liked to call him Joseph, but with the talk in the village thought better of it. She could not have the villagers putting two and two together and getting half a dozen. So she said, 'You have been so good to me, Bessie, I would like you to choose his name.'

'If that be the case, and if it be to your liking,' said Bessie, 'I think we should call him Robert.'

Emma smiled, as she reluctantly took her eyes away from her son and gazed up at Bessie saying, 'Robert Kyersh. I like it, Bessie. The name has a true ring with it.'

'Aye, it has,' said Bessie, 'and he will be a son to be proud of. I just knows he will.' She thought of Sara, saying to herself, Any bloodline from that lass is sure to be good. She wondered how Emma's predicament came about and why the girl had not been able to tell Master Tyler the truth of the matter. And what of Sara and Meleeka? They would know nothing of the grandson she had just delivered. She wished once again she'd not made that promise to Emma, but it was too late now. Then could not help herself saying, 'I think Master Tyler guessed the truth about the parentage of Robert.'

Once again Emma raised her eyes from the child and said simply, 'I know he did, Bessie. I think he has known from the beginning, yet he did not challenge me about it. Perhaps he could not, just as I could not tell him the truth. There must be some reason for us both to be silent with each other.'

'I think you are right,' said Bessie, 'For Master Tyler is not one for keeping things to himself. He likes them out in the open.'

As Bessie cooked the breakfast, she pondered upon the issue of Master Tyler and Emma. There was certainly something strange about the two of them not being able to speak to each other about the baby and its father, for she knew that Master Tyler worshipped his grandson. He'd brought her up to date with the events of Ilinka and Petraba and of how those she'd known were faring. But young Joseph was the one he spoke most often about, his eyes lighting up as he mentioned the lad's name. Master Tyler also liked Emma or he would not have taken so much care of her well-being, and that had begun long before he brought her to Maraldon.

She thought about what Emma had just told her, before she'd come downstairs to see about cooking the breakfast. She'd been about to leave the room when Emma called her back. It was then that Emma told her of the night that the baby was conceived, and of how at what must have been the very moment of the baby's conception, she knew she must leave Petraba. 'Of course, I had no idea that I was pregnant,' Emma had told her. 'I only knew that after what Joseph and I had done, I could not stay. I planned to go to Liverpool – how I was to manage when I arrived there never entered my head. Now I realize that from the very moment I conceived, I was to be protected. Mr Tyler told me that my baby was precious, but he did not mean it in a way that all babies are precious to a mother. There was some hidden meaning in the way that he said it, I'm sure there was, even though I still cannot fathom why.'

Now, as Bessie set up the tray, Emma's words were buzzing about in her mind. So too were the faces of Master Joseph and Sara. She was remembering how they came so unexpectedly to the farm more than twenty years ago. And how she'd known, but none would admit it, that the messenger sent to find Master Tyler had not done so. Yet he'd appeared and claimed his inheritance just the same. She thought of Sara and how she had healed Jamie. Why the lad was nowt but an idiot before Sara came. Yet when Sara left, no one would have taken him for the same lad. And now the blood of Sara ran through the baby upstairs. Of course the child was precious, it would have the power to heal in its hands. And that gift came from the Lord himself and the Lord had put the child in her keeping.

At that moment she decided that when Emma was well enough to travel they would move away from Maraldon. She had seen for herself that the child was a half-breed. Others in the village would also see it and there was no telling the taunting the child would get as it grew older. Besides, if the child's parentage became the talk of the village word might get back to Petraba and Emma did not want that to happen.

CHAPTER VIII

When Joseph opened his eyes and the vision faded, it was to see Archie grinning at him. Joseph smiled back at Archie saying, 'I'm sorry, I must have dozed off. It must be the jet lag catching up with me.'

Archie laughed, telling him not to worry about it. 'I'm always dropping off to sleep when I've got company but it be the first time my visitor's fallen asleep on me.'

Joseph looked at his watch, then said he must be leaving. He thanked Archie for an enjoyable afternoon and Archie told him he must call again sometime.

As he walked back to the farm, Joseph wondered what Archie would have said if he'd told him he'd not been asleep, but watching the story unfold of Emma Kyersh on his inbuilt screen. He had not wanted the film to end as he wanted to know what happened to the child. But he was grateful for what he'd been shown. His mission was to seek out the lineage of Robert Kyersh and bring them together.

He shuddered involuntarily, as he remembered the warning from the mountain. He gazed up into the sky silently, thanking the spirits for their help. He knew they would be with him and help to trace the lineage. They would let him see what had to be seen, all else would be up to himself. He ran the rest of the way to the farm not wanting to be late, as he was dining out with Jordana.

Jordana took him to the Mill House, a newly opened restaurant on the outskirts of Maraldon which was becoming a very popular eating place, not only for its excellent bill of fayre, but also because of its unusual decor. The restaurant itself was at one time a huge mansion, owned by a wealthy mill owner in the days when cotton was king and the mills flourished.

Now the old mansion was like a monument, fashioned not unto those industrialist men who lived off the fat of the land, whilst their workers almost starved and children fell asleep at their work with sometimes fatal results, but to the workers themselves, the ones who had really made cotton king. There were several small dining rooms at the restaurant, each one with a name sign over the door representing some aspect of cotton manufacturing, from raw cotton to the finest product.

The stone walls were adorned with relics from the old machinery that men, women and children once slaved over. There were also old pictures of the mill workers and newspaper articles of long ago.

Joseph was fascinated with it all, as Jordana hoped he would be. They chose the Mule Room to dine in and when the waiter had taken their order she said to Joseph, ''Tis a pity the mills have gone now, they were the heart and soul of Lancashire as the woollen industry was to Yorkshire. And when I read the history of it all, it saddens me to know that when working conditions in the mills improved, the mill owners decided to send machinery abroad so once again they would be able to use cheap labour. That's how I see it anyway.'

Joseph smiled at her saying, 'For a farmer's daughter you seem very interested as to what went on in the cotton industry.'

'I am,' she said, 'for it is something that was once the pride of Lancashire, now it is lost forever. The quality of cotton will never be the same again and I think the closing of the mills and taking the heart out of the people who spun and wove the cotton, is a disgrace.

'Do you know, I would not believe Archie when one day, as we stood in the farmyard looking down over the distant towns and villages, he told me that at one time on very clear sunlit days, it was possible to count two hundred factory chimneys from where we were standing. I thought he was pulling my leg, but it was true, since others have told me the very same thing, even Jack Farrel.' She smiled, saying, 'I bet the mill owner who once owned this house is turning over in his grave.'

'Why do you say that?' Joseph asked.

'Because, Jack Farrel, who owns it now and is responsible for all this,' she waved her hand into the air, 'comes from a long line of mill workers. His ancestors probably helped smash the looms when they were first introduced to the mills.'

'You know him then, this Jack Farrel?'

'Yes, I've known him a long time. He's abroad at the moment, but hopefully he will be back for my twenty-first birthday party next month. Will you still be here, Joseph? I would so like you to come.'

'I cannot honestly answer that but if it is at all possible for me to be there, I will.'

'I hope you will be able to make it. Ah, here's the waiter, let's get tucking in, I'm starving.'

As he ate, Joseph wondered about Jack Farrel and what the man meant to Jordana. It was obvious she thought a lot about him.

His thoughts turned to Archie, thinking how the old man would like this place and that he and Jordana might bring him one night. He'd asked Archie that afternoon if he would like to come with them tonight but Archie declined the invitation, telling him, 'The lads from the domino team are taking me to the Swan. There's a big match on tonight and if the team wins, we'll be the champions.'

He could not help but admire Archie, who at ninety-eight still knew how to enjoy life. Then he heard Jordana saying, 'There's a disco starts at ten, do you fancy going?'

The disco was held below stairs in what was once the servants' quarters. It was quite a large room with a bar in the corner. They made a striking couple as they danced together with an elegance unbefitting a disco, yet their bodies moved with the tempo of the music. And though they did not know it, many admiring eyes watched them. Joseph was not keen on the loud music, he thought there was no need to be deafened to enjoy oneself.

He was relieved when Jordana suggested they go out into the floodlit gardens to get some fresh air. The night air was warm and filled with the fragrance of night-scented stock. They strolled down the gravel path, then across the lawn towards the fish pond with the cascading water fountain reflecting the colours of the fairy lights which surrounded the pond. There was a bench for them to sit upon and as they did so, Joseph glanced up at the floodlit mansion. From the outside, he thought, no one could tell that it was not still a gentleman's residence. Any stranger passing by would think that whoever owned it must be very rich.

He did not know Jack Farrel, but he admired him for keeping the past together, both inside the building and out. He glanced about the lawns half hoping to see a croquet pitch marked out on them.

He smiled to himself on not finding one, then was brought out of his reverie on hearing Jordana asking, 'Whatever is amusing you Joseph?' When he told her, she laughed saying, 'I'll tell Jack about it when I see him. He'll probably agree with you and put one there.'

'He sounds quite enterprising, this Jack Farrel,' said Joseph, 'seeing that he comes from working-class folk.'

'He's very enterprising,' Jordana told him, 'but I feel sorry for him.'

'Whatever for?' he asked, hoping her answer would enlighten him as to her true feelings about the man.

'People will tell you Jack Farrel has the Midas touch, for it seems he cannot put a foot wrong. Everything he touches does turn to gold, but inside himself there is nothing there. No laughter, no joy, only sadness. Yet I am sure he could make money with the flick of an eyelid if he wanted to. But money is not everything and I'm sure Jack would rather be poor if he could have his wife Clare and the baby she was carrying with him today.

'Clare was killed in a car smash. They'd been sweethearts even at school. He's never got over Clare's death. That's why he's abroad now, once he'd finished this place and saw it was going to be a success. He could not stand Clare not being with him to see the fruits of his labour. He once promised her the world but now she's not here and he could give her so much, he cannot bear it.

'Yet when he returns there will be another idea running around in his head, then he'll not settle until he's worked day and night and it becomes a reality.

'So you see, Joseph, that's why I feel sorry for him. Behaving like he does it is unlikely he'll find happiness again.'

'How do you know so much about him?'

'He bought the land for development off the farmer that my father once worked for. He's been a friend of the family ever since. He often comes to visit when he's not swanning off abroad, especially when he's down in the dumps.'

Jordana rose abruptly, as if she didn't wish to discuss Jack Farrel any longer. 'It's getting late,' she said, 'I think that we had best be heading home. I've an early start in the morning.'

CHAPTER IX

When Joseph awoke the next morning, his first thoughts were of Emma Kyersh and her child. He laid there for some time, going over in his mind the things he had seen the day before. He was still puzzled by the fact that Emma's child had been kept so secret. He could not understand why the child's great-grandfather had shown no interest after he'd left Maraldon.

Later, after he'd taken a shower, and done his morning ritual, he'd cried out to the spirits of his ancestors, 'Let me see what has to be seen. Let me hear what has to be heard and help me now to understand why the secret of Emma and her child has been kept for so long.'

He waited for the vision to materialize, for only if the spirits wished it would he see or hear anything. It took only a moment before he was back in time, seeing Meleeka, Sara and her father. He could hear Sara asking, 'Are you sure of this, Father?'

'Yes, I am positive that the child Emma carries is young Joseph's. Many times I wanted to ask her outright but could not. I also felt that Emma wished to tell me the truth, yet could not do so. It was as if some force beyond our control was keeping the truth apart from us. And to be honest, though I have been home for many weeks, it is only now that I was able to mention it to you. And even now I cannot be sure I should have told you.

'I have this strange feeling that none of us were ever to know that Emma was with child. Yet I had no doubt about the child or its parentage from the moment I first heard Emma retching in the cabin. What the consequences of my telling you will be, I do not know, but I could keep it to myself no longer, you two being the grandparents.'

'And you its great-grandfather,' said Sara.

'Yes, I know, that is why I left Emma well provided for. But what are we to do about it?'

It was Meleeka who answered saying, 'Emma is wise beyond her years. She could not have known that day she came to you, Joseph, and told you she was leaving that she was pregnant. Yet all the same, she still planned to leave. We three have known for a long time the friendship between young Joseph and Emma would grow into something much deeper, even though we watched them both try to fight it. And your idea to send my son away on the grand tour, so they would be separated, was a good one. But it seems their young hearts were meant to fuse together and they did so. Maybe for the very reason my son was leaving.'

'But do we tell the lad when he returns?' asked Joseph, looking at his daughter for an answer. Sara, seeing her father was perplexed by the whole situation, told him, 'I think from what you have told us that it is not the wishes of the spirits of my ancestors that my son should learn of the child. So it would be unwise for us to tell him. If Joseph was to hear about the child, he would move heaven and earth to bring Emma back, regardless of the consequences.

'And we all three know what those could be with the hatred for the natives growing daily in the white men's hearts. Especially with some of the new settlers. They have brought much unrest while you were away, Father. The newcomers bring vile news of fighting and bloodshed. I have heard some say they are feared to sleep in their beds at night, living so near to Meleeka and his tribe. They do not tell of what the white men are doing to the natives. They sweep that under the carpet, as if it is not happening. But we know of what the white men are doing. We have heard from Chief Whiteband of how there is much bloodshed, in the slaughtering of all tribes, whether they be peaceful or warlike, it does not matter. Even Meleeka is getting frustrated with the vow he made, so too are his braves.

'Maybe that is the reason for Emma and her child, perhaps she is to protect the blood lineage of the Ilinkas. I hope that I am wrong in my thinking this, but the fact remains that for some reason Emma was to leave this place – the child was not meant to be born here. And as much as I love my son and Emma also, I think we should keep the secret of Emma's child between the three of us.'

Though it saddened them to do so, Meleeka and her father agreed with her and all three wondered what they would tell young Joseph when he returned.

It was here the vision of Meleeka, Sara and her father faded. Other pictures came into his mind, but they lasted only a few minutes, before he opened his eyes. He sat for a long time, deep in his own thoughts. He could understand now, why there was nothing in the chronicles about Emma. She could not be written about, for one day young Joseph would have read them. And it was obvious that even before she conceived, it was ordained by the spirits of Ilinka that Emma should have this child.

Three hours later, Joseph was driving over the Pennines. When he'd gone down to breakfast, he'd surprised them all by asking about getting a train to Leeds, especially Jordana who gave him a look which said, You never mentioned anything about going to Leeds last night. Yet they did not question him, for which he was grateful – he could not have told them of Meleeka and the things which he'd been shown only a short while ago.

It was Barbara who said, 'You don't need to bother about catching a train, Joseph, you can take my car.' When he told her he was not sure how long he would be away, she told him it did not matter. Now as he travelled up the steep winding road, he admired the panoramic view of the open countryside with the rolling hills that divide the two counties of Lancashire and Yorkshire. He was thankful to Peter for sending him on this route and not the motorways. He had no idea of where his journey would end, he only knew the spirits would guide him. He thought of Bessie and Emma and wondered what their journey was like for them, when they travelled to Leeds all those years ago.

He recalled the second vision he'd seen that morning. It was of Bessie, telling Emma of a dream she'd had the night before. 'And according to my dream,' Bessie was saying, 'we were both right in thinking Master

Tyler knew about Robert's father. He was discussing it with Sara and Meleeka.'

'But he promised he would tell no one,' Emma interrupted. 'Now Joseph will find out.'

'It was only a dream,' said Bessie, 'so wait until I'm finished telling you. Master Tyler was upset about breaking his promise to you, but he could hold it back no longer. They had a right to know and so too had his grandson. Sara told him that her son was not to be told, that the spirits of her ancestors wanted it this way. The spirits will protect Emma and her child so there is no need to worry about her. Besides, you left Emma well provided for. Bessie will take good care of her and will know what to do for the best. It will be hard, the child being a half-breed, especially in the village of Maraldon but it would be harder still here, no matter how influential its great-grandfather might be. The three of them then put their hands together vowing they would tell no one about the baby.

'That's all I can remember,' said Bessie, 'though it seems a strange dream for me to be having. What do you make of it, Emma?'

'The dream was telling you what I already know,' replied Emma. 'It explains why neither Mr Tyler nor myself could bring ourselves to speak about the matter. Ilinka is a strange place, Bessie, yet it is the most beautiful, with the Blue Mountain that dominates the area. Joseph told me the mountain has mystical powers and that when his father found Sara and her father dying of the fever, the mountain spoke to Meleeka, telling him how to save them. Sara also has some mystical power. You already know she has healing hands – you told me about her healing Jamie. But she also has her guide who tells her many things. So I have no doubt that what you dreamt last night was no ordinary dream. It was to let us know what was happening over there.'

'But why did I have the dream and not you?' Bessie asked.

'I can only assume,' replied Emma, 'that with Mr Tyler leaving me in your care, Sara wanted you to know what was happening so it was you she came to.'

When Emma told her this, Bessie pondered on what Emma told her and the dream itself. The thing that struck her most was Sara calling the child a half-breed. She thought about the child growing up in the village and the taunts that would befall him as he grew older. It was then she decided they would all pay a visit to Jessica who once worked at the farm but now lived with her husband and children in Leeds.

It was on the outskirts of Leeds that Joseph realized he'd taken a wrong turning to the one on the map that Peter had drawn for him. He pulled into the side of the road knowing it was no accident that he had done so.

On either side of the road there were modern houses with unfenced gardens that came down to the pavement. He wondered why he'd been brought here. Was this vicinity where Bessie had brought Emma but was now long gone from its former self with the coming of the modern age? Or was there someone from the Ilinka lineage that lived in one of these houses?

A moment later there came into his mind's eye a name, Rowens Lane. He drove down the road then came onto another one similar to the one he'd just left. When he saw the pub on the corner advertising Pub Grub and Morning Coffee, he decided to have something to eat and perhaps the landlord would know whereabouts Rowens Lane was. It would be better than driving around in circles. The spirits only guided you to where you had to go, they did not do the job for you. If they did, his mission could have been completed without him leaving home. He smiled to himself when he thought of this. Then he thanked them once again for sending him.

The landlord was very helpful in giving him directions, telling him to be careful not to miss the opening to the lane, as it was very narrow and some ruffians had smashed the nameplate.

He found it quite easily but was thankful for the landlord's advice. For the lane was practically hidden between the houses on the estate. He'd not travelled far up the lane when he saw it led out between the open fields. In the distance, he could see the rooftop of a house.

When the house came into full view, he brought the car to a halt in the lane. He wondered whether to get out of the car and walk around, then decided to sit quietly in the car to pick up any vibes off his surroundings. While he sat there he admired the house – it was a typical country cottage with a large garden surrounding it. It was well maintained with its white-painted walls and wooden leaded windows set into the original stone mullion that surrounded them. He got the impression that the house itself was once two cottages that had now been modernized and made into one.

No sooner had the thought come into his mind than the pictures came, though this time they did not come as they usually did, as if he was watching a film – they came to him in the form of a picture book with someone turning the pages. He saw Bessie and Emma being greeted, he assumed, by Jessica and the family. There were two girls standing beside Jessica; he could tell they were twins and about the same age as Emma.

By the time the picture book ended, he'd seen Bessie leaving Emma and Robert in Jessica's care and Robert growing into manhood. It was on the day Robert was to marry Jessica's granddaughter that Joseph's TV screen came into action. He saw Emma and Robert, both dressed in their finest clothes. Emma was showing something to Robert which was resting on the palm of her outstretched hand.

As his mind's eye zoomed in on the object Emma was holding, he realized it was the box that held the ring. Then he heard Emma telling her son, 'Keep this safe, Robert. Your father gave it to me, it has been my mascot for a long time. I've treasured it more than life itself. But now it is your wedding day and I want it to become your mascot. You might as well have it now than when I am gone. But promise me you will never part with the ring. Give it to your eldest child when it is their wedding day, be it boy or girl.'

Only when Robert promised did Emma open the lid of the box. Once again Joseph's mind's eye zoomed in and he could see it was an amber and gold locket ring. A ring that could keep a secret, he thought.

He saw Emma close the lid of the box then give the box to Robert, who put it in his waistcoat pocket. This action puzzled Joseph, for he knew it was a locket ring, therefore there would be hinges so the ring could be opened, just like one could open a locket that was worn around the neck.

Some such rings had been designed to hold a lethal drug that would kill one's enemy or oneself if need be. But mostly they were given as a romantic gift to hold a miniature painting or a lock of hair. Surely Emma must have known this, he thought. So why had she not shown it to Robert?

When the vision of Emma and her son faded there came another series of pictures mostly showing Robert with his two daughters. The last picture of all showed Robert, his wife and their two children, now fully grown, standing in front of a house. Standing beside each other, smiling at the group were Emma and Jessica. The house was clearly defined with its mullioned windows and two doorways side by side.

When the picture faded, Joseph had no doubt that it was the same house that he'd been guided to. He also felt sure that Emma and Jessica resided together next door to their offsprings.

Joseph was about to pick up his cigarettes when he saw the net curtain of the upstairs window twitch. He'd no idea how long he'd been sitting there – he was not in the habit of looking at his watch – before his TV screen had come into action. He glanced at the clock on the dashboard. It was half an hour since he'd left the pub, so he could have been parked outside the cottage for at least twenty minutes.

He became concerned for whoever was watching from behind the curtains. The cottage was in a lonely place and he supposed it could be unnerving to see someone parked outside gazing up at the house.

He wished now he'd checked in at the pub for an overnight stay, which he'd thought about doing while talking to the landlord, then he would have been able to explore the area on foot. But he was about to mention it when a crowd of lunchtime regulars had come in and the landlord had gone to serve them.

He'd finished drinking his coffee before going outside to the car to set off to find Rowens Lane. I cannot just drive away now, he thought, I must go and explain what I am doing here.

He was about to open the car door when he realized he'd parked too near to the barbed-wire fence and it was impossible for him to do so. He drove across the lane coming to a halt outside the garden gate.

Getting out of the car, he saw the door to the house open and an irritated woman coming up the garden path. 'I'm sorry, Ma'am, if I've alarmed you,' he said before she'd time to speak, 'and if I have, I was just coming to apologize for doing so. It was rude of me to park up outside someone's home and to sit there gaping. But in all truth, I believe that one of my ancestors once lived here and I have come to England to follow their trail, so to speak.'

It was as near to the truth as he could tell her and he was relieved to see her attitude change towards him. Though she had the figure of a young woman and was dressed in a designer tracksuit, he guessed that she must be in her early sixties.

His explanation must have satisfied her, for she smiled then opened the garden gate and with typical northern hospitality, invited him in for a brew.

CHAPTER X

She'd first caught sight of him as she came out of the back bedroom and glanced out through the landing window. How long he'd been sitting there, she had no idea. She'd gone closer to the window to get a better view for he was sitting so still she'd thought he was ill or something. Yet she'd not been able to move herself to assist him if he was. It was as if she'd been transfixed until she'd heard the engine of the car start up, then was able to run downstairs, curious to know what the young man thought he was doing. The lane was private and he'd no business to be there.

Now, after he'd explained himself, she welcomed him into her home. She had no qualms about doing so, even though she lived alone. She was a good judge of character and she liked this young man.

By the time she'd ushered Joseph into the living room, he knew that she was a widow, by the name of Ann Mills, but to 'call her Ann and not Mrs Mills'; that her late husband Tim was her second husband; and she'd two sons from her first marriage and three grandchildren.

When she told him all this, he wondered if any of them belonged to the Ilinkas, or was there some other reason he'd been brought to this house. He knew when she'd closed the garden gate and they'd introduced themselves, that Ann Mills was not one from his lineage.

Whilst waiting for her to brew the tea, he admired the room with its beamed ceiling and dark wood furniture. The curtains were made of chintz that matched the settee and two armchairs. A thick-piled Chinese carpet filled the centre of the room with polished floorboards surrounding it.

He liked the unusual design of the red-brick fireplace, telling her so when she came back into the room carrying a tray filled with two cups of tea, cake and buttered scones.

He saw her face light up with pleasure as she put the tray onto the occasional table next to him, then told him with pride in her voice, 'Tim and myself designed the fireplace, you'll not find another one like it.'

He could tell when she spoke about Tim how she must have loved him. She would smile before speaking his name, then her eyes lit up with pleasure. She was surprised when he asked if there had once been a doorway behind the Dutch dresser standing in the alcove by the side of the fireplace.

'However did you know about that?' she asked.

'I was trying to visualize, as I sat in the car, what the house must have been like in the old days, when my ancestors dwelled here. I imagined that it was two cottages.' He knew this was only partly true but could not tell her of the vision.

It was his turn to be surprised, as well as delighted, when he heard her saying, 'Now don't be trying to pull the wool over my eyes, young man. I wasn't born yesterday. You never imagined it at all, you've got psychic powers and the house as it once was came into your mind's eye. Tim could do the same thing, though he would deny being able to do so. Even though . . . oh never mind, it does not matter. But I'll say one thing, Joseph. If I had any doubts about your ancestors once living here, you have just dispelled them.

'Tell me,' she said, 'what really brought you to England to find your bloodline?'

So he told her that he'd been obsessed with coming, ever since finding the chronicles in the loft.

He was thankful for her interrupting him by saying, 'Ah, yes, it is surprising what the attics and lofts of old houses do contain, with the relics from the past hidden in them.' She rose abruptly from her chair telling him, 'It is strange that you chose to come today, for I have been cleaning out my loft and stacking things in the back bedroom to get ready for the dustbin. I think there will be something that will be of interest to you which I will go and get.'

When she returned, she handed him a small case saying, 'There is something in there that might be of interest to you. It belonged to my first husband's father and has been gathering dust for years. Yet it was only this morning that I could bring myself to throw it out. That is why I thought it strange you turning up today, for tomorrow it would have been in the dustbin cart with all the other rubbish.

'Come into the kitchen,' she said, 'I'll make you another brew of tea, then I'll leave you while I go and finish clearing up. Perhaps when I'm done, you will help me take the other rubbish downstairs.'

As he followed her into the kitchen, he told her to give him a call when she needed him. He did not open the case until she had gone, finding inside a leather-bound book, wrapped in a piece of blue velvet. The pages inside were handwritten and he was surprised to find the writer's name was Thomas Mills. Was it a coincidence that Ann Mills's two husbands bore the same surname or were they related?

There was no doubt about the writer's name – it was there on the first page: 'Memories and Things, by Thomas Mills'. Then underneath, 'I am writing this, for I am bedridden and there's naught much else to do.'

As he scanned the pages, Joseph found that Thomas Mills had written about things that amused or angered him as well as family events and remembrances of what he'd been told.

It was one such article that caught Joseph's attention when he read,

> It is funny what thoughts rush through one's head, when there is so much time for thinking. Today, as I lay here doing naught else, I began to wonder of something my grandfather told me. About some distant relative, who was a sailorman. Bob Townley was his name. When home on leave, he would visit this house to stay with his Grandmother.
>
> Next door, at the time, lived two pretty maidens. Their father be a foreigner, some thought his two girls be queer, for they'd been given the sight, so t'was said. Bob Townley took no heed of these notions, he'd known the lassies from being young bairns.
>
> It was after he returned from one of his long sea voyages, finding

the girls now grown into beautiful young women, that he fell in love with Emily and married her. Then took her with him to Australia. I cannot say what happened to them, perhaps I was told but have now forgotten.

Upon reading this paragraph, Joseph laid the book down, and lit a cigarette. He was now convinced the two girls were the daughters of Robert Kyersh, and Bob Townley was visiting Bessie's friend Jessica. And if I'm right, he thought, and they arrived safely in Australia, then part of Robert's lineage should be there.

Picking up the book again, he wondered if there would be anything written about their other daughter. A few minutes later, he was wondering if Ann Mills herself had read this journal and if so, it was good of her to let him delve into it. He'd just read of how Thomas Mills disliked his daughter-in-law, and wondered for a moment whether he should continue with the reading of it. But he knew that he must, it would help him with his mission.

He was pleased, therefore, when he began to read a later paragraph:

I have misjudged that lass and I hope she will forgive me. She has tended my needs while I am ill, no task is too much for her.

I believed Ralph, when he told me she was neither a good wife or mother. I should have known better. Ralph, like his mother before him is good at pulling the wool over my eyes. But I have heard today from a trusted friend that it is Ralph who is a no good husband or father.

He treats both wife and sons so cruelly as to beat them and fornicates with a trollop in Leeds. I was told also that Ralph waits only for me to die. Then he will sell this place and go away with that trollop.

How could I have been so blind? Living next door to them, yet knowing nothing of what has been going on. It pains me to write this but I must, for it is true. How Ann and the boys must have suffered, both mentally and physically.

On the last page Joseph read:

I feel my maker will not be long in coming. But I shall go to him with peace in my heart, knowing I put wrongs to right.

Over the long period of my illness, Ralph badgered me to make my will. So I have granted him his wishes and have done so. My lawyer and two trusted friends have just left. In my will, I have left everything to Ann, my daughter-in-law. For she has been to me like a loving daughter with the care and devotion she has given me.

Ralph will be in for a shock. But there be nowt he can do about it. Nor will he wish to do so.

I have written in my will, that I know of his ill-treatment to his wife and my grandsons and also of his fornicating. I have also written that if Ann wishes to be rid of her husband, she has my blessing to do so.

Neither must she feel guilty for what I have done. For there are also other reasons. I have pondered long over them. From childhood I have forgiven Ralph many things, turning a blind eye to his shortcomings. Not wanting to believe my mother's words, though many times they would ring in my ears. 'The child your wife carries is not yours, Tom, it belongs to that braggart, James Herbert.'

My mind nor my heart would not let me believe what my mother said, for I loved my wife. But in my guts, I knew my mother spoke the truth. I prepared myself to love the baby when it came. Whether it be mine or James Herbert's. The child did not ask to come into this world, and it was me that was married to its mother.

When Ralph was born, I did love him as my own. My mother seeing how happy I was held her tongue.

Only when Ralph came into manhood, did I open my eyes and let my mind accept the truth. Yet I had reared him, so in a way he was still my son. But his true father's blood runs deep inside him and I cannot forgive him for what he has done to Ann and the boys.

I think I will not be writing anymore, so when Ann brings me my tea, I will ask her to fetch the small case from the wardrobe and put what I've written inside and tell her to leave it there until after I'm gone and the will's been read.

As he closed the journal, Joseph felt guilty about having read such personal things. He was also disappointed, there'd been no mention of Robert Kyersh other daughter. Yet he felt sure, deep inside himself, that the journal held some clue as to why he was here at this house.

As Ann stacked the last of the rubbish at the top of the stairs, she thought she might as well take a shower and get changed. That nice young man Joseph will see to this lot.

While she showered, she wondered what he would be thinking as he read the journal. She'd really no idea why she felt compelled to give it to him. Well she did, really. Tim had told her, too, though she could not tell anyone about that. They would think she was mad. But she knew that even though Tim was dead, he was still with her.

The boys thought she was mad anyway, living in this rambling house in the middle of nowhere, all alone. They could not understand that she was happy living here and though she might live on her own, she was never lonely.

Perhaps, she thought, a shadow crossing her face, the boys cannot erase from their memories, their father beating them up, or worse.

She shivered as she remembered the aftermath of the reading of the will. Ralph had been on top of the world, the morning they were to visit the lawyer. He was the Ralph she'd fallen in love with, but loved no more. He even kept calm once the will had been read, even though it told of his fornicating.

He'd laughed, saying, 'Where did the silly sod get that idea from? Dad's left everything to Ann, 'cause he knew she will look after everything better than me. We will be alright, won't we love.' She herself had been too stunned to answer. There wasn't a fortune, just the two houses and some monies in the bank.

When they left the lawyer's office Ralph spoke not another word, though she knew he was seething inside. As soon as they were inside the house, he took off his belt, lashing into her with the buckle end, calling her among other things, a conniving bitch. She'd taken the beating, until Ralph himself was exhausted, thankful that the children were at school, or they too would have been given the same.

Afterwards, she'd told him to pack his bags and get gone to his fancy woman in Leeds. He'd been cruel long enough to her and the boys and she'd no need to put up with it any longer. His own father had seen to that.

It was only when she threatened to call the police and show them what he'd done that he packed his bags and left. The next day she'd gone back to the lawyer. He took one look at her battered body and told her to file for divorce. She was never to see Ralph again – he ran off with his fancy woman. Five years later, she heard that he was dead.

Ann finished brushing her hair and picked up the silver picture frame from the dressing table. It held her favourite photograph of Tim.

'You brought so much happiness to this house,' she said. 'You loved us all as we'd never been loved before. I laughed, when you told me that you had been sent to take care of us. Then I came to believe that you had not lied.' Tears welled up in her eyes as she remembered their first meeting at the grave of her father-in-law.

It was on the day she'd heard that Ralph was dead. On impulse she bought some flowers, then jumped onto the bus that would take her to the cemetery. As she walked through the grounds, she wondered why she'd come today. It was Friday and she would be bringing the boys on Sunday, as she usually did.

While she tended the grave, she thanked her father-in-law for what he had done for them. I will never forget you, she said. Nor will I let your grandsons.

She'd heard no one approach and was so startled when she rose and saw a man standing on the pathway holding a bunch of flowers that she stumbled.

He caught her, saying, 'I'm sorry if I startled you, but I did not wish to intrude. Are you alright?'

'Yes, thank you,' she'd said, too embarrassed to look at him.

'Don't go,' he'd said. 'Let me take you to the cafe down the road.'

She'd been about to refuse, then curiosity got the better of her. She'd never seen him before and wondered why he'd come to visit her father-in-law's grave. As far as she knew, there was only herself and the boys who ever came.

He told her he was a distant relative, he'd been working abroad for the last ten years and that his name was Timothy Mills.

As he spoke his name, a vision of Ralph had come into her mind, beating her and the children. For a moment she felt as though she must get away. Ralph could be charming and look how he'd turned out. She shuddered at the remembrance of it.

But Ralph was dead and though she had no intention of becoming involved with another man, ever, especially one with the name of Mills, she felt the warmth from this man oozing out to her. Then she looked up and their eyes locked together.

At that moment she knew that this man could never be like Ralph. This man was of a special breed – he would not harm a single fly, never mind a human being. She remembered reading her father-in-law's journal, then smiled to herself as she told Timothy she would go with him to the cafe. Ralph had not belonged to this man's bloodline. Ralph belonged to the Herberts.

As she replaced the photo frame, she said out loud, 'I never regretted marrying you, Tim, you were everything a husband and father should be. I felt your love surround me the first day we met when I gazed into your eyes.

'I laughed when you told me later that you'd been sent to me by my late father-in-law to love and protect me for all I had suffered at the hands of Ralph. Why else would we have met at his graveside, you asked when I said it was coincidence.

'You told me quite seriously, that you knew I would be there. I came to discover over the years, you had some kind of psychic power. Of course, you always denied it.

'And now, that young man downstairs reminds me so much of you. I can feel the warmth of love coming from him. He too in his mind's eye can see what others cannot. Just as you always could. He is seeking his bloodline and I have no doubts that you belonged to his lineage.'

While Ann made some fresh lime juice to take out into the garden, Joseph saw to the rubbish upstairs, then went to fetch the small table and the two loungers from the garden shed as Ann had asked him to do. He was glad of her suggestion that they should go outside, it was too beautiful an afternoon to be stuck indoors.

While he waited for Ann, he admired the immaculate mown lawns and the well-tended borders with their profusion of flowers. There was also a vegetable plot as well as a herb one. Over the back wall the fields were flat with new-mown grass, the aroma filling the air. He felt for a moment as if time stood still. For from here, there was nothing to show that he was in a modern world.

He would have liked to see, in his mind's eye, more pictures of Emily and Robert, as well as others that once dwelt here. But he knew, when the visions did not come, that it would be up to himself to sort things out.

He sat himself down in one of the loungers, then gazed up at the house, saying to himself, What secrets do you hold for me? Surely there must be a reason for my being here? He rose to his feet when he saw Ann coming out of the kitchen door carrying a tray with the jug of lime juice and two glasses upon it, as well as an ashtray.

As he took the tray from her they walked together across the lawn and he told her how he'd been admiring the garden. 'It is how one imagines an English country garden to be,' he told her.

She smiled, telling him. 'Tim loved this garden. He planned it all out. Then when it was finished, he could not bear to see a blade of grass out of place and the weeds were hoed out as soon as they appeared. I do my best to do the same but I think next year I will have to employ a gardener.'

When she spoke Tim's name, her eyes, as always, lit up with the love she still felt for him. Joseph was pleased after what he'd read in the journal that Ann had found such love.

He placed the tray onto the table, then lit a cigarette, while Ann poured the drinks. As he sat down, laying his cigarettes and lighter on the table, he was surprised to hear her asking, 'May I have one of those?'

'I'm sorry,' he said, opening the packet of Dunhill, offering them to her, 'I didn't know you smoked.'

'I don't usually,' she told him. 'I gave them up when Tim died, but today has been so strange.'

He saw her fingers tremble as she took a cigarette, putting it to her lips. He flicked the lighter, asking, 'In what way?'

They both sat down before she began to tell him.

'Well, in the first place, when I woke up this morning. I had no intention of clearing out the attic. Then when I do, you turn up. I know that could be coincidence, things like that do happen. But just now, when you came to take the tray from me, I thought you were Tim. He used to do the very same thing. Even my heart skipped a beat, then I realized it was my imagination playing tricks, for it was a gesture any gentleman would do. But when I saw you'd placed the table between the two loungers facing each other, just as Tim would have done, and lit a cigarette while I poured the drinks, the only difference in you doing that was Tim would light a cigarette for me at the same time. So do you wonder that I feel in need of having a cigarette with you?'

'I'm sorry,' he said, 'I have no idea why I placed the table and chairs in such a fashion, though I thought it unusual at the time. If it upsets you, I can move them. I don't want to be responsible for you picking up this bad habit I have of smoking.'

She smiled, telling him, 'If I begin to smoke again, or not, it will be my choice. I cannot blame you or anyone else.'

They both relaxed, each thinking their own thoughts.

Joseph was wondering for what reason he'd placed the table and chairs as Tim would have done. Ann was thinking about Tim and how much he would have liked Joseph. It always saddened her that Tim and herself were never blessed with children. Tim loved children – he'd shown that with her own boys and his nephews Jack and Martin. She stopped in her train of thoughts, knowing now how she could help Joseph.

Stubbing out her half-smoked cigarette she asked of him, 'Would you like to stay for tea? I usually treat myself to fish and chips on Thursday but I can soon rustle up something for us.'

Joseph, good at picking up vibes from people, felt the excitement within her. He also knew she'd thought of something that would help him with his mission.

He smiled telling her, 'I would be delighted to stay to tea. But only if you'll let me go to the chip shop. I passed it on the way here. The pavement was full of school kids, eating their dinners from paper trays.'

She laughed, saying, 'I used to do that when I was a girl. But in those days, the man behind the counter wrapped our chips in newspaper, made into a bag, then lashed them with salt and vinegar.'

It was after they'd finished their tea, Joseph telling her how much he'd enjoyed his first taste of English fish and chips, that the subject of the journal came up. Ann told him of what happened after her father-in-law's death, then of how she'd met Tim. She also told him of Tim's two nephews, Jack and Martin, who'd lived over the Pennines in Lancashire, and in the school holidays loved to come and stay with Uncle Tim, Aunty Ann and the boys. Joseph felt the excitement in him rising.

Then she continued, 'Martin was doing a project at school about his family tree. He wasn't really interested and only went back as far as his great-grandparents. We thought no more about it. Martin was satisfied, saying it would do. But when he was twenty-one, he was killed in a motorcycle accident.

'A few months later, and for reasons I never understood, Tim became obsessed with his own family tree, which of course Martin belonged to. I could understand Tim's interest but not his obsession. To be honest, I was glad when he could go no farther back. He tried of course but it was as if the Gods forbade him to search beyond what he'd already found.

'I sighed with relief the night he put the seal upon it, telling me that one day it would be given to his nephew Jack. "Why not give it to him now?" I asked. "Because it is not time for him to be given it," he said.

'I thought it was a perfect time. Jack getting married, it would have been a lovely gift. But Tim said no, and that was that.

'I never mentioned it again, until Jack rang telling me he was going to be a dad. "You're going to have to put a new addition to your family tree," I said. But as it turned out it was not to be.'

Joseph, who'd listened patiently to this family saga, was listening no more. He knew without being told who Ann was speaking about. It was Jack Farrel. There was no doubt in his mind at all. Neither was it by chance that Jordana took him to the Mill House. The spirits had guided her into doing so.

He brought his attention back to Ann, as she was saying, 'It came to me while we were in the garden, that Tim's family tree would be of more use to you than Jack Farrel. I've no doubt that your bloodline is connected with Tim. You remind me so much of him, not in his looks. more in mannerisms. Besides, Jack has vowed he will never marry again and he's the last of the Farrels.'

Whatever else Ann was going to say, Joseph did not know. He interrupted her, asking, 'Would that be the same Jack Farrel who renovated the old mansion into the Mill House?'

He saw the surprise on her face as she answered, 'Yes, do you know him?'

'No, I have never met him, though I have dined there with a friend of mine, Jordana Oakley.' He was hoping, with the mention of Jordana's name, Ann might have recognized it and in doing so answered volumes of questions of the connection between Jack Farrel and Jordana. Especially if they were lovers.

He was disappointed. It was obvious the name Jordana meant nothing to Ann when she said, 'Fancy dining out at Jack's place. I'll go and get Tim's drawing of the family tree. Oh, this is so exciting, it is like piecing a jigsaw together.'

Joseph smiled to himself as she left the room. He thought it more like a chain being linked together. How long that chain would be, as yet he had no idea. Only the spirits in the sky knew that.

When she came back a few minutes later, Joseph saw her hands tremble as she broke the seal before she unrolled the document, laying it upon the kitchen table. She was as eager as himself to see what it would reveal. Joseph could not believe his eyes. It was all there before him.

It began quite simply – Emma Kyersh, mother of Robert; and ended with the marriage of Timothy Mills to Ann Mills. The Farrel branch came into being when Tim's sister married John Farrel.

Like all family trees, it was an interesting document. Even Ann, who'd been 'relieved not so long ago, to see the back of it', was fascinated. It might have troubled her, the obsession that Tim had for tracing his lineage, then when it was done, not giving it to Jack Farrel. But Joseph knew now this document was not meant to be given to Jack Farrel, but to himself. And somehow, Tim also knew that this was how it would be.

The spirits moved in mysterious ways. He'd been guided to Archie's house because Robert was born there and to this house because it was from here that Robert's lineage began. Of course he could not tell Ann of what he was thinking. Yet he felt duty bound to tell her something of the history of it all.

She pointed to Emma's name, saying, 'Fancy, all this coming from her. I wonder who she was and where she came from? I remember Tim telling me her son had foreign blood in him, but Tim could find no trace of her parents. Poor lass, she must have suffered in those days, being an unwed mother.'

Joseph smiled at her words, telling her, 'Emma did not suffer, she was well provided for, and if you make us some coffee, I will tell you about her. It is the least I can do, for the way you have helped me.'

She would never know, he thought, how near the truth she had been when she'd said earlier about Tim's researching his family history, that it was as if the Gods forbade him to search beyond.

But now, though he could not tell her of his true mission, he could tell her the story of Emma Kyersh and of how he himself came from the lineage of Robert's father.

CHAPTER XI

It was nine-thirty when Joseph arrived back at the farm. He knew there would be no one at home as he'd phoned earlier and Barbara told him they would all be out.

He showered, then put on his dressing gown, intending to watch TV and have an early night, but for no apparent reason he decided to get dressed and walk down to the village pub.

Crossing the village square, he was surprised to see a brand new Mercedes parked outside the pub. Bet that cost a few dollars, he thought, admiring the car before entering the pub. The landlord greeted him like a long-lost friend, then told him Jordana was in the other room.

He turned to look through the open doorway. Jordana was sitting with her back to him, deep in conversation with a man dressed in grey gaberdine slacks and a grey silk shirt, his wrists adorned with a gold watch and bracelet. He looked to be in his late forties, but with his blond hair and tanned complexion, it was hard to tell. Joseph knew at once that it was Jack Farrel and the car outside belonged to him.

As he observed them, he was struck by the strong resemblance between them. If he'd not known Jordana, he would have thought them to be father and daughter. It can't be possible, he thought, yet he could not forget the electrifying touch of Jordana's hand.

He thought of Barbara, wondering, for a fleeting moment, if she'd once had an affair with Jack Farrel. Then he dismissed it as soon as it came. Peter and Barbara Oakley were a devoted couple – their marriage was made in Heaven, his father would have told him.

His puzzled mind came out of its reverie as the landlord put the pint of ale onto the bar, saying, 'Fancy chap, Jordana's with tonight. Worth a bob or two, I bet. Have you seen that fancy machine outside? It's his!'

A moment later, Jordana was standing beside him, introducing Jack Farrel. As they shook hands, there was no doubt in Joseph's mind that Jack Farrel came from the lineage of Robert Kyersh. So did Jordana. Neither Peter nor Barbara did, he was positive of that.

He accepted Jack's offer for him to join them. They were going to the Mill House, Jack told him. Once again, he was struck by the likeness of Jack and Jordana. No matter, he thought, when the time is right, all will be revealed.

Driving up the gravel path towards the Mill House, Jack could see the car park was full. He pulled in at the place specially reserved for himself. When they alighted from the car, he said, 'That's what I like to see – all those cars. It shows me my work was not in vain.' He smiled at Joseph, saying, 'Jordana's been telling me of your idea for a croquet pitch. I like it. It will be amusing to see whether this generation takes to what was once a pastime for the gentry.'

He ushered them through a private door, then into the Carding Room. Where in no time at all, they were being served with T-bone steaks and champagne to wash it down.

While they ate, Joseph observed Jack. Outwardly, he was flamboyant, laughing and joking with those who came to congratulate him on the success of his venture. But Joseph could feel the sadness that was eating at Jack's heart, a sadness that Jack would not let be seen to the outside world. Jordana was right, Joseph thought, when she told me Jack has everything, yet he has nothing.

He looked at her now. So young, so beautiful, yet she was able to detect the sadness being held in someone else. His eyes went to her outstretched hands as she twirled the stem of her glass between her palms. Those beautiful hands, and Jordana knows not what power is within them. The power of Ilinka runs through her, as it did with Sara. But it will not be the Blue Mountain that brings that power forth. It will be me.

His gaze once again fell upon Jack. He knew he would have to help him, release him from his sadness.

When the waiter finished pouring their coffee, Jack passed around his cigarettes. As he flicked his lighter, Jordana suggested they all go to Jack's place for a nightcap.

'It's alright by me,' Jack said, 'if Joseph doesn't mind.'

'I'm easy,' Joseph told him, knowing all the time he wanted nothing more than to be with Jack Farrel in his home surroundings, and that the spirits in the sky also wished it to be so.

It was 2 a.m. Jack was sitting in the soft leather armchair, staring into space, a goblet of brandy lodged between his fingers.

'If we are staying the night,' Jordana said to Joseph, 'I'd better show you to your room.'

'I'm sorry about this,' she said, as Joseph followed her, 'I should have known that Jack would hit the bottle, it is the anniversary of Clare's death. If you prefer, I could phone for a taxi for you, but I will stay here.'

'I don't mind staying,' he told her, 'and I'll put Jack to bed when he's ready.'

'Thanks for understanding, though I don't think Jack will go to bed. To be honest, when he gets like this, he usually sleeps it off in the chair. But just in case, that's his room over there, this one's yours. I'm on the landing.

'This room's en-suite,' she said, opening the door. 'You'll find pyjamas in the top drawer. Don't worry about Jack, if he wants to sleep in the chair, he'll be alright. I'm bushed. I'll see you in the morning.'

A moment later she was gone. Joseph admired the room; the thick pile carpet, walls, curtains and the bedspread were of matching blue, enhancing the hand-carved mahogany furniture. So rich, yet so poor, he thought as he went into the bathroom. Here too was the best that money could buy, with the marble floor and sunken bath with gold fittings. Pushing open a glass door, he found it led into a shower and sauna room.

Going back into the bedroom, he stripped off his clothes. It is going to be a long night, he said to himself, as he went towards the shower room, and I will need some help from the spirits in the sky.

He showered and dried himself before walking naked into the bedroom. Then he began to chant, dancing a sacred ritual as he did so. Raising his arms into the air, he called to the spirits in the sky to help him with the tormented man who was a brother to their tribe. When the spirits answered him, he bowed to the four corners of the room. He had seen what had to be seen.

As he dressed himself, he wished he could be wearing his doeskin pants. Then he smiled at the thought of Jack seeing him as an Indian brave standing before him.

When he left the room he felt refreshed and alert, ready for what lay before him.

When Joseph entered the room, Jack was pouring himself another brandy. He looked up as Joseph entered. 'Oh, there you are,' he said, 'thought you'd gone to bed. Help yourself.'

Though he'd no intention of drinking it, Joseph poured some brandy into a goblet. As he did so, he watched Jack fumbling towards the armchair. No sooner was Jack seated, the brandy glass halfway towards his lips, when Joseph said, 'Tell me about Clare.'

The hand holding the glass paused in midair as Jack replied, 'Clare's dead and I don't wish to talk about her.'

'I know she's dead,' said Joseph, as if he was talking to a stupid child. 'She's been dead a long time but I still want you to talk to me about her.'

'Well, stuff you,' said Jack. 'Who do you think you are, coming into my house, drinking my brandy, then wanting to talk about Clare? Why, you never even met her.'

It was too early yet for Joseph to tell him that not five minutes before, he'd seen Clare and the child. The spirits had shown her to him and also the child, the child that was not meant to be born in the earth world but was taken care of just the same.

'What the hell do you think you're doing now?' asked Jack, in a slurred voice as Joseph took the glass of brandy from him, putting it on to the mantelshelf.

Joseph ignored him as he took hold of Jack's hands, putting them palm to palm, with his own, then told Jack, 'Whether you like it or not,

I am here to help you.'

Jack tried to pull his hands away but they would not move. He stared at the man standing before him then felt his body become lighter as he seemed to be lifted out of the chair. It felt like a magnet was bonding his hands to the man's. He thought he must be dreaming when a golden cloud enfolded them.

Who was this bloody fellow anyway? He could vaguely remember he was a friend of Jordana. He must remember to tell her she had some funny friends, when they could bring a golden cloud into his sitting room.

He felt the man's hands release him, yet he still could not move. He heard a voice saying, 'It is alright, Jack, I am with you. You must tell me your innermost thoughts, or I cannot help you. What is it that eats away your soul? Is it the things you feel guilty about?'

For a moment Jack wondered how this man knew he felt guilty about anything at all and wanted to deny that he did. Yet he could not. He could feel the sadness inside of him ebbing away and felt so good inside this golden cloud, he did not want the feeling to leave him. He was also sure that if he lied to this man, he would never feel happiness again.

It had begun with the death of his brother Martin, then Clare, and finally his parents. After each death, he'd been told that time heals. Maybe it does for some, but not for me. You might pretend to the outside world that all is well, but inside yourself you know nothing will ever be the same again.

Only now within the golden cloud did he feel there might be hope for a new beginning. And when next he laughed, so too would his heart, his heart that for so long had been like a heavy weight inside him.

He felt a hand grip his; he was sure that at any moment he would be taken out of this golden sanctuary. Perhaps if he told the man of his guilty feelings, he would be able to stay; he did not want to return to his world of sadness.

A moment later, he was confessing of how he blamed himself for his brother Martin's death. If he hadn't lent Martin his motorbike that night, Martin would not have been killed. And of how he'd loved Clare from being at school. Yet he had not married her until he could afford to build her a house. All those years wasted, when all Clare wanted was for us to marry and have a family. She would have been happy to live in a tent with me. And the guilt he felt about his parents, working all the hours God sent, so he could go to college, when he should have gone into the cotton mill, bringing wages home to make life easier for them. I would have done but Uncle Tim drummed it into me that the cotton trade would soon be doomed. They were sending the machines abroad, so that the cotton could be spun and woven on the cheap. 'Go into the building trade, Jack,' he told me. 'In another fifteen years folks will be wanting to buy their own homes, they'll not be satisfied with paying rent all their lives with nothing to show for it.' He did not tell me that when the boom time came, my family would be wiped out.

He felt the tears well up into his eyes and tried to wipe them away – he was not going to cry. He'd not shed a tear when any of them died, he was not going to do so now. Boys don't cry, his mother always said.

He felt two arms embrace him and a soothing voice telling him to let the tears flow, they would take away the pain and also wash away the guilt.

With the last tears spent, someone took hold of his arm. He saw that it was Jordana's friend, Joseph. They were both standing in the midst of a golden cloud. Joseph was smiling, 'I have something to show you,' he was saying. Joseph gestured with his right hand, waving part of the cloud away, telling him to look into the open space.

As he did so, he saw Martin walking towards him. Martin's body was not mangled any more, as it was after the crash. It was the Martin that he loved, happy and smiling. Clare followed Martin, holding a child. She too was smiling, the smile he'd always remember. His parents came next. They walked hand in hand. They were not breathless or haggard with the cotton disease. They came and stood behind Martin and Clare. Clare lifted the child which was a girl, the image of her mother. They were all smiling, as if waiting for him to take a family photograph. And in a way, he was doing so, for the picture would be forever printed upon his mind.

He heard Joseph telling him, 'They have come to show you they are all together and that now you have seen they are happy, you must not feel guilty or blame yourself any more.' As if to confirm what Joseph had told him, he saw them all blowing him a kiss before they disappeared. It was a gesture that had always pleased him.

A moment later, the golden cloud burst and he was standing in his own living room with Joseph at his side. He felt relaxed and happy, not a bit befuddled with drink. Yet he could not believe what he'd just seen. He looked at Joseph who was smiling, and knew it had not been a dream.

Joseph walked away from him, returning a moment later with two glasses of brandy, then saying as he passed one to him, 'Here's to a new beginning, Jack.'

CHAPTER XII

When Jordana came into the kitchen, she was surprised to see both Jack and Joseph tucking into bacon and eggs. She scrutinized Jack. He looked different this morning. There was an air of happiness about him. And what was he doing eating breakfast? Usually when he'd been on a binge, the only thing he could stomach was black coffee.

She glanced at Joseph. He didn't look as though he'd been up all night either. Yet she knew they had not been to bed – she'd looked into their rooms on the way down.

She was even more surprised when she heard Jack asking, 'Want some breakfast? I'll make you some.'

'No thanks,' she replied. 'I'll just have some coffee. I'm going to have to rush you, Jack. I've a riding lesson at nine-fifteen and its eight o'clock now.' As she poured herself a mug of coffee Joseph began to clear the table.

'Don't bother with that,' said Jack. 'The cleaner will be in shortly, she'll see to it. We'll have a cigarette, then be on our way.'

It was a lovely morning and for once Jack was able to appreciate it. He took a swift glance at the garden – it was immaculate. He made a mental note to thank the gardener himself, instead of leaving his wages with the cleaner.

The morning traffic was heavy but once he'd turned off the main road and onto the cobbled lane, he drove the car expertly around the twisting bends.

Joseph, sitting in the back seat, wondered if Jack would drive up to the farm, for he could not imagine if the car had been his, tackling the narrow lane with such a machine as this.

A moment later, he could see that Jack had no qualms as he manoeuvred the car around the dangerous bend, as expertly as Peter had done with the Range Rover, and then on up the bumpy lane. As soon as the car came to a halt in the farmyard Jordana jumped out saying, 'See you both later.'

Jack made no attempt to get out, but turned to Joseph saying,

'I don't know what you did to me last night. I feel like a different human being this morning.'

Joseph smiled, saying, 'I will explain it all to you later. I presume you're coming into the house!'

'Yes!'

'Then you must come to my room. There is much that I must tell you.' Joseph opened the car door and stepped out.

As he watched Joseph making his way to the back of the house, Jack wondered what Joseph had to tell him that he could not have told him last night.

He got out of the car and followed. When he entered the kitchen, Barbara was telling Joseph she and Peter were going into town. Peter was standing by the table. He too greeted Jack as he entered, saying, 'And what might you three have been up to last night?' Then, laughing, said, 'On second thoughts, don't tell me, I probably won't believe you anyway.'

You never spoke a truer word, thought Jack, as he heard Peter continuing, 'Though I must say, Jack, you look in much better shape this morning than at other times you've brought Jordana home.'

'Don't be cheeky,' said Barbara. 'Whatever will Joseph think, saying things like that. Come on, away with you. You know I like to get to the market early. See you both later,' she said, ushering Peter out of the room.

Joseph observed the bantering closely. It was obvious they knew Jordana often stayed at Jack's place and they did not mind, but it was also obvious to him that Jordana and Jack were good friends and not lovers. And now that he'd seen Peter, Barbara and Jack together, he was certain Jack and Barbara had never had an affair.

Yet there was a connection somewhere, for the resemblance between

Jack and Jordana was uncanny. He'd noticed it last night, and again this morning. Perhaps when I speak to Jack the mystery will unfold, he thought.

He looked at Jack, asking, 'Shall we go to my room while the house is quiet? Or would you like some coffee first?'

Jack, intrigued after last night's experience and wanting to know what this was all about, said, 'We will have some coffee later.'

When a few moments later Joseph showed Jack his Uncle Tim's family tree, that Jack's Aunty Ann had given him, Jack became more puzzled than ever, saying, 'I can't think how Aunty Ann came to give you this. She usually won't part with anything of Uncle Tim's. In fact, I'm sure she still thinks he's in the house, the way she talks about him.'

Joseph smiled at this assumption, knowing that Ann was right to feel this way. Tim would always be with her. Watching over her as he did in life. So too would Jack's family watch over him, now he'd let them back into his heart. For so long, though Jack loved them all, he'd closed his heart to them.

Joseph pointed to the name Robert Kyersh, saying, 'She gave it to me because he is from the bloodline of my ancestral lineage.'

'Well, I'll be buggered,' said Jack, interrupting him. They were both sitting on the side of the bed, the family tree spread between them.

'I told you in the car,' said Joseph, 'that I had much to tell you and my story begins here at this very farm. So it seems appropriate to me that it is from this room the saga of the Tylers will be told to you.'

He took the cigarette that Jack was offering and when it was lit began to tell Jack about the Ilinka tribe and the power they held. He ended by telling Jack, 'That power runs through me and it also flows through you.'

'Me?' said Jack. 'Don't be daft. That might have been the power of Ilinka you used on me last night but I can assure you, there's nothing the likes of that inside of me.'

'The power of the Ilinka is within you,' Joseph told him. 'It has always been with you. All that it needed is for the power to be brought forth. This I will do.'

'So that was what last night was all about?' Jack asked him.

'Yes, but first you had to be healed from the guilt and remorse you held inside yourself. It was not good. Man has no control over being called to the spirit in the sky. No matter where we are, when the time comes, we must go. Even doctors can only help the sick. They cannot prevent the time of death.'

Jack understood all this. His father said much the same thing when he'd come back from the war. 'I was one of the lucky ones,' his father told him. 'My name wasn't on any bullet.' His father had seen nearly all his platoon gunned down at Dunkirk. Yet Jack could not understand why some people had to suffer so much before they died. As his parent had done fighting the cotton disease that filled people's lungs.

When he asked about this Joseph told him, 'That I cannot answer. I only know there is a reason for all things. Just as there was a reason for Emma Kyresh coming to England for the birth of Robert. I cannot explain to you why the spirits wished it to be so. I can only tell you I have been sent to find those of Robert's lineage and that you are to help me.

'The Great White Spirit in the sky is angered with the greed and destruction that is upon the mother earth. He wants peace and purity to be restored, as it was always meant to be when mother earth was first created. All things were put upon the earth that mankind did need. The tribes of old knew of all this and showed respect. Now, says the Great White Spirit, if mankind cannot respect the mother earth, then mother earth will not respect mankind.'

Jack was fascinated with all Joseph was telling him. Yesterday, he would have thought it all a load of bunkum, but now with his new enlightenment, he realized it could all be true. Was true in fact.

'But what is going to happen to mankind?' he asked, his own thoughts imagining some silly bugger pressing the red alert and starting an atomic war. This had been a threat for years now and he'd often wondered it this was the reason for the devil-may-care attitude of the youngsters of today.

'I cannot answer your question,' he heard Joseph replying. 'My mission is to bring the true lineage of the Ilinka tribe together. They must be sought out from the four corners of the earth. Only then will the Great White Spirit reveal what is to become of mankind. That is why I have been led to you. With your help and the appearance of this family tree, my quest will be much easier.'

He thought of Jordana and knew that somehow she belonged to this lineage. But how? The spirits of his ancestors had not enlightened him about Jordana. They would only show him what had to be seen. He knew that in all else he would have to find his own way. It would be up to himself to link the chain.

He thought once again of the resemblance between Jordana and Jack. With his forefinger he traced the lineage down from Robert Kyersh. When his finger came to a halt, he said to Jack, 'Tell me of those that still live and of what you know about them.'

As he followed the branch lines with Joseph, Jack thought it uncanny how his memory became so sharp and clear. Remembering long-forgotten relatives, some of whom emigrated to Australia and New Zealand after the war. There were others that had gone to South Africa.

'No wonder they call it a family tree,' he said. 'The bloody branches go everywhere.'

He saw Joseph's finger come to rest on the names of his mother and Uncle Tim. Then felt his heart beating fast, when he heard Joseph saying, 'Tell me about Jordana, I know she belongs to this lineage.'

Jack looked up into Joseph's eyes. He knew there was no doubt in Joseph's mind about Jordana but he still asked, 'And what made you come to that conclusion?'

'To be honest,' Joseph replied, 'it was the resemblance to yourself that put me onto it. I knew that the blood of the Ilinka runs through Jordana, yet does not do so in the rest of her family.'

'How did you know that?' Jack wanted to know.

'The same way I knew it ran through you, by the touch of the hands. But tell me about Jordana.' Joseph could not wait for this link in the chain to be connected, yet was unprepared for the story Jack was to tell him.

Jack's mind flashed quickly over the events of the night before. He was about to tell this stranger something he'd never told his parents and they should have had more right to know than anyone. But it was too late now.

A picture came into his mind's eye – it was as he'd seen them the night before, standing together with Martin, Clare and the child. Perhaps they know now, he thought. He gave a sigh of relief, then began to tell Joseph.

'You are right about Jordana, she does come from the Farrel bloodline. Jordana is my brother Martin's child. Martin told me the night before he died that he'd got a girl into trouble and was going to marry her.

'"Don't mention anything about it to Mum and Dad. I'll tell them myself when I've sorted everything out."

'"Who is she? Is she local?" I asked him. Martin wasn't like me, I only ever wanted Clare. Martin liked to play the field.

'"It's Susan," he said, "and she's three months gone."

'I knew Susan. Martin met her one night in Leeds, when we'd gone to stay at Uncle Tim's for the weekend. They'd been friends for two years, though they weren't courting. Sometimes Clare and I used to go out with them.

'"Are you sure you're doing the right thing?" I asked him, knowing he was also sweet on a girl down the road.

'"Susan will do me," he said, laughing. "I'm going over to see her tomorrow night. Then we'll tell her parents." That's where Martin was heading when he was killed. My parents were grief-stricken enough with Martin's death, so there was no way I could tell them about Susan.

'Clare wanted us to take a bus ride over to Leeds the weekend before Martin's funeral and tell Susan. But I was against doing so. It would have upset Mum and Dad all the more if they'd found out about Susan. So we waited until the next weekend. But when we got there, Susan already knew about Martin. She told us when Martin did not arrive as he'd promised, she had a feeling something awful had happened. Then she thought perhaps Martin had changed his mind about marrying her, after all they were not engaged and if he had, she was not prepared to come looking for him. Yet for days afterwards, she could not rid herself of the feeling that something awful had happened to Martin.

'She rang Uncle Tim, on the pretence of asking if Martin would be over at the weekend. Ironically, it was the evening after the funeral and Uncle Tim had just arrived home. When she told us, I felt guilty for not letting her know. When I told her this, she said she understood.

'Clare asked her about the baby and how she was going to cope. To our surprise she said everything was being taken care of. She'd been so upset when she'd heard the news about Martin, she told her mother about the baby. There'd been a family conference and it was decided her sister Barbara would rear the child as her own. Though they thought at the time only themselves knew about the baby, they'd no idea Martin had told me.

'Clare asked her how she felt about giving her child away, even though it was to her own sister. "I won't know until it happens," Susan told her. "But as neither Martin nor I planned to have a baby and Martin's not here now, I think it will be for the best."

'It was just after she told us this, her parents arrived home and with them was Barbara and her husband Peter. They were surprised to see us but later it was decided between us all to keep the arrangements already made. It was also decided, rightly or wrongly, that my parents were not to be told and that I, even as the child's uncle, would have no further contact with the family.

'At first I was reluctant to agree, wondering what Martin would want me to do. It was Peter who made up my mind for me. "Look," he said, "we have all decided what is best for the child. But one day, the child will have to be told the truth. I promise you, when that day comes, if the child wants to see you, we'll have no objections."

'I agreed to this, but Clare was reluctant to do so. She was thinking about my parents. "I know it will come as a shock to them," she said, "but in time the child might be a comfort."

'I knew what she was trying to say, and in a way I agreed with her, but in the end we did as the Oakleys wanted.

'Afterwards, as if by some unspoken agreement, Clare and I never mentioned the subject again. We never even knew whether the child was a boy or girl. Over the years, I wondered silently how the child was faring, asking myself many times what Martin would have done had it been me in his shoes.

'Then one day, fate played its part. By this time, the boom time Uncle Tim had predicted had arrived and people were wanting to buy bigger and better properties. After Clare's death, I'd put my heart and soul into my work, taking chances others would not take.

'I heard of a farmer in Yorkshire wanting to sell his land. I'd already had plans drawn up of the kind of houses I wanted to build. They were spacious with four bedrooms, more for the executive type than anyone else and I wanted them built in Yorkshire stone. It would be a challenge, but it could also make or break me. Anyway, I decided to take the risk. You could have knocked me down with a feather when the farmer introduced me to his farm manager and it turned out to be Peter Oakley.

'We recognized one another right away. Peter invited me into his house. Barbara was in the kitchen baking. She was surprised to see me but made me welcome while Peter explained to her why I was at the farm.

'Barbara made us a brew and some buttered scones. Then they told me about Jordana – she was a teenager by now and they were very proud of her and of their son Ashley. I wondered if they'd told Jordana the truth but didn't like to ask.

'As if reading my thoughts, Barbara said, "You must stay and have some tea with us. Jordana will want to meet you."

'"You've told her then?" I asked.

'"She knows the circumstances of her birth," Barbara replied. "Yet she's shown no interest in finding anything out about her real father's family."

'"Will it not be a shock for her seeing me then?" I asked. "I could go away, then come back later, when you've warned her."

'"Don't be daft," Barbara said. "You don't know Jordana, she takes everything in her stride." I agreed to stay and they showed me photographs of Jordana from being a baby to the present day.

'Jordana was the spitting image of Martin. I felt a twinge of guilt that my parents, now dead, had never known her.

'I brought them up to date with my own life, since we'd met.

'"And you've not married again?" Barbara asked me.

'"No, and I never will. My work is my life now," I told her.

'When Jordana arrived, my heart leapt. It could have been Martin walking through the door, especially with her short-cropped, curly hair. She was tall, like him, with the same happy smile.

'When Barbara told her who I was, Jordana said the strangest thing: "I knew that one day you would find me," she said.

'I wondered why she'd said this, for never once had I ever thought to look for her. Then she told me, "I will never call you Uncle. I would feel disloyal to my parents, but we could be friends."

'And that is how its been ever since, not only with Jordana, but with Peter and Barbara as well.

'So there you have it. Now you know how Jordana came to have the same bloodline as myself.'

Joseph, who'd listened with interest to all Jack told him, could now understand Jordana's reluctance to be questioned about Jack Farrel on the night they'd gone out into the gardens at the Mill House. Jordana would not wish to speak about her family history to someone she'd only just met. He could also understand why Jordana took care of Jack in his bouts of depression which hopefully, after last night, Jack would be rid of.

He thanked Jack for telling him about Jordana, then told him, 'I will need your help with my search for those abroad. Do you know of their whereabouts?'

Jack confessed he'd no idea, as the only relations he ever kept in touch with were his late Uncle Tim and now Aunty Ann. 'But there's an old box at my place belonged to Mam. She called it her treasure trove. I could never bring myself to throw it out. Perhaps there will be something inside that might be of help.'

Within no time at all, they were back at Jack's place sifting through the box. 'Me Mam loved writing to folk,' said Jack, picking up a bundle of letters, 'and she'd not throw anything away.'

'I'm glad she didn't,' said Joseph. 'If my guess is right, we should find a mine of information in here.'

The letters jogged Jack's memory to days long gone when his mam took him to visit aunts and uncles and their families. He was reading one such letter when Joseph heard him saying out loud, 'Well I'll be buggered.'

'What is it?' Joseph asked, as he saw Jack's eyes skimming across the page. Jack looked up, then laughingly told Joseph, 'I've just been reading about Aunty Jean's grandson. Right cock of the north, he was, Cedric Bell. Always bullying our Martin, until I challenged him to a fight. I broke his nose. Right thumping I got for that, I can tell you. But it was worth it, he never bothered either Martin or myself again.

'But I never knew he'd gone to Tenerife and bought himself a restaurant. Last I heard about him, he was getting wed to a girl he'd been living with for ten years. Fancy me not knowing about that. I often visit Tenerife. I would have looked him up if I'd known.'

At that moment there came into Joseph's mind a message, on what he called his ticker tape. He called it this because it was like a strip from a telegram being pulled through the inside of his forehead. The message read, YOU MUST GO TO TENERIFE. He did not question it, knowing there would be a reason, as to why he should go. So he said to Jack, 'I think we should seek out Cedric Bell.'

'OK,' said Jack, picking up his mother's old address book. It would have been all the same to him if Joseph had told him they were to visit the man in the moon. After last night's experience, anything could be possible.

When all the information they needed was gathered together, Joseph faxed a letter to his father telling him what he'd accomplished so far.

As Jack drove him back to the farm, Joseph smiled when he heard Jack telling him, 'I'm enjoying all this. And I can't wait for us to go and find Cedric in Tenerife. It is a fantastic place. I think you'll find it's worth visiting, even if we don't find Cedric.'

Then as if as an afterthought, Jack asked him, 'But what about Jordana? When are you going to tell her about belonging to the Ilinka bloodline?'

'Not until her twenty-first birthday,' Joseph replied. 'And you must give her no inkling of why we are going to Tenerife, or of our quest.'

Jack wondered what plans Joseph had for Jordana, but did not question him. He gave Joseph a quick glance, then thought to himself,

I don't know what is to become of all this, but there is no doubt in my mind that Jordana and Joseph would make a bloody perfect twosome.

CHAPTER XIII

A week later Joseph and Jack were in Tenerife. They'd found the whereabouts of Jack's arch enemy, Cedric Bell. His restaurant was situated on the south side of the island and they were now on their way to dine there.

'Do you think he'll recognize you?' Joseph asked, as they were about to enter the restaurant.

'Who knows?' replied Jack. 'It's such a long time since we saw each other, I might not recognize him.'

The restaurant was full, but they managed to get a table in the corner from which they could observe the whole place. As far as Jack could see, there was no sign of Cedric. He wondered if Cedric had bought the restaurant and like so many others on Tenerife, leased it out. He could imagine Cedric doing such a thing, letting someone else do the work for him.

They were halfway through their meal, when amid much merriment a party of six came in through the open doorway. Jack, glancing up, saw Cedric leading his guests towards the bar. He turned to Joseph, saying, 'That's Cedric, the one wearing the blazer.'

Joseph disliked Cedric as soon as he set eyes upon him. Neither did he take a liking to Cedric Bell's friends – they were all showy and loud.

He knew instantly that the reason for him being in Tenerife was not Cedric Bell.

At that moment his eyes spotted an old man sitting at the far end of the bar. He felt the old man's eyes penetrating into his own, and a kindred spirit flashing between them. He rose from the table, telling

Jack he would be back in a moment.

Jack, watching Joseph as he walked to the end of the bar and shake hands with the old man, wondered how Joseph knew him. The man looked like a native of the island; he also looked out of place in the restaurant which was filled with affluent holidaymakers. He could be from another era, thought Jack as he turned his attention towards Cedric.

When Joseph returned he told Jack he was meeting the old man down at the harbour in an hour's time. 'His name is Pelecoma,' he said, 'and he has something to show me. I will tell you more about it later. Now I think it is time you introduced me to Cedric Bell, then we will be on our way.'

'You don't like Cedric either, do you?' Jack asked.

'No!' was Joseph's simple reply.

When Jack introduced him to Cedric, Joseph knew for certain that Cedric Bell was not of Robert Kyersh's lineage. He was a big hunk of a man and if Joseph was right about him, not too honest in his business affairs.

Cedric asked them both to join him, but Joseph refused, saying they were on their way to keep another appointment.

Cedric, being the coarse man that he was said loud enough for everyone to hear, 'Got two dolly birds lined up, have you? Well, don't let me keep you. See you around sometime.'

There was much laughter from his friends when he made this remark, but Cedric knew he'd been snubbed as he watched Jack and Joseph walk out of the restaurant.

'We could at least have had a drink with him,' said Jack when they got outside.

'He is not of our lineage,' Joseph told him, 'so there is no point in wasting our time.'

It took Jack a moment to realize what Joseph was saying. How could Cedric not be of their lineage, if he and Cedric were cousins? Then he remembered – it was Cedric's father that was of the lineage, not Cedric's mother.

He laughed out loud when he realized the implication of these thoughts, telling Joseph, 'Me mam always said, "Cedric's mother was sweet on a yank during the war." Seems me mam was right all along.'

Pelecoma was waiting for Joseph when he went down to the harbour. He led Joseph to a small boat, then they headed out to sea.

Though Pelecoma spoke in his native tongue, Joseph had no difficulty in understanding him. The spirits had led him to this island; they had also sent Pelecoma to meet him. For what reason, as yet, Joseph did not know. He only knew that before the day was over, all would be revealed to him.

Pelecoma steered the boat into a small cove sheltered by the high mountain. 'I hope you are sure-footed like a goat,' Pelecoma said, as he secured the boat. Joseph looked up, wondering how far he would have to climb into this mountain. There was no sign of any paths that could have been travelled by others, then heard Pelecoma saying, 'If you follow my footsteps the way will not be hard for you.'

Joseph nodded, hoping Pelecoma was right. He did not know how far they had to go into the mountain and though he was used to climbing, he felt it would be no easy trek and silently thanked the spirits for being with him.

As if reading his mind, he heard Pelecoma saying, 'Do not be afraid. In this mountain there is hidden something very precious and of great importance to your tribe. The spirits will take great care of you, seeing that you will return safely.'

Joseph relaxed and smiled, then followed Pelecoma confidently until they came to a cave high up in the mountain. The cave itself was small – though Joseph and Pelecoma were able to stand at their full height, the cave only measured about eight feet by nine feet. The walls and floor were of what looked to Joseph like shining black coal. Joseph wondered how such a cave came to be here, for they'd passed no other on their way up.

Pelecoma sat down on the floor, Indian fashion, then motioned to Joseph to do the same. He did so. When he was seated he looked into Pelecoma's eyes and felt the power of Ilinka enter the cave.

He'd known from the beginning that Pelecoma was not of this world but of another, and had been sent to guide him. The light which entered the cave was brighter even than the sun that shone over the island.

As the light swirled into a golden cloud, Joseph could not see Pelecoma. He could only hear his voice telling him, 'In this cave are hidden the sacred writings of the Ilinka tribe. They were stolen by the men who discovered what was then called the New World. They came to the Ilinka settlement as friends and were made welcome. They stayed in the lodges of the people. The captain of the sailing ship told them they had travelled many miles, over much water, only by chance did they come upon this land.

'The sea captain and his crew stayed for many days. They were exhausted after the long sea voyage and the Ilinka tribe tended to all their needs. They were of a gentle nature with mystical healing powers that were used upon the sailors. They also owned a lodge that was filled with gold, silver and jewels that were given to them when the Great White Spirit in the sky saw fit to divide his chosen people, sending them to the four corners of the earth, giving each of them the same amount of wealth. But only to the Ilinkas that came to the land of the buffalo did he give the sacred scriptures of their tribe.

'They travelled thousands of miles to get to their destination, with no trouble from thieves. When they landed, the Great White Spirit guided them across the vast country to where they'd to build their lodges. A special place was built to hold their treasure and the jewelled tube which held the secret writings of their mother tongue. Nothing was moved again, even though many generations had passed before the arrival of the sea captain.

'Of course, when he and his men saw the treasure, their hearts became full of greed. All, that is, except a young boy who'd joined the crew as a deck hand. He'd known about the treasure and the scriptures long before anyone else but did not speak of them to the others, knowing they would pilfer the treasure as they had done in other places.

'He'd been told about the treasure by one of the squaws, and had then told her she must tell no one of this treasure and to warn her people that the sailors must not find out about it. But one day, when the young boy had been out hunting with four younger members of the tribe, they returned to find the whole settlement ablaze. Knowing what was happening he told the youngsters to hide. “Wait until I return,” he shouted, then ran into what once had been a peaceful settlement.

‘He heard the crying of a baby and followed the sound. Finding two babies hidden in a bush, he grabbed one in each arm and ran back with them towards the trees where he’d told the youngsters to hide. He handed the babies to them, telling them to keep them quiet and to go farther back into the trees. He’d seen enough to know the tribe were being slaughtered and didn’t want the youngsters also to lose their lives.

‘Once again, he ran back, hoping if he could, to save the jewelled tube with the secret writings. He could not forget what the girl had told him about the scriptures being worth more to her people than all the rest put together. When he got back to the village the crew were already loading the last pieces of the treasure and he could see for himself the tribe had all been slaughtered – there were dead bodies lying all over the place.

‘When the captain called to him, he quaked inside, wondering if the captain knew of those he had hidden, then sighed with relief when the captain barked out an order for him to help load the treasure and take it to the ship. He knew now there was no chance he could get the jewelled tube and return it to the youngsters, but at least they were safe and hopefully able to take care of each other.

‘He prayed with all his heart, that once on board ship, he would be able to get the sacred writings without being seen and one day return them to their rightful owners. That night his prayers were answered. As the men fought over their plunder, he managed to grab the jewelled tube, then hide it away.

‘When he returned home to his native island, he brought the jewelled tube to this cave. God had entrusted him with it when He’d answered his prayers. It was up to him to keep it safe and no one would find it here, so high up in the mountain. It was his own secret place. Perhaps one day he would be able to return it to those to whom it belonged, but that day never came.

‘The young boy grew into old age and was sorrowful for the sacred writings were still hidden. In death, he became keeper of the cave. His name was Pelecoma – he and I are one. I can rest in peace now, knowing you will find them and return them to where they belong.'

As Pelecoma spoke those last words, his voice was fading into the distance. Joseph opened his eyes, which had closed when Pelecoma first began to speak. He was alone, and the cave was in darkness. Not even the rays of the sun, which he knew must still be shining outside, gave any light to the entrance of the cave.

His thoughts turned to Cheeka, who all those years ago predicted that one day the sacred writings of Ilinka would be found. He wondered why they had been hidden for so long and why it was only now that Pelecoma was able to reveal himself and also the hiding place.

Though he was proud, that he'd been the one chosen to find the sacred writings, he could not help but wonder. Yet deep inside himself, he knew that there is a time and reason for all things and the time had now come for the sacred writings to be returned to the Ilinkas. The reason, he was sure, was because the Lord of the sky was angry with mankind.

No sooner had he thought of this when a small beam of light penetrated into the wall of the cave. He watched, fascinated, as part of the wall melted like molten lava. Then there came a hissing sound, like water being thrown onto hot coals. He rose to his feet, walking to where the beam had shone, and felt his hand begin to tremble as he raised it, putting it into the gap.

A moment later he was holding a narrow golden cylinder studded with precious jewels. He was surprised by the lightness of it, even though it was only six inches long. He carried it over to the cave's entrance, then sat down Indian fashion. He held the cylinder in both hands, raising them above his head as he spoke to the spirits in the sky.

Afterwards, while he waited for the spirits to answer him, he wondered for a moment, how he would get the cylinder through customs. This was not like the times of Pelecoma, this was a modern world, with high technology. Then he smiled to himself. If the spirits of his ancestors had preserved and protected the cylinder and its contents for so long, they would see to it that it would now be returned safely to the Ilinkas. He knew his faith in them was answered when he heard a voice telling him:

'You hold in your hands the sacred writings of the true Ilinka tribe. The seal of the cylinder must not be broken until your mission is completed and you return to your homeland. Only then can the words written by the scribes of long ago be read and on that day the Lord of the sky will decide the destiny of mankind. For he is angry with those who dwell in the earth world, saying the ways of the earth world are bad and will have to be changed.

'No more is there goodness in the hearts of the people. They lie and cheat then go to the churches and ask for forgiveness. Religion to them is but a word and they speak with forked tongues.

'The Lord of the sky sees into the hearts of all men and is displeased. But he knows that the Ilinka tribe who dwell below the Blue Mountain are true to themselves. They are pure of mind and loving of heart and they know the truth lays within their hearts. For if there is no goodness of heart there is no path which will lead them back to the Lord of the sky.

'That is why you have been sent on this mission. It is time now for those who's bloodline is connected with the Ilinkas to be brought together. It is the wish of the Great White Spirit.'

When the voice faded away, Joseph sat for a long time with his hands caressing the cylinder.

His thoughts turned once again to the chronicles of his ancestors and especially to the things that Cheeka had spoken of all those years ago. She'd predicted so much, which it seemed now was all coming true.

He remembered how she'd told Meleeka and Sara that their marriage was ordained and nothing on earth could have prevented the merging of the two bloods. Cheeka also predicted that a special lineage would be born to them who's nature would be of goodness, in both mind and heart. All this, Cheeka said, would be carried on for generations to come. It was a gift from the spirit in the sky.

And now, he thought, stirring himself, the spirit in the sky is calling us all home, though he still could not fathom why Robert Kyersh was born in Maraldon village.

As he made his way down the mountain, he could see Pelecoma's boat anchored in the tiny cove and marvelled at the workings of the spirits of his ancestors.

When Joseph arrived back at the villa, he showed Jack the cylinder, telling him all that had happened.

Jack could hardly believe what Joseph told him about Pelecoma. 'You mean to tell me,' he said, 'that the old man I saw you talking to at the bar wasn't real.'

'The spirits of my ancestors work in strange ways,' Joseph told him. 'Pelecoma rescued the cylinder with the sacred writings inside, so he was made the keeper of them until the time came for them to be taken back to the Ilinka tribe.'

'Bloody hell,' said Jack, wondering what other surprising things he would be finding out about Joseph and his ancestors. But he was glad Joseph had come into his life. People might envy me, he thought, saying I have the Midas touch, but what is money when your life is meaningless as mine was?

He looked at Joseph, asking him, 'What happens next? Will you be returning home now you've got the sacred writings?'

'I will not be returning home,' Joseph told him, 'until after Jordana is twenty-one. But I would be grateful, now there is nothing to keep us in Tenerife, if we could return to England as soon as possible.'

Jack said he would arrange it. Then he wondered how Joseph was going to get the cylinder through customs. He was about to ask him, then changed his mind, smiling to himself, knowing that Joseph would only tell him, 'The spirits of my ancestors will see to it that there will be no problems.'

Joseph was also smiling to himself, but for a different reason. He was hoping that Jack would behave himself going home on the plane, for Jack did not like flying, even though he was always travelling abroad, so when he travelled he took with him his own supply of brandy. When Joseph refused to join him in his drinking bout, Jack turned to the man sitting on the other side of him, pouring him drink for drink.

By the time they landed, the poor man was as drunk as a coot. They'd helped him to find his luggage, then taken him to his hotel, leaving him on the bed.

Jack had gone round later to see if the man was alright. The man laughed, telling Jack it was the best flight he'd ever had.

When Joseph turned to Jack saying, 'If you must drink on the plane, please don't be getting anyone else pie-eyed.' They both laughed at the memory of it.

CHAPTER XIV

It was the evening of Jordana's twenty-first birthday. Jack was waiting for Joseph to come downstairs so he could drive him to the Mill House where the party was being held. He'd given Jordana a gold watch for her birthday but there was also an extra present for her inside his jacket pocket. As if to reassure himself it was still there, he put his hand inside the pocket, gripping the box tightly.

He loved Jordana like a daughter and he'd waited a long time to give her this present. But now, as he held it, his thoughts went to Joseph and the events of the last few weeks for he was unsure as to whether to give the present to Jordana or Joseph.

He'd learned so much from Joseph and though he was old enough to be Joseph's father, 'and wished so many times that he was', he'd felt young again in Joseph's company. They'd laughed and joked, as he and Martin had once done when they were young.

He was so deep in thought, he did not know that Joseph had entered the room until he heard him asking, 'Is anything wrong, Jack? You look troubled in your thoughts.'

As he turned towards Joseph, Jack took the box from his pocket. 'This is what's troubling me,' he said, placing the box in the palm of his hand.

'What is it?' asked Joseph, though he knew without Jack telling him that inside the box would be the ring he'd seen Emma Kyersh give to her son Robert.

Then he heard Jack telling him, 'It is a ring given to me by my Uncle Tim, who told me it was to be passed down through the family. And as he'd no children, I was to have it. I was going to give it to Jordana as a surprise gift, being as I've no children either. But just now, I was torn between whether I should give it to her, or to you, Joseph. I cannot even think why such a thought crossed my mind. After all, Jordana is my niece. Even though she was adopted by the Oakleys, it is still Martin's blood that runs through her. So one would think it only right that this should be given to her.'

With beating heart, Joseph took the box from Jack's hand and opened it. There was no doubt the ring inside was the one Emma gave to her son Robert. As he admired the ring, he asked Jack if he'd ever opened the clasp.

'I've never taken the ring out of it's box,' Jack told him. 'I knew when Uncle Tim gave it to me I was going to give it to Jordana when she was twenty-one. Uncle Tim thought that one day I might marry again and have children of my own. Of course I knew I'd no intention of doing such a thing but Uncle Tim knew nothing about Jordana and I couldn't tell him. In fact, it was only a month after I'd met her myself that Uncle Tim gave me the ring.'

He was about to say something else, then something registered in his mind. So he asked Joseph, 'But how did you know about the ring having a clasp?'

Joseph, putting the ring back in the box, answered, 'I will explain everything to you later. But can I ask you not to give Jordana the ring? We can all three of us discuss the matter later when we come back here. Right now, I think we should be on our way to the Mill House. The others will think we have got lost.'

It was two a.m. when they arrived back at the farm. Jordana's party had been a great success, with guests being in no great hurry to leave. All the girls wanted to dance with Joseph, asking Jordana where she'd found such a handsome man.

Jordana herself had danced with him many times and was glad Joseph was able to be there, for she was sure, though he'd not mentioned it, that he would shortly be returning home.

At one stage the dance floor emptied, the crowd of dancers moving away to watch Jordana and Joseph dancing to the tune of 'Midnight

Blue'. It was a song Jordana had always loved and she had brought the record with her for the disc jockey to play.

Though most of the guests had forgotten the record ever existed, Peter and Barbara Oakley had not. They both remembered how Jordana used to play the record over and over again until it drove them to distraction.

Now as they watched her dancing to the music with Joseph, it was as if the beat of the rhythm was etched, not only into Jordana's soul, but in Joseph's as well. They could have been watching one dancer and its shadow. Their unison was such that their every movement was as one.

When the music ended, everyone clapped and shouted, 'More, more.'

Joseph and Jordana smiled at each other as they bowed to the audience.

Jack, who'd been watching them closely, thought that the two of them were made for each other. He hoped the man who was videoing the party had got them dancing together – he would like to see that again. A moment later, the man was beside him telling Jack he'd never filmed anything so fantastic. And all the time hoping his video wouldn't run out of film.

'Thank God it didn't,' said Jack. 'I was just hoping you'd captured it all.'

'Perhaps,' said the young man, 'the couple would like to see themselves dancing together. If you like, I could go home and put it on tape for you and have it back before the party is over. Or would you rather me reload and carry on here?'

'Put it on tape,' said Jack. 'It will be a surprise for them, when we get home.'

Now, with the others in their beds, the three of them were in the living room, watching the tape for the third time. When it came to an end Jordana said, 'Well I never even knew I could dance like that.'

She went over to Jack, kissing him on the cheek. 'And thank you, Jack,' she said, 'for the best party I ever had.'

'Your day of wonderment is not over yet,' he told her. 'There is something Joseph wants to tell you.'

When she looked across at Joseph, his face was so serious she wondered whatever was the matter with him.

Then Joseph smiled, and began to tell her of his quest and the reason for his coming to Maraldon. He left nothing out, telling her in the end that it was now time for her to have the true power of Ilinka opened up inside her.

She'd listened to all Joseph told her and was not afraid of what would happen to her. Joseph explained everything and she trusted him, and Jack would be there as well.

By some instinct, when she'd danced with Joseph to the music of her favourite record, she'd known that this night was to be like no other. She'd felt then as if they were the only two people in the universe, and as she'd watched the recording of it, with their bodies moving in unison, yet never touching. It was as if they were one.

Now Joseph was waiting for her to take hold of his hands. She knew if she did so, she would have to leave Maraldon, the farm and her family.

Jack was also watching and waiting for her to decide.

She thought of how she would be sorry to leave all that was held dear to her heart but knew that she must do so. She also knew that when her family was told, they would understand.

She hesitated only for a second, then took hold of Joseph's outstretched hands. As she did so, a brilliant light entered the room and shone around them.

They stood together like a bride and groom, with Jack standing before them holding the ring. She saw him give the ring to Joseph, then felt Joseph lift her left hand. She was expecting him to place it on her finger, but he did not do so. Her eyes sought out Jack's but his eyes were focusing on something behind herself and Joseph. She tried to turn around and find out what had caught his attention but she could not move.

She felt that something was crawling down her left leg, then her right leg. A moment later, though she could not believe it, came the sensation of someone stepping into her body. She imagined a diver getting into his wet suit, first one leg, then the other, dragging it up until his whole body was enclosed. But the sensation felt more like she herself was the wet suit.

Jack was standing before them and though Joseph had warned him what to expect, he could not believe what he himself was seeing.

Oh, Joseph and Jordana were standing before him alright, but standing behind them were, he assumed, the spirits of Sara and Meleeka's first-born, Joseph Tyler the second, and Emma Kyersh. They were not aged but young, like Joseph and Jordana. Both were smiling as if at last, after so long, they would now come together as it was always meant to be.

He watched amazed as the Joseph of yesteryear stepped into the body of the Joseph of today and Emma stepped into the body of Jordana.

When this was completed, he returned his gaze to the couple standing before him. They were both smiling as Joseph placed the ring onto Jordana's finger.

A moment later, Joseph released the clasp and Jack gasped as he bent down to see what was inside the opened ring. There was no doubt after what he'd just seen that etched out in silver were the faces of Emma Kyersh and Joseph, the father of her son, and it did not take an idiot to realize that when the ring was closed their lips would be sealed and that in a way their spirits had never been parted.

Joseph and Jordana were also kissing each other and as he watched them Jack thought of his brother, Martin, who's daughter Joseph would be taking with him to Ilinka.

Why the Great White Spirit wished them to return, Jack did not know. He only knew that when the time came, he was to gather those from the bloodline of Robert Kyersh together. Then they too would travel to Ilinka.

PART IV

CHAPTER I

Jordana was oblivious to the activity going on around her, as she unconsciously toyed with the ring Joseph gave to her on the night of her twenty-first birthday, the ring, she knew now, which was to seal her destiny.

She relived again the sensation she felt when the ring was placed upon her finger – the sensation, that someone was stepping into her body. At the time, she thought she was imagining it all. Then Jack told her of how he had seen 'the spirit of a young girl entering into your body, Jordana, and of a young man's spirit entering into Joseph's.'

'I could not believe my own eyes,' he said, 'though I can assure you, that is what I saw.'

Recalling it all now she wondered why she'd not, for even a moment, been afraid of what had happened to her. Perhaps, she thought, there'd been no time to be afraid, not even when Jack had told her what he had seen. For, a moment later, Joseph was explaining everything to her: about the Ilinka bloodline, and of how herself and Jack belonged to that lineage; and of his mission, which was to bring that bloodline together. Lastly, he explained about the two young spirits Jack had seen, and the story of Emma, and Meleeka's son Joseph.

'Why it was ordained,' he said, 'for Emma's child to be born in Maraldon, I do not know. Neither can I tell you, why the spirits of those two lovers have been reborn again, so to speak, within your body, and my own. I only know, after what has happened here this night when I placed the ring upon your finger, the spirits of my ancestors wish for us to be married, as soon as possible. And you, Jordana, and also Jack, are to help me with my mission.'

He'd taken hold of her hand, kissed the ring, then looked deep into her eyes as he said, 'You are willing to marry me, Jordana?'

She told him that she was, because at that moment she felt it was the most natural thing he was asking her to do.

He'd given a sigh of relief, then said, smiling, as he gestured for her and Jack to sit down on the sofa, and he sat down on the chair facing them, 'The three of us have much to discuss before we tell your parents in the morning of our forthcoming marriage.'

He told them both of the power of the Ilinka bloodline. Jack also told her of what had happened to him, on the night they'd all been to the Mill House. The more she listened to what they had to say, the more intrigued she became. She also realized life, as she knew it, would never be the same again.

'The power of the Ilinka bloodline runs through your veins,' he said. 'It is a gift, a very special gift, that others could not even comprehend. You need not be afraid, for I will be the one who opens up that power. Then you will see and hear many things which will hopefully be for the good of mankind.'

There'd been so much during that long night that Joseph enlightened them about, and she'd been surprised how neither herself nor Jack questioned anything about what he told them. Not even about the marriage that was to take place between herself and Joseph.

The next morning, Joseph told her parents about his mission. He left nothing out, except the extraordinary happening when he placed the ring upon her finger. They'd all decided this would be too much for her parents to understand.

She'd watched her parents as they listened to Joseph without interrupting him. Even her mother, who usually wanted to know the why and the wherefore about everything. Of course they were both dismayed when Joseph said the marriage would have to take place as soon as possible. They'd glanced her way, as if silently asking if this was what she really wanted. She'd given them the answer by nodding her head, in consent.

Her father took hold of her mother's hand as they sat staring at her, unable to speak. It was Jack who broke the silence when he said, 'Peter,

Barbara?'

Her father let him say no more. 'It is alright, Jack,' her father said, 'I think we understand what Joseph has been telling us. Don't we Barbara?' he asked, turning to look at his wife, looking at her as if they shared a secret only the two of them knew about.

Her mother smiled as she said, 'You have not forgotten then, Peter, what I said all those years ago?'

'No, I have not forgotten,' her father said.

Her mother looked at Joseph, telling him, 'We never lied to Jordana about the circumstances of her birth, and I would often tell Jordana, when she was little, that when I first held her in my arms, how I felt there was something special about her. Her father laughed at me that day when I told him how I felt. "Barbara," he said, "all babies are special," which I knew to be true. Yet I could not explain to him the feeling inside me when Jordana's eyes stared into mine. It was as if her eyes were talking to me, telling me she'd been put into my arms for safe keeping. Somehow, I knew at that moment Jordana had been put on this earth for some special reason. I have never forgotten that moment. Now it seems I was right. And though Peter and myself may be stunned by what you have told us, especially about the marriage, we understand perhaps better than anyone else would why it should be so. It is an incredible story, Joseph, that you have told us, yet I believe it to be true.'

'So do I,' her father said. 'You have spoken, Joseph, about the links in a chain which have brought us together. Well, I have often wondered why it was me who was selected to take care of this farm, when there were others more qualified than me to do so. Now, after what you have told us, there is no doubt in my mind the first link in your mission was for us to be here when you arrived at the farm. So now, Barbara and myself give you our blessing for you to marry our daughter.'

A week later their wedding took place at the Register Office by special licence. It was not like the wedding she'd always dreamed about, which would take place in the village church, filled with family and friends.

Afterwards, Jack had driven them to the airport to catch a plane.

Joseph was taking her to Tenerife to show her the cave where he'd found the Sacred Cylinder.

He'd told her all about Pelecoma, and if anyone else but Joseph had told her that story, she would not have believed them. At the entrance of the cave he'd held her close, telling her, 'Whatever happens inside the cave, Jordana, do not be afraid, for I will be with you.' He'd taken hold of her hand and led her into the darkness. Then he placed her hands onto the wall from where he'd taken the cylinder.

Her hands felt the coldness of the wall. Then they became warm, and began to tingle, as if some magical power remained in the wall, where the cylinder had been.

When she told him this, he took both of her hands into his own, and led her to the centre of the cave, where they'd sat down, Indian fashion, facing each other. He kissed the palms of her hands, then told her: 'The spirits of my ancestors guided me to this cave, Jordana. Not only to find the cylinder, which holds the Sacred Scriptures of our tribe. I was also to bring my bride. I knew before I came to the farm there was going to be more to my mission than finding the lost ones of our tribe. What I did not know, not until the first night of my arrival, was that you, Jordana, would be that bride. The spirits showed me this when I did my ritual, though I could speak of it to no one.

'When we dined together the next evening at the Mill House, and you spoke so much about Jack Farrel, I wondered if you had already given your heart to him. And though I did not doubt what the spirits had told me, I was relieved when they led me to the true facts about yourself and Jack.' He'd gripped her hands tightly, as he went on, 'I am telling you all this, Jordana, because I truly love you, and I would have done so no matter what the spirits had ordained for me.'

There'd been no need for him to tell her this for she'd felt the same about him – she'd seen it in his eyes when they first met, and her own heart quickened, when she greeted him from astride her horse !

'I do not know,' he said, 'the reason for bringing you to this cave, but whatever happens, as I have already told you, you must not be afraid. Are you ready, Jordana, to go into the unknown?'

She'd told him that she was, knowing she would trust him with her life!

'Then you must listen carefully,' he said, 'to what I tell you. First I will place my forefinger upon your brow. You must also do the same to me, with the forefinger of your right hand. My finger will trace the sacred marking of the Ilinka tribe upon your face. Your finger must move in exactly the same direction as mine does.'

He placed his finger upon the temple of her brow, and she did the same to him. She concentrated hard, when his finger began to move, feeling as light as a feather upon her face.

It had been no easy task getting her finger to move in unison with his, when all the time, even in the darkness, she could see his eyes staring into her own. And even if she had wanted to, she could not have drawn her eyes away. A strange feeling had come over her when her finger reached his chin, and he linked their fingers together.

A blue mist swirled around her. When the mist disappeared, she was in another time, another place. Standing below the Blue Mountain of Ilinka which Joseph had told her so much about, Sara was there, standing with her arms wide open, like a mother, waiting for her child to run into them.

Then Sara's arms enfolded her as she told her, 'The bloodline of my ancestors runs through your veins. With Joseph by your side you will be shown many things together, be led to many places. You must not be afraid of what you are shown, or of where the path will lead you.'

Sara hugged her close before turning her around. Meleeka appeared before her. He also hugged her close before he said, 'The spirit of our son, and the spirit of Emma, are happy now. For they live again in yourself, and Joseph!'

'This is true,' Sara said. 'Our son, and Emma, have waited for many moons for their spirits to find yourself and Joseph, and now they have found you, they will become lovers again. Living with a love they shared all those years ago, a love which at the time was not meant to be.

'The spirits of my ancestors work in mysterious ways, ways that we do not question. But Meleeka and myself are also happy that our son and Emma live again in yourself and Joseph. You must not be afraid of what you have been told. No harm will come to you. For I will be your guide, as Meleeka is the guide of Joseph.' They hugged her then, between them, and a moment later she was back in the cave with Joseph, still staring into his eyes.

She was going to tell him what she had seen, but Joseph closed his eyes, and she knew she must not disturb him. She'd been surprised when he opened them and told her, 'Jordana! Sara and Meleeka wish for us to go to Australia, to seek out the bloodline of Emma's lineage from the siblings of Emily and Bob Townly.'

He raised himself in one swift movement. 'There is much for us to do,' he said, taking hold of her hand and pulling her into his arms, kissing her, before he led her out of the cave into the brilliant sunshine.

She'd been disappointed they would not be going first to Ilinka. For before they entered the cave, their plans had been that when they left Tenerife they would return to the farm, then Joseph would take her home. As she walked down the mountain, she'd wondered what lay before her on the special path of life the spirits had chosen for her to take with Joseph.

She came out of her reverie on hearing Joseph telling her, 'Jordana, our flight number is being called.'

She glanced around the table where they'd all been sitting, having drinks. Her mother was rummaging in her handbag. She looked up and smiled as she took out a handkerchief, in case it was needed. Her father, raising himself from the chair, winked at her. Ashley and Jack were standing beside Joseph, who was picking up their flight bags.

As her parents hugged her close, she wondered when she would see them again, or if she ever would Then she went into Ashley's arms and saw the tears well up in his eyes as he said, 'I'm going to miss you, Jordana. It will not feel the same, you not being at the farm.'

She gave him one last hug, before she went into Jack's arms. There was no need for them to speak. They both knew what the other was thinking. Their lives had changed so much over the last few weeks and were about to change even more. Yet neither of them knew what lay before them. Nor could they understand the mystical forces that Joseph said lay within them.

Jack hugged her to him one last time, and as he watched Joseph lead her away, he wondered why their plans had been changed. For now they were en route for Sydney, he'd been entrusted to take the Sacred Cylinder to Ilinka.

CHAPTER II

Joseph smiled at Jordana's childlike wonder as she gazed over the balcony railing onto the view of Sydney Harbour. When they'd arrived at the hotel an hour earlier, she'd been so tired she wanted nothing more than to fall into bed. The journey had been a long haul for her, especially as she'd not been able to sleep on the plane. He'd realized too late that it would have been better for her if they had taken a couple of days stopover en route.

He told her to have a shower. 'It will refresh you, and you will sleep better.'

While she was in the shower, he ordered salmon salad and champagne. He'd no idea whether or not Jordana was hungry, but he was.

He was glad he had done so, for when she came out onto the balcony, the sight of the harbour put new life into her.

'Oh Joseph,' she said excitedly, as she went to stand by the railings. 'What a beautiful sight.'

'Well,' he said, 'it is supposed to be the most famous harbour in the world. Now, shall we eat, drink and be merry before we go to bed?'

'You spoil me,' she said when she saw the champagne and the food on the balcony table.

While they ate, they watched the ferry boats with their twinkling lights go sailing by; and listened to the merriment the travellers were making.

Now, Jordana was standing by the railings, savouring the scene below. The expression on her face was like a child's on its first visit to a fairground.

His heart quickened as he watched her. Then he gazed up at the starlit sky as he silently thanked the spirits of his ancestors for sending him to her, and keeping her pure until that time came. He felt his manhood rise when she turned to face him, waving the empty glass she was holding. He reached for the bottle so he could refill her glass, and saw the mischief in her eyes. As he was about to do so, she said, 'I have a better idea, Joseph. Let us take the champagne to the bedroom and drink it in bed!'

Pretending to be shocked he said, 'Jordana, I never thought the virgin I married would suggest we take champagne to bed with us. But now you have done so, you wanton woman, lead the way.'

As they made love together, Jordana was surprised by the passion that raged between them. They'd never made love like this before – Joseph had always been gentle with her, and she'd enjoyed it that way, not knowing, in her innocence, the act of love could be so different. What surprised her most were her own actions when her passion became as savage as Joseph's.

Even when she climaxed, and her whole body shook with joyousness, she could not understand how she could be acting this way. Then in one split second, her thoughts turned to Sara, and what she had said about Emma.

Now, as she lay in Joseph's arms with her body exhausted, wreathed in sweat and still tingling with excitement, she wondered why she'd thought about Sara and Emma. Yet deep in her heart, she knew why. It was not only Joseph and herself who had just made love, it was the spirits of the two young lovers as well.

She felt Joseph relax, then listened to his gentle breathing until she knew he was asleep. She brought her thoughts back to Emma, and relived again every moment since she'd got into bed with Joseph. She smiled to herself, thinking of how the spirits of the two young lovers would be happy tonight, for she was sure it was their spirits that had dominated the lovemaking.

Why she thought this way, she had no idea, for she could not even understand how their spirits could be reborn again in herself and Joseph. She only knew this phenomenal event had taken place, and was predestined a long time ago by some omnipotent power she was not even going to question.

She raised the hand that wore the ring Joseph gave her and opened the clasp. She kissed the faces of the cameo carving as she said, 'I hope you are both happy now. You must have waited a long time to be united with each other. And now, I am happy also. For I know you will travel with us on the path that will lead us to Emily's offspring.'

She closed the opened head of the ring slowly, trying to see if their lips touched before the clasp was fastened, and was disappointed to find she could not see if they did so.

The next morning, when she awoke, Joseph was still sleeping. She could still smell the muskiness from their lovemaking the night before. She lay there for a moment, wondering whether she would tell him of her thoughts before she'd gone to sleep, then decided not to.

She crept out of bed, put on her robe, and went out onto the balcony to see if the harbour was as beautiful in the daylight as it had been the night before. It is still a wonderful sight, she thought, leaning on the railings, watching the morning traffic of the river jets skimming across the water, and the ferry boats sailing at a more leisurely pace. But I would rather see the Opera House when it is floodlit – it looks more majestic, she said to herself as she went back inside to have a shower.

As she massaged the rich, foaming gel into her body, she wondered what Joseph's plans would be for today. The very thought of him brought a yearning desire to her young, lithe body. Before she could rinse the foam away, she felt two strong arms enfold her and knew, as he lifted her and carried her into the bedroom, still covered in foam, her desire would soon be satisfied.

Later after they'd eaten breakfast, which was brought to their room, Joseph performed his morning ritual, then helped her with her own ritual, which he'd told her was to bring forth the power that was laying dormant within her.

'Soon,' he said, 'your hands will hold the power to heal and you will see visions within your mind's eye.'

When it was over, she wondered about the path they were about to embark upon and where it would lead them to. Yet she did not mind where the path would lead them for they would be travelling it together.

It was mid-morning when they emerged from the hotel. They were both dressed alike in white, linen slacks and jade green shirts. Many admiring glances were directed at them as they strolled hand in hand around Circular Quay. They made their way towards the Opera House, and on the way read the name plaques, set in the pavement, of famous writers, then went to the old part of the city known as The Rocks, a place lovingly preserved from the days of long ago. Joseph was fascinated by the old part of the city. And though they strolled around like any other tourists, Jordana knew Joseph's interest was more profound than anyone else's.

Joseph thought Sydney was the likeliest place that Bob Townly would have brought Emily, and he was hoping he might pick up some vibes that would set them onto the trail of the Townly descendants.

When nothing came to him, they ate lunch in a quaint little restaurant. Afterwards they went back to the Quay and caught one of the river jets which took them to Darling Harbour.

It was late evening when they got back to the hotel, and Jordana could not believe they'd seen so many sights in one day.

They were relaxing outside on the balcony with ice cold drinks, when she said to Joseph, 'I have enjoyed myself today. In fact it has been a perfect day. I am only disappointed that you got none of your vibes, as you call them, to tell you of the direction you have to take for you to begin your mission.'

Joseph smiled as he took hold of her hand, saying to her, 'You must not feel disappointed, Jordana. It has been a wonderful day, and I too have enjoyed it immensely. Neither must you be concerned about our mission. I know not when, or where, we will find the first link in the chain that will lead us to Emma's lineage. I only know, when the spirits of my ancestors are ready, they will show me the path we must follow. As they did when I came to the farm and they led me to yourself and Jack.'

Jordana knew what he said was true and she would have to be patient. She also knew the disappointment she felt was for herself. She wanted so much for this mission to begin, and end. Not only because of the importance of bringing the tribe together – the real reason was she could hardly wait to see Ilinka. To be there where it all began.

As the cold water washed over him, Joseph's mind was filled with the events of the day.

It was true what he'd told Jordana about having to wait for the spirits to show him the way, for he could do nothing until they did so. He also wanted to return to Ilinka, as soon as possible, though his reasons were different from Jordana's. Hopefully, when he returned, the lost tribe would follow.

He towelled himself dry, then walked naked into the bedroom. He picked up the doeskin trousers which Jordana had laid on the bed in readiness for his nightly ritual. Earlier, he'd been with Jordana when she performed her own ritual, and he was pleased with her progress. Jordana was outside on the balcony and would not disturb him.

He put the trousers on, then relaxed his whole body, taking deep breaths as he did so. Then he began to chant in the language of his ancestors. His body moved gracefully as he danced the sacred dance, which would bring his spirit guide to show him what had to be seen. When he knew the spirit guide was with him, he sat down, legs crossed, on the floor and waited for the visions to come.

A pure white mist came into his vision, then changed into white, foaming breakers that ebbed backwards into the sea, leaving dark, wet sand behind. A moment later, with the heat from the blazing sun, the sand dried into fine, golden grains. An eagle flew down from the sky, landing upon the sand. It flapped its wings, as if making ready to take off again and soar back into the sky. Instead it flew low, just above the sand, then came to perch in front of Joseph. He knew then, he would become as an eagle, and what was to be shown to him, he would see through the eagle's eyes.

A moment later, he felt himself rising from the ground. Then he was high in the sky, scanning the horizon. In the distance, tall ships were anchored, with their white sails billowing in the breeze. Below him in the bushland, not far from the beach, a tribe of natives were going about their daily tasks, living, he supposed, in much the same way as his own ancestors must have done. He felt a great sadness, as he passed over them, knowing only too well, what the coming of the white man would mean to those natives.

He flew on to where the ships were anchored, then perched on one of the mast poles so he could see what was happening. He watched the soldiers make themselves ready for any trouble that might occur, when the ship was unloaded of its convict passengers.

When the convicts came ashore, they were in a sorry state. Many of them shaded their eyes from the hot, blazing sun, and they also moaned and groaned with the weakness that was within them. Men, women and children were treated like cattle being sent to the slaughterhouse. Some fell to the ground as the soldiers butted them with their rifles, to make them hurry along. Then they would drag them to their feet. The men who were stronger cursed the soldiers, and helped their fellow men as best they could. They also cursed the long sea journey and the foulness of it all. And they cursed the captain of the ship for bringing them to this godforsaken place.

There were mutterings of agreement from all around, until a voice from the crowd shouted, and was heard above all the commotion, 'I do not care where we have come to. Anywhere is better than England, where they could have hung us all. Even myself who stole a few pennies so I could feed my family.'

Those nearest to the man nodded their heads in agreement with him. Then another voice was heard saying, 'This man is right in what he says, and I for one will take my punishment. Making the best of whatever the good Lord did spare me for. For I am sure the Lord has forgiven us for our sins. Otherwise, He would not have given us this chance to make amends for whatever we might have done.'

This little speech seemed to put new life into those who were listening, and as they were marched away, many of them raised their eyes to the sky, as if silently asking God to take care of them.

A woman came onto the deck as they were marched away. She raised her parasol, opened it, then stood watching the activity below until a sailor dressed in officer's uniform came to join her. They kissed fondly, then strolled hand in hand towards the gangplank.

Before they stepped onto the wharf, Joseph came out of his eagle-like trance, and knew that he'd seen Emily and Bob Townly arrive in Sydney. He was not disappointed in not being shown what happened when they came ashore, for he knew the spirits would enlighten him about that when the time came for them to do so.

As always when he came out of his trance visions, he sat for a while, recalling what he'd been shown. He knew, the spirits had their reasons for making him become as an eagle, and letting him see through the eagle's eyes the native dwelling place, the arrival of the convicts and most of all, the arrival of Emily and Bob Townly.

He rose to his feet, bowed to the four corners of the room, thanking the spirits as he did so. He smiled to himself as he went to join Jordana, wondering what the convicts he'd seen in his vision would have thought if they could have been with Jordana and himself today, on their sightseeing tour. For after all, it was those convicts who helped to build the first dwelling places and industries, and in so doing, they did not only put Sydney on the map, it was the beginning of making Sydney and New South Wales into what they had become today.

CHAPTER III

'I do not know,' said Joseph smiling, 'why I bothered to hire a car. It has been in the hotel parking lot ever since we arrived two nights ago.'

They were on the ferry boat heading for Manly and were standing together by the side of the boat, taking in the view of the harbour.

Jordana looked up at him as she said, laughing, 'Joseph. This is a wonderful way of getting from A to B. No traffic jams, no petrol fumes and beside that, if you were driving the car, we would not be standing with our arms entwined around each other while our eyes take in the magnificent scene that surrounds us.'

'I have to agree with you,' he said hugging her close, 'and I suppose we might as well enjoy ourselves.' Then he whispered into her ear, 'Perhaps it is the wishes of the spirits that we enjoy ourselves and relax before it is time to begin our mission.'

Yet as he spoke those words, he wondered why they were going to Manly and not Botany Bay where he'd first intended to go. He'd thought, after his vision the night before, Botany Bay would be the place to start his quest. But this morning, while Jordana was getting ready, he'd looked through the itinerary in their room of places to visit, and it was a picture of Manly beach which kept drawing his attention. Jordana also said she would prefer to visit Manly.

Before going to the beach they bought fresh fruit and cans of soft drinks. Walking down the busy Corso, Jordana saw a huge beach umbrella outside one of the shops and insisted that Joseph bought it. There were many people on the promenade, sitting on the benches under the trees, shading themselves from the hot sun. But Jordana was surprised to find the beach was almost empty. She thought of the beach in Blackpool, where on a day like this, the beach would be full of holidaymakers and day trippers, and you would be hard put to find a place to sit.

They walked for a while bare footed along the water's edge. Then to her surprise, Joseph threw the umbrella like a spear and they walked over to where it landed.

'There is a reason for us coming here,' he said, picking up the umbrella and opening it, before sticking it into the ground.

Jordana looked at him in amazement. In the first place, she could not believe Joseph had thrown the umbrella like some ancient warrior throwing a spear at his enemy. And there was no reason to stay at this particular part of the beach for there was no one around. So out of curiosity she asked him why he'd thrown the umbrella and why he thought there was a reason for them staying where it had landed.

'In all truth, Jordana,' he replied, 'I cannot tell you. I only know this is where we have to be. The spirits have guided us here, for what, I know not.' Then he smiled as he said, 'But I am not complaining when we have got this part of the beach to ourselves and that beautiful ocean for us to swim in.'

She had to agree with him, though she wondered if she would ever get used to the spirits guiding him to where he had to go. She laughed as she voiced her thoughts to him, then said, 'What are we waiting for? The sea looks so inviting, let us go for a swim.'

They were both wearing their swimwear underneath their shorts and shirts, so they stripped off their clothes, then ran, hand in hand, into the water.

Later, some surfers came along; there were six of them, all boys who looked to be in their teens. Sitting under the beach umbrella, Joseph and Jordana watched them for quite a while. When she saw the boys pick up their surf boards and walk across the beach towards the promenade, Jordana laid down and closed her eyes. Joseph was about to do the same, when one of the boys turned back and ran into the sea. Joseph watched him go farther out into the water than any of the boys had done previously. As the boy raised himself onto the board, Joseph knew the boy was in danger. He raised himself from the ground in one swift movement and ran out into the ocean.

As he swam towards the boy, who was now riding on the crest of the wave, he saw in his mind's eye a freak wave which was about to erupt. A voice within himself told him to dive, and when he did so he felt the changing current swirling about him. He felt as though his own lungs would burst as he swam under the water, and in his mind's eye, he could see the boy being thrown into the air, then crash down into the water. He thought his lungs could bear it no longer, and was about to swim upward to get some air. Then he saw the body of the boy coming towards him, sinking as though it was made of lead. He caught the boy between his arms and swam to the surface.

He paddled his feet as he gulped for air, making sure the boy's face was also above water and swam on until his feet touched the sand below. He was about to lift the boy over his shoulder and carry him ashore but gave a sigh of relief when the boy coughed and spluttered. He felt the boy's feet sink into the sand near his own feet. He released his hold and the boy grabbed his shoulder to steady himself.

'Give me a minute, mate,' he said, 'then I will be alright.' He coughed some more, then took deep breaths before saying, 'Thanks, mate, I thought I was a goner!'

Jordana, seeing them both standing there, could not believe her eyes. When Joseph raised himself, she'd opened her eyes. There'd been no time to ask what he was doing. He'd run like the wind across the sand and into the ocean.

She'd seen him dive, just before the giant wave threw the surfer into the air. Then he crashed down into the water, the surf board following him. She could not be sure, but she thought the board had hit its rider before they both disappeared. Then the waves washed ashore the wreckage of the surf board. It was split in half. The two halves now lay in the sand, on either side of her. She shivered as she looked at them. They reminded her of two sharks getting ready to pounce. She was glad the boy looked to be alright when he came out of the sea. The first thing he did was to pick up the pieces of the damaged surf board and examine them.

Joseph came to stand beside her as they both watched the boy who picked up the two halves of the surf board, then came over to them.

'Thanks again mate,' he said.

'Do you feel alright?' Jordana asked him, and before he could answer she said, 'Come and join us, you must have had a terrible ordeal out there. We have some fresh fruit and cans of soft drinks.'

'OK,' he said, 'and thanks.'

'In that case,' said Joseph, 'we'd better introduce ourselves.' The boy told them his name, Andrew Gibbs, and said nothing more as they walked across the beach.

He's not very talkative, Jordana thought, as she got the fruit and cans out of the bag, and put the bag on the sand with the fruit on top of it.

'Did the board hit you?' she asked, remembering what she thought she had seen.

'I don't think so,' he replied, picking up an apple from the pile of fruit. 'I don't hurt anywhere, which I would if the board had caught me.' He took a bite of the apple, then continued, 'Though to be honest, I did think the surf board was going to crash down onto me just before I hit the water. I also thought I was a goner as I felt myself sinking deeper and deeper. I tried to swim but the current was too strong. I became frightened when I felt my lungs were going to burst, and I imagined myself being washed ashore with the ingoing tide. I gave up trying to save myself. I was ready to let the sea take me as I sank down into its depths.'

He looked at Joseph as he said, 'And but for you, mate, being there, I know I would have drowned. Though I must confess, in my semi-conscious state, when you grabbed hold of me I thought you were some kind of sea monster come to get me.' He turned to Jordana, smiling, 'But I really do feel OK now.'

'I'm glad you do,' said Jordana. 'It must have been a terrible ordeal!'

Joseph took some grapes from the bunch and absently ate them as he looked out into the ocean where it all happened. He recalled the warning he'd had as he'd watched Andrew, and how he'd run without question out into the water, knowing Andrew was in danger. He finished eating the grapes, then lay down on the sand, arms folded beneath his head.

He could hear Jordana talking to Andrew, though he did not listen to what she was saying. He was deep in his own thoughts, wondering if Andrew was the reason they had come to Manly. If he was, he could not fathom the reason why, for he knew Andrew was not of the Ilinka bloodline. He heard Andrew laugh at something Jordana had said, and he wondered about him. Though Andrew seemed alright now, he'd noticed a sadness in the boy's eyes that had nothing to do with his recent ordeal.

He raised himself from the ground on hearing Andrew saying he must be making tracks, his father would be worrying about him.

Andrew shook hands with them and thanked them both. He picked up the broken surf board, said 'See you,' and walked along the beach following the water's edge.

'He's not a very talkative boy,' said Jordana. 'Apart from telling us what happened after he was thrown into the ocean, he's hardly said a word. Perhaps,' she said, taking hold of Joseph's hand, 'the ordeal upset you both for I noticed you were also very quiet and left me to do the talking.'

'I think,' said Joseph, thoughtfully, 'there is a sadness within Andrew that should not be there in one so young. And it has nothing to do with what happened out there. I also believe the reason we came to Manly was so I could save Andrew's life.'

Jordana was used by now to Joseph's way of reasoning and linking things together. But what he'd just said was beyond her understanding. She looked at him aghast as she said, 'Joseph, what are you saying? Are you telling me if we had not come to Manly, Andrew would have been drowned?'

'In all truth, Jordana,' he replied, 'I cannot answer your question. For I am not the only one to have been in a certain place at a certain time to save someone's life. I only made that remark because I feel our coming here today was no coincidence.'

They sat down under the beach umbrella and Jordana was thoughtful for a moment before she asked, 'So you think we will meet Andrew again? But how can we? We know so little about him. He could be a beach bum for all we know.'

He smiled at her assumption, then told her, 'Jordana, if the spirits wish for our paths to cross again with Andrew, then it will be so. How this will come about I have no idea. But there is one thing I do know, Andrew is not of the Ilinka bloodline.'

Jordana picked up the remainder of the bunch of grapes, knowing she would have to be satisfied with what Joseph told her. She popped one into her mouth and thought about Andrew. 'Did you notice the colour of Andrew's eyes?' she asked. 'They were deep amber. Is that not unusual for someone as blond as Andrew?'

She could not keep the surprise from her face when Joseph told her, 'The native blood of the island runs through Andrew's veins. Andrew is of mixed blood.'

'Are you sure about that?' she asked. 'I would never have thought of that being the reason for his amber-coloured eyes.'

'Well it is,' he said, taking hold of her other hand as he raised himself from the ground, and pulled her to her feet. 'Now how about going for a swim? Then we will go and catch the ferry.'

As they ran laughing across the sand, neither of them knew Andrew was the first link in the chain which would lead them to the bloodline of Emily and Bob Townly. And the path they would take was already mapped out for them, in bringing that bloodline together.

When they entered the hotel and went over to the desk to collect the key to their room, the desk clerk was speaking to someone on the phone. Joseph was surprised when the clerk signalled that the phone call was for him. The clerk passed the phone receiver over to Joseph, then went to get their key.

Jordana wondered who could be calling Joseph. No one, except their parents and Jack, knew where they were staying. Then she remembered she'd told Andrew. It surely can't be him, she thought, as the friendly clerk handed her the key.

'Have you had a good day?' he asked smiling.

'Yes thank you. We have been to Manly.'

As Joseph was holding the umbrella he guessed they'd been to the beach. 'Nice place,' he said. 'One of the best beaches by far in my opinion. Much better than Bondi. Catch you later,' he said, as Joseph handed the receiver back to him, then took hold of Jordana's arm.

'That,' said Joseph, leading her towards the lift, 'was Andrew's father. He's invited us over to meet him this evening, and guess what? He's sending a chauffeur-driven car to pick us up. By the way, what have you been saying to Andrew? His father seems to think we are on our honeymoon.'

She smiled as they entered the empty lift and Joseph pressed the button. 'I could not tell Andrew the real reason why we are here. And I do feel as though we are on our honeymoon. Even more so than when we were in Tenerife.'

He laughed out loud. 'I know what you mean, Jordana,' he said. 'And when we get to our room, I will prove it to you.'

They made love in the shower, then afterwards relaxed on the bed.

While Jordana dozed, Joseph's thoughts were on Andrew Gibbs and his father, Mathew. There was no doubt in his mind now, his mission of finding the lost tribe was about to begin. Why the coming together of Andrew and himself should have happened in such unusual circumstances, he did not know. He only knew there must be a reason for it happening that way. He recalled the sadness he'd felt that lay deep within Andrew, and wondered what could have been the reason for bringing it into Andrew's young life.

He glanced at his watch, then woke Jordana. It was time for them to make ready for their visit to Mathew Gibbs.

As the chauffeur-driven car wove its way in and out of the city traffic, Jordana thought she could have been in Manchester or Leeds as there were shop windows boarded up and covered in graffiti, which continued onto the walls and doors. The sight displeased her, more so than it would have done in England. She would never understand why people deface their own cities and towns. Or why the authorities let them get away with doing so.

As they crossed the Harbour Bridge, she wondered about Andrew's parents. Her hand caressed the leather upholstery of the car seat; and she smiled to herself when she recalled saying to Joseph that Andrew could be a beach bum. Yet Andrew had told her very little about himself. Though he'd asked her questions about herself and Joseph, she'd not asked him questions about his family, and Joseph had been no help at all. For although he'd been sitting next to them, he'd been lost in his own thoughts.

When she saw the signpost for Manly, she wondered where this quest Joseph said they were about to embark upon would lead them. She also marvelled at the way Joseph was led, by some unseen force, to the people and places that would, as Joseph said, connect the links together.

Yet at this very moment Joseph did not know the reason why they were being taken to meet Mathew Gibbs, for his son Andrew was not of the Ilinka bloodline. So neither could his parents be. What Jordana did not know, nor did Joseph, was that Mathew Gibbs was a self-made millionaire, and though he was not of the Ilinka bloodline, he would be the one to help them link the chain together.

They were both impressed when the car turned into a long driveway, with immaculate lawns on either side, then pulled up outside an old colonial-style house.

'There is much sadness here,' Jordana heard Joseph whisper as the driver opened the car door.

There was no time to question him before they got out of the car, and she was surprised by what he had said. Yet, at the same time she marvelled at the acuteness of his senses; when he could feel within a moment that there was sadness in this place, and the way he'd said there was a sadness within Andrew.

She presumed he was right, yet the man who came out of the house to greet them looked anything but sad. He was tall, smartly dressed in khaki, tailored shorts with matching shirt. He wore knee-length socks and his brogues were made of the finest leather. He was smiling as he introduced himself and welcomed them to his home.

'It is our pleasure, Mr Gibbs,' Joseph said as they shook hands. 'We appreciate the invitation.'

'In that case, Joseph,' he said, 'you will refrain from calling me Mr

Gibbs. My name is Mathew, as I told you over the phone. That goes for you as well Jordana,' he said, taking hold of her arm as he began to lead them around the side of the house. 'I thought,' he said, 'as it is such a lovely evening, we would dine outside.'

Jordana could not believe her own eyes when they came round the corner of the house. It was as if she'd been transferred onto some Hollywood film set. There was a large swimming pool, and by the side of the pool there were tables and chairs, as well as brightly coloured loungers that matched the garden umbrellas which hung over the tables. The tiled walkway leading to the pool was filled with tubs of flowers, making a profusion of colour. The borders of the garden surrounding the immaculate lawn were also filled with plants, and beyond all this was a view of the ocean.

'Oh, Mathew,' she said awestruck. 'It is beautiful!'

'I am glad you like it, Jordana,' he said, smiling at her enthusiasm.

Then he gestured for them to follow him up the verandah steps. The verandah was huge, and there was a table upon it which was already set. He held a chair away for Jordana, then when Jordana and Joseph were seated, he excused himself. 'I won't be a moment,' he said.

He'd put some champagne on ice for when they arrived, and went inside to get it. As soon as he was gone, Jordana, not forgetting what Joseph said in the car, asked him: 'What did you mean when you said there is much sadness here? How can there be when there is all this?' She gestured with her hand, taking in the house, the garden and the pool.

'All this, Jordana,' he said, making the same gesture as she had done, 'does not automatically bring happiness. One can be as poor as a church mouse, yet inside one can feel great happiness. I told you this afternoon there was a sadness in Andrew. That same sadness is also within this house, and also in Mathew.'

'I wonder why you feel this way?' she whispered as Mathew returned.

She watched Mathew closely as he poured the champagne into the glasses. He did not look at all sad and as he passed a glass to her, his eyes lit up with a genuine smile. She wondered if he had a wife, for he had not mentioned one. And if he had, where was she? But she did not doubt what Joseph had said, his senses were too acute for her to doubt him.

She saw Joseph give her a secret smile when Mathew raised his glass and made a toast to the newlyweds, who, Mathew thought, were on their honeymoon.

Mathew took a sip of the champagne, then sat down. 'I also want to thank you,' he said, 'for taking care of Andrew. Especially you, Joseph, for saving his life.'

Joseph, sensing Mathew was becoming upset, waved his hand to dismiss the subject. Mathew ignored him. He gave a deep sigh, then continued, 'Andrew told me what happened out there. I can imagine what it must have been like. Those freak waves are very treacherous. And you, Jordana, also played your part, when you sat and talked to him. He told me how you calmed him, for he'd been so shocked and shaken when he thought he was going to drown that when he sat with you, and knew he was safe, all he could think about was his mother.'

Mathew toyed with the stem of the glass, as if wondering what next to say. Then he told them, 'You will never know the gratitude I am feeling at this moment for what you did for my son. And it is no wonder all Andrew could think about was his mother. Six months ago, our eldest son David died. My wife has not left her bedroom since the day we buried him. To have lost Andrew would surely have killed her. Well, I assume it would, for I do not even know if she knows what is going on around her. She lies in her bed like a zombie. The medical profession tell me that with time and patience she will recover. To be honest, I am beginning to disbelieve them.'

As he listened to Mathew, Joseph thought he must have been led to this place so he could help Mathew's wife, and also Mathew. So he said, 'You must not give up hope, Mathew.'

'I know,' said Mathew, 'but it hurts me to see Anna in the state she is in. Anna was always so full of life.'

Joseph watched Mathew as he refilled their glasses. He knew he must get Mathew to talk about the death of his son, for Mathew was hurting inside himself. Not only because of his wife's condition but also because of the son he had lost.

He waited until Mathew had filled the glasses, then he said, 'It must be the hardest thing in the world to lose one's child. Perhaps more so for the mother who gave birth to that child, for a mother's love is different than a father's. Yet they both have to grieve for their loss and that grief can affect them in different ways.' Joseph hesitated before he added, 'Perhaps, Mathew, though Jordana and I are strangers to you, you might feel like talking to us about your son?'

Mathew gazed at Joseph. He'd liked this young man from first speaking to him on the phone. Now that he'd met him, he liked him even more, and it was not only for the gratitude for saving Andrew's life. He felt Joseph was wise beyond his years and at this moment he felt he could talk to Joseph, telling him the things he'd not even been able to speak about before concerning the death of David. He also liked Jordana who he noticed, as he turned his gaze towards her, was smiling sweetly, yet her eyes were full of concern.

He wondered how he could begin to tell them of the hurt he was feeling deep inside. Not only hurting because of the death of his son, or because his wife was lying in her bed like a zombie – of course this contributed to the way he felt – but most of all, it was the way Anna had accused him of being responsible for David's death. His guts churned as he recalled that night, and then, whether Joseph and Jordana were strangers or not, he found himself saying:

'Perhaps you are right, Joseph, in what you say about a mother's love. She can spend more time with her children. While a father has to go out to work so he can feed and clothe them. The trouble with this father is I'm a workaholic!'

'Surely there can be no shame in that,' said Joseph.

'Maybe not,' Mathew replied, 'until it affects one's family.'

He gave a rueful smile, then he continued, 'If David had died in an automobile accident, perhaps Anna might have reacted differently. But David died because he'd been dabbling with drugs. Neither Anna nor myself could believe what had happened to David. Coming home in the car after we identified him, we were too shocked to speak. Then, as soon as we entered the house, Anna began to scream. Then she lashed out at me, thumping me with her fists, and with her tongue she called me all the names under the sun and blamed me for David's death.

'"You gave the boys too much," she shouted. "If you had spent more time with them David would still be alive, and before long Andrew will go the same way." I could do nothing to calm her down as she ranted and raved. Terrible, hurtful things spilled from her mouth, all of them directed at hurting me. Even as I rang for the doctor, she would not relent. When the doctor came he gave her an injection and we carried her to bed. The doctor, Adam Glenn, is also a friend, and he kept her sedated until the day of the funeral.

'On the day of the funeral Anna was calm. We even held hands at the graveside and she cried on my shoulder as they lowered the coffin into the grave. Under the circumstances, Anna seemed to be doing fine. We came home and some of the mourners came back to the house. Irene, our housekeeper, had put on refreshments for anyone who felt like having something. And I was pleased to see Anna was being the perfect hostess.

'I was standing outside, saying goodbye to Adam Glenn, when someone came to get me. "Anna is screaming her head off," they said. Adam ran to the car for his medical bag. He gave Anna an injection and we carried her upstairs. She has not left her room since that day!'

When Mathew saw they were both staring at him, he felt guilty for burdening them with his troubles. 'I'm sorry,' he said. 'I don't know why I am telling you all this. I am usually a private person, and what goes on in my home I usually keep to myself.'

'Don't apologise, Mathew,' Joseph said. 'It does one good to talk. Especially about the things one bottles up inside oneself. And I assume that is what you have been doing since your wife's outburst accusing you of David's death, and saying Andrew would go the same way. I can understand how hurt you must feel by what she said that night!'

Mathew marvelled at Joseph's understanding of the situation. 'You are right, Joseph,' he said. 'Anna hurt me deeply, and even though I know she was in shock when she said those horrible things, it still hurts me when I think about them. Perhaps more so because of the way Anna is now.

'I know, if Anna was well, she would not be able to take back her words that have caused me such pain, but she would know I have forgiven her for saying them. And as for what Anna said about Andrew going the same way as David, I have no qualms about that. Andrew is dead against drugs, and from what I can gather, always has been. What does worry me is the effect his mother's illness is having upon him. He won't even go into her room. He cannot abide to see her this way and he's cursed David many times for his mother's condition.

'"It isn't fair, Dad," he will say to me. "David had a choice about taking the drugs. He also knew they could kill him. Mother had no choice at all. She is like she is because of David's stupidity. Why did he do it, Dad?" And for the first time in Andrew's life, I could give him no answer.'

Mathew picked up his glass and took a long swig. 'I have been talking too much,' he said, putting down the empty glass. 'I invited you here to dine with me, not to listen to my woes. And as it is Irene's night off, I thought we might as well have a barbecue. So if you will excuse me?'

'Do you want any help?' Joseph asked as Mathew raised himself from the chair.

'No thanks,' he said smiling, 'you are my guests. Relax, take a stroll around the garden, it won't take long.'

They watched him in silence as he made his way to the back of the house where the electric barbecue was installed. Then Jordana turned to Joseph as she said, 'No wonder you felt the sadness. It is so tragic what Mathew has been telling us. But I don't understand why we have been led here. I know it is possible you may be able to help Mathew's wife. But you already know this family is in no way connected to Emily's bloodline.'

'I cannot answer your question,' he said, raising himself from the chair. 'I only know there is a reason for us being here. And we will be shown the way on the path we have to take.' He held out his hand to help Jordana to her feet. 'Come on,' he said. 'We will do as Mathew suggests and take a stroll around the garden.'

When Mathew called to them, they went back onto the verandah. Jordana was surprised to find the table was filled with a platter of huge steaks, a bowl of salad, an assortment of dips and wafer-thin biscuits.

There was also a bucket of ice, which held a bottle of champagne.

'My, you have been busy, Mathew,' she said. 'It all looks delicious!'

'Help yourselves,' Mathew said, as he pulled out a chair for Jordana to sit on.

While they ate, they talked about things in general. Anyone seeing them would have thought they'd been friends for years.

Later, they went inside the house, where they relaxed in huge leather chairs. When Mathew poured them all a brandy, Joseph noticed the brandy was the best that money could buy. He was also becoming intrigued by this man who the spirits had led him to. For with all the wealth that surrounded Mathew, he did not flaunt it as some might do.

He also liked Mathew, and he assumed, rightly so, that before the death of David, this household had been happy and filled with love, And, above all else, Joseph wanted to know, before he committed himself, all about Mathew.

When Mathew offered him a Dunhill from the silver cigarette box, Joseph took one. Mathew flicked his lighter and held the flame for Joseph to light the cigarette. As he did so, Joseph looked deep into Mathew's eyes, then said, 'Tell me about yourself Mathew.'

For a moment, Mathew could not take his eyes away from Joseph's. There was something in Joseph's eyes he could not fathom. He flicked the lighter shut as he asked, 'What do you want to know?'

'Everything,' Joseph said, without taking his eyes away from Mathew's.

Mathew felt a queer sensation run through him. It was as if Joseph was looking into his soul.

He took a cigarette out of the box, put the box on the table beside Joseph, lit the cigarette, then walked over to his chair. He sat down, stared first at Joseph and then Jordana. And though they were both smiling at him, he felt mesmerized by their presence, yet wanted more than anything to tell them about himself. He picked up his goblet, took a swig, then relaxed in the chair.

Joseph, watching him, also relaxed. He was here to help these people and he would do so. But right now, his sole interest was to listen to Mathew, to let Mathew tell him about his life. Then later, he hoped, he would be able to help Mathew get rid of the torment which festered inside him. For Mathew had not mourned for his son, and the spirit of David would not be set free until Mathew did so. He sighed with relief when Mathew began by saying, 'I came to this country with my parents after the war, when my dad came out of the Army. While he was away, I lived with my mother, in my grandmother's house in Manchester. When the war was over, my father could not settle down. And to make matters worse, his mother, whose house it was we lived in, decided to remarry. This did not go down well with my father who was her only child. So my father decided we would emigrate to Australia. My mother was not too keen on the idea. She wanted to get a house of our own and stay in Manchester. In the end she agreed to go when she saw the rift between mother and son was not going to be mended. And my father said if she was not prepared to go with him, he would go alone. My mother was sad about the whole business. She thought the world of my father's mother. She'd always treated her more like a daughter than a daughter-in-law. My mother was always thankful for that, for she'd no other family to call her own. Her parents were both dead, and she also was an only child.

'We came to live in Sydney. Ironically, it was my mother who loved being here. My father did not like it. We moved around so many times, there was hardly time for me to go to school. It was when we went to live in Paramata my mother put her foot down, telling my father she was not going to move any more. Two months later, my father left us. I never saw him again.

'For a while, we lived pretty rough, until my mother got a job. Even then there was no money to fritter away, but we managed OK by ourselves.

'I was about thirteen when she brought Luke Bowen home. He was the first man who'd come to our house since my father left. I could see my mother liked him, and I did not resent him coming to the house. I was told he'd just moved into the district, and had got a job at the store where my mother worked.

'Luke began to call at the house a couple of nights a week. Then eventually he came to live with us. We were all happy together until I was nearly sixteen. It was then I realised they were drinking too much. The house became so neglected I was ashamed to bring any of my mates home with me. When it became obvious they were both alcoholics, I begged them to stop drinking. But it was all in vain. One day I came home to find my mother had collapsed on the kitchen floor. Luke was on the couch, snoring his head off. Two days later my mother died. The doctor at the hospital told me her liver stopped functioning because of the amount of alcohol she'd consumed.

'I was furious, both with myself and Luke. I should have suspected long before what was happening. And if Luke had not been there, my mother would not have been drinking.

'The day after the funeral, I packed my bag. I left Luke lying on the couch in a drunken stupor. His face was swollen and ugly from the fight we had the night before. There was vomit all around him. As I stood looking at him from the open doorway, I hoped he would die.

'I'd given no thought to where I was going. I jumped onto the first bus that came my way. As I gazed out of the window, all I could see was Luke's battered face. And all I could think of was if Luke died, the authorities would be after me.

'I jumped off one bus onto another until I ended up out in the bushland, after thumbing a lift. For a while I shacked up with some Aborigines, until two blokes came along who were trekking around the country in a Jeep. I said goodbye to my native friends and tagged along with Geoff and Alan. We had a great time going from place to place, sometimes working our butts off to make sure we could do so.

'We struck lucky when we decided to do some opal mining. After we sold the opals, we split the money, then went our separate ways. I went back to the old house and was relieved to find Luke was long gone. There was a young couple living in the house we once rented. They'd no idea who Luke was or where he'd disappeared to. They'd heard the gossip about him always being drunk, and the neighbours sending for the police when he got out of hand. And of how no one could believe it when Luke suddenly changed and became as sober as a judge. Then Luke shocked them all by running off with the butcher's wife.

'By the time I heard all this, I was old enough to realize my mother had brought on her own downfall. And I hoped Luke would be happy with the butcher's wife. I walked away from the house happier than I had been in a long time. Happier even than when we found the opals, for always, at the back of my mind, was the picture of Luke, lying there on the couch.

'I was twenty-two years old, Luke was alright, and I had a bag full of money. There wasn't a fortune, but there was enough to start making my own way in life. Strangely enough, it was the young couple I'd been speaking to about Luke who put me, unknowingly, on the road I was going to take.

'During the conversation we'd had about Luke, the young woman told me, though she had never met Luke, she was truly grateful he'd run off with the butcher's wife. "How come?" I asked, surprised by her statement.

'"Because," she said quite seriously, "if he hadn't run off, we wouldn't be living in this house. And we had a devil of a job finding accommodation when we arrived from England."

'Her words kept ringing in my ears, so I decided I would put my money into property. I bought a ramshackle old house and made the large rooms into flats. I never looked back. Yet never once have I forgotten when my father left us. How sometimes my mother and I survived on jam and bread. I made a vow a long time ago that if I ever married and had children, my family would want for nothing. By the time I met Anna, I was a very rich man. And that, Joseph,' he said, his voice choking with emotion, 'is why my son is lying in the graveyard. Because, Anna said, I gave the boys too much, but did not give them my time. And, consequently, why my wife is upstairs, lying in her bed like a zombie.'

Tears came into his eyes and he tried to hold them back. Joseph, seeing this, said to him, 'Let the tears flow, Mathew, they will take away the pain. You must cry for David, the son you loved and lost. Let your tears wash away the seed of guilt that festers within you. Jordana and I will go outside. Join us when you are ready.'

Mathew let the tears spill forth, making no attempt to stop them as they rolled down his face, dripping onto his shirt.

Outside, in the now floodlit garden, Jordana was sitting beside the pool. Joseph was sitting on the verandah, where she had left him, deep in thought. Her own thoughts were on Mathew and the story he had told them.

She could understand now why Joseph had wanted Mathew to talk about himself. Joseph knew Mathew had not grieved for his son. He'd been more concerned with the seed of guilt Anna had put into his mind, the seed of guilt that was festering inside him, like a cancerous growth. She marvelled at the way Joseph could get Mathew to talk, and in doing so, hopefully, the sadness Joseph felt in Mathew would come to a head. She glanced over her shoulder and looked back at the house, wondering about Mathew's wife, and if Joseph, when he saw her, would be able to help her.

Joseph was also thinking about Mathew, hoping, when he came outside to join them, the pain Mathew had kept inside himself for so long would be washed away. He could understand, after hearing about Mathew's childhood, why Mathew made that vow. He could also imagine Mathew spoiling his sons, as Anna had accused him of doing.

Joseph gave a deep sigh. When it came to family values, he was for the old school of thought. If he ever wanted anything out of the ordinary, he'd had to earn the money himself to pay for it. He smiled to himself as he recalled getting a job at the general store, and going to work there when he came home from school so he could save the money for a racing bike he wanted. His friends made jibes at him for doing so because his parents were more affluent than their own and could quite easily have afforded to buy him a bike. Yet, he could also understand a father's desire to give his children more than he ever had. It is a vicious circle, he thought, coming out of his reverie when he heard Mathew come out onto the verandah.

'Feeling better?' he asked, as Mathew sat down beside him.

Mathew nodded in answer to his question. He was still too overwhelmed by his feelings to speak.

When Joseph had left him alone, he'd thought about David.

Especially about the devastation that David's death had left behind, with Anna lying in her bed day after day; Andrew being so upset about his mother, he could not even enter her room; and himself, who'd been so hurt by Anna's accusation, he'd not even mourned for his son. And through it all, he'd put on a brave face, so no one would know about the sadness inside himself.

Then he cried out 'David, I love you, I always loved you. I miss you, son, and I hope you will forgive me for shutting you out.'

Lying back on the chair, he recalled the memories of David, from the day of his birth until the night he died. It was then he felt a stirring within his heart, as if someone was pulling on his heart strings. The tears were still flowing and he thought he was going to faint when he felt a tug within his heart, as if something had broken away, releasing itself. A moment later, the tears stopped flowing. He'd given a great sob, which made his whole body shudder, leaving him feeling relieved, as though he'd let go of something. As he rested himself, legs sprawled out in the chair, he wondered why the youth of the world were turning to drugs. If only, he thought, they would realize what the consequences of their actions could bring.

He felt Joseph touch his shoulder and ask again if he was alright. 'Yes,' he replied, as if coming out of a daze. 'I feel better now, I have just wept for my son.'

'I am glad,' said Joseph, 'that you have done so. The spirit of your son David will be happy now you have released him from your heart.'

'Why do you say that?' asked Mathew, turning to face Joseph, and recalling the sensation he'd felt around his own heart.

'My people,' he replied smiling, 'believe we are born, we live and we die. When death comes, those who live on must bear no guilt or blame themselves. For the spirit of the dead one will be unhappy, knowing of the sadness that festers in the heart. We also believe, those who are left behind must not grieve overlong, for they must live on. And the spirit of the dead one will raise itself in peace.'

Mathew was bemused by what Joseph was saying, yet he could understand there was some logic in what he said.

He thought about Anna, and wondered if she'd released David's spirit. He would ask Joseph about that later. Right now, he wanted to know more about what Joseph's people believed, so he said, 'What you have told me, Joseph, is very interesting. I am not a religious man, not in the true sense of the word. Tell me more about your culture, especially about life and death.'

Joseph was thoughtful for a moment, putting his hands together, placing the fingers to his lips. Culture and religion were difficult subjects to talk about. Everyone had their own culture and belief.

Then he said thoughtfully, 'Our culture is much changed from the old days. Like others, we have moved on with the times. We have cars and TV sets and buy our food from the markets. Yet our values have not changed, we follow the path of the heart and believe the Great White Spirit in the sky controls our destiny. Even to the span of our lifetime on earth. For it is the Great White Spirit who controls who will live and who will die.

'Sometimes, I have found this hard to believe. Especially with the history of my homeland and the killing that went on there all those years ago, and the wars that have followed. When you think deeply about these things as I have done, you wonder about the poor, unfortunate, lonely souls who commit suicide. Were they meant to do so at that particular moment of their lives?

'I have found no answers to my own questions. Nor do I think I ever will. So now, I accept the wisdom of my ancestors. When death comes, in whatever shape or form, the living must let the dead one's spirit go free.'

Mathew turned over in his mind all that Joseph had told him. It had been an interesting conversation and freeing the dead one's spirit seemed to be logical enough. He'd never thought about the dead one having a spirit. He'd always believed that when you were dead, you were dead, end of story.

'Let us go inside,' he said. 'I will make us some coffee.' And, he thought, I will talk to Joseph about Anna.

Joseph raised himself from the chair and called to Jordana. He waited until she joined him, then they went inside the house.

Mathew went into the kitchen, put the percolator on the stove, set up a tray, then went upstairs to Anna's room. She was fast asleep as he knew she would be. He'd given her her sleeping tablet before his guests arrived.

He stood looking down at her, wishing with all his heart she could come downstairs to meet Joseph and Jordana. He knew she would have liked them. He also knew, she would have been surprised if she had heard him pouring his heart out to them, telling two strangers of his private affairs and innermost thoughts.

He bent down, kissing her on her lips. For all the hurt and anguish she had caused him, he still loved her, very, very much.

He felt so relaxed as he sat drinking his coffee with Jordana and Joseph, he invited them to stay at the house.

'There is plenty of room,' he said, 'and you can come and go as you please. Your staying here will be no trouble at all, even though I have a sick wife on my hands. Our housekeeper Irene takes care of Anna. In fact, she is so good with her, there was no need for me to get a private nurse. And I know Irene will be delighted if you stay – she loves taking care of people.'

Joseph accepted the invitation, knowing full well it was what the spirits wanted. 'We will be delighted to stay with you,' he said, 'if you are sure that is what you want?'

'Of course I am sure,' said Mathew, smiling, 'it will be good to have you around. I have enjoyed myself this evening. I am only sorry Anna is too ill to be with us and that Andrew could not break his date with his girlfriend. Her parents invited him to dine with them. He's not met them before.'

'I understand,' said Joseph. 'There is no need for you to apologize. We will see Andrew tomorrow when we come to stay.'

Mathew refilled their cups and all three of them sat in silence, content in each other's company.

Mathew was wondering about what Joseph said about him holding on to David's spirit and if he should ask him if Anna was doing the same. But in all honesty, he could not believe it was possible for two people to hold on to one spirit. In fact, he did not know if what Joseph said was true, though at this moment, he felt better than he had done since David died. Then he heard Joseph saying, 'I do not want to build up your hopes, Mathew, but I may be able to help your wife.'

'How? Are you a doctor?' Mathew asked.

'No, I am not a doctor!'

'A shrink, then? Adam's already tried one of those. With no results.'

'I am not a shrink either,' said Joseph, smiling at the way Mathew had pronounced the word.

'Then how can you help Anna?' Mathew asked, bewildered.

Joseph was thoughtful for a moment, wondering how best to put into words what he had to say. Then he held up his hands, palms facing Mathew. 'I possess in these hands,' he said, 'the power to heal. But that does not mean I can cure all things. If that were possible, I would be a very busy man. I do not wish to give you false hope, Mathew. Though if you agree to let me see Anna, I will do all I can to help her.'

'Of course you may see Anna,' Mathew said, without hesitation. 'I will try anything to make her get well again. I will take you to her room if you would like to see her now.'

'We will wait until tomorrow,' Joseph told him. 'It is late and time we returned to the hotel.'

Mathew would have liked them to stay overnight, and return to the hotel in the morning to collect their belongings, but he did not suggest it. Instead, he went to the phone and rang for Thomas to bring the car round.

When they had gone, he went upstairs, kissed Anna goodnight, then went through the connecting door into his own bedroom. He lit a Dunhill as he walked out onto the balcony, his thoughts were on Joseph and Jordana.

He was glad they had accepted his invitation to stay with him. He'd felt truly grateful to them when Andrew came home and told him what had happened. He'd also had the strangest feeling he should meet them and thank them personally. Why this should be, he had no idea. But he'd followed his feelings, and was glad now he had done so. There was a serenity about them both, but especially Joseph, which calmed him. He smiled to himself as he stubbed out the cigarette. He was hopeful Joseph would be able to help Anna.

He saw the headlights of Andrew's car as it turned into the driveway, then went into his room, knowing, somehow, he would sleep peacefully tonight, more peacefully than he'd slept for many months.

Jordana was deep in thought as the chauffeur-driven car turned onto the Harbour Bridge. Joseph had just told her that he was sure now their meeting with Mathew Gibbs would set off a chain of events that would lead them to Emily's bloodline. 'How this will come about I have no idea, because first and foremost, I have been led to the Gibbs' household to help his wife.'

'Will you be able to do so?' she'd asked.

'I think so,' he'd replied. 'Otherwise, there would be no point in going there. Though I could not tell Mathew this.'

Going over in her mind what Joseph had told her, she marvelled at the way he was led to the places he had to go. Not only because of this day's events. It had happened before when he'd come to the farm and was led in a roundabout way to herself and Jack.

She gave a contented sigh as she snuggled up to him. It was exciting being Joseph's wife, you never knew what was going to happen next.

As the car drew to a halt outside the hotel, she wondered about Mathew's wife and hoped Joseph could make her well again. She liked Mathew, and for all his wealth he did not flaunt it. He was a quiet man and unassuming.

They said goodnight to the chauffeur and as she went into the hotel, she could not help but wonder what tomorrow would bring.

CHAPTER IV

Anna was sitting up in bed when Mathew came into the room. She'd eaten her breakfast and Irene had given her a bath. She thought how handsome Mathew still was as he gave her a good morning kiss. She would have liked to have responded to his affection, but she could not do so. Neither could she be bothered to listen to what he was saying, about a young couple coming to stay with them. He could have invited the Queen of England for all she cared. She was still not going to leave this room. All she wanted was to be left alone, then she could think about David, even though, when she thought about him, it brought back memories she did not wish to remember.

She saw the hurt in Mathew's eyes as he gazed down at her, and gave him no response that she even knew he was there. He shrugged his shoulders as if in despair and walked out of the room, closing the door behind him.

She just lay there, as she'd lain there every morning, she knew not for how many, watching the same procedure, and her heart cried out for her husband.

As the door slammed shut, Mathew banged his fist on the wall in frustration. He'd done this many times before and when he calmed himself, he wondered if he'd done it this time from force of habit. For when he'd awoken, his first thoughts were of Joseph, and he'd felt deep down inside him that if Anna was to be cured, Joseph would be the one who would make her well again. Then when he saw her, in that zombie-like state, he lost all hope. But I must not lose hope, he said to himself, as he went down the stairs. I must keep my faith in Joseph.

He was delighted to find Andrew was already sitting at the breakfast table, and Irene was pouring the coffee. He bid them good morning as he sat down. Then he told them about Joseph and Jordana; that they would be arriving this morning, and would be staying until they decided to move on.

Andrew looked pleased as he said, 'Gee, Dad, that's great. I like them, they're a smashing couple.'

Mathew laughed as he said to Irene, 'I think Andrew here has taken a shine to Jordana. He spoke very highly of her yesterday.'

Andrew blushed, as he said, 'Well, Dad, you have to admit she's a great looker. And you must really have liked them or you would not have invited them.'

'I do like them,' Mathew replied, 'and as you say, Andrew, they are a smashing couple.'

'And I,' said Irene, 'will look forward to meeting them. Especially for what they did for Andrew.' She ruffled his hair and winked at Mathew as she said, 'Even though it means I will have to put up with Andrew tormenting me every time we meet.'

When Joseph and Jordana arrived, it was Andrew who went to greet them. Joseph was glad to see Andrew looked fit and well, with no after effects from yesterday's ordeal. He also noticed, as Andrew opened the car door for Jordana, how Andrew was smitten by her beauty. But who can blame him, he thought as he got out of the car.

Andrew helped Joseph with the luggage, then led the way upstairs, showing them to their room.

'I'm glad you have come to stay,' he said, as he put the leather holdall onto the floor, 'and I know Dad is pleased. He's usually a workaholic, but he said this morning, while we were having breakfast, "The office can run itself for a while, I pay enough people to make sure it runs smoothly." Oh, by the way, Dad says to make yourselves at home. He was on the phone when you arrived, but he will meet you by the pool.'

When he'd gone, Jordana glanced around the room. It was full of olde worlde charm, in keeping with the house.

'Shall we unpack?' she asked smiling. 'Or might you be getting another of your visions? Then we will have to move on again, at a moment's notice.'

Joseph took no offence at her jibe, understanding how she must be feeling. Since they'd been married, they'd done nothing but move from place to place. Besides, he knew she was only teasing. She'd already told him how she loved every minute of it all.

'We will leave the unpacking until later,' he said laughing.

They went down the stairs holding hands and met Mathew coming out of his study. He greeted them warmly, then took them into the kitchen and introduced them to Irene.

'I don't know what I would do without Irene,' he said, when the introductions were over. 'She's more like a mother to us all than anything else.'

'Get away with you, Mathew,' she said laughing. 'I know my place when need be. Now let me thank this lovely couple for taking care of Andrew yesterday. God only knows if anything had happened to him, what it would have been like in this house. It is bad enough already.'

She shooed them all out of the kitchen, telling them to go and sit by the pool, and even though she had work to do, she would find time to bring them some long, cool drinks.

'She's quite a character,' said Joseph, as they made their way to the pool.

'She is,' said Mathew, 'but I wouldn't like to be without her.'

As they sat beside the pool, Joseph questioned Mathew about what the medical profession had said about Anna. He listened to Mathew with interest, then told him, 'I can make no promises Mathew. But I will do all that is in my power to help her.'

He knew from what he'd been told, there was something very deep seated that was troubling Anna, and until she could speak about it, she would not recover. He also thought that whatever was troubling Anna was not solely the shock of David's death, or what she had said to Mathew, which had made Anna take to her bed and, to put it into Mathew's words, act like a zombie. He believed something had happened after the funeral which had triggered Anna's hysteria.

He waited until they'd all finished their drinks before suggesting they all go to her room. When they got there he was surprised when he walked over to the bed to find Anna, though fair of skin and with blonde hair, was a true native of the island. He'd already guessed the island's blood was in Andrew, though he'd not suspected it came from his mother. He'd assumed, it seemed wrongly now, that the native blood within Andrew had been passed down from an earlier generation.

He took hold of Anna's hand and even though she seemed unaware he was there, he began to speak to her softly. So softly, in fact, neither Mathew nor Jordana, who were standing only a few feet away, could hear what he was saying.

As Mathew watched Joseph massage Anna's wrist with his thumb, speaking softly to her all the time, he could not believe his own eyes when Anna raised her face and smiled at Joseph. It was the first time he'd seen Anna smile since the death of their son. He heard Joseph raise his voice a little as he told Anna to close her eyes and relax. A moment later, Joseph took away the pillows and turned down the bed sheet. Anna was laying prostrate on the bed in her silk nightie.

Mathew thought he and Jordana might as well not be in the room. Joseph took no notice of them as he raised his hands above Anna and waved them above her prostrate body several times. Then placing his right hand above the crown of her head, he began to move his hand slowly, following the outline of her body, until his hand was back where it started. Next he placed both hands together as if in prayer, and with fingertips pointing downwards he once again followed the outline of Anna's body.

Mathew was fascinated by the movement of Joseph's hands. What he did not know was Joseph was putting a protective aura around Anna.

Joseph himself could see the gold outline as it followed his fingers down one side of her body and up the other, until it met at the crown of Anna's head. That is good, he said to himself, it is the colour of all healing. He kissed the tips of his fingers before pulling the bed sheet back over Anna.

He turned to face Mathew and Jordana saying, 'Anna must sleep now.'

'Will she be alright?' Mathew asked in almost a whisper.

Joseph smiled as he said, 'Hopefully Anna will feel much better when she awakes.' He looked at his watch, 'Which should be in about five hours. Though no one must disturb her until then and I would prefer to be alone with her when she awakens.'

As they came out of the room Mathew said, 'I will tell Irene not to go into Anna's room. But knowing Irene she will want to know the reason why. May I tell her?' he asked, looking at Joseph.

'Of course,' Joseph replied. 'For now I have met Irene I cannot imagine you will get away with not telling her the reason why. And I am sure Irene will not think ill of me for trying to help your wife.'

'I'm sure she won't,' said Mathew smiling. 'Irene is devoted to Anna. She would like nothing more than to see her well again. And I am sure, Joseph, though I do not understand what you were doing in there, if anyone is to help Anna, it will be you.'

Tears came into his eyes and he became so emotional that he gave Joseph a bear-hug. 'Now,' he said, composing himself, 'if you would like to go and unpack your things, I will go and tell Irene.'

'May we go for a swim after we have unpacked?' Jordana asked.

'Jordana,' he said, 'while you are here, my home is your home. You do not need to ask. You must feel at home here. Come and go as you please. I only ask that you let Irene know if you will be dining with us. She is a stickler for wanting to know who will be in or out at meal times. But she will willingly prepare a picnic basket for you if need be, so don't be afraid to ask.'

Jordana thanked him for his thoughtfulness.

'My pleasure,' he said, before going down the stairs.

Jordana could not wait when they got into their room to ask Joseph what he'd been doing to Anna. She'd been fascinated by it all.

'I was putting the aura of protection around her,' he said. 'And I was relieved to see, when I drew around the outline of her body, the colour of gold. It is the colour of all healing.'

'Will you be able to make her well again?' she asked.

He was thoughtful for a moment before he replied. Then he told her, 'I feel hopeful that when Anna awakes she will speak to me of what is troubling her. I am also sure her condition was not solely brought on by the shock of David's death. There is something more which she wants to block out from her mind!

'And only if I can get her to talk about it will she recover. It will be up to Anna whether she wants to do so or not. And though I may be hopeful, I am not a miracle worker, Jordana. I cannot wave my hands in front of the blind and make them see again, or make the lame get up and walk by touching them.

'I only know I have been given the gift of the power to heal and I use this gift to the best of my ability. How the power works, I have no idea, and there are far greater men than myself who can neither understand nor explain it. Yet even the most sceptical of scientists are beginning to believe such a power exists.'

He took hold of her hands and kissed the palms, then said, 'The power to heal is also within you, Jordana. Soon, with your development, it will come into fruition. For you are progressing well.'

She looked at him wide-eyed for to have the power to heal must be a most wondrous gift. She was so overcome with emotion she threw her arms around him, saying, 'Oh Joseph. I'm so glad you married me.'

'I had no choice in the matter,' he said, teasing her as he pulled her away from him and looked into her eyes.

He knew how overwhelmed she was by the changes that had come into her life. And there is so much more I have to teach her, he thought, as he pulled her to him.

He felt his manhood rise when he kissed her and saw her eyes light up at his unspoken question. They fell laughing onto the bed.

Mathew smiled as they came towards him. He guessed what they'd been doing. Oh, what it is to be young, he thought, as they joined him at the poolside table.

Jordana smiled, slipped off her bathrobe and dived into the water. Joseph draped his bathrobe over the back of the chair, then sat down beside Mathew.

'You have a beautiful wife,' Mathew said, picking up a packet of Dunhill cigarettes and offering them to Joseph. 'In fact I think you make a very handsome couple.'

'Thank you,' Joseph said. 'Both for the compliment and the cigarette.'

Mathew flicked the lighter, saying as he did so, 'And thank you, Joseph, for coming into my life. I don't know what it is about you, but I feel more at peace with myself when you are around.'

'I am glad you feel that way,' said Joseph. 'Let us hope I have the same effect upon your wife.'

'Yes, let us hope so,' Mathew said thoughtfully. 'We have all been devastated by the death of David. But to be honest, I never thought Anna would have taken it so badly. She always used to be strong willed. I have asked myself many times why Anna should be acting this way, yet I can find no answers. But I suppose when death comes amongst you, everybody reacts in different ways. And no one expects their children to die before themselves, even though we know it happens to others.

'It seems strange now, seeing Anna this way, when I remember how we once laughed when I told her of my grandmother's attitude towards death. And Anna agreed my grandmother had the right idea. I told her of when I was young and lived with my grandmother in Manchester during the war. And of how, when the sirens went off, my grandmother would not go to the air-raid shelter. She would make us go into the cellar instead telling us, "If we are going to get killed, we will die in our own home."

'Ironically, one night, a bomb dropped on the shelter and killed everyone that was in there.' Mathew stubbed out his cigarette. 'Come,' he said, suddenly rising from his chair. 'Let us go and join Jordana in the pool.'

Later, Irene served them lunch out on the verandah. Then afterwards Mathew took them out through the back garden, showing them a short cut to the beach. Within minutes they were walking along the water's edge, all of them knowing they were killing time until Joseph was to return to Anna's room.

Mathew had never known in all his life the minutes tick by so slowly. Yet he had faith in Joseph, even if he did not understand the mystical power Joseph held in those hands of his. He believed deep down that those hands would bring Anna back to her senses.

* * *

Anna was still sleeping when Joseph entered the room. He sat down on the chair beside the bed, watching her. When she stirred, he raised his eyes, asking the spirits to guide him.

He took hold of her hand, stroking her wrist with his thumb until she opened her eyes. His voice was gentle as he asked, 'Do you remember me?'

Anna stared at him before she answered as there was a soothing sensation running through her whole body. She'd never felt anything like it before and she did not want it to go away. 'Yes, I remember you,' she said. 'Have I been sleeping?'

'About five hours,' he replied. 'How are you feeling?'

Without hesitation, she told him. 'I feel very relaxed, though my head feels a bit fuzzy!'

Without saying a word he took both of her hands into his own and pressed them together. He looked deep into her eyes as he said, 'Mathew is worried about you, Anna. He tells me the medical profession has had no success in finding out what ails you. I am here to see if I can help you. But before I can do that you, Anna, you must also want to help yourself.' This wasn't strictly true, though he wanted her to think it was as he continued. 'And in doing so you will help Mathew, and also your son Andrew. Andrew is terribly upset, as no boy should be, at seeing his mother wasting her life away. The death of your son David brought a dark cloud over you all. It is time for that cloud to be lifted. You must let David go.'

He felt her flinch at the mention of David's name. She tried to pull her hands away, but he would not let them go. Her body grew tense, her hands began to tremble within his own. He let his thumbs find the inside of her wrists and began to massage them to calm her.

Anna relaxed as she felt the pent-up tension draining away. At this moment she felt better than she'd felt since the day of David's funeral, despite the pills and potions she'd been prescribed. Who is this stranger, she wondered, who in only a few minutes, can make me feel like this?

Then as if reading her mind, she heard him saying, 'I am a healer, Anna. I can help you, but only if you are truthful with me. I can already feel it is not only the death of your son that is the cause of your illness.

There is something else. Something known only to yourself, which you keep hidden.'

She wondered how he could possibly know this, because what he said was true. She closed her eyes, thankful that she could do so. She'd tried to close them before when she thought this man was looking into her very soul, but she'd been unable to do so.

She opened them again, as he said gently, 'I assure you, Anna, whatever you tell me will be repeated to no one. Not even Mathew.'

She saw he was smiling the most serene of smiles she had ever seen, and though she tried hard not to do so, she lifted her gaze to his eyes. There was a look in them which she could not fathom, yet made her want to tell him of what she'd kept hidden within herself.

I wonder how he knew about that, she thought. When even the shrink who came to see me went away without a clue as to what was troubling me. She smiled to herself at the memory of it, though at the time it had not been funny.

She brought her mind back onto this man who wanted to know her innermost thoughts. She knew, without a shadow of a doubt, that she could trust him. She also knew she wanted to be with Mathew again, happy as they had always been until . . . no, she would not think about that, not today. Today was going to be different, she was going to speak out to this stranger, tell him what troubled her. For if I don't, she thought, I will lay in this bed until the day I die. She felt so calm and soothed, it would be a relief to tell him.

Joseph, sensing this, said to her, 'Tell me Anna, what happened to make you take to your bed and shut out your world?' He gave a sigh of relief when he heard her begin to speak, telling him:

'When we were told David was dead, I could not believe it. Even when I saw him lying there, it was still hard to believe. He looked so peaceful. Yet I did not cry, or even speak. Only my heart cried out to God, asking him why he had taken David, when I would have willingly gone in his place.

'When we arrived home, something snapped inside me. I blamed Mathew for the death of our son. Mathew always gave the boys anything they wanted. And I thought if David had been short of money, he would not have been able to buy the drugs the police believed had killed him.

'I was vile to Mathew, I kicked, I clawed and spat out the vilest of accusations. And all the time I knew I was hurting Mathew deeply, but I did not care. I can remember all those things quite well, though I cannot remember the days that followed, until the day of the funeral in fact.'

Joseph felt her hands begin to tremble and could see she wanted to turn her head away. He willed her to keep looking into his eyes. He knew for certain now that whatever happened that day was the cause of Anna's illness.

His thumbs gently massaged the inside of her wrists as he said, 'I know it will be hard, Anna, for you to recall what happened that day, but you must tell me. Tell me from the beginning. Perhaps then it will be easier.'

Once again Anna felt the soothing sensation run through her body, and as if in a trance she told him, 'When I awoke, I wondered where I was. I'd been having a horrible dream. I gazed around the room, not even knowing I was in my own bed. My head felt woozy as though I'd been drunk, or drugged. I saw the black dress hanging outside the wardrobe door. For a moment I wondered who's it could be. Then it all came back to me. David was dead and I'd done and said terrible things to Mathew. Irene came into the room bringing me some toast and coffee on a tray. I drank the coffee, but left the toast. I could see the sadness in Irene's eyes. Neither of us spoke. What was there we could say? When Mathew came into the room, I was dressed, ready to go to our son's funeral. Mathew's eyes were full of sadness. They also reflected the hurt I had caused him. I wanted to say I was sorry, but how could I? This was not the time. He'd already told me they were waiting downstairs and it was time to go.

'When we held hands as they lowered David into the grave, I knew Mathew had forgiven me for what I'd done and said. And even at that sad moment, I knew everything was going to be alright between us.

'When we came back to the house, I felt quite calm, as I mingled among the guests. Then I found out the terrible truth. It was myself who was responsible for the death of our son, not Mathew.'

As she recalled that moment, the pain she had felt then came back to her. The pain in her heart, which had nothing to do with David, the pain was for Mathew. And it was so intense, she thought her heart would break. She'd hurt him so much with the vileness of her words and actions. She felt as if her world had crashed around her. Mathew would never forgive her, nor would he forget the things she'd said and done. Not now, when he found out it was her who was responsible for the death of their son.

Joseph watched her closely, not knowing what thoughts were passing through her mind. He did not know, as she lay there and he waited for her to continue, she could still hear her own screams and see her guests staring at her with pity in their eyes when Mathew came to her!

As he watched, her body began to writhe about, and when she tried to pull her hands away from his, he let go of them. He lifted her from the bed and sat her upon his knee, like a child in need of comfort. He stroked her brow with his fingers, making circular movements as he did so. When he felt her body relaxing he said gently, 'Anna, tell me the truth. Why do you think you were responsible for the death of your son?'

Anna could feel his fingers brushing as light as a feather over her forehead. She felt safe in his arms, yet only a moment ago she'd wanted to get away from him. Wanted him to leave her alone. The thoughts she'd been having had frightened her. She'd heard her own screams and seen Mathew and Adam rushing towards her. She'd even felt the prick of the needle when Adam injected her, which had sent her into oblivion. For how long? She did not know. Since then she'd lived in her own little world and she wanted to go back to that world. I cannot, she thought, face Mathew. Even if he is not told what I have done, I will know.

She heard a soothing voice break into her thoughts, telling her, 'Anna, I don't know what you have done, or what you think you have done. But what I do know is your husband Mathew, and your son Andrew, love you very much. They need you, Anna, need you so very much.'

Somehow, Joseph had sensed what her thoughts might be. That she wanted to go back to her silent world, and if he was not careful, she would do so. He called upon the spirits of his ancestors to help him. To bring this tormented woman back into the world of reality.

He lifted her onto the bed and she curled herself up like an unborn baby lying in its mother's womb. He stood beside the bed, silently watching her, until he saw the spirit of Sara standing at the other side of the bed. She bent down, putting her lips close to Anna's ear.

Joseph saw her lips pucker as if she was going to whistle, though no sound came from them, as she breathed her gentle breath into Anna's ear. There were words coming from her gentle breathing, but only Anna could hear, the whisper of silence. And as she listened, her body uncurled itself until she lay there relaxed on the bed.

Sara smiled at Joseph, then gestured for him to take over before she disappeared. Joseph was not surprised by what she had done and immediately began to speak softly to Anna.

'Tell me now, Anna,' he said, 'of the guilt you feel about David, and why you blame yourself.' He was relieved, even though he knew Anna was in a semi-trancelike state, when she began to tell him.

'I blame myself because I closed my eyes to David's faults. And it was me, not Mathew, who inadvertently gave David the money to buy the drugs. I know,' she said, giving a deep sigh, 'I accused Mathew of spoiling the boys, but I also did my share. And on the night David died I had given him two hundred dollars. He came to me, asking for some money. He'd met this girl, he said. "She's something special and I want to take her somewhere nice, somewhere out of the ordinary." I gave him the money and thought no more about it. A mother does not suspect her children of messing about with drugs, even though she's heard the rumours that her children's friends might be doing so.

'On the day of the funeral, when we came back to the house, the girl David had taken out that night came over to me, offering her condolences. Andrew had invited her, along with some of David's other friends. She seemed a nice girl and I could understand why David thought she was special.'

Joseph heard the emotion come into her voice. He'd no idea what she was about to say next. He took hold of both her hands, pressing them between his own, as he said, 'Anna I know this is hard for you, but tell me what you felt at that moment, and what was said.' He knew, whatever had triggered her hysteria, must have come while she was talking to the girl.

'I felt quite calm,' she said, 'as the two of us spoke about David. Whether I would have stayed that way, I will never know. I'd felt, that day, when we came back from the funeral, so calm and relaxed. Perhaps the feeling of calmness came from the medication Irene gave me earlier. Of course, I cannot be sure of this. I only know, when Paula – that was her name – made her way over to me and told me who she was, I liked what I saw.

'I could see she was embarrassed and did not know what to say. After all, it is hard enough for your adult friends in such circumstances to know what to say, never mind someone so young who you have never met before. To put her at her ease I asked her if she'd enjoyed her night out with David, and which restaurant had he taken her to. I saw the blush come to her face and also the shock.

'I realized, then, it was a silly question to have asked her. But at that moment, to me, this was the girl who David was so happy about taking out. This was the girl who David had spent his last night on earth with. There were no thoughts in my head of the way David had died. It was as if I'd blocked that away as I imagined them spending a romantic evening together. I could see, as I waited for her to answer me, she didn't know what to say. "Please, Paula," I said, touching her arm. "Tell me about that night."

'I saw her fighting with herself as if she was wondering whether to say anything at all. Then she said: "I've no idea what David told you, Mrs Gibbs. But we did not go to a restaurant. In fact, it was only by chance I met David that night. He said he was going to a party and invited me along. The party wasn't my scene so I only stayed for a short time. David wanted me to stay, but I wouldn't. I got a taxi home. I was devastated the next day when I heard about him dying like that. I also felt guilty about leaving him, though it was as well I did go home. My parents would have gone spare if I'd been interviewed by the police, like the others!" She began to say,' Anna told Joseph, 'something about the inquest, but I wasn't listening to her any more. I was thinking about Mathew and the terrible things I'd accused him of.

'I could hear loud screaming, then realized it was coming from myself. Then I saw Mathew pushing his way towards me. My precious Mathew, who I loved so much. He will never forgive me, I thought, when he finds out the truth. That it was me, and not him, who gave David the money which enabled him to buy the drugs that killed him.

'I saw Adam following Mathew, and when he gave me a shot in the arm I hoped I would die, as David had done. I did not want Mathew to hate me when he found out what I had done. I just wanted to die and I did my best to do so. I have not left this room or spoken a word to Mathew or anyone else since that day.' She looked at Joseph's kindly face as she said, 'Until now.'

Joseph saw the tears well up into her eyes. He smiled, then said softly, 'Let the tears flow, Anna. Let them wash away the pain from your mind.'

She raised her hands, covering her eyes with them, as if to catch the tears. He sat there, quietly watching her, as her whole body began to shake with her sobbing. When her tears were spent, she reached for the box of tissues on the bedside table. Taking out a tissue, she wiped her face and hands. She felt much relieved, as if her whole body had been washed clean, inside and out. She smiled timidly as she said, 'Do you really think Mathew will forgive me? After the anguish I have caused him.'

'Mathew,' Joseph said smiling, 'wants nothing more than for you to become well again, Anna. You must believe that.'

'I do believe it,' she said. 'For have I not watched him come into my room, day after day, and seen his sadness? My heart, though he did not know it, cried out for him. Yet I could not speak to him. My lips would not let me do so. Even though I knew how much it was hurting him, seeing me this way. And at night, I would know, even if I was sleeping, that Mathew came into my room and brushed his lips against mine. Yet though I knew all this, I still wanted to die.

'If it had not been for Irene, I think I would have willed myself to do so. But Irene would not let me. Her will was stronger than mine. Several times a day she would drag me out of bed and make me walk around the room, telling me "I may not be able to get you to speak, but I will be damned if I'll stop letting you move your limbs." Sometimes I would be stubborn and refuse to move. But Irene always won. She would not leave me until I did what she said.'

Joseph could imagine the trouble Irene went through, and silently thanked her for it.

'And now,' he heard Anna saying, 'you have made me speak again, and I do not even know your name.'

When he told her, she took his hands into her own. There was a smile upon her face as she said, 'I do not know from where you have come, Joseph Tyler, or what you have done to me, but I thank you from the bottom of my heart. For I feel like my old self.'

Joseph closed her hands together, kissed the tips of her fingers, then told her, 'If that is the case, Anna, I think it is now time for you to see Mathew. He will be pleased when he sees you are well again.'

For a moment, he saw her brow pucker and the light go out of her eyes. Then she smiled when he said, 'You must not be afraid, Anna. Nor must you blame yourself for the things you have spoken to me about.' He hesitated before he continued, 'I feel for you all, that you have lost a part of your family. But none of you are to blame for the way he died. Mathew tells me your son Andrew said that David had a choice in whether or not to take the drugs, and when he decided to do so, there was no going back. I'm afraid,' he said, giving a deep sigh, 'what Andrew says is true. For we are all of us responsible for our own actions, sadly though, some of those actions bring distress to others.'

He did not mention about Andrew not being able to go into her room because it distressed him too much, and that he blamed David for making his mother suffer that way.

'Now,' he said smiling, pressing her hands between his own and glancing at his watch, which showed he'd been alone with her for over an hour, 'I think it is time for you and Mathew to speak to each other. So I will leave you and send Mathew up to his wife.'

There was a slight tremor in her voice when he heard her saying, 'Will you come back with him, Joseph, if only for a moment?'

'Alright,' he said. 'But as you say, only for a moment.'

'Is she alright?' Mathew asked, as he followed Joseph up the stairs.

Joseph had not spoken to him. He'd come out onto the verandah, seen Mathew talking to Jordana, then called to him and gestured for Mathew to come inside.

Joseph turned his head to face Mathew. He did not speak but gave him a brilliant smile. Even so, Mathew could not believe Anna was going to be alright. Joseph had only been with her just over one hour, and the shrink, over a period of time, had spent many hours with her.

'See for yourself,' Joseph said, opening the bedroom door.

Mathew stood there transfixed when he saw Anna sitting up in bed, smiling at them both standing in the open doorway. Mathew, with tears in his eyes, gave Joseph a bear-hug. 'How can I ever thank you?' he said. He did not wait for an answer as he let go of Joseph and ran across the room to Anna, flinging his arms around her.

As Joseph closed the door, he was not surprised to see they were both crying.

Later, in the evening, they all dined together, even Irene, and Thomas the chauffeur. As they ate, Joseph saw that, sitting across from Andrew, the sadness had now gone from his eyes. Those same eyes were now laughing at something his mother had said, and Andrew touched her shoulder as if to reassure himself that his mother was sitting beside him.

From across the table Irene's gaze let upon Joseph, and then Anna, and she marvelled at whatever it was that Joseph had done to make Anna recover so quickly.

She was glad Joseph and Jordana were staying for a while. It was a long time since she'd seen this house, and the family within it, as happy as they were at this moment.

Tears welled up into her eyes as Mathew made a toast to Anna's recovery, and to Joseph for making it possible. As she raised her glass she said a silent prayer, thanking the Lord for what had happened today.

She'd no idea how Joseph had managed it, and she'd hardly been able to believe it when Mathew came into the kitchen all happy and smiling, telling her Anna would be coming down to dine with them;

and herself, as well as Thomas, he hoped, would be able to join them.

She'd wanted to go and see Anna there and then, but Mathew had firmly told her no. She'd not taken offence or asked any questions. She'd been happy enough in knowing Anna was alright. Besides, Anna herself would tell her later; for the moment, as Joseph's eyes let upon her and he smiled, as if knowing what she was thinking, she was content to wait.

Much later, when at last she was alone with Anna in her room, she could contain herself no longer, when she said, as soon as Anna's bedroom door was closed, 'I don't know what Joseph did to you, Anna, but I am truly grateful. Tell me. What exactly happened in here?'

Anna smiled to herself at the sheer awe in Irene's voice as she spoke. She'd known all evening that Irene had been dying to hear how it all came about. She laughed out loud as they both sat down on the bed, like two sisters who'd been on their first date, and were now ready to confide in each other what had happened.

Anyone seeing them, who did not know them, could be forgiven for thinking that was just what they were, sisters. For there'd been a comradeship between them ever since Irene had come to work at the house that went far beyond employer and employee, for they were also friends.

So Anna laughed as she said, 'And I am truly grateful to you, Irene, for not only making me, but forcing me, to walk around the room when I did not want to.'

It was Irene's turn to laugh now at the memory of it. Many an employer would have sacked her on the spot for saying some of the things she had said to make Anna walk.

'You did give me a hard time,' she said, laughing, 'but don't keep me in suspense, please. Tell me what Joseph did to make you recover so quickly. I have seen healers on TV, but with all the razzmatazz that goes with it, I have always thought it a load of bunkum.'

Anna smiled at this statement, for she too, if anyone had asked her before, would have said the same. Now her face became serious as she told Irene, 'When Mathew first came into my room with Joseph and Jordana, I wondered who they were. I was surprised when the man walked over to my bed. He began to stroke my wrist with his thumb. A soothing feeling came over me, I could feel myself begin to relax as he whispered, "You must begin to live again, Anna. You cannot lay here forever, wallowing in what troubles you in your mind. There are people out there who love you. I am a healer, Anna. I have come to help you. I cannot do so if you do not wish to help yourself!" Oh, Irene,' she said, with deep emotion in her voice. 'His wording was so precise and so direct, I thought, I must listen to what he is saying.

'I looked into his eyes and I knew at that moment, I wanted to come home again, to come back into the world of the living. To be with Mathew and my son Andrew. Andrew who I knew, deep inside of me, could not bear to come into my room any more. Joseph must have known what I was thinking, for he said, "You have much to live for, Anna. You have a wonderful husband; and a son to be proud of."'

Anna looked at Irene, as she said, 'Then he surprised me by saying, "I know all about the loss of your eldest son David. And I am sorry. But you must let him go, Anna. Not the memories of him, you will always have those. It is David's spirit you must let go of. His spirit needs to be free, and at peace, to wander the great plains of the sky above."'

Irene interrupted her, saying thoughtfully, 'I never heard that one before, but being as Joseph's of Indian blood, I suppose it's natural for him to believe in such things. And who is to say he is wrong? What happened next? Did you pick up your bed and walk?'

'No, I did not,' Anna said sternly. 'And if you are going to be flippant about what I'm telling you, I shan't tell you anything else. Even though I had the most wonderful experience I ever had in my life.'

'How come?' Irene asked, her eyes nearly popping out of their sockets.

Anna could not help but smile as she told her, 'Joseph took the pillows away, telling me to lie down and relax. He took the sheet away and as I lay there, I watched his hands raise above me, and I closed my eyes. I could feel his hands gliding over my body, and also feel a warmth coming from them. I felt I was floating on a white cloud, which changed to blue, then green. As I lay there, still feeling the warmth from Joseph's hands, I felt so safe, as if nothing ever again would harm me.

'I felt Joseph's hands move away from above my body, though the warmth from them was still there. The white cloud took over from the green one and Joseph placed his hands above the crown of my head and began to move them, drawing an outline around my body. Though I could not see what he was doing, for I could not open my eyes, it felt to me as if he was drawing a line around me, like you see on the films when someone's been killed and they've moved the body. I could still feel the heat from his hands as he moved them down one side of me and up the other, until they came back to where he'd begun.

'Then in my mind's eye, I could see myself laying there on a white cloud, with a gold line as thick as a rope surrounding me. I heard his voice, as if coming from a distance, telling me he'd put a protective aura around me, and that I would sleep now.

'When I awoke, he was sitting beside the bed. He was smiling and asked me how I was feeling. Then he went to bring Mathew.'

She'd no intention, good friends as they were, of telling Irene what she had talked about with Joseph. That was between herself and him. So she said laughing, because it was the first time she'd seen Irene so dumbstruck, 'That is when I picked up my bed and walked!'

Irene saw the funny side of what Anna said. Then laughing with her, she said, 'And it was about time too. How you could lie there like that for all these months, hurting those who loved you, I will never know. Why, you even had me scared, and I don't scare easily as you know.'

Irene raised herself from the bed as she said in her usual bossy way, 'I think you have had enough excitement for one day. In fact, I think we all have, so I will say goodnight.'

Anna said, 'Goodnight, Bossy Boots, see you in the morning.'

Irene pulled a face, then laughed: 'Not if I see you first,' she joked.

As Irene went to her own quarters, she felt happier than she'd felt in months. The whole house feels different, she thought, as if it has come alive again.

It was 2 a.m., and only Joseph and Jordana were still awake. Joseph had just done his nightly ritual and was thanking the spirits of his ancestors for helping him with the healing of Anna.

As always, when this was done, he sat quietly, letting his mind drift on whatever was to come into it. He smiled as his mind recalled the look upon Andrew's face when he saw his mother coming down the verandah steps with his father. Andrew had no idea what had been going on while he'd been out with his girlfriend.

He'd come home and he found Joseph and Jordana sitting beside the pool. He greeted them, then challenged Jordana to a race across the pool and back. Andrew won, and as he was lifting himself out of the water, Joseph saw a look of wonderment come upon his face. In one swift movement he was out of the pool and running towards his parents. Joseph, watching him, could hardly believe himself the change in Anna as she held out her arms for Andrew to run into them.

Anna was dressed in a pale blue safari-type dress, and she looked wonderful. No one would have believed it was the same Anna who'd laid in her bed like a zombie for so long. Her face lit up with happiness as she hugged Andrew close, not minding at all that her dress became wet from the water still dripping from his body.

Jordana had come to stand beside him, putting her wet arm around him. 'Oh, Joseph,' she said, her voice choking with emotion at the scene before her. 'I can hardly believe what I am seeing.'

Andrew's face, as well as his parents, was a picture of delight, as all three came towards them, their arms interlinked around each other with Andrew in the middle. Joseph saw the gratefulness in Anna's eyes as he introduced her to Jordana.

'I'm so glad,' said Jordana, as Anna gave her a hug, 'that you feel well enough to join us.'

Anna smiled as she said, 'All thanks to this handsome husband of yours, Jordana.'

Andrew looked from his mother to Joseph. He'd no idea what was going on, but he was too happy to care. Even when he heard his father saying, 'Thank you Joseph. We will be forever grateful.'

Joseph came out of his reverie. As yet he had no idea what part the Gibbs family had to play in the quest to find Emily's lineage. But at least he was thankful he'd been able to help them.

He went out onto the balcony where Jordana was waiting for him. He was ready now to take Jordana through her own ritual. He was pleased with her progress. She was his pupil, accepting everything he taught her without question. He also thought it would not be long before Jordana would see her own visions in her mind's eye.

He found her gazing up at the moonlit sky and the twinkling stars. She turned her gaze away when she heard him and smiled at him as he held out his hand, which she took hold of, and without either of them saying a word, he led her into the room. She noticed he'd pushed the bed against the wall so there would be more space in the room. He'd also placed the Chinese rug near the open doorway.

He gestured for her to stand on the centre of the rug, then brought his hands together as if in prayer, kissing the tips of his fingers, before he moved away.

When he did so, she closed her eyes. Her left hand raised itself and began to swirl around her head, making circular movements as it did so. Her right hand swirled around her body, as though binding something around her. A moment later, she heard the beating of the drums. Her body began to sway in unison with the rhythm.

Joseph, watching her, waited until this ritual came to an end and Jordana stood still with her eyes closed. Only then did he go to stand before her. He raised his hands above her head, then brought them down on either side of her until they reached the floor. He did these movements several times, and each time he saw a different colour surround her. The colours were a powerful protection against all evil.

In her trance-like state, Jordana felt a shroud of many colours surrounding her body. She knew as she felt his hands wafting around her, Joseph was responsible for making that shroud. She was not afraid even though nothing like this had ever happened to her before.

When the wafting of his hands came to an end, there was only silence. And then she was standing at the entrance of a cave which was filled with a golden light. She looked in and as she gazed up at the roof of the cave, she saw droplets of clear water forming on the roof. The droplets began to fall, turning into different shaped raindrops. Then they were like raindrops no more as each one changed into brilliant colours, making them look like precious jewels.

The jewels sparkled and shone when they landed on the ground, but above them the cave went dark. Jordana tried to look deep inside the cave, but she could see nothing. Yet she felt she was not alone. She felt a powerful presence of something which could not be seen and though she knew not what it was, she also knew she had been touched by it.

When she realized this, the jewels faded, one by one. Her eyes opened and Joseph was standing before her. He took hold of her hands and they lowered themselves onto the rug, then sat down side by side facing the open doorway. Joseph put one arm around her shoulders and gestured with the other to look out of the open doorway. All this was done in silence, as if by mutual agreement.

Jordana was still in a wondrous state from the things she had just seen and felt, and only for a moment did she wonder why they were sitting on the rug. Then she gazed out of the doorway as Joseph had gestured for her to do. His hand was still raised as she did so, and she could see nothing in the night sky, only darkness. A moment later, when Joseph dropped his hand, the moon seemed as if it had fallen from the sky and landed in front of the doorway. The moon was so big and bright, Jordana thought if she reached out she would be able to touch it with her hand. The light from the moon shone into the room and engulfed their bodies in a kind of halo.

Jordana turned her head so she could look at Joseph, thinking as she did so, there would never again be a night like this, and when he looked at her, then kissed her lips, she was sure there would not be. For as their lips met, she felt they were both at one with the Universe. When he drew his lips away, she wanted to tell him how she felt, but some instinct told her she must not speak.

Joseph touched her chin with his finger, then gently turned her head so she could see the doorway. She saw the moon moving away, rising up into the sky, as if the moon had performed some duty and now it was done.

As the moon moved away, Jordana saw something else was taking its place. To Jordana, it looked like a mist that was hiding something inside. Then the mist cleared and Sara was standing in the open doorway, smiling down on them.

Sara's eyes sought out Jordana's as she said, 'On this night, Jordana, you have been shown the power of the Ilinka tribe. This power, Jordana, was brought forth from the very core of your heart. It is a great gift you have been given. You must use it wisely on the path you have to travel with Joseph. In both seeking out the bloodline of the lost tribe, and beyond. For when the bloodline has been brought together, there will be still much for you to do.'

When Sara had spoken, the mist returned, and a moment later, Sara was gone.

Jordana turned to Joseph with an expression of wonderment upon her face. When she was able to speak, she said, 'Oh Joseph, I hope I am worthy of all that has happened to me this night. For I feel that I have been touched by the spirit of all things. Tell me I am not dreaming.'

He held her close as he told her, 'You are not dreaming, Jordana. I also have seen what you have seen, and from now on, because we have been shown these things, you will be able to perform the Sacred Ritual by yourself. But you must always remember, the ritual must be done each morning and each night before you retire to your bed.'

He raised himself from the ground, bringing her up with him. Then they went out onto the balcony where Jordana gazed in wonderment at the moonlit sky as she recalled all that had happened to her that night.

Joseph, standing beside her, was thinking about Jack. Who should, he thought, glancing at his watch, be in Ilinka by now.

He gave a deep sigh, as a picture of the Blue Mountain came into his mind, and he wondered how long it would be before he was able to take Jordana home.

For a moment, he envied Jack. He'd wanted more than anything, after he'd married Jordana, to take her home as soon as possible. The envy was only momentary, for he knew the pleasure of taking Jordana to Ilinka would have to wait. But the pleasure of taking Jordana to bed was imminent, and he smiled when he heard her asking him to do so.

CHAPTER V

Jack was standing below the Blue Mountain, thinking what a magnificent sight it was, and that Joseph had not exaggerated when he'd told him about it.

He'd arrived at the Tyler residence four hours earlier. Joseph's father met him at the airport and there'd been a gathering of the clan, waiting to greet him when they arrived at the house. He'd been introduced to them all before being shown to his room. He'd unpacked, showered and put on a change of clothes before going back downstairs, taking the Sacred Cylinder with him. He'd smiled to himself as he carried it downstairs, recalling how he'd told them when he'd come through customs, he'd nothing to declare, and wondered what would have happened if they'd opened his case. Yet he'd had no fear of them doing so!

When he entered the room, everyone looked up, and stopped whatever it was they'd been doing. It seemed to him as though time for a moment stood still, for no one moved – they could all have been made of wax. For that, to Jack, was what the scene looked like – a setting from a wax museum.

Then Joseph's father came over to him, and when he gave him the cylinder, he held it in his hands as if it was more precious than life itself. He turned to face the others with his arms outstretched, his cupped hands holding the cylinder. He did not speak, but it was as if he had when they all moved as one and came to look. Joseph's father raised his cupped hands to his mouth and kissed the cylinder, then lowered his hands.

One by one, from the eldest to the youngest, they came to stand before Joseph's father, and bowed their heads to kiss the cylinder. Jack watched it all and when they were done, Joseph's father turned to him and he did the same. When he looked up, he saw the tears in the eyes of Joseph's father as he said, 'Thank you, my friend. Perhaps now the spirits of our ancestors will be happy, with this Sacred Cylinder being returned to the Ilinka tribe.'

The tears, Jack knew, from what had been said in the car on the journey here, were not only for the safe return of the cylinder but also for the son who could not bring it himself. And as the cylinder was being locked away in the safe behind the picture on the wall, Jack recalled how he'd said in the car that he thought it was sacrilege him bringing the cylinder, when it should have been Joseph's privilege to do so.

Then he was told, 'My son has a mission to complete, my friend. And he takes heed of the spirits who guide him. Though I must admit my heart is sad that Joseph could not bring the cylinder himself, and also his bride.'

When the safe was closed and the picture put back in its place, Joseph's mother said it was time to eat. She'd made a special Thanksgiving dinner for their guest and did not want it spoiled.

After they'd eaten, Jack went upstairs for the video recording he'd brought with him of Jordana and Joseph's wedding day. And also spliced into it was them dancing together at Jordana's birthday party. Jack watched for the reaction of Jordana's in-laws when she came up on the screen. He was not disappointed when Joseph's parents turned to him smiling and said in unison, 'Jack, Jordana is beautiful.'

They watched the rest of the tape enthralled, and when it was over Joseph's mother was unashamedly crying when she looked at him, saying, 'My tears, Jack, are tears of happiness. I can see my son is happy with the bride the spirits chose for him. And Jordana is happy also.'

When she demanded the tape be played again and her husband obliged, Jack excused himself, saying if they did not mind he would go for a walk. Joseph's father offered to go with him but he declined the offer.

He came out of the back door into the garden, then through the gate which would lead him onto Ilinka soil. Closing the gate, he looked back at the house, and let his thoughts dwell on the man who had built it all those years ago. Joseph had told him the history of it all. About Ilinka, Petraba and the Tyler residence. And he could not help but wonder about the man who'd been born at Topmount Farm and came to dwell here. He also wondered how that same man had left behind him a chain of events that were still being linked together to this present day.

He followed the wooded path, which he knew would lead him to the Ilinka village. Coming out into the clearing, his eyes let onto the snow-capped mountain. He'd seen the peak of it from his bedroom window, but the tall trees hid the rest. He'd heard so much from Joseph about this mystical mountain but he was unprepared for the effect it would have upon him when he saw it for the first time.

If he'd been of the Catholic faith he would have crossed himself. He stood there transfixed as a strange feeling washed over him. It lasted only for a few moments, yet he knew he'd been touched by some mystical power.

He gazed down onto the settlement below. Like everywhere else, Ilinka had moved on with the times, there were cars parked outside the cabins and TV aerials everywhere.

He recalled the plans he'd seen for the building of Ilinka, and also those for the building of Petraba – the plans drawn up by Joseph Tyler which were framed and hung in the hallway of the Tyler residence. With his builder's eye, he imagined how it all would have been when Joseph and Meleeka first came to develop the settlement. And he was glad to see nothing had changed, except for the cars and the TV aerials. Everything else had been lovingly preserved by the generations that followed.

He made his way to the stone-built house, the same house that Joseph Tyler had built as a wedding gift for Sara and Meleeka. It stood empty now, waiting for Joseph to bring his bride home. Jack stood there, admiring the workmanship of the men from Maraldon Village who had come thousands of miles to build this house. He restrained himself from taking a peek inside – he would wait for that pleasure until Joseph and Jordana returned.

He made his way to the foot of the mountain and now, as he stood before it, he wondered what would be in store for them all, when those, like himself, the lost tribe as Joseph called them, were brought together. For it was then that the Sacred Cylinder would be opened to reveal its secret.

He sighed as he turned away from the mountain and made his way to where the founders of Ilinka and Petraba were buried. As he walked between the graves, he marvelled at the way destiny had brought them all together, and was still doing so, with not only his own, but with others whose bloodline was linked to those of Meleeka and Sara. He also marvelled at the way he'd come to be standing beside these graves of the ancestors he'd known nothing about, until Joseph had come to the farm.

He felt like weeping when his hand caressed the headstone of Meleeka and Sara. For when he touched it, a vision of Clare came into his mind, and he recalled that when she died, all he'd wanted to do was die himself. Once he'd even contemplated taking his own life. It would have been easy, all he needed to do was run the car off the road and drop down the thousand feet into oblivion. He'd driven up that road three times with every intention of going over the top, yet could not find the courage to do so. Instead, he'd thrown all his energy into his work, hoping the stress of it all would eventually kill him. Whereas, all it had done was make a lot of money.

He still missed Clare and would always do so. But as he glanced around the graves he wondered about the unknown force which had brought these people together, the very same force which had now brought him here to where it all began.

He followed the road leading to Petraba and found the place where Jenny's cookhouse once stood. From the front, it looked the same as it must have done when it was first built, but now there was an extension built on the back making it into a mini-market store.

He bought some sweets for the children who were back at the house. While he was being served, he wondered if the young couple behind the counter knew the history of the place.

Joseph had told him about Jenny and her ambitions and how she came to Ilinka. He'd thought, as Joseph narrated to him the story about Jenny, that in the end she would have married her benefactor, or at least, Adam the lawyer. He'd been disappointed when he found out that Jenny married no one.

Coming out of the store, still thinking about Jenny, he walked up the hill to find the house that had been especially built for her. When he found it, he was pleased to see it had also been lovingly preserved. And he could imagine, as Jenny said she would, her sitting on the verandah watching history being made!

What sights she must have seen, he thought, as his gaze moved to the township below. It must have been wonderful to see a town come into being, both with the development of it and the immigrants who had come and settled there from all walks of life. He smiled ruefully as he thought about how there would soon be an influx of strangers arriving at the Ilinka settlement and he wondered what the inhabitants of Petraba would think.

He'd been told by Joseph's father that when the time came the lost tribe would gather below the mountain. Then, and only then, the seal of the cylinder would be broken and the Sacred Scripture the cylinder contained would be read to the people. When this was done the mountain would speak. He'd no reason to doubt what he'd been told would come to pass. He only hoped that whatever the Scriptures and the mountain revealed, it would be for the good of mankind.

He was not a religious man, not in the way of going to church, yet he believed that there was some omniscient power which had created all things. And most of all, the beauty of nature could not be denied. Even in one's deepest sorrow, the beauty of nature could lift a person's heart.

He'd realized this after Clare had died as he'd roamed over the moors of his home town with his heart feeling like a lump of lead. Then, all at once, he'd come upon a scene so tranquil it would take his breath away and he would feel at one with whatever had created such beauty. Sometimes the tranquillity of it all made him want to pray to the God he'd been taught about as a child. Yet he'd never been able to do so.

For a long time, religion to him had been nothing, only a word. For if there was only one God, he could not understand why the different religions fought over him. And how, in the name of a God they professed to love, they killed and maimed little children who'd done them no harm.

He gave a deep sigh as his thoughts turned to Joseph and his quest. He could understand why, as Joseph said, the spirit in the sky was getting angry with mankind.

He walked on, making his way back to the Tyler residence, and as he did so he thought about the two men who had created the village of Ilinka and the township of Petraba, two men from different cultures, who, at the time, should have been enemies. But instead of fighting they'd shown respect for each other and they'd achieved so much. He hoped, when he got back to the house, he would be allowed to read the chronicles they left behind, which Joseph had told him so much about.

CHAPTER VI

Joseph awoke early and quietly slipped out of bed so as not to awaken Jordana. He crept out onto the balcony which overlooked the secluded part of the garden. In the distance, he could see the calm breakers of the ocean rolling in towards the shore.

The leaves on the trees began to rustle with the awakening of the birds. He listened to their chattering, which sounded as though they were waking each other, so not one of them would miss the coming of a new dawn.

When the sun began to rise, the birds came out of the trees. Their beautiful coloured plumage was a sight to behold. They swooped around the garden, as though they were happy to be alive.

As Joseph surveyed the scene – the rising of the sun, the beauty of the birds, as well as the incoming tide and the garden below – his heart soared with thankfulness at being a witness to this morning glory. Then was saddened when he wondered why the human race was hell bent on destroying such beauty. Not only with weapons, he thought, which were now more dangerous than ever before, but with chemicals that seeped into both land and air.

As he watched the birds happily going about their morning routine, he thought of the creatures who could die from the pollution. For there was no one to tell them what was happening. And he hoped that the powers that be would come to their senses before it was too late.

He went back inside where Jordana was still sleeping. He opened the wardrobe door quietly, taking out the doeskin, in readiness for after he'd taken a shower. As he did so he wondered how long they would be staying here and the reason for them doing so. Anna was fine now and they'd been here five days already. Yet the spirits had shown him nothing of where they would go next.

After he'd showered he went back out onto the balcony to make himself ready for his morning ritual and was surprised to find the birds had all disappeared – there was only silence, as if the whole world was sleeping. He relaxed his body and began to breathe in the fresh, morning air, before performing the Sacred Ritual.

When the vision came, he saw a dirt road with men and women on either side of the road. The women carried parasols to shade them from the hot sun. Two dogs were playing in the middle of the road, oblivious to the heavy wagon being pulled by bullocks which was heading towards them. The road carried on, winding its way to a new development under construction.

Sitting under the shade of a tree was a woman with a babe in her arms and a young boy standing beside her. Two men were standing by a plot of land, one of them holding some papers. They came over to where the woman was sitting. The man with the papers raised his hat, spoke a few words, then left. The other man sat down beside the woman and they both smiled as he spoke to her. And there was no doubt in Joseph's mind as to who they were.

By the time his vision came to an end, he'd seen the history of the Townly sibling up and until the present day. As always when his vision came to an end, he sat quietly, going over what he'd been shown. This time, his thoughts dwelt on the menfolk of the family who had fought with the Anzacs and were never to come home again. A generation later war came again and there were other menfolk of the Townlys who did not return.

With these thoughts running through his mind, he shuddered involuntarily as he imagined what the power of modern weapons could do today – annihilate the world.

He raised himself from the balcony floor and brushed these thoughts away. He leant on the railing, looking up into the cloudless sky, and thanked the spirits for showing him what had to be seen.

He knew now, by what they had shown him, it would not be long before the bloodline he was seeking would be brought together. And he also knew the reason for being led to Mathew.

He went into the bedroom and as he picked up his lighter and cigarettes from the bedside table he glanced down at Jordana. She will be happy, he thought, when I tell her what I have seen.

Going back out onto the balcony, he relaxed on one of the loungers, lit a cigarette and let his mind drift. With the bloodline being uppermost in his mind, his thoughts drifted to Ilinka, then to the white man who's name he bore, the man who had left a legacy of wealth that had enriched the Tyler tribe for all the generations that followed. Yet that wealth had not hindered the gift which came from Sara, the white man's adopted daughter.

From her, came the power to heal; the purity of mind; the loving of heart. He'd realised a long time ago he was truly blessed. For wealth alone could destroy many things and bring greed to mens' hearts.

He recalled reading the chronicles of when the settlers came to Petraba. His namesake said it was progress and of course he was right. Progress had to come, but how far could progress go? He'd thought then, as he was doing now, of the native tribes of long ago. They'd been happy with their daily lives, hunting and fishing to feed and clothe their families. Then all that was changed with the coming of men from other nations. These men found gold and jewels on the plains the natives had roamed for so long, not only in his own country but others as well. Much blood had been spilt as the men searched for the precious metals and jewels which had been hidden in the land for thousands of years.

The natives could not stop their lands being invaded. They fought, of course, though it was all in vain. Nor could they stop the building of towns and cities that would come later.

He'd been glad when he read the chronicles – there'd been no bloodshed on Ilinka soil, or Petraba. The two men, from different cultures, who helped each other to create both places, had been too wise for that to happen. Yet even now, he wondered, as he'd wondered before, why the natives of those lands were allowed to roam the plains for so long, living with nature and what nature provided. Then to change it all with the coming of the strangers.

He knew, as he stubbed out his cigarette, he would never find an answer to his own question. There was no malice in his thinking this way. For he himself, had much to thank a white man for, and one could even marvel at those other white men who, coming from an island so small, conquered vast continents. And in doing so changed the world.

And the world is still changing, he thought. For now, some of the offspring of those long ago conquered tribes who were ruled over by the white man, are now invading the white man's country. But they come in peace, bringing their own cultures with them.

I hope they have come in peace, he thought, for while I was there I felt a smouldering of unrest. And Jack had confirmed when they discussed the subject that there had been many fights among the younger generations of different cultures, fights which erupted without any just cause.

He gave a deep sigh as he raised himself from the lounger and said to himself: There is so much unrest in the world; the sooner my mission is completed, and I can return to my home, the better I will feel.

Later in the day he rang his parents and told them of his vision. His father was pleased and said he would start preparing things. His father also told him of the recording Jack had given to them and how he liked Jordana, even though he'd only seen her on TV. His mother said the same, though her voice choked when she told him, 'I can see you are happy my son. And I think Jordana is wonderful. I can see she loves you.'

When Jordana came back from a shopping spree with Anna, he told her his parents were delighted with their daughter-in-law, even though they'd only seen her on the video tape recording Jack had given them.

Jordana smiled as she said, 'I'm glad they approve, Joseph. For it would be a bit late for them to be disappointed in me now, when, in the short time I have known their son, he has changed my life completely.'

He smiled back at her as he reached for her hand across the poolside table. He knew what she meant.

'Did you speak to Jack?' she asked.

'Yes I did. And he says to give you his love. And he can't wait to see your reaction when you see the mountain for the first time. He says it had the most peculiar effect on him. He loves Ilinka, but he is leaving in a couple of days to make ready for the gathering.'

He'd told her earlier of his vision and she knew it would not be long before they would be going to Ilinka. For a while they spoke about Jack and the mission he was about to embark upon. Then they sat quietly, holding hands, both of them deep in their own thoughts.

When Mathew came out onto the verandah, this was how he saw them, sitting together as if they were both at peace with the world. As always, he thought what a perfect couple they made. Yet there was something about them which he could not fathom. He'd met many people in his life, from all walks of life, but none of them compared with these two. He knew that although Jordana looked stunning in her white bikini, and Joseph, wearing only white shorts, had the physique of a warrior, it was nothing to do with their looks or appearance that intrigued him. It was something else, yet he knew not what.

He stood watching them, not making a sound. Then they both turned their heads in unison as if they'd sensed he was there, and greeted him warmly. It is uncanny, he thought, as he went to join them, the way they both sensed me standing there.

Jordana gave him a brilliant smile as he sat down. 'Where is Anna?' she asked. 'She told me she would meet me by the pool!'

'Anna is in the kitchen with Irene,' Mathew replied. 'She shouldn't be long.'

Jordana told him of her shopping spree with Anna. And when Joseph challenged them to a race in the pool, Jordana accepted the challenge, but Mathew declined. He watched them dive into the pool then, lighting a cigarette, lay back on the lounger, blowing smoke-rings into the air.

While he relaxed, and without any reason he could think of, his thoughts turned to Anna, to when he'd first met her twenty-eight years ago.

When Anna had come into his life he had been thirty years old and had never been involved with a woman before. The property business he'd set up when he sold the opals was booming, thanks to the immigrants who were arriving by the boatload. Today they would have called him a wizz kid, making so much money in so short a time. Though it had been hard work, buying old property and renovating it, his whole life revolved around doing just that. Then he decided to open an estate agency. It was there that he first saw Anna who'd been pinning pictures onto the board of houses for sale.

With her long blonde hair and fair complexion, he'd no idea she was of Aboriginal descent. And if he had known, it would have made no difference, for as soon as he saw her, he felt as though he'd been struck with a thunderbolt. He'd been so alarmed by this unusual feeling that when the rest of the staff bid him good morning as he made his way to the manager's office, he could not even acknowledge them.

When he entered the office, Ian Ross the manager, was speaking to someone on the phone. He'd closed the door quietly, then watched Anna through the plate-glass window. Any other man, so suddenly struck by the beauty of a pretty girl, would have asked Ian Ross about her, but not him. He'd got on with the business he'd come to see Ian Ross about.

When he came out of the office there was no sign of the girl. He realized it was lunchtime, and though some of the staff were still working, she was not one of them. Like a fool he'd stood there glancing around until he realized the office girls were all staring at him.

He went outside, thinking he would come back later, then he saw her as he was opening the car door. She was coming out of the delicatessen farther down the street. He closed the car door, then followed her down onto the Plaza where she settled herself onto one of the benches and opened the bag containing her lunch which she'd bought from the delicatessen.

The pigeons were swarming all around her. She took a bite from her crusty roll sandwich, then broke a piece off and threw it to the birds, watching their antics as they fought over the crust of bread. She absently broke off another piece of roll and threw it as near as she could to the one-legged pigeon that had not had a chance against the others. She smiled as the bird pecked at the bread contentedly.

His heart was thumping as he walked over to the bench. 'May I sit here?' he asked as he looked down at her. When she glanced up, he knew she'd no idea who he was.

'It's a free country,' she said, turning her attention back to the pigeon. His heart leapt at the sound of her voice – she'd spoken pleasantly, as if she'd said those words a thousand times to a thousand strangers.

He watched the expression on her face as she tried to entice the one-legged pigeon closer by throwing pieces of the roll nearer to herself. What she would have done if she had achieved this aim he'd had no idea. Nor did he find out. For the other pigeons turned their attention to what she was doing and swooped over, picking up the bread with their beaks.

This should have given him an opportunity to speak to her, but he'd just sat there, like a besotted schoolboy, trying to conjure up in his mind what to say. He'd panicked when she rose from the bench and began to walk away. Then, taking the bull by the horns as he would have done over a business matter, he leapt to his feet and tapped her on the shoulder. The very act of touching her made his heart pound so much he thought it would break.

When she turned to face him, her amber-coloured eyes, as they gazed into his own, made him feel as if he was going to faint. For a moment he'd not been able to speak, standing there like a tongue-tied idiot. Then he'd calmed himself and blurted out, 'I believe I'm in love with you! Yet I do not even know your name.'

She'd looked at him as if he was some kind of nutcase, but before she could turn away he grabbed hold of her arm, saying, 'Please don't go. I know what you must be thinking, but I assure you it does happen to be true. I'm sorry if I have offended you but I have never fallen in love before. I just didn't know what else to say.'

She'd blushed with embarrassment, then said kindly, as if talking to a child, 'You must let me go. I will be late for work and that will make a poor impression on my first day there.'

'There is no need,' he'd said, 'for you to go back to work. You will take the rest of the day off. I am your boss, and that is an order!'

'Now I know you are a madman,' she replied, giving him a scathing look. 'Ian Ross is my boss. Now will you please leave me alone, or I will—'

He'd not let her finish whatever it was she was about to say. He'd regained his confidence as he told her, 'I know Ian Ross happens to be your boss. Ian works for me and runs the estate agency that employs you. I am Mathew Gibbs, the owner, and I apologize for the way I have been acting.'

He could see the name meant nothing to her and she was still unsure if what he'd said was the truth.

'Come with me,' he'd said, pointing to a phone box not far away from where they were standing. 'I will phone Ian and prove to you who I am.'

Without more ado he took hold of her and guided her over to the phone box, knowing as he did so she was only allowing him to because she was so young and did not know how to handle the situation.

'What is your name?' he asked, as he dialled the number.

He could hardly hear her as she whispered, 'Anna Carosea.'

He held the phone between them so she could hear the conversation. When he replaced the receiver, he turned to her saying, 'Now you know who I am, Anna, will you please spend the afternoon with me? You need not be afraid. I have no ulterior motive. I only want to be with you, and I want that more than anything I have ever wanted in my life!'

His heart soared when she smiled shyly, then nodded her head in agreement.

He did not know, as they came out of the phone box, that when Ian Ross put the phone down, he announced to the rest of the staff, 'The white Abbo will not be coming back this afternoon. She's spending the rest of the day with the boss.'

If he had known, he would have sacked Ian Ross on the spot. But by the time he found out, it didn't matter.

When they came out of the phone box he'd felt like a schoolboy on his first date as he took hold of Anna's hand and they walked across the Plaza, making their way to the wharf.

He bought two tickets for the ferry that was going he knew not where, until the ticket collector said it was bound for Manly.

When the ferry revved its engine they were standing on deck. Anna looked like a child who was playing truant. Then, as the ferry began to move, she surprised him as she laughed out loud and said, 'I shouldn't be doing this, you know. Mr Ross will not be pleased. But now that I am here, I intend to enjoy myself.'

He'd wanted to take her into his arms but refrained from doing so, not wanting to spoil the magical moment of pure happiness which he hoped Anna was feeling as well as himself.

By the time the ferry reached Manly he felt as though he'd known her all his life. She'd told him about her family and of how she was the youngest of five brothers and four sisters. She also told him about her tyrant of a father.

'He would dislike you on sight, Mathew' she said. 'Just because you are white.'

He'd laughed, telling her, 'Your father can please himself whether he likes me or not, but he will have to accept that I am going to marry his daughter.'

'Mathew,' she said. 'You hardly know me. How can you be talking of marriage?' She looked at her watch. 'It is less than an hour ago that you picked me up.'

He thought he'd offended her with his talk about marriage, then she smiled, saying as she looked into his eyes, 'Mathew, it may be only a short time since we came aboard this ferry, yet I feel as though I have known you all my life. There is happiness here,' she pointed to her heart, 'that I have never felt before, never, in all my life.'

His heart soared as she continued in her truthful, childlike way that later he would come to adore. 'If I feel this way now, Mathew, what am I going to feel when we really get to know each other?'

His voice was choked as he told her, 'You will feel happiness always, Anna, there in your heart.'

'And will your heart feel the same, Mathew?' she asked.

'Yes, yes, yes,' he replied. 'You must never doubt that, Anna.'

Later, when he'd met her father, he found out Anna had not lied – her father disliked him on sight.

Mathew stubbed out the cigarette and for a moment watched Joseph and Jordana, still swimming in the pool. Then absently took a Dunhill from his cigarette case, lit it and lay back on the lounger, recalling how he could not wait to marry Anna, but she'd been under age and needed her father's consent.

In the Carosea household her father's word was law and her father did not approve of his daughter marrying someone not of her own kind, as he put it. He was hostile towards both Anna and himself. But in the end agreed to give his consent on condition Anna be married at home, with only a few guests in attendance, and the reception be held there also. He'd agreed to this, even though he would have liked Anna to have the biggest wedding in town.

On their wedding day, her parents did Anna proud with the food and drink. But the reception had been a nightmare. How he'd kept his temper that day, he would never know.

They'd sat at the head of the long table laden with food. Her family on one side, his guests on the other, and neither side had been at ease with the other. As he sat there holding Anna's hand, he could feel the tension in the air between her family and his guests as they eyed each other across the table. It was as if they were enemies at war, ready to do battle. Anna had warned him of what it would be like.

'My father may have given his consent,' she said, 'for in the end it would be pointless for him not to do so. But he will not give us his blessing, nor will the rest of my family, including my mother. My father's displeasure will also reflect upon my family. So do not expect them to be sociable at the wedding.'

When she'd told him this, he'd asked her why she agreed to be married from home. 'We could have waited,' he said.

Without any hesitation she told him, 'Neither you, nor I, wanted to wait, Mathew. And, because that is the last order, and it was an order, I will ever take from my father!'

He'd hardly believed it would be as bad as she said, yet it turned out to be worse.

From that day on, he'd cherished her more than ever and they'd been happy together. Only the death of their son had marred that happiness, when he thought he'd lost her both in mind and body. But now, thanks to Joseph, Anna was her old self again and he was a happy man.

He came out of his reverie when he felt two arms enfold him around his neck and Anna asked: 'Whatever are you thinking about, Mathew? You were so deep in thought you never heard me put the tray of drinks onto the table.'

He looked up and smiled. 'Believe it or not,' he said, 'I was thinking of our wedding day.'

He saw the surprise on her face, then she laughed, saying, 'Mathew, please don't remind me, it is something I try my hardest to forget.'

And as if to prove it, she called to Joseph and Jordana, pointing to the tray of drinks.

They all looked at Mathew when he suddenly excused himself and went into the house.

'I won't be a moment,' he said.

While they were talking, all sat around the table, Mathew had only been half listening – there was something niggling him at the back of his mind, something about a wedding invitation. And he vaguely remembered there'd been some talk about a wedding before David died. He'd no idea, as he went into the study, why he felt an urgency to sort the matter out. He opened the top drawer of the desk, taking out a pile of letters. Most of them were letters of condolence from when David died. He put these to one side – he would burn them later. Anna had not seen them and he certainly wasn't going to show them to her now.

He found what he was looking for – a wedding invitation from Helena. He hoped, as he took out the invitation, that the wedding had not been and gone, for with Anna's illness he'd forgotten all about it. When he saw the date was in ten days' time, he picked up the receiver and dialled Helena's number. Helena had been his secretary when he'd first gone into the property business and the invitation was for her daughter's wedding.

'Hi, Helena,' he said, when he heard her voice on the other end of the phone. 'It's Mathew here, and I'm in a bit of a dilemma. I'm calling to confess that until a moment ago I'd forgotten about Judith's wedding. And now I'm wondering if I replied accepting your invitation?'

He sighed with relief when he heard her saying, 'Of course you accepted Mathew. I would have been onto you before now if you had not done so. In fact, I was going to ring you to see if Anna would be able to come; and also apologise for not ringing sooner to ask how she is. But to be honest, Mathew, what with the trip abroad, the wedding arrangements and everything else, I don't know where the time has flown to.'

When she asked about Anna, he told her how well Anna was, and of Joseph's involvement. 'That is another reason why I rang you,' he said. 'Joseph and his wife are staying with us and I was wondering if they could also come to the wedding. I know it is short notice.'

'Say no more, Mathew,' she told him. 'Of course you must bring them. It is not too late to squeeze in another two guests. Besides, they sound a very interesting couple. Especially Joseph and the way he has healed Anna. You must be truly grateful to him.'

'I am,' he said. 'In fact, Helena, you will never know how grateful, or how much I appreciate them staying with us. Anna and I get on so well with them. And you will never believe this, since they arrived I have not set foot inside the office.'

For a moment Helena was stunned into silence for she, above anyone, knew what a workaholic he was. He heard her laugh as she said, 'Then I am doubly looking forward to meeting them.' They reminisced for a while before he put the receiver back on the hook.

As he went out onto the verandah he heard the laughter. Then he stood there watching Anna laughing. He could hardly believe it was the same Anna who only a few days ago had been causing him so much despair. He went to join them, telling Anna as he sat down that he'd been ringing Helena about Judith's wedding.

'Oh,' she said. 'I had forgotten all about that.'

'To be honest,' he said, 'so had I. And I do not even know what prompted me to think about the wedding invitation.' He turned to face Joseph and Jordana as he said, 'I hope you don't mind, but I have wangled an invite to take you with us. If you have any other plans for a week on Saturday, I will understand, and I will call Helena back right away.'

'We will be delighted to accept,' Joseph said, smiling. He was not surprised they'd been invited to the wedding as he'd seen it in his vision that very morning.

Anna was also delighted – nothing had been said about how long Jordana and Joseph would be staying with them, and in truth, she did not want them to leave. Though she felt like her old self, the thought of those long, lonely days and nights she'd spent in her room still haunted her. She felt safe when Joseph was around for if it had not been for him, she would be still there.

She smiled at Jordana, as she said, 'I think that gives us an excuse to go shopping tomorrow for new outfits for the wedding!'

Mathew laughed, 'The treat's on me,' he said, 'and there is no need to spare the expense.'

'We won't,' said Anna, laughing, as she winked at Jordana. She knew how Mathew felt about this young couple he'd brought into their home.

Joseph was also laughing as he raised himself from the chair and said he was going for a swim. He wanted to be alone with his thoughts. He knew, now his mission was being made easy for him, the reason for being led to this house and the part Mathew was playing in leading him to the bloodline of Emily and Bob Townly. The bridegroom was of their bloodline and there would be others there from the same ancestry, bringing many of the tribe into one gathering. He would meet them and know which of them truly belonged to the Ilinka tribe. Later he would tell them of his mission and of their roots.

The spirits work in mysterious ways, he thought, as he rested upon the water, letting his body float. He recalled the warning from the mountain and thought the spirits were doing all they could in bringing the tribe together as quickly as possible. He wondered what the outcome would be if he was able to complete his mission in time. He had an idea what it would be if he did not. Yet he could not believe he would have been sent on the mission if he was not able to complete it in time, though he could not be sure he was right in thinking this way.

He began to swim again and swam two lengths of the pool before getting out and joining the others. As he got out of the pool his thoughts were on Ilinka, wondering how Jack was getting on.

CHAPTER VII

Jack was sitting by the fireside at the Tyler residence. The chronicles lay on the table beside his chair – the founding of Ilinka and Petraba had made fascinating reading.

Relaxing in his chair, he lit a cigarette, then gazed up above the fireplace to the painting in the gilt frame of Topmount Farm. He thought it was a good likeness of the farm which still stood there to this day, and wondered who had painted the picture all those years ago. As he gazed at the painting it was hard for him to believe that the man who'd been born there was responsible for so much of what he'd read in the chronicles, simply because he'd been led to dwell in a place not of his own choosing.

When he'd studied the portrait of that man, Joseph Tyler, which hung in the hallway he'd liked what he'd seen. The artist had captured not only Joseph Tyler's kind and gentle smile but also the wisdom in his eyes. And now he'd read the chronicles, he admired the man even more for what he'd achieved.

It could not have been easy in those days – a white man, living with a tribe of Indians. Yet he'd become a prominent man who was loved by the natives he'd chosen to live with and the pioneering settlers as well.

Stubbing out his cigarette, his thoughts turned to the Sacred Cylinder, hidden in the safe behind the picture, and he wondered about Joseph and Jordana, and how they were coping with the mission they'd been sent on. He recalled the night in England when Joseph first told him about the mystical mountain speaking to him, about the spirit in the sky being angry with mankind and of the mission he'd been sent on.

He could not say he disbelieved Joseph when he'd told him, though he'd found it hard to understand.

Now, he wondered what secrets the cylinder held for the future of mankind. And if the spirits of Meleeka and Sara would show Joseph and Jordana the way to bring the lost tribe home before it was too late. And himself also, for tomorrow he was going on his own mission, to bring his own branch of the lineage together, making them ready to travel to Ilinka.

He did not relish going on this mission for he would be flying to the four corners of the world, but he knew it had to be done. The mission itself did not bother him – it was the thought of spending many hours on aircraft that did.

He looked up and smiled when Joseph's father came into the room and sat down opposite him on the settee.

'Did you enjoy reading about our ancestors?' he asked.

'Very much so,' he replied. 'And thank you JT for letting me read them.' He'd come to address Joseph's father as JT because everyone else did so. 'Your ancestors left behind an incredible story.'

JT smiled. 'And to think,' he said, 'if my son Joseph had not found the chronicles in the loft, and been fascinated by them, they would still be lying there gathering dust.'

'I don't think so,' Jack said. 'I think Joseph was meant to find them. Joseph and no one else. They must have been in the loft for generations, yet no one else had touched them.'

'Perhaps you're right,' said JT, 'for I certainly did not know they were there. Nor, as far as I know, did my father.'

'I know I am right,' Jack told him, raising his eyes to the picture on the wall. 'Joseph had to find the chronicles because it was Joseph who, out of the long line of the Tylers before him, was the only one to come to the farm, the very same farm where it all began. The farm, where Joseph Simon Tyler was born and brought up before he was destined to come and dwell with Meleeka and his tribe.

'In all truth, JT, as I read the chronicles, I marvelled at how the dynasty had worked out. Especially as no blood of the man himself runs through the Tyler veins. And also, how the two men from different cultures accomplished all they did, when there was at that time so much prejudice about the natives.'

JT smiled ruefully as he put his fingers to his lips in the same mannerism as his son. 'The prejudice is still there, Jack,' he said. 'The Tylers may be rich and affluent, but we are still of the same blood, some people think, of those natives who fought with their ancestors. They try not to show it, of course, but I know it is there. It is as if the hatred of the natives of this land has been handed down from one generation to the next.'

'It is the same in my country,' Jack told him. 'With the influx of different creeds who are infiltrating the cities and towns. They come in peace, yet they come to a country whose people once ruled over their ancestors. Sometimes you can feel the growing resentment between the different cultures. Especially between the younger generations. I sometimes wonder how long it will be before that resentment erupts.'

JT gave a deep sigh as he said, 'There is unrest between different cultures all over the world. Let us hope that when my son returns and the cylinder is opened, the contents will hold some master plan which will bring peace to the people of all nations.'

Jack hoped so too. No one had any idea what the cylinder contained for it could not be opened until the lost tribe were all brought together. Then, JT had told him, there would be a grand ceremony below the mountain. There'd been no doubt in JT's mind, that his son would complete the mission he'd been sent on and return home before it was too late.

Jack sighed as he looked at JT and remembered the warning that Joseph had told him about, which came from the mountain. Tomorrow he too was going on a mission. But his was not as complex as Joseph's. He knew where he was going and who he would be meeting.

As if reading his thoughts JT rose from the chair, picked up the chronicles and said; 'I think it time we went to our beds, Jack, and got a few hours sleep before I take you to the airport in the morning.'

CHAPTER VIII

Mathew was listening intently to the weather forecast on the radio and could not believe what he was hearing. That thick fog was covering the city. Not today of all days, he thought, as the weather report came to an end. He excused himself from the breakfast table, saying he was going to make a phone call.

'I wonder what he's up to,' said Anna to Joseph and Jordana. 'Mathew doesn't usually listen to the weather forecast.'

'Perhaps,' Joseph said, 'it has something to do with the day out he's planned for us. After all, it is a surprise, and Mathew has given no hint about where he is taking us.'

Mathew smiled as he put down the phone. The trip was still on despite the fog. He'd planned this day out like a general who would not tell his troops their destination. The fog could have spoiled it all.

'Where are you taking us?' Anna wanted to know when he told them to be ready in ten minutes.

'Just do as you are told,' he said, smiling. 'I've already told you it's a surprise and I am not giving you any clues as to what it might be.'

The trip he'd booked for the four of them was in a helicopter and he'd been fearful when he'd heard about the fog that it would have to be cancelled. As it turned out, and because of the fog, the helicopter flight became the highlight of the day.

They'd all, but more especially Jordana, been enthralled as the helicopter rose above the fog. Jordana gasped as they came out of the mist into the blue sky above and in the distance saw the top floors of the city skyscrapers. With the fog swirling around them it gave the effect of the buildings rising into the sky. The sun's rays caught the tallest building of them all and its reflection shone on the glass window panes, throwing out rays of golden light into the sky above and the fog below.

'I feel as though I'm in heaven,' Jordana whispered through her mouthpiece. 'I shall never forget this scene until the day I die. And I can imagine that when I die the Spirit of all Being will be waiting to greet me in a light such as this.'

Though they all agreed with what she said, no one spoke as they were all awestruck by what they were seeing – it was a breathtaking sight.

For a moment Mathew thought the pilot had cut the engine, for there was nothing but silence as if they were suspended in time between heaven and earth. Then the pilot's voice broke the spell as it came through the headphone saying, 'Just think, if I had delayed the flight because of the weather forecast we would have all missed a sight to behold.'

A moment later he was telling them to look down below. 'The fog is clearing,' he said. 'You can see the early morning traffic.'

He headed out towards the coast where he would begin the journey he'd been instructed to take them on, over New South Wales. It was mostly to be a sightseeing tour from the air, except for a visit to Old Sydney Town, the Wineries, where the best of Australian wine was made and the Blue Mountains.

The trip would take most of the day, though he did not mind as he loved flying and it was a change from his daily sightseeing tours over the city. He'd also earned more for this trip than he would have done all week. There was an added bonus for through his earphones he could hear Mathew giving a running commentary on the landmarks they passed over. The guy is better at it than me, he thought, all I'll be needing to do today, is to relax and fly the machine.

By the time they returned to the landing strip it was early evening. As they walked over the tarmac to the pilot's office, they were all surprised to hear Mathew asking him if there was anywhere they could freshen up.

'In here,' the pilot replied, unlocking the office door.

Mathew gestured for them to go inside, then went over to the car and took out a holdall. He'd no idea what was in it except that there was a change of clothing for them all, which Irene had packed after he'd told her his plans, and asked her to commandeer the clothes and get them into the car without any of them knowing.

He smiled as he went into the pilot's office and saw them look up in surprise. It was Anna who spoke first when she said as she looked at the holdall, 'Mathew. What are you planning now? I thought we would be going home.'

Then her eyes lit up with surprise as he told her, 'We are not going home yet, Anna. I have booked a table at the Tower Restaurant, where we are taking Joseph and Jordana to dine. Then we shall go on to the Casino.'

They all laughed, including the pilot, when he unzipped the bag and asked, 'Now which one of us is going to get ready first?'

Jordana was so tired after their wonderful outing that when they arrived back at the house, she refused to have a nightcap.

'No thank you, Mathew,' she said when he offered her a brandy, 'I have enjoyed everything you planned for us today, but if you don't mind I will go to my bed, for if I don't, I am sure I could fall asleep standing up!'

She bid them all goodnight and when she got to the bedroom she stripped off her dress and fell into bed. It was 2.30 a.m.

She awoke an hour later feeling wide awake as if she'd been asleep for several hours. She thought Joseph must have disturbed her when he got into bed, but he was sound asleep. She slid out of bed, took off her bra and panties and put on her silk dressing gown, then went out onto the balcony.

As she gazed up at the sky, she remembered she'd not done her nightly ritual before going to bed – she'd been so exhausted, she'd forgotten about it. That is why I feel so wide awake, she thought. Joseph warned me I must never forget no matter how tired I might feel. Though he had not told her if she did not perform the ritual the spirits would waken her, which, she thought, was what had happened now. She knew she was right in her thinking when her body began to sway and she performed the Sacred Rites that Joseph had taught her.

She'd not seen any visions since the night Sara appeared when she'd been shown the cave where the droplets of water turned into jewels. Nor did she expect to see any now as the ritual came to an end.

She rested for a moment, thinking she would now be able to go back to bed and to sleep, even though she still felt wide awake. She put her hands onto the railings, drew her body close to them and looked up at the sky, just in time to see a falling star. She was about to make a wish, as she used to do when she was a child and she saw a star fall from the sky, but there was no time. For as it fell, she lowered herself to the balcony floor, crossing her legs as she sat down.

A moment later a blue mist surrounded her. She felt her heartbeat quicken with excitement, knowing the spirits were with her, and she would be shown what had to be seen. She was not afraid even though Joseph was not with her, and it was the first time she would go into the unknown without him being there.

When the mist cleared she saw a young man who for all the world could have been her own husband. He was walking towards a house where a woman dressed in black was sitting on a rocking chair on the verandah. Her eyes were closed as she rocked to and fro. The young man, also dressed in black, stood for a moment as he came to the verandah steps, watching her. Then he said softly, 'Jenny, it is time to go.'

Jenny opened her eyes, raised herself from the chair and took hold of his outstretched hand.

'Ah, Joseph,' she said as he led her down the steps. 'I was just reminiscing about your grandfather. I was only a girl when he first brought me here to start my little venture, as he called it. I can see him now on the day we stopped here, on our way to Ilinka. I told him then, as we stood on this very spot, he would build me a house here. And one day I would sit in my rocking chair and gaze down at the township your grandfather would create. Your grandfather laughed out loud but I knew these things would come to pass, and they did,' she said as she gestured with her gloved hand to the township below. 'I will never forget that day,' she said, as they reached the waiting carriage.

'Nor I, Jenny,' he said, helping her up the step. 'I remember when we came to meet Grandfather, to welcome him home. I was sitting up front with my father, upon his horse. You were the first white lady I had ever seen and I wondered why you had come.'

As they seated themselves, she patted his hand, as if he was still a child. 'I can see, young Joseph,' she said, 'we both have fond memories of your grandfather. But we will keep them until after the funeral, they will comfort us.'

The carriage moved away and as it did so, Jordana thought that when the blue mist returned, the vision had come to an end. But as she sat wondering why she'd been shown Jenny and young Joseph, obviously going to his grandfather's funeral, the mist cleared again and she saw Meleeka dressed in his chieftain robes surveying the crowd who had come to pay their last respects to the man who was being laid to rest.

Sara stood beside Meleeka and the natives of Ilinka stood on either side of them. Four of the tribe still held the ropes that had lowered the coffin into the grave.

Meleeka's gaze let upon Adam, Jenny and his son Joseph, who were all standing together at the other end of the open grave. Adam was old and grey now, and he also had requested when his time came to be buried on Ilinka soil, near his old friend Joseph. Jenny too, had requested the same. He marvelled at their loyalty, both to himself and his tribe, and also to the man they'd all loved.

Standing behind Adam was Jamie with his wife and children, and for a moment Meleeka recalled how fate had brought them all together. Then his eyes surveyed the townspeople of Petraba who had also come to pay their last respects to the man who built them their town. They were all looking at him now, waiting for him to speak.

Taking hold of Sara's hand, he lifted his head towards the mountain, then turned his gaze back upon the crowd as he said in a clear and loud voice, 'Today, my truest friend has been laid to rest. It was his request to be buried on Ilinka soil with the natives of Ilinka. Some of you here today will understand why! Others will wonder why such a prominent man as Joseph Simon Tyler wished to be buried on Ilinka soil.

'But all who are here today will know we are laying to rest a kind and loving man. And if all mens' hearts were the same as his then my native country would be a better place for all who dwell within its vast plains.

'But it is good to see,' he gestured with his hand to take in the crowd, 'that you have not forgotten this day the man we all owe so much to. And I thank you all for coming.'

He bowed to the mountain and when he raised his head, he saw Adam coming towards him, smiling, as he said, 'I bet you hit a few raw nerves there, Meleeka!'

'I know,' he replied, smiling. 'And I think Joseph would have been proud of me. Do you not think so, Adam?'

'I do, I certainly do,' Adam replied, as they watched the crowd disperse.

Meleeka left Sara with Adam and went over to Jenny who was crying unashamedly, with her head resting on young Joseph's shoulder. Taking hold of her arm Meleeka turned to his son saying, 'We will leave you, Joseph. You need to be alone to speak to the spirit of your grandfather. I know you have not done so yet and that there is something in your heart which has been kept hidden.'

It was here the scene faded and Jordana could not believe what she had seen or heard. Joseph had told her how his own visions were like watching a film, but he had not explained to her how it was better than that. Why, it was as if she'd been there and even knew what Meleeka was thinking.

She was about to raise herself from the ground, then somehow knew there was more to come. She closed her eyes and saw young Joseph standing alone, looking down into the open grave. He raised his head and looked up to the sky above, then began to move his body and arms in some kind of ritual.

When this was done, he cried out, 'Grandfather, I loved you more than life itself. If I could have died and let you live, I would have done so. You taught me so much, Grandfather, and you were always there when I needed you. Especially when I came home from my grand tour and found Emma was gone. And though you explained to me Emma's reasons for leaving, I felt you were keeping something from me and were being economical with the truth.

'I was heartbroken that day, as you know. Yet deep in my heart I'd somehow known Emma would not be there when I returned. And if I am to be honest, I had known this even before I went away. All the same, I hurt you that day, and also my father, when I vowed that because you would not tell me where you had left Emma, I would never marry.

'But in all truth, Grandfather, you not telling me of her whereabouts was not the reason for my vow. I'd realised a long time ago that Emma and I were falling in love and a marriage between us could never take place. I made that vow because I felt I was already married to Emma, both with the heart, and with the spirit.'

Tears came into his eyes and he let them flow. He began to sob, as though his heart would break. And as his tears gushed forth as big as raindrops, he bent his head over the open grave and let them fall onto the wooden box where his grandfather lay.

After a while he sat down on the newly dug earth, crossing his legs as he looked up to the sky, above the peak of the snow-capped mountains. His tears were still flowing down his face as he said out loud, 'Grandfather, I am weeping now, not only for you or for Emma, but for the promise I gave you which I cannot keep. When I was a boy you gave me the amber stone ring, telling me also the history that went with it. You also said I was to give the ring to my bride on our wedding day and I promised that I would do so. But I must confess to you now, I gave the ring to Emma. It is a secret I have kept long in my heart. Emma, to me, was my true bride, there would be no other who I would give the ring to.

'I worked many hours making the cameo faces of Emma and myself and placing them inside the ring, which I gave to her the night before I left on my grand tour. I felt no qualms about giving Emma the ring. Nor do I do so now.

'I make this confession to you now, Grandfather, because one day, in the none too distant future, I will break my vow. I will marry, for it is my duty to do so. There is no one else to carry on your name.'

Jordana's face was wet with tears as she saw him raise himself from the ground, raise his arms to the mountain and call out; 'If you forgive me, Grandfather, show yourself to me. My heart grieves so much, I know the Spirit of all Beings will allow you to do so.'

Jordana could not believe what she was seeing when a tall man with snow white hair appeared, standing before his grandson. He embraced his weeping grandson in his arms, then held him at arms length as his grandson said, 'I know you will watch over me, Grandfather, as you did in life. And I beg of you to ask the Great White Spirit that one day, in another lifetime, Emma will come to me as my bride.'

His grandfather turned to face the mountain, and as they both gazed upon it, a voice was heard saying, '*It shall be done*.'

Once again his grandfather hugged him close. And before he disappeared his grandson said, 'Now it is time to tell my parents I am ready to marry.'

When the vision faded Jordana was unashamedly crying. Whether her tears were for the young man who looked so like her husband, and the parting with his grandfather, or because the Great White Spirit had kept its word in bringing the two young lovers together within herself and Joseph, she did not know.

Before raising herself from the ground she looked up into the sky. Then thanked the spirits for showing her what she had just seen. She went back to bed; her face was stained with tears, but she did not mind.

When she awoke, Joseph's head was propped up on his hand and he was staring down at her. She smiled as she propped herself up so their faces were nearly touching. Then she told him what had happened during the night.

He listened eagerly to all she had to say. Of course the speech that Meleeka made was in the chronicles, but Jordana had been shown what happened after the funeral, and the spirit of the grandfather coming before his grandson. Even Joseph himself knew nothing, nor had been shown anything, about that.

It is unusual, he thought, for Jordana to have been shown so much, so early in her development. Yet he was glad for Jordana's sake as he watched her press the clasp on the ring and gaze at the cameo faces when the ring opened. She had seen the truth now of how it was all ordained that one day she would wear the ring herself.

He nearly laughed out loud when she took the ring from her finger, held it close to her eye and tried to close the ring slowly. He knew she wanted to see the cameo faces of the two young lovers kissing. But that only happened when the ring was closed and the clasp brought into place.

CHAPTER IX

It was the morning of Judith's wedding and as he waited for Jordana to put the finishing touches to her hair, Joseph wondered what the day would bring. And more to the point, how many of the Townly bloodline would he have made contact with before the day was over.

He looked up as Jordana said she was ready, thinking she looked stunning in her cream, sleeveless, silk dress with the matching hat held in her hand.

'It is no good me putting the hat on until we get there,' she said. 'I cannot believe we will be travelling to this wedding in a helicopter. Mathew certainly does things in style, doesn't he? I wonder what he would say if he knew about us and the reason for us being invited to the wedding?'

'I don't know,' he said, taking hold of her hand and leading her towards the bedroom door. 'But you are right about him doing things in style. Though I am not supposed to tell you because he doesn't want Anna to find out, Mathew has also booked us in at the hotel where the wedding reception is being held for a couple of days. He asked if it was alright by me, of course, and I told him that it was.'

They were out on the landing and Jordana whispered, 'But what are we to do about clothes?'

'Don't worry,' he said, 'Mathew's taken care of that. He is good at planning things, is Mathew. Remember what happened the other day when we arrived back after, as Mathew called it, our little trip out in the helicopter?'

Jordana grinned as they went down the stairs. She was secretly delighted with Mathew's plans. It would have been, even in the luxury of the chauffeur-driven car, a long drive to Shoal Bay where the wedding was taking place.

Anna was also delighted with Mathew's plans when she found out about them. So too was Andrew.

Later, as they watched the bride and groom walk up the aisle, tears pricked in Jordana's eyes when she thought of the village church back home where she'd always imagined her own wedding would have taken place on a day such as this, with the sun smiling down on her, the church filled with family and friends, and she, the virginal bride, all dressed in white.

Then she smiled as the young couple passed by. She'd no regrets about marrying Joseph, or that the wedding had taken place in the Register Office. In fact, it had been quite exciting at the time. She'd felt like one of those war brides in the old films her mother watched on TV.

She felt Joseph's arm slip around her waist and hug her. He was sensitive to her thoughts, so he would know what she'd been thinking about.

She was right of course. Joseph had sensed her feelings as the young couple walked up the aisle, but his interest was more in the groom than the bride. After all, that was why they were here. He also thought it was ironic for them to be on the bride's side of the church when it was the groom who was from the bloodline of his own ancestors. Taking hold of Jordana's hand, he led her out into the aisle and followed the procession outside.

While the photographs were being taken, Joseph excused himself from the others and went to strike up a conversation with an old man. It was no coincidence that he did so, he'd seen the old man in his vision, and he knew it was this man who was to help in bringing the tribe together. The man's name was Paul Rudge. He was eighty years old and the groom's great-grandfather. He was tall, with snow white hair, and still handsome despite his age. Like all old people he loved to talk, but found like so many did, there were few who listened to his ramblings. For sometimes he forgot what he'd been talking about and sometimes he even forgot where he was. He'd even heard folk say he was senile.

At this moment he was pleased, especially with all the activity going on around him, that the young man standing beside him, who'd introduced himself as Joseph Tyler, was asking him questions and really listening to his answers. He'd no idea who this young man was but he liked him. So he was annoyed when his daughter Eunice came to tell him it was time to go. Eunice was one of those who'd no time to listen.

Before moving away he took hold of the young man's outstretched hand and was pleased, as they shook hands, to hear the young man saying, 'I will see you later at the reception.'

'I will look forward to doing so,' he said as his daughter dragged him away.

Joseph watched them walk away, then went to join the others. They were standing with Helena who, when Mathew introduced her to him, eyed Joseph with interest. She was intrigued by what Mathew had told her about Joseph, not only on the phone, but just now, when she'd spent a few moments alone with Mathew. Nor could she believe, when she'd seen Anna in church, how well she looked – after all the money Mathew must have spent on the specialists and the shrink had been to no avail. Then for Joseph to come along and in no time at all, according to Mathew, make Anna become her old self again was just incredible.

Mathew had also, a few minutes ago, out of earshot from Anna, told her how the young couple had come into his life.

'And I'm truly grateful they have,' he'd said. 'Yet do you know, Helena, there is something about them I cannot fathom. Neither can I explain why I feel this way. They are both of them always so calm. And there is, especially with Joseph, a serenity about him beyond belief. He makes me feel so good I would not complain if he and Jordana stayed with us forever.'

Mathew is right, Helena thought, as she let go of Joseph's hand after they'd been introduced. There is something about Joseph. But there was no time to dwell upon the subject. Her husband was making signals that it was time to go.

Joseph watched her walk away, then scanned the crowd for Paul Rudge. He knew that Paul was suffering from dementia and if no one was taking care of him he would be more confused than ever, being in a strange place with crowds of strangers milling around. When his eyes let upon Paul, he was standing beside a group of people who were totally ignoring him and to say the least was looking bewildered.

Joseph smiled to himself when the group began to move away, taking Paul with them, then said to himself, 'Soon Paul will be demented no more, I will see to that. I will make him the chief over those that ignore him, then they will ignore him no more.'

He was also glad, as his own little group began to make their way to the hotel down the road from the church where the reception was being held that Mathew had booked them into it for a few days. For later he would take Paul Rudge to their room and would be able to be alone with him.

As they came out of the church gates he wondered if it was Mathew's own idea they should stay here for a few days, or was it the spirits who put the idea into Mathew's head? He believed it was the latter.

It was later in the evening when Joseph sought out Paul Rudge. Nearly everyone was dancing when Joseph made his way over to the table where Paul was sitting alone. The old man's eyes lit up with pleasure when he saw Joseph coming towards him. His usually bemused mind had not forgotten the young man who'd taken such a great interest in him earlier, though how they were going to be able to talk with all the racket that was going on, Paul couldn't imagine. So he was pleased, therefore, when the young man leaned close to him saying, 'It is very noisy in here, Paul, and I would like to speak with you on a very important matter. Would you mind very much coming to my room?'

Paul nodded in reply. He wished he could remember the young man's name but he'd met so many people, and even been introduced to them, he could not remember who he was even though he'd recognised him.

He raised himself from the chair, glad to be getting away. Then he hesitated, glancing around the room. His daughter would not like it if he just disappeared. He'd wandered off earlier and Eunice had been very displeased!

'It will be alright, Paul,' Joseph said, seeing Paul's hesitation. 'My wife knows where we are going, she will tell your daughter where you are.'

Since speaking to Paul outside the church, Joseph had learned that Paul lived with his daughter Eunice. He'd also been told she was a good daughter, in the way she kept her father fed, clothed and clean. Yet he could imagine the exasperation her father must cause her with the mental state he was in.

Joseph guided Paul up to his room, then settled him down in the armchair before going over to the drinks cabinet, pouring each of them a tot of brandy and dry ginger. He handed a glass to Paul and sat down on the edge of the bed facing him.

'Cheers,' said Paul, as he clinked his glass with Joseph's. He'd no idea why this young man had brought him to this room, but it was much more comfortable than being downstairs.

While they sipped their drinks, Joseph looked into Paul's eyes, then told him of the Ilinka tribe and of his mission. As he listened, Paul felt a queer sensation run through his body and wondered if the brandy was the cause of it. I've had too many drinks already this day, he thought, as he continued to listen to what was being told to him. He was also pleased he could understand all that was being said for sometimes his mind lost all train of thought, and when it did so he could not remember what had been done or said only moments before.

Joseph, watching the changing expressions on Paul's face, knew that he had a clear understanding of all he was being told. So he was not surprised, when he'd finished telling Paul of his quest, that Paul said to him, 'It is a wonderful story that you have told me and I pray your quest will not be overlong in coming to an end.'

'I think,' said Joseph, putting his hands together and resting his fingers on his chin, 'that now I have been led to you, Paul, it will not be long before I will be returning home. For with your help in bringing the tribe together, it will make my mission much easier.'

'I hope you are right,' Paul said, surprised at how he felt in full possession of his own faculties when he continued, 'for from what you have told me it seems the whole of mankind might be in danger.'

Joseph smiled ruefully as he said, 'That is true. But until the time comes for the Sacred Cylinder to be opened, we will not know what the Great White Spirit has in store for the whole of mankind. What I do know is the sooner the lost tribe are brought together, the sooner the cylinder will be opened. And you, Paul, are the one the spirits have chosen to help me.'

Paul felt tears prick in his eyes. How could he do what was being asked of him when he was old and senile, a burden to his own kith and kin? Especially to his daughter Eunice, who he realized now, he must have driven to distraction, not once but many times, with his befuddled mind and his wandering off, not even knowing himself where he was going.

He held back the tears as he said to Joseph, 'I think the spirits have chosen the wrong man. I am too old and too senile to do what you are asking of me!'

'I think not,' said Joseph. 'You have been chosen by the spirits to help me with my quest and I have been led to you so that you may do so. But, before we go back downstairs, there is something I must do. You must not be afraid, Paul, of whatever happens in this room. For I will be helping you to gain the strength and clarity of mind that will be needed, with all the things you have to do.'

He smiled as Paul stared at him in disbelief, then continued, 'Tomorrow, Paul, your family will find a great change in you and show you much respect. No more will you be like an old man in his dotage. You will be strong and your mind will be as clear as the mountain stream. It is the spirit of our ancestors who have chosen you. For after all, even though you are aged, you are still the head of your tribe, and in so being you will be shown the way.'

Joseph raised himself from where he'd been sitting on the edge of the bed, and asked Paul to stand before him. Joseph looked deep into Paul's eyes, saying, 'Before your own mission begins, there is something that has to be done. You must not be afraid for I will be with you. And when it is over, you will have been given the strength of a young brave, the courage of a warrior and the wisdom of a chief. Are you ready now, Paul, to go into the unknown?'

'I am ready,' Paul replied, as he kept his eyes locked with Joseph's.

He had no qualms in doing what Joseph asked of him. In fact, he was enjoying himself more than he'd done for a very long time. Nor was there any doubt in his mind that what Joseph said would not come about. How it was to be accomplished, he'd no idea. But it would be good not to be a burden on his family any more. And though he knew how lucky he'd been with his family taking good care of him, he also knew, sometimes he could also be a nuisance to them.

For a moment, as he stood before Joseph, he recalled the many times he'd prayed to the Lord to take him to join his beloved wife who'd been dead these last ten years. And he'd wondered why the good Lord did not answer his prayers, when all the time he felt he was becoming more and more of a burden to his family.

Now, standing before Joseph, he realized why his prayers had not been answered. My prayers were not answered, he thought, because I had to be here when Joseph came so I could help him bring the lost tribe together.

Joseph told him to close his eyes, and as he did so he felt his heartbeat quicken. As if from a distance he heard chanting in a language he did not understand, and he felt as if someone was wafting something in front of him. Then the wafting sensation circled around his whole body several times, and only came to a halt when the chanting also ceased.

A moment later he felt, and assumed they were Joseph's, two hands resting upon his shoulders. The fingers on both hands spread themselves open before being dragged down the back of his body like tiger claws, from shoulders to ankles. This was done several times and he felt as though his whole body was being rejuvenated.

As Joseph worked his clawed fingers over Paul, he could feel the changes taking place inside Paul's body. When he'd first laid his hands upon Paul, he'd felt the frailty that one would expect in a man of his age. Now he could feel a new strength building up in Paul. Not until he was satisfied that he was strong both in body and mind, as he'd told Paul he would be, did he cease the clawing movements of his hands. Then he rested for only a moment before bringing his hands above Paul's head, closing them together as if in prayer. When his hands opened, leaving only the fingertips touching, he brought them down on either side of Paul, then moved them up again above the top of his head until they rested above him in a prayerlike fashion. He repeated the same procedure, circling around Paul as he did so, until he could see a protective aura was covering every part of his body, giving him protection for all that Paul would be called upon to do.

When he was satisfied, he told him to open his eyes, then gestured for him to be seated. He smiled when Paul asked him: 'What have you done to me? I feel as though I have been reborn!'

'I have done nothing,' Joseph replied. 'It is the spirits of our ancestors who have made you ready for the mission that lies before you. I am only the instrument, so to speak, which they have used to enable them to do so. But you must tell no one, Paul, of what has happened in this room. When your mission begins, you will be guided in all you have to do and say. In the meantime, your family are bound to begin to see the change in you, if not tonight, then certainly by tomorrow.'

Joseph touched Paul on the shoulder and as Paul looked up at him, Joseph smiled as he said, 'And tomorrow you can tell your daughter Eunice the things I have already told you about the Ilinka tribe, and of your bloodline which is connected to them.'

Paul smiled ruefully at the mention of his daughter's name. Eunice, he thought, will be the first to notice the change in me. He told Joseph what he'd been thinking.

'I know she will,' Joseph said. 'But when you have explained to her about the Ilinka tribe, the spirits will see to it that not only Eunice, but your family also, when you have told them, will understand. It is then, Paul, when your true mission will begin.'

Before they left the room, Joseph gave Paul Mathew's telephone number. 'It is imperative,' he said, 'that you and I work closely together in bringing the tribe together as quickly as possible!'

'What about Patric?' Paul asked. 'He will be going on his honeymoon in the morning. Shall I speak with him before he goes?'

'No,' Joseph replied. 'The newly-weds will be home in a week. You can wait until then. There should not be a problem with Patric not knowing before then.'

Paul laughed as he said, 'The biggest problem we have, young man, is to get my tribe, as you call them, to listen to me in the first place. No matter what you say about the spirits helping me, my family will think I am telling them some cock and bull story I have made up just to annoy them.'

Joseph smiled at Paul's humour. 'I know what you mean,' he said. 'They will find it hard to believe the old man that was in his dotage is now telling them he is the chief of the tribe. But have no fear, Paul, for they will see their chief is strong, both in mind and body.'

They both laughed as they made their way to the door. And as Joseph opened it he said, 'But remember, Paul, for the rest of this night, you must act like the three monkeys. Do you think you can manage to do so?'

'Leave it to me,' Paul said with confidence, knowing it was the best for all concerned. For as Joseph had told him, no one else knew why Joseph was here, except his wife Jordana and now himself.

Jordana was watching out for Joseph so was relieved when she saw him take Paul Rudge back to his table, and was now making his way towards her. Helena was sitting next to her, bombarding her with questions about herself and Joseph. She was now asking where Joseph had disappeared to with that silly old man.

Joseph, overhearing her, and aware of Jordana's emotions, winked at Jordana as he sat down at the table and said to Helena, 'I took Paul up to our room for a while. He was getting a bit agitated with all the noise.' Then he could not help but add, 'He is a very interesting man, to those who find the time to listen to him. We have had a wonderful discussion.'

Helena, who thought Paul Rudge was a rambling old fool, could not tell by the tone of Joseph's voice whether or not there was some inner meaning in what he was saying about the old man.

Like Mathew, she felt there was something about this young couple which she could not fathom. Usually she was good at sizing people up, but not these two. Even her conversation with Jordana had not made her any the wiser. And Joseph's interest in the old man more than intrigued her. She'd seen them together outside the church and now they'd been together for more than an hour in Joseph's room. Whatever could a young man like Joseph, she wondered, find to discuss with the old fool? Knowing she was not going to find out from Joseph, she excused herself, thinking as she left the table, I will go and sit with the old fool for a while. Maybe I can get some sense out of him.

Jordana, watching her walk away, said, 'I was glad when you came back, Joseph. Helena was beginning to probe too deeply into things that were no concern of hers.'

'I sensed that,' said Joseph. 'She is a very inquisitive woman and Mathew will have told her all about us. There is a strong bond between Helena and Mathew. I mean a friendship bond,' he said laughing, as Jordana raised her eyebrow. He laughed even more when he saw Helena sit down beside Paul who ignored her, as if his mind was on something where angels fear to tread.

'Come,' he said, taking hold of Jordana's hand. 'Let us mingle. The onus is on Paul now to bring his people together. But I would like to get to know them before they find out who I am.'

Later, in their room, they discussed the day's events. And Joseph was pleased with what he'd accomplished.

'I like Paul,' Jordana said, 'And now he has been given the power to help him with his mission, I can imagine him going about it with great pleasure.'

'Of course he will,' Joseph said. 'He is now the chief of his tribe. He will take great pride in doing what is being asked of him. Also, he now has the stamina of a much younger man. Nor is his mind befuddled as it has been for so long.'

They were lying on the bed; he laughed as he hugged her to him and said, 'It is a pity we will not be there to witness what Paul's family's reaction will be to the change in Paul. Especially with his daughter Eunice, who deals with him every single day.'

'It will be a shock to them, Joseph,' Jordana said. 'And I can see nothing for you to laugh about.' But in all truth, she herself was amused by the thought of it. When she recalled Helena sitting at the table with Paul after he'd been with Joseph to his room, Helena was drumming her fingers on the table as she tried to get Paul to converse with her, but he just sat there, staring into space, acting like the imbecile Helena thought he was, when all the time Paul was now as sane as anyone.

Jordana smiled to herself as she wondered what Helena would have said if she'd known about Paul, or found out why Joseph was taking such an interest in the groom's side of the family, for she knew Helena had been watching them as they mingled with his guests and relations.

Joseph broke into her thoughts when he took hold of her hand and caressed the amber ring with his finger, saying, 'I do not think it will be long now, Jordana, before I take you home to Ilinka! Now the wheels have been set in motion through the meeting with Paul and those I have seen this day, my mission here will soon be over. He will introduce me to those of his tribe I have not met. Then it will be Paul who gathers them together to bring them to Ilinka.'

Jordana became thoughtful. She was glad Joseph would soon be taking her to Ilinka but she was thinking about Mathew and Anna, especially Mathew and how good he'd been to Joseph and herself. Of course Mathew was grateful to Joseph for what he'd done. But all the same, there was a true friendship which had developed between the four of them. She thought it a shame that Mathew could not be told of Joseph's mission, and though Mathew may have his reasons for being grateful to Joseph, Joseph should also be grateful to Mathew for leading him to Paul Rudge. She voiced her thoughts to Joseph and was pleased when he told her, 'I know how you feel, Jordana. I also have been thinking the same. I should have asked the spirits for guidance when I performed my ritual. But I will do so in the morning. Right now,' he said, unzipping her dress, 'I think it is time I made love to my wife!'

Joseph was not surprised the next morning when the spirits of his ancestors said he could reveal the truth to Mathew. He'd felt for two days now that, though Mathew was not of the Ilinka tribe, he was playing his part in bringing the tribe together. Last night, when Jordana had voiced her own thoughts to him on the subject, he'd known it would be acceptable for Mathew to be told, though he could do nothing until he had spoken with the spirits of his ancestors.

Jordana was delighted when he told her the news. She'd been sitting up in bed reading a magazine. Joseph had not been in bed when she awoke and she assumed he had gone for a walk along the beach which was not far away from the hotel. Joseph was always an early riser, no matter how late they went to bed, and it was not only the performing of his ritual that made him so. 'It is the best part of the day,' he'd told her.

It was eight o'clock when he came into the room smiling. 'Good morning, Lazy Bones,' he said as he came across the room, gave her a kiss, sat down on the side of the bed and told her that the spirits had approved of him telling Mathew about their mission.

'I'm so glad,' Jordana said, throwing her arms around him to show how delighted she really was. 'When are you going to tell him?'

'After breakfast,' he replied. 'I have just seen Mathew. He wants us all to meet in the dining room at nine o'clock. Apparently, he has been down to the quayside and booked us a trip out on one of the boats to see the dolphins. The boat doesn't set sail until noon, so there will be plenty of time to get him on his own.'

Later, Joseph found no problem in getting Mathew alone. After breakfast, he suggested they take a stroll along the beach, and out of politeness asked if anyone wanted to join them.

Anna told him: 'No thank you, Joseph. If we are going sailing later, and if you don't mind, I will return to my room.'

Andrew said he would do the same as he had a bit of a headache. Of course Jordana declined and suggested they should all meet at the quayside at a quarter to twelve. That will give Joseph plenty of time, she thought, when they'd all agreed it was a good idea.

Mathew listened attentively to what Joseph was telling him. Joseph left nothing out as he told him about the lost tribe, his reasons for being here and of the warning from the mountain.

They were sitting on a bench on the grass verge overlooking the ocean. There was not another soul in sight, nor any sound from what one would expect of the usual activity of the morning.

As Mathew listened he felt the peace and tranquillity which was surrounding them at this moment, and could hardly believe that in effect, what Joseph was telling him was that the prophecies of Nostradamus, and others like him, could in the not too distant future come true.

He was glad now that Joseph had sworn him to secrecy about what he was going to tell him, and he'd given his oath that he would do so. For if any of this got out the world would go mad, madder even than it was already.

He turned to face Joseph and asked in an awestruck voice: 'What will happen when the lost tribe are all gathered together?'

'I honestly do not know, Mathew,' Joseph replied. 'No one knows the answer to that question. Nor will they, not until the Sacred Cylinder is opened. That is why the bringing together of the lost tribe is of the utmost importance. And with the help you have given me by inviting Jordana and myself to Judith's wedding, which led me to Paul Rudge, I do not think it will be long now before Jordana and I will be returning to Ilinka.'

'It wasn't all my doing,' Mathew said. 'The spirits of your ancestors also played their part.' He smiled for the first time since Joseph had told him of his quest, when he said, 'Speaking of Paul Rudge, I like the idea of making him chief of the tribe. Even though I hear tell he is a senile old man!'

'You must not believe everything you hear, Mathew,' Joseph replied. 'Paul was chosen because he is the eldest of the lost tribe. And Paul is now as sane as you and me.'

'So,' said Mathew, 'that is why you disappeared with him to your room. Helena was very inquisitive about the interest you were taking in Paul. But,' he said ruefully, 'as much as I like Helena, it always annoys me when she pokes her nose into things that are no concern of hers. In fact, I think I must apologise to you, Joseph, for telling Helena so much about you. For if I had not done so, she would have taken less interest in you and Jordana. And though I am not making excuses to get myself off the hook, Helena is one of those women who fire questions at you and gives you no time to think before you reply.'

'Think no more about it,' said Joseph. 'It was good of Helena to let us attend the wedding of her daughter. Though it seemed ironic that my interest in being there was for the groom's side of the family. Now,' he said, raising himself from the bench, 'I think it is time to go and meet the others at the quayside.'

'Before we go,' Mathew said looking up a Joseph, 'I want to thank you for trusting me. And if I can help you, in any way, you know I will be willing to do so!'

Joseph smiled as he thanked Mathew. He was counting on his help and that was the reason for telling Mathew of his mission.

Mathew was deep in thought as they made their way towards the quayside. He'd been shocked by what Joseph had told him and could only wonder why the lost tribe were being called back to Ilinka. He only hoped that they would make it in time. For according to Joseph, time was running out. He gave a deep sigh as he thought, whatever the future holds for any of us, I cannot change the way it will be.

They crossed over the road and he saw Anna standing on the corner, waiting with Jordana. A moment later Andrew joined them, putting his arm affectionately around his mother's shoulder. And as Anna and Andrew smiled at each other, Mathew, as he went to join them, thought for a moment what might have been – he could have lost them both.

CHAPTER X

Paul Rudge was sitting at the kitchen table, where he'd just finished eating his breakfast. He could not believe the change within himself for he felt like a young man, both in body and mind. He glanced over to the sink where Eunice was washing the dishes and began to tell her about Joseph.

Eunice, with her thoughts on something else, was not really listening to her father who was always rabbiting on about something and nothing. She nearly dropped a plate into the sink when her father raised his voice, speaking to her in a voice that brought back memories of her childhood when what he said was a law unto itself.

'Eunice,' he was saying now. 'Will you leave that be. Come and sit down and listen to me. This is important, what I have been trying to tell you.'

She dried her hands then, like a child, did as she'd been told. As she sat down at the table she looked at her father. There is something different about him this morning, she thought. Both in speech and manner. He was not gabbling his words as he usually did. She could understand every word he spoke, but she had no idea what he was going on about and she told him so. She felt a twinge of guilt when her father gave a deep sigh and said to her in an authoritative voice, 'It is a long time, Eunice, since you actually listened to your father. But you are going to listen to me now, for it is very important.'

As Eunice listened, she could not believe what her father was telling her about this young man, Joseph Tyler, though she remembered the interest he'd shown in her father yesterday at Patric's wedding. Nor could she believe, despite the way her father was acting this morning, that this same young man wanted him to be the chief of the tribe. For a moment, she thought the whole damn thing was something her father had dreamt up just to annoy her, until she realized the story was too incredible for him to have made up himself.

She was also annoyed because her father was explaining things to her as if she was some imbecile child, when all the time it was he who was the imbecile, and had been for some time.

She sniffed three times, as she always did when someone or something annoyed her. And although she had to admit to herself there was a great change this morning in her father, she could hardly believe, even from what he'd been telling her about this Joseph Tyler, that the change in him would be permanent. So she said sarcastically – because this morning she was not getting the better of her father, and was in awe of him for the first time in years – 'I don't know who this Joseph Tyler might be, Father, but if he thinks you are fit enough to become chief of our tribe, as he calls us, then the man is insane!'

Eunice sniffed again three times. This time she was annoyed with herself for she could think of nothing else to say.

Paul, despite his daughter's last remarks about Joseph, was enjoying himself. It had been a long time since his daughter had been in awe of him, but she was now. Though he knew she must also be shocked by what he'd told her and was not believing what he'd said. If the roles had been reversed, he too would have had his doubts. So his smile was gentle as he said to her, 'Eunice, Joseph Tyler is far from insane. In fact, if there were more men like him, this world would be a better place for us all to live in!

'I have already told you what Joseph said to me when I asked him if I was not too old for the quest he had set before me. But I will repeat it to you again. "You may be old Paul," Joseph said to me, "both in mind and body. But after this night you will be a wise and strong chief, who will lead his tribe where they have to go."' He took both of his daughter's hands into his own, then continued, 'And as you can see Eunice, with your own eyes, Joseph did not lie to me.' He gave a deep sigh as he asked, 'Or are you still blind, Eunice, to what Joseph has done?'

'I am not blind, Father,' she said. 'Though it is hard for me to accept that only yesterday . . .'

She did not finish saying what she was going to say. Paul said it for her.

'Yesterday,' he said, 'your father was a gabbling old fool who drove his daughter to distraction.'

The tears welled up in her eyes as he spoke. This was the father who she'd always loved and admired, not the father who, these last few years, had worn her out with his senile ways and dirty habits. How this transformation had come about overnight, she could not imagine. If she was to believe her father, it was because of his meeting with Joseph Tyler that this phenomenal transformation had taken place.

She felt the tears on her cheeks as she thought, I may not yet believe my father could become so changed overnight, yet neither can I deny what I am seeing with my own eyes.

She drew her hands away from her father's, telling him as she did so, 'I will put the kettle on and make us a pot of tea, and you can tell me once again about Joseph Tyler.' Then her emotions overcame her. She felt so happy for her father she threw her arms around him, hugging him close and kissing the top of his head before going to put the kettle on.

Tears pricked Paul's eyes as he watched her go over to the stove, though his tears were not for the affection Eunice had just shown him. They were for the love and care she had given him through all the trials and tribulations he must have caused her. And in doing so, his once beautiful daughter looked tired and weary. There was a gauntness in her face, making her look old before her time, and he blamed himself for the way she looked.

He gazed down at his hands, turning them over as he did so, inspecting them closely. Joseph had told him he'd put some kind of power into his hands to help him with his mission. Joseph had also given him instructions on how to use that power if the need arose.

'There is no need to be afraid, Paul,' Joseph had said. 'You will know instinctively on whom you will use that power, and the spirits of your ancestors will guide you in what you have to do.'

He clasped his hands together and as he did so, felt the need to use that power upon his daughter. Perhaps, he thought, raising his eyes to look at her, these hands will erase the weariness from her body.

She was stirring the tea in the teapot and looked up in surprise when she heard her father saying, 'Eunice, leave that be. There is something I have not told you about which is very important!'

CHAPTER XI

Two weeks after Judith's wedding, Joseph was able to make plans to return to Ilinka. The spirits of his ancestors had been wise in choosing Paul Rudge to bring his tribe together, and Joseph had been in constant touch with Paul. Paul had rung him at the hotel the morning after the wedding to tell him of his daughter's reaction, and how Eunice could not believe the change in her father!

'Well, Paul,' Joseph told him, 'you have to admit it must have given Eunice quite a shock seeing her father as he used to be, and not the senile old man she'd taken care of over the years.'

'I know it must have,' Paul told him. 'And it also pained me when I realized what my illness had done to Eunice, with the trials and tribulations I had caused her. Her face was gaunt, and she looked old before her time. I could have wept when I looked at her. It was as if my eyes had been opened and I was seeing her for the first time, for she was not the daughter I remembered.'

Paul's voice broke with the emotions he'd been feeling as Joseph waited for him to continue. Then he'd heard Paul telling him, 'I looked down at my hands and felt a queer sensation come over me. I prayed to God that I would be able to use the power you said now lay within me on Eunice, not only to make her understand the mission you had set before me, but also to take away her weariness. I called Eunice over to me as she was making a pot of tea. She sat down before me and I followed your instructions in what I had to do. Eunice is just fine now. She understands all I have been telling her. And I know she will be a great help in the quest to bring the tribe together.'

Joseph had been pleased with what Paul told him and Paul had been proved right – Eunice had been a great asset to their predicament. She'd travelled everywhere with her father, visiting the families that had to be told of Paul's mission.

When they returned, Joseph went to see them and gathered all the information he would need. Before he left, he told Paul, 'You have done well, my friend. The spirits of our ancestors were wise in choosing you. Jordana and myself can now return to Ilinka to prepare the way. When all is ready you will receive instructions about bringing your tribe to Ilinka.'

He gave Paul a bear-hug, then told him, 'The next time we meet will be on Ilinka soil. My people will welcome you and rejoice, for you will be bringing the lost lambs back to the fold!'

Joseph was now in the study with Mathew. The arrangements for them to leave the next day had just been confirmed.

'I am going to miss you both,' Mathew said sincerely. 'Even though I know it is of the greatest importance you return to Ilinka as soon as possible. And whatever the consequences might be, whether it is the annihilation of us all, or the salvation, I thank you now for what you have done for Anna, and also for taking me into your confidence. Forewarned is forearmed and whatever the outcome, I intend to make the most of it, before your Sacred Cylinder is opened.'

Joseph smiled ruefully. What Mathew said was true. When the cylinder was opened it could go either way and he admired Mathew for his way of thinking.

'If it is at all possible, Mathew,' he said, 'when the day comes for the cylinder to be opened, I will inform you of what the Sacred Writing contains. And of course I will keep in touch with you before then!'

'You cannot be fairer than that,' Mathew said, raising himself from the chair. 'Now shall we go and tell Jordana the news she has been waiting for?'

Jordana was with Anna, relaxing after their swim in the pool. Jordana was thrilled when she was told the news. Anna was disappointed and she showed it as she turned to Joseph saying, 'Joseph, you can't possibly return home yet. I thought you would be staying much longer. There are so many places you have not seen. I was hoping Mathew and I would be showing them to you. I also thought you would be staying for at least another month.'

'I'm sorry, Anna,' Joseph said, glancing at Mathew for support, 'but I have been recalled home on an important matter.'

Mathew, understanding, said to Anna, 'Let us be thankful Joseph and Jordana have been able to spend so much time with us. I am also disappointed they are leaving. It has been a pleasure having them here.' He paused for a moment before adding, 'And they both know they are very welcome to come again.'

Joseph, knowing how much it had cost Mathew to say this, not knowing what the future held for any of them, said, 'Thank you, Mathew, Jordana and I would love to visit you again. And when we are settled in our home, you must come and visit us.'

'What a splendid idea,' Anna said excitedly, forgetting her disappointment. 'That will be wonderful, won't it, Mathew?'

'It will,' Mathew replied, glancing at Joseph, knowing what they were both thinking. Then, changing the subject, he said to Jordana, 'What would you most like to do on your last night here? Make it something special for your wish is my command.'

'Then I wish, kind sir,' Jordana replied, 'that you take us to dine out on one of the ferry boats that sail around the harbour.'

'Your wish will be granted,' Mathew said, laughing. 'You will have a night to remember!'

As the ferry sailed across the harbour, many of the other passengers wondered who the two handsome couples were for the four of them seemed oblivious to everything except themselves. One passenger even remarked how there appeared to be something mystical about them. Another was heard to say, enviously, how she thought the older couple shared a love that was as intense as the young couple.

She could not know, as her unromantic husband stuffed food into his mouth, not even listening to what she'd said, that Mathew, who had always loved Anna more than life itself, would now, because of what he knew, cherish every moment he spent with her. Anna, of course, though for different reasons, felt the same about Mathew. So it was no wonder they looked so much in love.

Later they went up on deck and as the ferry glided over the water, passing the famous Opera House, Jordana thought what a perfect way it was to end their stay in Sydney. Resting her head upon Joseph's shoulder, she glanced over to where Anna and Mathew were standing like two young lovers as they gazed up at the stars.

She wondered if she would ever see them again. For at this moment, none of them knew what the future would hold. Then she marvelled at the way they'd all been brought together and the reason for them being so. She also wondered what Mathew was thinking about. It seemed incredible to her on this special night that they could all be so carefree, when three out of the four of them knew that in the not too distant future this beautiful world could be no more. Yet here they all were, acting as if they knew nothing of what might come to pass.

And it is a beautiful world, she thought, raising her eyes to the sky and recalling what she'd seen up there when the helicopter raised itself above the fog. She'd thought that day God was about to show himself in those golden rays; the God who had masterminded the creation of such a beautiful planet; the same God that no one has ever seen, yet millions pray to every day. Now, as she gazed up at the stars, she wondered what thoughts must have been in God's mind when He put temptation in Eve's way, and the reason for Him doing so. If the temptation had not been there, perhaps the world would have been filled with a different kind of people who did not fight over the same God they all worshipped.

As a child, she'd loved listening to the stories from the Bible, though even then she'd not been able to understand why there was so much slaying of others. Best of all, she'd loved the stories of Jesus. And she'd cried when He died on the cross, taking upon Himself the sins of the world. At the time she'd not understood what it all meant.

But she knew now and she was no blasphemer when she said to herself, The sins of the world are more terrible now than ever before in the history of this planet.

She was appalled, on such a night as this, at the profoundness of her own thoughts. Yet with them came understanding of the urgency of Joseph's mission, and she was glad that tomorrow he would be taking her home.

She saw a star in the sky shining brighter than any of the others. A moment later it began to fall and she made a wish. She thought it was a childish thing to do, but even so she wanted this wish to come true, more than anything she'd ever wished for in her life before.

And though she did not know it, Joseph and Mathew wished for the very same thing when they too saw the falling star.

CHAPTER XII

Jack was waiting for them at the airport. Jordana saw him first and ran into his outstretched arms. Joseph gave him a bear-hug before they went outside to where Jack had parked the car. Jordana was surprised to see the car was a white limousine. When their luggage was loaded Joseph said he would take the wheel. 'If I drive,' he said smiling at Jordana, 'you and Jack can sit in the back seats. There is, I know, much for you both to discuss.'

Joseph opened the car door and Jordana got in. Jack followed and sat facing her. She was glad Jack had come to meet them – he would be with her when she met Joseph's parents for the first time.

As the car sped away, Jack leant forward, taking hold of Jordana's hands, placing them in his own. Their faces were serious as they gazed into each other's eyes. There was no need for words, they each knew what the other was thinking. Joseph was going home, his mission was completed, and none of them knew what the consequences would be.

It was Jordana who broke the silence when she asked, 'What is Ilinka like, Jack? Is it as beautiful as Joseph described it?'

'More so,' Jack replied. 'You have to see Ilinka for yourself, Jordana. Ilinka is the most beautiful place on this earth in my opinion.'

He would not reveal the effect the mountain had had on him when he saw it for the first time. She must see the mountain for herself without any forewarning of the magic it held. Then he told her, 'You will also love Joseph's parents, and of course the rest of the tribe. Joseph's mother wanted to come to the airport but his father told her, "Jack will go alone. Jordana is coming to a strange land to meet her in-laws for the first time, an ordeal for any young bride. So we will have no argument."'

'It was very thoughtful of him,' Jordana said. 'And to be honest Jack, I am grateful to him. I do feel a bit nervous about meeting them all.'

'You need not be,' he said laughing. 'They feel as though they know you already. They have watched the video tape of your wedding many times and Joseph's mother sings your praises daily!'

For the rest of the journey, they brought each other up to date on what had been happening since they last met.

As soon as Joseph stopped the car outside of the house, the large oak door was flung open and his parents came dashing down the steps. His mother was crying as she welcomed Jordana with open arms.

'Don't mind my tears, Jordana,' she said, 'for they are tears of happiness for you and my son.'

There were also tears in Joseph's father's eyes as he hugged her close. When they got inside the house, it was filled with Joseph's uncles, aunts and cousins, all waiting to greet them.

Later, after the Thanksgiving dinner, which had been especially prepared to welcome them home, Joseph's father raised his glass to make a speech. When all eyes were upon him he said, 'We have celebrated the homecoming of the newlyweds, and welcomed Jordana into our fold. We have also heard their story of how the lost ones of the Ilinka tribe were brought together. And before long, thanks to the accomplishments of the newlyweds, and Jack, our people will be arriving from the four corners of the world.

'Then, our Sacred Cylinder will be opened and we will know the truth of what the future holds. But now,' he said, smiling gently as his gaze let upon Jordana, 'I think it is time for my son to take Jordana home to Ilinka. So everyone, please raise your glasses, to Joseph and Jordana.'

Joseph took hold of Jordana's hand as everyone saluted them with their glasses, then drank the wine.

Her eyes questioned him when they all left the table, then left the room one by one. He smiled as he put his finger to his lips, warning her to say nothing. He gestured that they were to follow when the room became empty, then led her through the house to the open kitchen doorway.

It was pitch dark as they stepped outside onto the back porch and he held her close as they stood together in the darkness. Then, as if by magic, a light flared, and two burning torches leapt into the air, revealing two rows of people with a path running between them. More torches were lit as Joseph led her down the steps. The torches were held up like crossed swords making an archway.

Joseph told her to jump over the sticks on the ground before they began to run between the burning torches which were lighting the way for them to go home.

Jordana, without knowing why, kicked off her shoes before she began to run, holding Joseph's hand under the flaming torches. When they got to the end Joseph's father and Jack were waiting. They held their torches high in the air, ready to lead them through the garden gate and down the garden path that led on to Ilinka.

Before they reached Ilinka soil they doused their torches and left without saying a word. Jordana wondered why they had done so for the night was pitch dark and there was not a light anywhere to be seen.

For a moment she wondered what lay before her as Joseph let go of her hand and brought her close to him. His lips found hers and as he kissed her passionately she closed her eyes. Before their lips parted, she felt a light shining upon them. The light was from the moon rising above the mountain.

She opened her eyes and Joseph turned her face so she could look down upon Ilinka, where the settlement could now be seen from the light of the moon. The light came brighter still as the moon lowered itself below the mountain peak. And as she raised her eyes, she was awestruck, for she was sure the moon was smiling just for her! She felt as though she had been struck by some mystical power that would live in her heart forever.

She thought of Emma, and of how, on such a night as this, she must have conceived her baby. The very thought of it brought tears to her eyes as she wondered if herself and Joseph would be blessed in the same way. Or was it too late for that now? Yet she could not believe they had come home to Ilinka for no specific reason. Surely, she thought, even if the Great White Spirit in the sky was angry with mankind, as Joseph said he was, there must be a reason for the Ilinka tribe being gathered together in one place.

She felt the tears roll down her face as she heard Joseph saying, 'Welcome to Ilinka, Jordana!'

When she turned her face to look at him and he saw her tears, he swept her into his arms and carried her home across the soil of Ilinka. He guessed what she'd been thinking about Emma and the baby, and why she was crying. He wanted to reassure her, tell her everything would be alright. But how could he when he did not know himself?

Tears welled up in his own eyes as he buried his face next to hers, then let his tears flow to mingle with Jordana's.

When he reached the house, he lifted his head and raised his eyes to the mountain, then cried out, 'Be merciful. Let the bloodline of the Ilinka continue!'

As he carried her into the house he wondered if their tears were a bad omen for this was not how he expected it to be when he brought Jordana home. He wondered if his mission had all been in vain. Or was the most important part of it to bring Jordana home, and in doing so bring home the spirit of Emma, which now resided in Jordana, and the spirit of Sara and Meleeka's son Joseph, whose spirit resided in himself?

They were both still crying when he opened the door to the house. The door was not locked so he'd only to turn the knob. He carried her over the threshold, put her down and hugged her to him. His thoughts were mixed as he comforted her. The mission he'd been sent on was completed, the wheels would now be set in motion for them to be brought to Ilinka. As for what had happened to himself and Jordana, that was ordained a long time ago. So why should they both be weeping now when they were home?

He felt his heartbeat quicken and also Jordana's, then he knew that their tears were not of sorrow, they were tears of happiness being shed by two spiritual lovers who had come home to where they belonged.

As these thoughts crossed his mind, the darkened room flickered with moonlight, throwing shadows all around. Jordana stirred in his arms, drawing away from him. It was then the room became so bright it was as if someone had flicked a switch to lighten it up.

Jordana's thoughts turned to Emma, who, if things had been different, would have lived in this house a long time ago. She felt a great happiness flow through her body as she turned to Joseph and said, 'We will be happy here, Joseph. The two young lovers have come home. The tears we have both shed were not because of the unknown, they were their tears, not ours.'

He did not speak as he lifted her into his arms and carried her to the bedroom. And even there, there was no need for him to switch on the light – the room was already lit up from the light of the moon.

In the weeks that followed, preparations were made in readiness for the bloodline to be brought together.

The townspeople of Petraba wondered what the Indian tribe were up to when they saw the settlement of Ilinka being transformed. Speculation was that the Tylers were making ready for some kind of tribal anniversary when tepees were seen being erected. Yet strangely enough, none of the townspeople interfered. They'd no idea the tepees were for the Tyler tribe, who, when the time came, would move into them. And the expected visitors would reside in the vacated cabins. With help from the spirits, Joseph and his father were shown how it all had to be.

There was much merriment among the tribe as they went back in time to the old ways of their ancestors when they went hunting for animal skins and other things that would be needed for the ceremony that was to take place. Even the children helped in any way they could. Jack, watching the preparations taking place, could imagine how it must have been when Meleeka first brought his tribe to the Blue Mountain.

Jack himself had just arrived from England and was surprised at the transformation which had taken place while he'd been away. Since the night of Joseph's return, he'd travelled many miles, giving final instructions to his relatives, who because of their bloodline would be coming to Ilinka. England had been his last port of call.

On his last day there he'd made a quick visit to the farm. When he arrived Barbara was alone in the kitchen. Peter and Ashley had gone to Skipton market to buy some cattle and would not return before it was time for him to leave.

Barbara was delighted to see him even though she knew his being there meant it would not be long now before the cylinder would be opened. She could not hide the tears that welled up in her eyes as Jack came towards her.

Since being told about Joseph's mission, and him taking Jordana away, she'd thought long and hard about it all, coming to the conclusion there was nothing anyone could do about what the future might hold for mankind. Seeing the tears Jack hugged her close. She brushed the tears away with the back of her hand and said she would put the kettle on.

Jack watched her brew the tea, then butter some scones before asking her, 'Do you remember, Barbara, when I first ate one of your delicious scones? It was the day I met Jordana.'

She gave him a rueful smile as she carried the tray over to the table, and said, 'I remember the day well enough, Jack, but none of us knew then what that meeting would lead to.'

She poured the tea into the cups and told Jack to help himself to a scone. As he did so, he knew he'd said the wrong thing and tried to make amends by telling her, 'Joseph would have found Jordana and myself even if we had not met. The spirits would have guided him to us.'

'I know he would,' she said, putting her hands around the cup, as if her hands needed to feel the warmth from it. She took a sip before she said, 'I agree with you, Jack. But all the same, it hurts, knowing your daughter is on the other side of the world, and you have no idea what is to happen to that world!'

Then she thought of how she missed Jordana, which was only natural as any mother would miss her daughter, especially when they'd got married and gone to live in another country. Jordana had done both of these. She'd also gone into the unknown, though Jordana always seemed happy enough when they'd spoken together on the phone!

'Tell me, Jack,' she said, picking up a scone. 'Is Jordana really happy? She always seems to be when I speak to her on the phone. But then Jordana always was one to take everything in her stride.'

Jack smiled as he told her truthfully: 'Jordana is very happy, Barbara. There is no doubt about that. And the Tylers love her as if she was their own daughter – they welcomed her with open arms!'

'And what about Ilinka?' she asked. 'Is it as beautiful as Jordana tells me it is?'

'It is more than that, Barbara,' he replied. 'It is a mystical place.' He told her of what he'd read about in the chronicles, the history of how it all began.

'And to think,' he said, when he'd related everything to her, 'that a baby born in this very house, all those years ago, was to grow into the man who would create that history.' He saw her smile at the very thought of it. Then he added, 'I cannot believe in my own heart and with all the preparations going on to bring the lost tribe together, that it is all being done for nothing. There is no logical reason for bringing them from the four corners of the world if the world is going to be destroyed.'

'I agree with your way of thinking, Jack,' she said. 'But the Lord works in mysterious ways, and it was He who created this world. So I have no doubt that if He is angry with the human race, He could easily uncreate it.'

She took a sip of her tea before saying, 'For a long time, many have prophesied the coming of the end of the world. Dates have been given which have come and gone. Yet from what we know that time may well be near. Or perhaps, from what you have told me, the Lord has other plans for the human race. Either way there is nothing any of us can do to change the way it will be.'

Jack agreed with her as he poured himself another cup of tea. He offered her a Dunhill, she took one and as he flicked his lighter she gazed into his eyes over the flame. When her cigarette was lit, she blew smoke rings into the air.

He lit his own cigarette and was surprised at the profoundness of her perception when she asked, 'Has it ever occurred to you, Jack,

Ilinka might be a sacred place? And the bloodline that comes from Sara, might that not be sacred also?'

'Barbara,' he said, awestruck, 'Whatever has been going on in that head of yours?'

'I have been thinking about the bloodline,' she replied, 'ever since Joseph took Jordana away. And, of course, about Joseph himself. It was no coincidence he came to the farm when he did. He came for Jordana.'

She stubbed out her cigarette and asked for another. When it was lit she said, 'From what you have told me about Ilinka, and the bloodline being called home, so to speak, I got to thinking about Joseph. We both know Joseph holds what is, to me, some strange power. You perhaps know more about that than I do.'

Jack was getting the drift to the way Barbara's mind was thinking. Of course he knew more about Joseph's power than Barbara did. That power had been used on himself and Jordana. He saw her hands begin to tremble and her voice was choked with emotion as she told him, 'It seems to me the bloodline is being brought to Ilinka so the mountain can protect it, while the rest of the human race is wiped out!'

Jack, who only a moment ago thought he knew what Barbara was thinking, was appalled by what she'd said. And though he confessed to himself she might be right, he'd not thought about that himself, so he asked, 'And then what do you think will happen, Barbara?'

'I believe,' she replied, 'that the same power Joseph holds lies dormant within Jordana, yourself and the rest of the bloodline. And when Joseph wants to, he can open up that power.'

Jack knew this was true, but said nothing as Barbara continued, 'I may be wrong, Jack, but I believe that if the human race as we know it does come to an end, and the bloodline of the Ilinka tribe does survive, then Joseph will use his power to open up what has lain dormant in that tribe for so long. They will be given a loving heart, and purity of mind. Then they will multiply and become a perfect species for a brand new world!'

Jack did not know what to say for he knew Barbara could be right, as he recalled what Cheeka said when he'd read the chronicles. Of how the world was meant to be when time began. He had not mentioned

Cheeka to Barbara and he was not going to do so now, not when Barbara was smiling at him and telling him, 'I am happy with these thoughts, Jack. And even if I am wrong it does not matter for Jordana is safe in Ilinka and that is where I want her to be. You know how much I love her, even though by birth she was not my own.'

She took hold of his hands as she said, 'Besides, you will be there with her.'

'Barbara,' he said, gripping her hands tight within his own. 'No one knows what the opening of the cylinder will reveal. But deep in my own heart I feel the cylinder will contain some master plan that will save the human race.'

'Let us hope you are right, Jack,' she said, taking her hands away from his. She raised herself from the chair and stacked the cups and saucers onto the tray.

Jack watched her as she went over to the sink. He was thankful they had spoken together and been alone. If Peter and Ashley had been there, the conversation they'd just had would not have taken place, though he was sorry Peter and Ashley would not be home before it was time for him to leave.

He said his goodbye to Barbara inside the house. Usually she would have walked with him to the car, but this time she said she preferred not to do so and he respected her wishes, knowing how she felt.

Before getting into the car he stood beside it, taking in the panoramic view that he'd come to love of the distant Pennine Moors, and the villages and towns that swept out to them. There must be millions of people down there he thought, as he got into the car and wondered what the future held for them.

He eased the car into the narrow lane and drove away without a backward glance. There was one more thing he had to do before going to the airport and it would give him great pleasure to do so. He might not have any idea what the future held, but before he caught his plane he would make someone happy.

He drove to his favourite pub, situated half a mile away from the airport. He'd visited the pub many times and a brother-like friendship had been formed between himself and Fred, the landlord. Fred had always admired the Merc and there was no way he was going to leave the car in the parking lot at the airport when Fred could be using it. He smiled to himself as he came to a halt outside the pub – Fred was in for a big surprise.

He opened the compartment in the dashboard, taking from it all the documents Fred would need, picked up his valise from the front seat, got out of the car and locked the door.

Fred, seeing him enter the pub, began pulling him his favourite pint. It was ready for him by the time Jack reached the bar.

'On your travels again, I see,' Fred said, nodding towards Jack's valise.

Jack perched himself on the bar stool, threw the documents and the car keys onto the bar and said, 'Yes Fred. I'm away again, in ten minutes in fact. Can you do me a favour and order me a taxi to take me to the airport?'

Jack picked up his pint as if he was dying of thirst while Fred picked up the phone at the end of the bar and ordered the taxi. Then went to serve another customer.

Jack smiled to himself as he watched Fred. He'd decided earlier in the day what he was going to do with the car. Fred had always admired it and it was a dream of his to own one like it. Well, Jack thought as he finished his pint, and saw the taxi draw up, Fred's dream is about to come true. The car is of no use to me where I'm going. And if, by some miracle I do come back, what does it matter?

He called Fred over. 'Here,' he said, handing him the documents and the keys. 'You have always admired my car. It belongs to you now. I don't know if I will be coming back from this trip I am going on.'

He laughed out loud at the astonishment on Fred's face and the other customers around the bar. 'I'm not joking, Fred,' he said, as he got off the stool, picking up his valise.

Fred was too stunned for words as he watched Jack walk towards the door, though he managed to raise his hand to the wave that Jack gave him before walking out of the door and into the taxi.

Jack laughed out loud as the taxi sped away. He could imagine the conversation that would now be going on around the bar, and Fred not being able to believe his luck. The taxi driver could not believe his luck either when Jack gave him a twenty-pound note and told him to keep the change.

When Jack reached his destination, Joseph's father was waiting for him and on the long drive to the Tyler residence brought him up to date with what had been happening. By the time they reached the house, Jack knew all the wheels had been set in motion and it would not be long now before the gathering of those from the Ilinka bloodline took place.

Later, after he'd showered and put on a change of clothes, Jack went out into the back garden, then made his way to Ilinka. His thoughts were on Barbara and her theory. He'd thought a lot about what she'd said and come to the conclusion, if Barbara was right, Ilinka would in effect be like starting a new Garden of Eden.

When he came out into the clearing he gazed down upon Ilinka, then he raised his eyes to the mountain. 'What mystery do you hold?' he cried out. 'What secret will be revealed when the cylinder is opened?'

He did not expect the mountain to answer him but he felt better for speaking his thoughts out loud. He followed the path that led to Ilinka where he would find Joseph.

Joseph greeted him with the usual bear-hug, then asked, as if Jack had been on holiday, 'Did you enjoy your trip and meeting your long-lost relatives?'

When Jack replied yes to both questions, Joseph asked more seriously, 'Did everything go as planned?'

'Better than I expected,' Jack replied. 'Your father has all the details. I also went to visit the farm.' Though he refrained from telling Joseph what Barbara had said about the Ilinka tribe, telling him only that Barbara was well and he'd not seen Peter or Ashley. He also told him what he'd done with the car. Joseph laughed – he'd met Fred and could imagine his reaction.

'I'm glad you went to the farm,' he said, as he gestured for Jack to follow him.

'I can see,' Jack said, 'you have been busy while I have been away.' He was referring to the Indian-like settlement, with the cone-shaped tents made of animal skins, and the dyed feathers and hides that were hung up outside the tents.

'Yes, we have,' said Joseph. 'But there is still much work to be done. The womenfolk are working hard making our native dress. When the time comes to open the cylinder there will be a grand ceremony. And now you are home, Jack, I do not think it will be long before that ceremony takes place, for soon the influx of the lost tribe will begin to arrive.'

Joseph smiled as he opened the flap of one of the tents to show Jack inside, then told him: 'I spoke to Paul Rudge on the phone yesterday, he should now be setting the plans he received into motion. Those plans are much the same as you have given to your bloodline, Jack. The influx of the lost tribe into Ilinka will be gradual – we cannot have the townspeople of Petraba getting too inquisitive. And this,' he gestured with his hand around the tent, 'when they begin to arrive, will be the home of Jordana and myself.'

Paul Rudge had followed Joseph's instructions like a field marshal in command of an army. Eunice, his daughter, could not believe, as the days flew by, how her father, who not so long ago had driven her to distraction by his idiotic ways, was now in complete command of the quest Joseph had set before him.

She was only half listening as he spoke on the phone, making the last-minute arrangements with those who would be going to Ilinka. She was thinking of those who would be left behind, for only those who held the bloodline would be going, which was twenty in all.

It had been no easy task for her father to convince Patric that he must go with them. Patric, like the others had been sworn to secrecy, and being newly wed did not want to leave his bride, which in the circumstances was understandable. For none of them knew what would be the outcome of their journey to Ilinka. In the end it had been Judith who had persuaded Patric to go, even though she did not know the true circumstances of what was happening.

When Paul put the phone down, he smiled at Eunice. 'Everything is going as planned,' he said. 'Put the kettle on, I could do with some coffee.'

He picked up the fax which Joseph had sent and marvelled at modern technology. And also at how the whole operation had been planned for getting them to Ilinka. The telex revealed a list of names and beside each name was a date on which they were to travel. They would pick their tickets up at the airport. The timing of the flights were varied. All were scheduled to arrive at their destination in the hours of darkness; they would be met at the airport and be taken to Ilinka. Himself and Eunice would be the last to leave.

It was on that day, a week later, that Eunice roamed around the house from room to room, the family home where she'd been born, and later her brother Robert had come along, then her sister Mary. And before them her father and his father. She'd always loved this house and never wanted to leave it, even when she'd got married to her late husband. It broke her heart when he took her away to live in the city. Then by some quirk of fate she'd been the one to come home and take care of her father when her mother died. Now, she thought, giving a deep sigh, I am to leave it again.

She lovingly caressed some of the family treasures, many of them left by past generations. Sometimes she'd complained about the dust they collected and even threatened to throw them all out. Now she fingered them like precious jewels as the memories came flooding back of when she was a child and was told stories of how these treasured possessions were come by. And she recalled how the house was always warm and cosy, full of laughter and love.

She sighed again as she replaced the ornament back on the dresser. They would be leaving soon. The others, she mused, should be in Ilinka by now.

She heard her father call her, telling her it was time to leave. Then he was standing in the doorway, holding out his hand for her to take hold of. She felt the tears prick her eyes as she took hold of it. He is like a captain of a ship, she thought, who is taking the last passenger overboard. And like the others who had gone before them, they would not know what was out there once they jumped into the unknown.

CHAPTER XIII

It was the evening of the night of the full moon. Joseph, his father, Jack and Paul Rudge were all together as Joseph's father unlocked the safe, taking from it the Sacred Cylinder. He carried it over to the table, placing the cylinder on a blue velvet cushion in the centre of the table.

Joseph, Jack and Paul Rudge were already seated. Joseph's father lit the candles in the candelabra at either end of the table, switched off the lights, then sat down next to Joseph. They raised their right arms, resting their elbows at the nearest corner of the cushion from where they were seated. They joined hands, Joseph with Jack, his father with Paul, making a pyramid-like structure around the cushion.

Joseph closed his eyes and began to speak in a language neither Jack nor Paul could understand. Then he began to chant, which sounded to Jack like 'Oka Eaka, Oka Eaka' over and over again. Joseph's father joined in.

Moments later, not of their own free will, Jack and Paul Rudge also began to chant. When the chanting came to an end, it was as if someone had given them a signal to stop for they all stopped chanting at the same time.

Both Jack and Paul realized they'd been performing some kind of ritual, but when they opened their eyes they were unprepared to see Meleeka standing behind Joseph and his father.

No one would have believed it was only the spirit of Meleeka – he looked as real as any of them as he stood there smiling at the awestruck faces of Jack and Paul. Then he spoke to them saying, 'You have done well, my friends, in bringing the bloodline of our first-born home to

Ilinka. We have waited for many moons for this night to arrive.

'My son never knew of Emma's child. If he had he would have moved heaven and earth to find her. So he could not be told. It was a secret to be kept by myself, his mother and his grandfather. Kept hidden within our hearts.

'My son gave his heart to Emma, as she gave hers to him. When death came to them both, their spirits roamed the empty plains until they could be reborn again in the hearts of two young lovers. Many moons passed over the earth and they waited patiently until the Great White Spirit let them know who those two young lovers would be.

'My son, and also Emma, are happy now for they live again in Joseph and Jordana. And this night I am here to thank you,' he gestured to Jack, saying his name, and then to Paul, 'for bringing the fruit of their love home to Ilinka.'

As he spoke, their four hands were still entwined over the cylinder. Placing his hands over theirs he told them, 'I cannot tell you what the cylinder will reveal when it is opened. Only the Great White Spirit knows of its secret. I can only give thanks that Joseph completed his mission to find the lineage in time!'

A moment later, Meleeka disappeared.

As the full moon raised itself above the mountain the people of the township of Petraba were all in their beds sound asleep. Not a soul awoke as the moon shone down, making the settlement of Ilinka as bright as a summer's day.

The tribe below the mountain gazed up at the moon, and to them the whole of the world could have been sleeping as they all waited, wondering what this night would bring.

Joseph wore a replica of Meleeka's chieftain robes and feathered headdress. Jordana was beside him wearing a replica of Sara's dress that Sara wore on the night they welcomed Meleeka home and she'd danced before him with her father! They were standing on the mountain, looking down onto the gathering of Sara's lineage.

As the drums began to beat, Joseph recalled the things he had read about Cheeka and of how all those years ago Cheeka predicted this night when the true Ilinka tribe would be gathered together from the four corners of the earth.

His eyes let upon Jack. It was Jack's lineage which had enabled Cheeka's predictions to come true, and Jack had done well to track down his long-lost relatives who had emigrated to different parts of the world soon after the War.

All eyes were upon Joseph as the drummers softened their beat and Jordana went to stand before him. She watched him close his eyes then raise his arms to the heavens above. Both his arms and hands moved gracefully, his fingers too, as if he was speaking with them to some unseen force.

Everyone watched, mesmerized, until the soft beating of the drums came to an end and Joseph lowered his hands.

No one spoke, as Joseph's father proudly carried the cushion holding the Sacred Cylinder towards his son. The spirits have been wise, he thought, in choosing my son to open the cylinder.

Jordana stepped to one side. Joseph's father stood beside her and held the cushion towards Joseph. With bated breath Jordana watched Joseph take hold of the cylinder and caress it in his hands. Then she turned to gaze down upon those who were waiting for Joseph to speak. Their faces were solemn. They were all wondering, she supposed, what was to be their fate. She caught Jack's eye and he smiled as if he was trying to reassure her!

She heard the click as the seal of the cylinder opened, then turned her head to see Joseph taking out the contents. He handed the cylinder to his father before unrolling the delicate parchment!

Joseph scanned over what was written down. The writing was in code, a code that until this moment, he knew, he would not have been able to decipher. He marvelled at the ingenuity of whoever had written upon the scroll!

Jordana saw his hands tremble. He looked up to the moonlit sky, as if he was saying a silent prayer. When at last he began to speak his voice was so powerful she wondered for a moment if it was Joseph who was speaking. Then she listened as he read from the scroll.

I the first-born of the Ilinka tribe weep
As I write down what I have seen.
The prophecies are of the future
Many, many moons from now.
My tears drop upon the parchment
as I write.
And as I place the parchment
Into the jewelled cylinder
I pray the seal will never
be opened. Even though I know
My prayers will not be answered.

Joseph paused for a moment as his own tears fell onto the parchment. He could not hold back his emotions, knowing he was truly blessed. Then he continued,

For I have also seen in my vision
The breaking of the seal.
Only one man can open the cylinder,
And break the secret code written
Upon the parchment.

When this day comes, there will be
Much unrest in the world.
No love, or peace, in the heart.
Only greed, for more power and
monetary and material possessions.

No love of family life,
Husbands will leave wives,
Wives will leave husbands,
And the children, the very fruit
Of the parents who professed to
Love each other, will be lost.
The heart of the child will

split into two.
Never again to be mended.

There will be wars fought
With lethal weapons. More powerful
than ever before.
Many fought in the name of religion
For a God they profess to love.

When all of this comes to pass
The Great White Spirit will be
angry.
He sees into the hearts of everyone
and knows the truth.
He did not create this beautiful
earth
To be spoiled by the greed of
the human race.
Or create the human race for man
and woman to break their children's
hearts.

But the Great White Spirit
Still loves, even in His anger
And the one who breaks the seal
To read the coded message to his
people
Will be the one whose path
Must be followed.

Joseph rolled up the parchment and turned to face the mountain. This action was done so swiftly there was no time for those who had been listening to speak among themselves.

They could only gasp in awe, for as he turned, the voice from the mountain boomed out.

Sara of Ilinka

You, who have witnessed the
breaking of the seal
And listened to the prophecies
that have all come to pass
Are of the true Ilinka
blood lineage.
When the Great White Spirit
gave life to the people of
the earth
He brought forth the tribe
of Ilinka.
He knew of the trials and
tribulations, which would
lay before them, and of
how some would stray
from the fold.
He also knew, when mankind
was lost in its own destruction
They would be brought back
into the fold. Like a sheep
brings its lost lambs, back
to the safety of their mother.
And when that day comes
The Ilinka tribe will listen
in awe, as the voice from a
mountain speaks.
I am that voice.
I have waited long to
tell you the secrets of
the Great White Spirit.
But now that time has
come, and I say to
you all.
There is only one path
in the world of religion.

This path comes from
the heart.
Where there is no goodness
of heart,
There is no path.
Listen to what the heart
tells you. If you cannot
hear, no heart exists.
This is the path, which will
open the eyes, that
have been closed for
so long. And open the
ears that have not listened.
The Ilinka tribe must go
forth.
Open those eyes, and ears
before it is too late.
These are the wishes of
The Great White Spirit.

Joseph waited for a moment in silence, then bowed to the mountain before turning to face the gathering of the Ilinka tribe.

He was relieved, as they all must have been, that the Great White Spirit, who loved all things, had given them the chance to go forth into the world, hopefully, to bring peace into the hearts of its people.

Taking hold of Jordana's hand he walked with her down the mountain. He knew it was no easy quest that had been set before them. To open the eyes and ears of the people of the world would be difficult.

Yet with the power they held of the Ilinka tribe, they would pass on that power. Then people from all nations would be given the purity of mind, the loving of heart, and the healing hands. Then peace would come upon the earth. And when this was done the Great White Spirit would rest in peace himself.

He smiled as he saw Jack and Paul Rudge coming towards him, and as they did so, the crowd behind them cheered.

He looked back over his shoulder towards the mountain. And the mountain whispered to him alone:

'It shall come to pass.'